Hate and Fury

REYHAN GABALALI

Order this book online at www.trafford.com
or email orders@trafford.com

Most Trafford titles are also available at major online book retailers.

Print information available on the last page.

ISBN: 978-1-6987-0373-2 (sc)
ISBN: 978-1-6987-0372-5 (hc)
ISBN: 978-1-6987-0374-9 (e)

Library of Congress Control Number: 2020923642

Trafford rev. 01/07/2021

www.trafford.com

North America & international
toll-free: 844-688-6899 (USA & Canada)
fax: 812 355 4082

Introduction

THE NOVEL *HATE AND FURY* IS THE AUTHOR'S first work in a foreign genre. As we read the novel, we feel the alternating tense moments, the emotions that historical periods evoke in human destinies; we see the causes, roots, scale of complex and tragic events, and get acquainted with the deeds and struggles of patriotic sons. The author tries to reveal the character of the work, Special Officer Michael Grady, to reveal his character, including his spiritual world as a human, and personality, and to show the psychological aspects that make him constantly proactive in the ups and downs of life. The work reflects the difficulties faced by the hero in his childhood and adolescence, his great leap into life, career advancement, worries, desires, dreams, love, suffering in this way, betrayal, evil, crime, and punishment. The hero's victory is the culmination of the work. But this victory is not easily won by him.

In the first part of the work, readers get acquainted with the artistic image of a hero who served in a peacekeeping force in Afghanistan with his group during a difficult and complicated period. The main goal of the hero is to fight against the enemy to ensure the security of the civilian population. He is not alone in this struggle, and around him, there are enough brave, friendly, principled comrades in arms. But the hero is always in tension. On the one hand, he is always worried about the horrors of war, the lives lost; on the other hand, he feels the longing for the people he loved whom he left behind in his homeland and, for some reason, could not hear about them for days. Michael Grady, who returned from the war crippled, is not alone. Along with him, his closest friends were discharged from the army for some reason and returned home. But the moral damage he received at home is more serious. The book clearly reflects the series of tense events, the difficulties faced by the hero, his sufferings and struggles for love, even if he is a victim of betrayal. The culmination of the work ends with the victory of the hero.

Hate
and
Fury

I T WAS ABOUT THE BEGINNING OF SUMMER, but the weather was still quite cold. As the nights became shorter, the sun would rise much earlier.

It was one of the ordinary days. It was half past six. Dawn was breaking; the sunshine was gradually illuminating the horizon. You could feel the cold breeze and hear the chanting of the birds.

It was close to noon in the dormitory of a military academy in one of the largest states in America. While everyone else was sleeping, military cadet Michael Grady was awake since midnight. He was very much worried about his mother, who was taken to the hospital just a day before because of her deteriorated health condition, therefore could not fall asleep. He was looking forward to the morning, hoping to call and find out about the well-being of his mother and, if possible, even pay her a visit. Michael looked at the green through the open window and got lost in the deep thoughts. His thought took him to the depths of the past. He remembered his rough childhood.

Michael was raised by his mother because he had lost his father while he was a little child. After the death of her husband, despite the difficulties of life and suffering many hardships, she was able to raise her son as an educated and well-behaving child.

Michael earned the respect of everyone at his school with his sincerity and kind behavior. At the age of seventeen, Michael graduated from the military school with excellent marks and, as planned, entered the military academy. When his mother heard of her son's desire to become a soldier, he wished her success on this path. He wanted to see his son as a patriotic child in the future.

Michael, like many of his other friends, had left behind the difficulties of the military academy and was about to finish his academy. After receiving his undergraduate degree with his close friends and fellow students, Michael would begin to fulfill his military duties in various fields of the military. His main goal was to serve as a special unit intelligence officer in the U.S. Army. Two of his best friends, George Bradley and Indian American Roger Thomas, would be graduating together with him from the academy that year.

The sudden wake-up call brought him back to reality. In five minutes, along with the other soldiers, he put on his military uniform and, like everyone else, fixed his bed and waited, ready for the commander to arrive. The commander inspected the uniform and bedding and ordered all the soldiers to line up in the courtyard as usual.

Col. Scott Cordell had been training them for over a year. He was a tall man with large shoulders and looked very strong. He was a man of great stature, with broad shoulders and sheer muscle. Colonel Cordell looked great in the uniform he wore. He stood out from others in terms of perseverance and high standards.

Colonel Cordell had returned home after completing his military mission after taking part in the war in Afghanistan. For over a year, he had been providing military training and education to the students in this school. The colonel was also a skilled warrior who knew the secrets of hand-to-hand combat and skillfully taught these skills to his students. Unlike the other students, Michael and George were athletes who had already mastered the mysteries of this martial arts before coming to the military. Therefore, the colonel has always appreciated the abilities of both students. Michael was very different from the students around him because of his academic achievements and military training skills, in addition to being a skilled martial artist.

The national flag was raised. The soldiers, standing in line, rested and sang the national anthem under the raised U.S. flag. The spectacular sound of the splendid anthem spread around and woke all the inhabitants of the sleeping forest. As soon as the anthem finished, the colonel started his speech.

"Special Forces soldiers! A month later, you will graduate from the academy and be granted a bachelor's degree and start working in various military areas based on your appointments as an officer. Your knowledge and skills as members of the Special Forces unit are very high. To test your skills in martial arts, we will hold competitions at the academy starting from today until the end of the week. There will be ten winners in this competition. Then those ten soldiers will compete against the ten best students of the police academy. The best team will win. Starting from today, we will be working on identifying ten of your most talented peers and preparing them for the weekend. One of them has already been identified. Michael Grady, step forward!"

"Yes, sir."

"You are a skilled warrior who knows the secrets of hand-to-hand combat. The team that you are going to lead will defend the honor of our academy. I believe in your ability. Starting from today, you will have to work hard to prepare the team for the competition. I will also participate in the selection process and help you to identify the potential team members. Good luck to you!"

"Yes, Colonel."

"Free!"

Michael Grady left his fellow students and approached the colonel.

"Sir, let me ask."

"Go ahead."

"Colonel, last night, my mother was hospitalized because of acute pain. I would like to visit her, if you would permit."

"I give you an hour. Hurry up!"

Michael got out of the courtyard with a permit in his hand and rushed straight to the hospital.

He contacted the hospital admissions office and said he wanted to meet the doctor on duty. Michael went into the doctor's room and explained the reason for his visit. The doctor showed him a place to sit and gave him an update about the situation.

"Ms. Clara Grady was brought to the hospital in an ambulance because of acute appendicitis in the gallbladder. Although the pain has diminished significantly after first aid, it is still ongoing. It is recommended that she stay in the hospital for a few days for a complete examination and accurate diagnosis and treatment. Because of the large number of stones in the gallbladder and the persistence of pain, the operation is inevitable. We are also worried that additional issues might be identified after the complete checkup."

Michael thanked the doctor and stepped out to the corridor and started walking toward the unit where his mother was being treated.

When he entered the room, his mother was asleep. Michael approached his mother's bedside and stared at her. The mother had changed considerably over the years. She had lost weight, and her hair was grayed out. Michael was very much worried to see her mother's yellowish skin color. As if she felt it, his mother woke up and turned her head aside. Near him stood a tall, broad-shouldered military soldier. The mother thought it was a dream when she saw her smiling son. But it was reality—it was actually Michael. She wanted to get up. Michael stopped her and gave her a big hug. The tears of the mother, who hugged her son tightly, soaked his son's cheeks.

"How are you, Mom?"

"All my pains disappeared as soon as I saw you, Michael."

"I was very worried to hear the news."

"I have been suffering from severe liver problems for a month. I had to call an ambulance this evening."

"Do not worry. I got permission for a short time. I was very worried about what was happening. I had to see you."

A nurse with a big smile on her face entered the room.

"Good morning. How do you feel?"

"Thank you very much, my daughter. The pain is still there, but it is a little better than yesterday."

"I will just give you a shot, and you will feel better."

"Meet my son, Michael."

"Good morning. I am Beth Francesco. I am glad to meet you."

"Beth is a nurse. She has been taking care of me since last night."

"Thank you, Beth."

"My shift is almost over. I will see you tomorrow night. Take care of yourself. Shortly, the doctor will arrive."

"Excuse me, when exactly can I meet the doctor?"

"Unfortunately, there is still half an hour for the doctor to arrive."

"I have to leave. This is very important."

"You don't have to worry. All the necessary examinations will be done. You can give me your phone number. During my next shift, I will inform you about the condition of Ms. Grady after I get the doctor's permission. If he's OK, you can also speak with him yourself."

"Thank you very much. Thank you for your help."

"Michael, you may be late. Do not worry about me."

"I hope you understand, Mom. Be strong. I will take a vacation after school and spend some time with you. Take care of yourself."

Michael was sad and had many things going through his mind. He was very much worried about the color of his mom's skin. He was worried that his mom's sickness could turn out to be something very serious.

Michael stepped out into the hospital yard and pulled the fresh air into his lungs. The sun began to rise above the horizon. He looked around. There were a lot of people in the yard. The majority of them were people rushing to work.

Michael suddenly noticed the nurse whom he just had a conversation with in his mom's hospital room standing outside. She was waiting for someone. Beth turned her head for some reason and smiled when she noticed Michael's attentive look at her. She was looking beautiful. The sun's dusk fell on her face and made her look even more beautiful. The breeze was swinging her hair across her face. She frequently used her hands to fix her hair.

A woman walked out from the building and greeted Beth, and they returned to the building together. Michael sat in his car and returned to the academy. Now, he knew the nurse's phone number. He would be able to get information about her mother's condition from time to time. Beth was not only friendly and kind but also beautiful. Michael could not forget her smile.

It was nearing the end of the week. Most of the military personnel expected to participate in the competition were already identified. Today, George Bradley was to be confirmed. He had already won two rounds. Michael was expecting that George would also win the third round.

The competition was intense, and the advantage was on George's side. Suddenly, George was hit by an illegally thrown heavy blow and fell down on his right arm. He felt a severe pain on his arm and back. He quickly got back up and tried to finish the fight but was not able to use his arm. He needed to see a doctor urgently. According to preliminary doctor examination, George Bradley suffered severe damage to the nerve and bones in the arm. He was transported to the hospital for a better examination.

After a thorough examination at a military hospital, the doctor reported that the arm and nerve unit were severely damaged, with a diagnosis of deformity in the base area. Physiotherapy was also needed. He was not allowed to move his arm for a while. Thus, George was eliminated from the competition.

Michael Grady was excited. The game was to be held that day. The venue for the competition was already decided. The competition was to be held at the gym of the military academy. Since the gym was large, it enabled the academy to hold many different types of competitions there. Numerous supporters from police departments and military units had come to cheer for their teams and support them.

They called Michael Grady's team's name, and they entered the arena first. Roger Thomas could not qualify for the finals after losing in the qualifying round. Michael was sad by the fact that he had another friend who had already left the competition at the earlier stage. He was thoughtful and staring at the audience. A familiar face from the ranks of the rival team's supporters caught his attention. Michael, for some reason, could not remember exactly who he was, but the person was also staring at Michael.

The second team had already arrived. The name of the person who was to lead the other team was announced. It was Reid Wincher, who was expected to graduate the same year from the police academy. Michael suddenly remembered who the police officer was looking at him a while ago. It was Carl Caster. Michael attended the same school with them. Carl Caster was good friends with Reid Wincher. Not only did he attend the same school but also he lived in the same street with Michael. Carl was a tall and strong-looking man, which separated him from others. He came from a very wealthy family. Carl was jealous of Michael because of his great academic performance. Michael was admired and recognized by his teachers, which made him very jealous. Michael's friendship with George, on the other hand, also made him upset. Somehow, everyone knew and felt how Carl thought negatively about black kids in general. Even his father was called to the school regarding this issue. Carl's father was left with no other option but to apologize for his actions and explained the reason for his son's behavior, which he cited to the murder of his grandfather.

Although Reid was in a different class, he was always with Carl out of class and during breaks. Carl could not accept Michael's friendship with George. They both had filed complaints with the school administration citing the misbehavior of Carl. This time, along with Carl's father, Reid's parents were also invited to the school. They were informed about the behavior of their children and how they treated their classmates. The school administration warned the parents of Carl and Reid that they would make a final decision to expel their children from the school if their actions repeated.

The next day, Carl did not come to school.

Observing his changed manners and lower esteem, Michael and the other kids could tell that Carl was reprimanded by his father. Michael thought it was over. But he was wrong. One day, on his way home, Michael was stopped and beaten up by those two boys. When he got home, his mother saw a lot of blood coming from his nose. Michael had blood all over his body. No matter how hard his mother pushed him, Michael did not say who had done it to him and strongly objected to informing the police.

After a while, there was a knock at the door. Carl's father entered the house with him. He apologized to his mother for what happened to Michael and asked Carl not to repeat it. In the next few days, not seeing Carl coming to the school, Michael found out from their mutual friends that Carl was transferred to another school. A few days later, Reid Wincher had also left school. He and his friend would continue their studies at another school where they attended together.

A month later, Michael began to take some hand-to-hand combat classes.

The next meeting of Michael and Carl took place five years ago. Michael had decided to have fun with friends at one of the nightclubs to celebrate the last day of school. Carl, who also had happened to come to the same club with his friends and a couple of girls, ran into Michael. Carl, who again tried to bully Michael when they were partying, encountered his hard fist. Carl was caught by surprise. He had to redeem himself. So he called Michael outside to the club to settle their issues like a man. A fierce fight broke out between the young men. Reid, who was watching the fight closely, could not handle watching his friend getting beaten up. So he decided to rush to help his friend. But Michael was prepared well. He was able to handle both men single-handedly. Michael returned home like a hero that day.

A month later, Michael entered the military academy and left his home for five years to attend college.

Finally, they met again today. Both friends were police officers. One of them is studying at the police academy, while the other one was serving as an officer at the department.

According to the jury's decision, the match was even. Next round, Michael was matched with an opponent team member. The match was short and intense. Loud cheers were made for Michael, who beat his opponent with one hit. While taking his seat, Michael met Carl Caster's angry looks.

The final match was on. As an outstanding athlete in all the matches, Michael was to meet Reid Wincher at the finals. It was the decisive match. Michael witnessed Reid Wincher's masterful skills throughout the competition. Sometimes, the match was paused by the coach because of Reid's use of illegal blows. Reid was warned that he will be eliminated if it occurs again.

Everyone was expecting the match between Michael and Reid to be intense because both fighters were master athletes in hand-to-hand battle. Michael won the first two rounds of a three-round battle. Reid was very angry. He was trying to use all of his might to conquer the opponent. Even though they both were tired, the will to win was pushing them to the next round. Finally, the coach announced the beginning of the third round. The fight began. Like the rounds before, Michael skillfully handled the opponent's blows. Reid tried with all of his might to win the fight, which resulted in a mistake that was decisive. The competition finished with Michael and his team's victory. Even though the coach announced that Michael was the winner, protests from the tribune rose, and he agreed to continue the battle. The next match lasted ten minutes, and Michael was the winner again.

Nobody understood the reason why Reid refused to congratulate Michael except for them, even though all the other contestants congratulated each other in a gentlemanly manner at the end of the competition. Carl and Reid angrily left the military academy before everyone else.

George Bradley joyfully hugged his friend.

"Well done, Michael. I'm proud of you."

"It was a friendly match. I did not expect Carl and Reid to be there."

"Michael, their aggressive behavior shows their hatred against you. Be careful!"

"Of course, but they are law enforcers and civilians now. Their current aggressive behavior might be understandable."

"You are right, but violence does not solve anything. Civilians must understand that. Victories should be achieved with dignity, patience, and conscience."

The exams were going to start in a few days. Like the other cadets, Michael was preparing for the exams. Michael was helping his friend George, who was struggling because of his arm injury. His mother's condition was improving. Beth was informing Michael about it without Michael calling her. Michael was looking forward to Beth's calls. He was falling in love with her.

George was supposed to go to the doctor's checkup after the morning exam. Michael was also planning to go with him.

After the X-ray scan, the doctor said that the bandage can be taken off. The nurse took George to the bandage room. Michael was waiting for his friend in the hallway. After a while, George got out of the room and left the hospital with Michael.

"George, I think I have seen that nurse somewhere."

"Her name is Luisa. She works here. She works shifts at the hospital. Today was her afternoon shift."

"I have seen her at the hospital where my mother is being treated. She was with another nurse who was working there."

"Maybe they are friends. She is very friendly."

"Perhaps you like her?"

George smiled without saying a word.

Carl Caster was very upset because of what happened, spreading false rumors about how the match was not ruled fairly and bragging about how he was going to teach Michael a lesson if they ever meet again. Some of his peers played along with this scenario not to hurt his feelings, but some of them thought that he still can't accept the loss and it's his tactic to deal with it. Actually, his friend was just as mad at Michael as him. Since the time Michael beat them up real good, they both wanted to get back at him. After this, they started doing sports actively and learned the secrets of hand-to-hand combat.

News about the competition made him happy. Reid told the news to Sheriff Carl Caster and asked him to come and watch the game. Carl was happy that the game was on his rest day. They knew that Michael was a cadet at the military academy and he was going to attend the competition. In both friends' opinions, the result of the match was another blow to them personally. Finally, after passing all the exams, the two friends graduated from the academy and became bachelors. Each one of them was going to serve their duty to their country as a special unit officer. Because of his achievements in education, sports, and his discipline, Michael Grady was ranked to captain lieutenant directly. All the graduates of the academy were given a vacation.

Roger Thomas was planning to spend his vacation with his parents in the neighboring state.

George Bradley had nowhere to go. He grew up as an orphan. His father's house was in another state. After losing his parents at a child age, George's uncle took him in. His uncle had a house on the street where Michael lived. He sheltered George before passing away because of severe illness. George grew up with his aunt. Since then, George and Michael went to the same school. After getting accepted to military school, the two friends continued their education together. Later on, George Bradley heard the news of her aunt; she sold the house and moved to a neighboring state to get married with someone. On the other side, news of his father's house burning down devastated George. Trying to comfort George, Michael said that his doors were always open for him.

Roger Thomas was the only child of a wealthy family. At first, his father was a master jeweler; later on, he opened his own workshop and hired skilled workers. As the number of workshops and stores increased, his father became a wealthy business owner. Despite his vast wealth, his father always worked and taught his son the secrets of this art. Despite all of this, Michael went against his father's wish and chose the military. Roger stood out among his friends with his excellent behavior and his good grades. During his academy years, Roger established strong friendship relations with Michael and George. Finally, today, he was graduating alongside his friends and was given vacation release.

It was past noon when the three friends left the academy territory. Roger bid farewell to his friends and went home with a private car his father sent. Michael knew his friend had nowhere to go. He approached and put his hand on his shoulder.

"My mother is waiting for us. Let's hurry, food is getting cold."

George hugged his friend.

"I am also alone in life, George. Consider me your brother. I am with you until the end of my life."

Clara was very happy that day. Her son graduated from military academy and was coming home. To celebrate the matter, she opened a big table and cooked all of Michael's favorite meals. Michael told Clara that he will be coming with his friend, so she was well prepared.

Clara took her pain medicine. Her illness was severe. She couldn't hold her tears when the doctor revealed the diagnosis. She was diagnosed with gallstone disease and liver cirrhosis. She knew it was serious, but she asked Beth not to tell her son about it. The mother did not want her son to worry and be distressed before the exams. Exams were plenty stressful.

At last, a car stopped in front of the yard. She looked out the window and ran toward the door joyfully as she was taking off her apron. As soon as the door opened, she hugged both officers in uniform with pride. Her heart was about to explode; she could not hold back her tears.

She couldn't get her eyes off her son.

Michael left five years ago. During these years, he grew taller, became more handsome, and resembled his father more.

The military uniform he was in deservedly suited him. Michael noticed the changes on his mother's looks right away. Her skin's color change and weight in the last three weeks were not hard to notice. First thing he asked about was his mother's health. His mother, using an excuse to avoid upsetting her son, was telling him that she only has gallstone and she just lost her appetite. Michael understood that what his mother said was not true and she was hiding something.

Mother and son were fond of George. Clara Grady knew about his life. His childhood was lived in this house. Michael had already told Clara that he will be coming home with George. Therefore, Clara prepared a bedroom for her son and for George, as if he was her own son. George Bradley was shy and worried. Michael thought about it and tried to make him feel at home.

After supper, the friends discussed their vacation plans. The first thing for Michael to do was to go to the hospital and find out the truth about his mother's condition. George needed to go through an X-ray scan at a military hospital.

"My friend, I see you get excited when you hear 'hospital.' Your mood changes."

George smiled.

"Yeah! There is something else here. Perhaps you are in love with the nurse?"

George's face became red. Seeing his friend get so embarrassed, he knew it was true.

"Is that so? That's great, man. I'm happy for you."

"Yeah, Michael, I like her."

"You watch out! What if she is married or has a boyfriend? You'd get beaten up," he said, laughing.

"No, man! I found out everything. She is single, and I think she likes me too."

"Love is a beautiful thing. Life is short. We don't know what will happen in the future."

"They will probably assign us somewhere."

"Of course. Let's put this matter aside for now. What time are you going to go to the hospital tomorrow?"

"Probably early in the morning. I have got a doctor's appointment. I was supposed to go two days earlier, but because of my exams, I missed it."

"You must not joke around with this kind of injury, and you are hiding something from me. Tomorrow we are going to the hospital together."

"Michael, don't worry about me. Maybe you have important things to do."

"George, to be honest, I'm worried about my mom. I can't get her to tell me everything. I think she is hiding something serious from me. I have to meet her doctor tomorrow."

"That's what I wanted to talk about with you, man! Ms. Clara's condition worries me too."

"I don't know the doctor, but I have the nurse's number. I'll call her and find out the doctor's work hours."

"He works the night shift. Shouldn't call now, just be there in the morning before the doctor's shift is over. It's better this way."

The friends left the house early in the morning. His mother knew why they got up early and where they went, but for the first time ever, Michael lied to his mother using work as an excuse.

There was little time left before the shift was over when he arrived at the hospital. He approached the reception and asked for Beth Francesco. The nurse called someone on the phone and asked him to take a seat and wait in the hallway. Beth arrived in a few minutes. She looked around, saw Michael, and approached him. Michael got up and greeted Beth.

"Hi, Michael."

"Hi, how are you? I hope I'm not bothering you."

"No worries, my shift is over anyway. How are you?"

"I'm good. I have been at home for vacation since yesterday."

"How's Ms. Clara?"

"Not well. She still has pains. Beth, I want to thank you for taking care of her while I'm gone."

"It's my job. If you want, I can wait for the doctor with you. You will get some information."

"If it's no trouble for you. You just finished your shift. You must be tired."

"Don't worry, Michael."

"Beth, my mother's condition worries me. I would like to know the real analysis, diagnosis of the doctor."

"Michael, her analysis results are ready. She was going to come to her next session and be informed today."

"You probably know something. Is there something serious?"

"I am forbidden by law to tell you something about it. The doctor will come soon, and we will find out together."

After some time, Beth and Michael went upstairs to the second floor. Beth asked Michael to sit and wait, and she entered the doctor's room. After a short time, Michael got invited to the room. After introducing himself, the doctor asked him to sit.

"Mr. Michael Grady, I understand your concerns about your mother's illness. After the first test, we diagnosed her with gallstone disease, but later tests revealed liver cirrhosis. It's serious. Treatment takes a long time and is currently ongoing. I'm sorry to tell you, but this illness leads to liver cancer in many cases, and considering that fact, we had to do extended tests to reveal cancer-related diagnosis. We got the result of the test yesterday. Our patient was going to be called and informed about the results. Unfortunately, we discovered liver cancer. As you are the only relative of the patient, we share this information with you. She will be treated stationary for some period. After she is sent home, she will be recommended to come to test appointments from time to time."

"Doctor, maybe my mother shouldn't know about this."

"We are obligated to share our patient's health condition with the patient."

"I didn't expect such disappointing results. I feel terrible. I don't know how I will look into her eyes. Can I bring her to tests tomorrow?"

"Mr. Michael, of course, you can. I'm sorry."

Michael got up, said good-bye to the doctor, and left the room.

The news was terrible. He didn't know what to do. He sat in the hallway. He was shaken. Seeing Michael, Beth was also saddened. She sat near him, put her hand on his shoulder, and tried to comfort him.

"Be patient, Michael. If you go like this, she will feel worse."

"You are right. The news hit me hard. I don't know how I will look at her face."

"Maybe I should come with you."

"Don't worry. You must be tired. If you want, I can take you home."

"No, Michael, don't worry. Be patient. I will pay a visit to Ms. Clara sometime soon."

When Michael arrived home, his mother was not there. She has probably gone somewhere. He went to his room and lay facedown on the bed. He could not hold back his tears. Life was preparing to hit him hard for the second time since his father's death.

A car stopped at the street. He looked out the window. It was his mother. He quickly ran to the bathroom to wash up. He didn't want his mother to see him this way. He still didn't understand why his mother would hide her illness from him. Perhaps it was money issues. But her insurance account had plenty of money; it was enough for medication. He was also worried about the news he heard today. He knew that cancer medication is very expensive. He had to go to the hospital with his mother and discuss the treatment thoroughly. Perhaps this is why she was hiding this from him.

The door closed. Michael went into the room and greeted his mother. She was out of breath and tired. He could see that she was at the market from the grocery bags she was holding.

"Mom, why didn't you tell where you were going? I could have bought those on my way home."

When the mother looked at her son, she saw his eyes were red and answered the question with a question.

"Michael, what happened to you? Why are your eyes red?"

Michael tried to hide it but couldn't. Trying to hide his wet eyes, he came close and hugged his mother. Clara Grady could guess what was going on.

"Mom, please, as long as I'm here, I will go with you everywhere."

"I understand, my son. Looks like you know something. You are worried, but listen to me carefully . . ." she said and sat on the sofa and put Michael's head on her shoulder.

"Michael, your job is hard, and you carry a lot of responsibility. You are a big boy now. You are smart and educated. Your future is ahead of you. You can't trust the air we breathe. We are all guests in this life. Everyone passes away one day. You are my only wealth. Don't worry, my son. Treatment goes on. I'm getting better day by day."

"Mom, we will go to the hospital tomorrow. You need to get tested again. If the doctor suggests, you will stay at the hospital."

"Michael, I've missed you a lot. At least let me spend this month with my son after five years, and then I will go for stationary treatment at the hospital. You are trying to strip me off this happiness."

"You must understand, Mom. Your illness may get worse."

"I'm getting treatment anyway. Why does it matter at home or at the hospital?"

"OK, I don't want to argue with you. We will decide after the tests. George is coming. We should have lunch together."

George Bradley arrived after some time. When he arrived, clocks were showing lunchtime, but he went straight to his room without eating. Michael got up and followed him.

"George, what happened? Why are you upset?"

"Michael, the news I heard worried me too. Luisa told me everything. She heard it from Beth. I feel your pain. I can't look at your mother's face. I don't want to distress her in her condition."

"I understand, my friend. I can't get her out of the kitchen no matter how hard I try. She promised me she will go to the hospital tomorrow for stationary treatment. But if you don't eat what she has prepared, it will hurt her feelings."

"Don't worry, let's have lunch together. If you wish, you can go and rest somewhere after noon. Don't worry about me. I can't leave her alone for now. I'll go to the seaside with her later."

"Yeah, I have somewhere to go as well."

"I see you are also hiding something."

"None, I would never hide anything from you."

"Is it about Luisa?"

George didn't say anything.

"Don't be embarrassed, my friend."

"Yes, I have a date with her tonight."

"I'm really happy to hear that. Looks like you really are in love."

"What did the doctor say about your arm?"

"It's OK. Starting tomorrow, I'm attending an hour-a-day treatment session."

"Congratulations. Can you move your arm freely?"

"Yeah, but the doctor said that I shouldn't move it too much."

"That's right. You need to attend treatment sessions on time."

"Michael, Luisa is Beth's friend. I found out today. The reason she was at the hospital that day was her relative was getting treatment there."

"Beth is a nice girl. She supported my mother emotionally."

"My friend, I can see you have feelings for Beth."

Michael smiled.

"You see? I'm not mistaken by my feelings."

The conversation was cut short as soon as Clara entered the room.

"Looks like I'm interrupting."

"Do not worry, ma'am."

"I heard Beth's name, that's why I came. You went to the hospital today?"

They both didn't know how to respond.

"Yes, I was at the hospital."

"What about, Michael?" she said, staring at Michael.

"You didn't answer my question."

His mother looked at Michael. She could tell that they both were embarrassed. Clara Grady understood this in a different way and left the room.

His mother was happy. It looked like Michael was in love with Beth. Her only wish was to see Michael's wedding. She couldn't wait for the day for her son to have a family and be happy.

Come evening time, they both sat on the sofa and watched TV. Michael put his head on his mother's knee as she sleeked his hair and noticed the white ones.

There was a knock at the door. Who was it? George left an hour ago. When Michael opened the door, he could not believe his eyes. It was Beth at the door.

"Good evening. I guess my arrival was unexpected."

"Welcome, Beth. Come inside."

Ms. Grady heard Beth's voice and came to meet her.

"Welcome, Beth. Happy to see you."

She went inside as she smiled. Michael's face became red; his mother noticed that.

"I came to see you about your condition."

"I'm fine, my girl. I take my medicine on time, and my son is with me to take care of me. What else does a mother need? Do you have any news about my test results?"

Beth realized that they have not visited the hospital today.

"I think it will be ready in the morning."

"Great. I was supposed to be there for treatment with Michael in the morning anyway. How are you doing?"

"All is good, ma'am."

"I'll leave you two alone and you can have a chat. I will make some coffee."

"Mom, don't trouble yourself."

"It's no trouble, my pleasure."

They chatted for hours without realizing how late it got. Beth got up to leave.

"My girl, thank you for coming. Perhaps you should stay the night here."

"Thank you, ma'am. I don't want to disturb you."

"Michael, go and see Beth off. I will be waiting for your next visit."

"Good night."

She went out with Michael to the yard.

"Maybe we should take a walk in this nice weather?"

Beth was thrilled with the offer, therefore she agreed without a word. They walked up to the park nearby. Moonlight was illuminating. A soft breeze blew; birds were chirping. It was past nighttime; it was silent all around. Michael smoothed Beth's hair. As she was enjoying this, she put her head on Michael's shoulder. Their hearts were racing. Michael squeezed Beth close to himself and started kissing her lips and chest. Beth responded in a similar manner.

By the doctor's orders, Clara Grady started getting stationary treatment. Days passed. After a while, Clara Grady's treatments started paying off, as her health condition was improving. Michael visited his mother every day. Mother knew about his relationship with Beth; she was happy about it.

Michael and Beth's relationship was getting serious. Beth was spending most of her free time in Michael's embrace. George Bradley had moved to Luisa's house. George had no time, and since Luisa was living alone, she asked him to stay with her. George's biggest dream was to get married and have children. Even though they already agreed to get married, George hesitated a little bit.

Michael was happy. After hearing positive news from the doctor, Michael left the hospital after saying good-bye to his mother. He put his phone on silent mode as he was meeting with the doctor. He looked at the caller's number. It was George. Michael got worried and called back.

"Hi, man! You called me."

"Hi, Michael. How's Ms. Clara?"

"She's OK now. I just met with the doctor."

"Glad to hear that, man! There's a party tonight. I am going to make reservations. Maybe you and Beth should also come?"

"I like your offer. Great, of course, I will come. What club is it?"

"It's a club located downtown. It's good."

"See you tonight!"

Michael took a deep breath. Today was Beth's rest day. He called her. She was waiting at the hospital yard for him. It looked like she didn't go home after her shift. He was happy today.

As he arrived at the hospital yard, he saw Beth sitting on a bench and approached her. Considering that Beth was tired after her shift, he sat behind the wheel and drove her to her house. Michael did not want to be seen because he knew that Luisa and Beth are neighbors. Therefore, he parked the car behind the house. They went in from the backdoor and through the kitchen.

Beth invited Michael in, even though he wanted to leave. She offered him breakfast. Michael agreed to a coffee. He sat on the sofa, turned on the TV, and started to listen to music.

Beth took a shower and changed her clothes. As she walked into the kitchen, she was more pretty and fresh. When she started making coffee, Michael embraced her from behind and kissed her. This scene continued in Beth's room.

Michael was also tired. They snuggled and slept. It was past noon when they woke up.

They were planning to go to the nature side after lunch. When Michael asked Beth to go to one of his favorite nature places with him, she agreed.

Michael drove the car to the woods just outside the city. Michael loved these places since childhood; sometimes he would come alone, sometimes with George. They went into the depths of the woods holding hands. Even though today was warm, inside the woods was chilly. They sat under the willow tree near the lake and gazed at the beautiful nature. Soft breeze was blowing; birds were singing as if they were racing with nature. They were both happy to be in silence and listen to birds singing. They wanted to forget all of their pain and suffering even just for a while and just enjoy the moment of happiness. Michael lay on the ground under his favorite willow tree. Wind was waving Beth's hair. She also lay near Michael and put her head on his shoulder. Michael touched her hair and started kissing her.

They were madly in love and did not realize how fast the time had passed. Michael had an idea. He took out his knife and engraved both of their names on the tree.

"Let these engravings forever be the sign of our love."

She smiled and kissed Michael.

"I love you very much."

"I love you too. Let's promise each other that we will always be together."

A phone call woke them up from their beautiful daydream. At first, Michael hesitated to answer the call from an unknown number, but he decided to answer. He was not mistaken. He was asked to come to the land troops military headquarters urgently. He started to worry. He moved aside and called George.

"Michael, I was about to call you. They called me to the headquarters too. I wonder what it is."

"I don't know either. I'm returning home with Beth. Wait for me. We will go together."

"OK."

When they arrived at home in half an hour, George was dressed in military uniform and waiting for them. Michael approached him.

"Have you talked to the other guys?"

"Of course, they called everybody. It looks serious. There is still a week of vacation left. Something is going on."

"Whatever. Let's hurry, we will find out soon."

"We had a reservation at a restaurant tonight. Looks like we're going to have to cancel."

"I don't think they will hold us very long. This place is far away from the city center. Returning would take a long time. Perhaps Beth and Luisa should go to the restaurant together, and we'll join them afterward directly from headquarters. I think it's better this way."

"Don't worry about us. We will come after you call."

They arrived at the headquarters. Everyone gathered at the meeting hall was wondering the reason for this sudden call-up.

Finally, several high-ranking military officials along with the headquarters board entered the hall. Everyone got up, saluted the officials, and sat down. After his short speech, the headquarters chief gave the word to U.S. Army general-major Barton Coleman.

"Greetings to all Special Forces. You all have earned a bachelor's degree graduating from the academy, which many can only dream of. You have earned this with your hard work and discipline. I want to congratulate all of you for earning the right to be an officer, and I hope that you all will fulfill your duties with honor. Difficult years of studies are behind. Today, you all are fully qualified military officers. You will be assigned to various military fields, where you will serve your country with honor and pride. As you know, our nation has been actively involved in an anti-terror operation for the freedom and prosperity of Afghan people. Most regions of the country are in devastation because of the conflicts between Taliban and other extremist radicals. Results of internal war for power are terrifying. Many innocent civilians have lost their lives. We have had our share of loss during these years. Special Forces' bravery in these clashes is undeniable. We bow down to those who lost their lives while serving their country with honor."

Everyone got up to honor those who have fallen with a minute of silence.

"You have a grave responsibility in the U.S. Army as special unit officers. There are few days left until the end of your vacation. You have been ordered to gather here for important reasons. As you may know, anti-terror operations in Afghanistan are fairly successful. We cannot allow any civilian casualties.

"The terror act that happened in Kunduz was terrifying and unbearable. The news of suicide car bomb explosion near the bazaar, which resulted in many deaths and injuries of innocent people, devastated us. As a result of the Taliban's growth of power in the region, the number of terror acts has been increasing. Unfortunately, the casualties of medical staff alongside civilians are horrifying news. Terrorists are more active lately. Terrorists hiding in tunnels and caves periodically implement their terror plans, killing many civilians, local police, and soldiers.

"Special Forces, soon you will be sent to Afghanistan as a special unit army intelligence agent to implement your missions. You will be informed of your main objectives when you are in Afghanistan. Starting tomorrow, you will start your training. The purpose of the training is to make you sure your intelligence diversion group locates the enemy location and destroys the enemy without getting innocent people involved. After the training period, you will serve your duty by participating in operations in Afghanistan as special unit intelligence agents. Good luck, gentlemen!"

Col. Scott Cordell stood up.

"Officers, whoever's name gets called comes to my room."

Michael Grady, alongside several officers, entered the colonel's room. Everyone left the room with given orders.

"Michael, the situation in Afghanistan is tough. You will participate in training actively starting tomorrow. Main goal of the training is to make sure officers are well prepared for hand-to-hand combat situations, scouting behind enemies, going through rough terrains, and several other situations. You will be tested by your military training habits before being sent to Afghanistan. Knowing your abilities and education, I am certain that you will be successful. Headquarters board has a very high opinion of you. You have a great responsibility as the commander of an intelligence diversion group to be sent to Afghanistan. We believe in you!"

"Thank you, sir! It's my duty. I am always ready to serve my duty with honor and pride."

Michael went down the stairs to the academy yard where George was waiting for him.

"That was long. Is everything all right?"

"Training begins tomorrow."

"So they are sending us to Afghanistan?"

"You worried?"

"Of course not. We knew what we were getting into when we chose this path."

"Yeah, man. Not everyone is being sent there. Maybe you won't even go!"

"I won't leave you alone, Michael. I will have my say about this very soon."

Michael smiled.

"Don't worry man, just kidding. Nothing is certain yet. But training is vital. We'll talk about it later. Let's go to the club."

Beth looked at the time.

"Luisa, I think it's time. We should go. They'll probably come directly."

"But, Beth, Michael said that they will call. We don't know for sure whether they'll come or not."

"I'll call them."

"Don't. Their job is very strict. Their phones are probably turned off."

"Let's go, then. We'll meet them there."

Even though Luisa was hesitant, Beth turned on the ignition of the car.

"Come on, they are not gonna stay there. They'll come eventually."

Luisa got into the car reluctantly.

"Beth, if we start our relationship like this, we will have problems in the future."

"I don't know about you. I'm in no hurry to marry an army man. You don't see the situation? Their job is very hard. Something military might happen any minute, any day. I wouldn't rush it if I were in your place. You gotta take everything into consideration with things like this. Battlefield or even a war awaits them. You don't even know how they will return from

Afghanistan. I hope everything will be fine, but the war there is very hard."

"It seems that love for you is just fun and games. But I think Michael really loves you. Don't play with his feelings."

"Luisa, honey, you have your life, I have my own. I do love Michael, but like I said, I'm in no hurry to get married, and I think so should you."

They went inside the club after parking the car. Slow music was playing. There were a lot of people in the club. They sat at their reserved tables.

Even though Beth was happy, Luisa could not enjoy herself, especially after what Beth said. She started to think that maybe she doesn't deserve Michael.

"Why are you upset?"

She did not reply. To make her relax, Beth started moving her body to the music's beat. She noticed men sitting on the other side of the club. For some reason, all three guys sitting there were looking at her. One of the guys said something to the other guys. Ignoring them, one of the guys started approaching Beth and Luisa's table.

"Do not agree if he invites you to dance."

"What's wrong with that? We are civil people."

"Would you like to dance, ma'am?"

She smiled and stood up to dance with the guy. After dancing for a while, the guy ordered another dance song and approached Beth again. They danced to the Spanish dance music. Luisa was worried. Michael and George could come any moment now. Michael could get mad if he saw Beth dancing erotically with another guy. A phone call shook Luisa. It was George. She said that they were at the club. They were on their way. The dance finished, and the guy escorted Beth to her table. They both were out of breath.

"Beth, Michael and George will arrive soon."

"Oh, Luisa, I danced nicely."

She didn't mind Luisa, ignoring her, and asked the waiter for two more drinks.

"Luisa, honey, you act like you don't know me. I am the same Beth. I like to have fun. Michael should know it beforehand."

Carl was starting to like this girl.

She is beautiful and her dancing is awesome. Her name is as pretty as herself. Who makes such a beauty wait?

Reid noticed two guys entering the club and turned his head to his friends.

"Boys, looks like their men have arrived."

Carl looked at the entrance. His color changed as soon as he saw Michael and George. His friends could notice that he got mad.

"Damn, I should've kept dancing with her," as he was watching him kiss Beth and take a seat near her.

"Carl, this is a private club, and you are a police officer. We don't need trouble. Calm yourself."

"It's about time someone teaches that bastard a lesson."

"Be patient, man! Don't spoil your fun over him. Time will come and we'll meet him again. You are drunk. Let's go home. You've had plenty of fun."

"I think I'm gonna confront him today."

"Guys, I gotta—" Brook Cletus got up.

"Come on. I'm just joking."

"Carl, I think we better get going. You are drunk."

"Are we not allowed to drink? I'm just trying to relax after work, that's it. Sit down. We will go in a while. So it looks like they are their cavaliers. A cavalier will never make their lady wait. They are garbage to be dumped."

"Looks like Carl did good!" Reid mentioned.

Slow music playing, everyone was dancing. Suddenly, Carl stood up and approached Beth to ask her to dance. Michael got up and pushed his hand to the side.

"Looks like you've forgotten ethics rules."

"You are so wrong, man. Everyone has already seen how I danced with her. I'm gonna dance with her again. You are late."

"Carl, we don't need this. Let's go. I'm sorry, gentlemen. He is drunk." He grabbed his arm and tried to pull him outside.

"No! I'm not drunk. I'll go after I dance with Beth."

Michael was shocked. As he looked at Beth, he didn't know what to say. He suddenly grabbed Carl's arm and twisted. Carl curled with pain. His attempt to punch Michael with his other arm was blocked by his friends.

"Gentlemen! Looks like you don't know where you are. This is a private club. Please leave the club, or I will have to take measures!" screamed the club security.

"Don't worry, Mister. Apologies for what happened. We are leaving." They all left the club together.

"That bastard has been a coward since childhood," said Carl, cursing him. Brook Cletus apologized to the club owner for what happened and left with his friends.

Michael couldn't calm down all the way home.

"I'm sorry, Michael. Forgive me for what happened. I just danced with him. If I knew that you have a history with them, I would've never done that."

Michael kept on driving the car in silence. When Beth tried to hug and give him a kiss, Michael didn't allow that to happen.

"Honey, I love dancing. He asked me very politely to dance, and I accepted."

Michael didn't say a word until they arrived home.

"You can get off."

"You aren't coming?"

"No."

"You still haven't forgiven me. I apologized many times."

"Beth, I'm asking you, let's not talk about this. You see that I'm still mad. I need some quiet." He got out of the car, handed the keys to Beth, and walked away.

He had to be at the headquarters early in the morning. He asked the taxi driver to drive to the hospital before going home. As soon as Michael walked into his mother's ward, she hugged him with great joy.

"Michael, what happened? You look upset. Are you hungry?"

"No, Mom. Don't worry. How are you feeling?"

"There is a final test tomorrow. The doctor will give the final opinion. There's even a possibility that I resume my treatment at home and only come to the hospital for the tests."

"Mom, starting tomorrow, I will be at home only at night. I will be at the headquarters all day for training. I don't know how you will come to the hospital and go back. You shouldn't drive in your condition."

"But, Michael, you still have few days left on your vacation. Are they taking you to a war? Please tell me the truth. Are you hiding something?"

"There's no word about it yet. It's just usual army training. And one more thing—I am an army man. You should always consider that. Those who go to war have mothers too. If needed, I will also go. My mom should keep her head high. As a soldier, we must be prepared for everything."

"Afghanistan is not my land. Why must a mother lose their children? Let them solve their own problems."

"Mom, you watch TV more than me. I'm sure you've seen what is happening in Afghanistan and other parts of the world. So many innocent lives are lost because of terrorism. Wives lose their husbands, mothers lose their children, kids lose their parents, lose their arms, legs, and eyes, people dying. What's their fault? So many innocent people die in the middle of a bloody fight for position, wealth, power among various groups. Whole world is against terrorism. To sustain tranquility, NATO sends its troops to regions. If the clashes are not stopped, terrorism will spread to my and many other countries, which will result with the death of many innocent people."

"I understand, son. May God protect you all. They are all cursed—"

"Don't worry, Mom. If you end up coming home in the morning, I will ask the neighbor to pick you up from the hospital."

"Beth will help if I ask her."

Michael didn't say anything.

His mother finally understood what her son's problem was.

"Oh, Michael, you are young. These things happen. If you fight over little things, either your relationship will be short lived or your life. Don't worry about me, Beth has a shift tomorrow. Go home, get some sleep. You gotta wake up early. Pick me up before you get home at night. I'll wait for you."

"OK, Mom." He kissed her good-bye and left the hospital.

Training was ongoing for more than a week now. Michael was always tired when he got home. Beth was taking care of her while he was gone, visiting her frequently and taking her to the hospital. Even neighbors Lucas Marchelo and his wife never left her alone; their only daughter, Sarah, would always visit after school to keep her company. Michael didn't know how to thank all these people; he loved Sarah the most.

Relations with Beth were back on track, and love sparkles were growing between them. Even though he was tired, he would always manage to take her out for a walk. As Beth got to know Michael closer by this time, his courageousness strengthened her feelings for him.

Michael was actively involved in training. He was teaching soldiers rules of army secrets of hand-to-hand combat. A terrible thing that happened to him made him choose this road.

The commander let them go early today because it was the weekend. When they arrived at Luisa's house, she wasn't there and her phone was off. George was really worried. Michael was surprised at how worried George was over something like this. Even though he was really tired, he didn't refuse when George asked him to go to the hospital with him.

There were a lot of soldiers in the hospital yard. This surprised both friends. When they saw ambulance cars among military cars, they understood what was going on. They knew about the terror attack in Afghanistan; they also knew that the wounded would be returned to military hospitals in the country. Everyone was trying to help the wounded. George saw Luisa among the nurses treating the wounded. Both officers came running to help get the wounded to the stretchers. Michael and George had never seen the terrifying results of terror so closely. The injured were in bad condition. Michael was sad on his way home because of what he had seen at the hospital with George. Ms. Grady just assumed that he is tired as always and turned on the TV for Michael after supper. It was a news program on TV talking about local and international news. His mother tried to change the channel.

"There's plenty of bad news around. Hearing more bad news is only going to make it worse."

"Mom, no, leave that channel on. I wanna hear what they say," he said and increased the volume.

"Today, our borders have been breached once more. A group of dangerous criminals has entered the country secretly after committing big crimes in the neighboring country. Two of them have been eliminated during the shootout with the police force. A sheriff was murdered, and two more police officers were wounded. Unfortunately, the rest of the group is still at loose. They were careful. They hid their faces from cameras. They are very dangerous. With the help of the witnesses and the officer involved in the shootout, their facial composite sketches have been created. If you see anyone matching these characteristics, inform the department immediately. They have fake passports.

Passports taken from dead criminals support that evidence. The police department and the federals are doing everything possible to get the criminals in custody. In other news. Another terror attack in Afghanis—" Michael quickly changed the channel.

"Michael, that was the most important part. Maybe something important happened."

"They are just gonna talk about another terror attack."

Michael did not want his mother to worry too much. He was heading to Afghanistan in two days. His mother would be worried even more.

The wounded brought back from Afghanistan were treated at the resuscitation department and operated on. The doctors were unable to save two military officers' lives.

Luisa came home exhausted after a hard shift. News from George devastated her even more. George was heading to Afghanistan with Michael. Tonight was their last night together. Tomorrow they must say good-bye. The duration or the result of this farewell was unknown. They were both very sad because of this. George didn't know when or whether he would see Luisa again. They decided to spend their last night together at the restaurant.

Seeing Michael get up early to get ready for work was normal for Clara until she realized that it was Sunday. That made her worried. She hesitantly tried to look through her son's gatherings. She knew something was up.

"Michael, where are you going? It's Sunday today."

"Mom, I'm gonna be gone for some time. Beth and the neighbors will take care of you."

"Michael, what are you saying? Why did you hide this from me?"

"Mom, I don't wanna trouble you with every little thing. It's a short trip. I'll be back soon."

"Are you going to Afghanistan? Why did you hide this from me? I would have gone to the general to explain the situation and maybe take some time off for you. What if something happens to me by the time you come back? At least I could live the rest of my days with my son. Why didn't you think of me?"

"Mom, I understand you. You think it's easy for me? I was supposed to be there three months ago. Most of my classmates are already in Afghanistan. With all of these happening, how can I just sit and watch? You are the reason I'm not there right now. Your health is good for now. Don't worry, it won't be long."

His mother was crying. Michael hugged his mother. Even though he tried hard, he couldn't hide his tears.

"Mom, you must not cry today. It's not a good sign. You know these things better than me."

"OK, Michael. I won't cry anymore. May Holy Mary protect you."

"There you go, Mom. You must hold your head high. Clean your tears and wish me luck."

The news hit Ms. Grady hard. She didn't know what to do. She couldn't get the idea of losing her only son on the battlefield. No matter how hard Michael tried to comfort her, she couldn't hold back her tears.

The moment has come. Even though his mother made a big breakfast table, Michael only had a cup of coffee. When he got to the living room to say good-bye, he stopped. Beth, neighbors, and his mother were there. Everyone knew about his departure and came to bid farewell. His mother was sitting on the sofa with her head down. Michael said good-bye to the neighbors first. Lucas Marchelo hugged Michael and wished him luck, and so did Sarah and her mother. Michael got down on his knees and put his head on his mother's knees.

"Good luck to you, my son. Don't worry about us. Don't you see how friendly our neighbors are? Beth is like my daughter now. As soon as you return, we'll have your wedding." She stood and hugged her son.

"I won't cry anymore, son. You should be careful out there."

"I'll be back soon, Mom, I promise. Don't worry."

Beth was going to drive with Michael to the headquarters. Michael stopped the car before arriving.

"I love you, Beth. Are you going to wait for my return?"

"Michael, I will always love and wait for you."

"I'll write letters to you. I want you to answer them."

"OK, Michael. I love you."

"I'm not gonna say good-bye. See you soon."

As the hours passed by, the plane was approaching the destination. The trip was tiring. Michael Grady thought about his mom throughout the trip. What if something happens to her? She shouldn't be alone in this state. He trusted Beth and his neighbors, he was sure of them.

The soldier sitting next to him distracted him from his thoughts.

"I know you. I have seen you at the academy many times. I can't forget the day you won the tournament a few months ago. My name is Buster Bufford."

"Nice to meet you, man. Where are you from?"

"I'm from Virginia. We moved to your state after I got accepted to military school. I lived alone with my mother. I was a baby when my father died in a car crash. After high school, I got into the military academy. My mom lives in a two-bedroom house in the suburbs. I've always wanted to be a tankist. That's what brought me to the academy. I graduated this year. I'm a tank commander. Few friends of mine are going to Afghanistan too."

"I only have my mother too. She's very sick. After the academy, I spent a few months with her. I'm really worried for her. She takes lengthy treatments at the hospital."

"I'm sorry to hear that, man. It must be hard. If I'm not mistaken, you will go as a special unit intelligence agent to Afghanistan for a mission."

"Yeah."

"It's a really tough job."

"You are right. There is no easy job in the army."

"You're right."

Even though there was airspace in Kunduz, they have been ordered to land in Kabul for safety reasons. Soldiers knew the situation in Kunduz was bad even before they got on board. Even the flight from Kabul to Kunduz in a helicopter was dangerous enough. Highway was safer, but still everything needs to be considered. They could be confronted by Taliban or Islamic groups. They needed to be prepared for anything.

The plane conductor announced that they will be landing in Kabul soon. Michael was looking through the window as they were approaching the ground. The capital used to be just a quiet eastern Muslim city. But now there is war at hand. They had a difficult task.

Soldiers were on the ground. Special units took their place in a designated area. Long trip and warm weather had already worn them out, but they were withstanding. Several military officials were discussing something nearby, and it seemed like they were expecting someone to arrive.

As the military car was approaching with high speed, it created a cloud of dust behind. It was a colonel-ranked army official. He approached the line; it was obvious that he was tired. It was Col. Bill Carmen, commander of the special unit regiment in the U.S. Army. The colonel saluted the soldiers.

All the soldiers saluted back. The lower-ranked officer standing next to the colonel started calling special unit agents' names. As the colonel was walking in front of the line, he was checking the soldiers' uniforms and their stance. It looked like vigorous training sessions had paid off, as the colonel had seen nothing incorrect. When he came to Michael, he checked Michael from head to toe.

"Commander, two steps forward!"

Michael came forward and stood still.

"Special unit intelligence commander Michael Grady at your service, Colonel!"

"At ease! As a commander, I'm sure you are aware of your responsibilities."

"Yes, sir!"

"You will be informed of your mission and passwords before heading out to Kunduz. You may get back to your place."

"Special units! There is a tough task in front of you. The Taliban has been very active lately. Terror attacks are nonstop. Streets filled with dead people. Blood lakes are everywhere. It's terrifying. You all know why you came to Afghanistan. This is a battlefield for the brave and strong. You have been chosen among thousands regardless of your religion, nationality, or race. Only by sticking together we can win the war. No words such as 'Where are you from,' 'What is your belief' to be heard here. You have important missions to complete and a war to fight. You must be aware at all times. Never forget, terror can happen any moment. You have to be careful with every step you take. It's a war zone. You may lose your arm, your leg, even your life here, but you must hit the enemy hard. You have been through military training. You know the war tactics. Any male can become a man, but not every male can become a special unit agent. Don't underestimate the enemy. Don't be overconfident. Don't ever think that you are untouchable.

"Commander Michael Grady! There are soldiers from each race and nationality that live in America in your battalion. I'm certain you understand what I mean. It's time to put your knowledge to work that you obtained in the past five years. Soon, your battalion will head to our headquarters located in Kunduz with armored military vehicles. Attacks on the road from Taliban and other Islamic groups are inevitable. You must be prepared for attacks. You will implement your mission in Kunduz and nearby regions. You will have five tanks and their crew members with you. Good luck, gentlemen!"

North of Kunduz Province. Mountainous region, located to the border of Uzbekistan. North of Afghanistan is considerably colder compared to other regions of the country. In the desert surrounded by hills and rocks, there are a lot of civil-dressed native soldiers and military vehicles. The vehicle stopped at the destination. One of the three people inside the car moved rapidly toward a group of armed men and said something in Persian. After chatting briefly, with the guidance of two other soldiers, the same man went through the tunnel. One of the armed men ahead showed him to stop with his hand; the first man had to squeeze through rocks to get into the cave. The cave resembled a house. There were mats and sheepskin on the floor. Ten people could easily have a comfortable seat inside. Three people were inside. A man in his sixties, white beard, was sitting at the top, moving his misbaha, and reading Quran verses under his lips.

The sheikh lifted his head up to see who had come and resumed to finish prayer.

"Amen! God, protect us from misfortunes!" He turned his head to the newcomer.

"I'm listening."

"Your Highness, one of the caravan leaders has come bearing important news."

"Let him in!"

The sheikh looked at the man from head to toe with suspicious looks.

"I have never seen you before."

"Sheikh, I am replacing the caravan leader who died in the last battle."

"Do you know him?" he asked the armed guy.

"Sheikh, honestly, I see him for the first time."

"Your Highness, Gunduz Saeid Omar personally appointed me the caravan leader. It's my first time here."

"Saeid is my most respected and trustworthy caravan leader. I believe him. How did you find this place?"

"Ex-caravan leader's driver brought me."

"OK. Tell me, what is the news? What is the rush for?"

"Important news from Kabul. Sheikh, I have heard a battalion of America's best soldiers are heading toward Kunduz."

"Special units?"

"What!"

"Do you think it's the first time?"

"Of course not. But these are very skilled intelligence agents. It's obvious why they are here."

"So I guess intelligence agents."

The sheikh changed the topic as if he was suspecting something.

"Where do you live?"

"I'm from a nearby village."

"Where are your documents?"

"All here, Sheikh," as he showed the piece of paper.

The soldier standing next to him grabbed the paper and handed it to the sheikh.

"Do you know the rules? If you don't, you should learn. You must give complete information about you and your close ones. If you betray or lie to me, I will destroy you and your loved ones. I have different plans for a traitor. Betrayal is unforgivable. Hear me good. Your information will be checked."

"Sheikh, unfortunately, my family lived in Kunduz. I lost my wife and two sons in an explosion."

"May their souls rest in peace."

"He is telling the truth, Sheikh. I lost my relative in that explosion too."

"It's understood. Looks like they have sent their best soldiers again. They are probably planning something. This is how things are. What else are they saying?"

"Sheikh, they landed in Kabul and are moving toward Kunduz in armored military vehicles."

"They are coming to Kunduz. OK, let them come. It's not the first time. We will teach them a lesson. Don't you worry. These special agents need to be destroyed in their place. You should know, they came here for us. Don't forget, a small campfire in the woods can create a very big bushfire. The fire needs to be put off as soon as possible. Destroy them before they regroup with the troops located in the center. You must catch at a place where you can destroy them before air and land support arrives."

"Your Highness, my caravan is in the mountainous region near the area. Main purpose of my visit is to ask for your blessing and ask for your help for the troops in need of help. It's scary to meet these kinds of fighters with just a few of us. It's not easy to win against them."

"Do not worry. We will take care of them. As you can see, they are aware of my power, that's why they have landed in Kabul first. They are not coming with a helicopter. Why? Because we will hit their helicopter. Highway is less dangerous for them. Let them be. Get all the troops together and control the highway. Let other caravan leaders know of my order. It's suicide to confront them in the desert. Put a trap in a mountainous region near Kunduz. Surround them. After destroying their vehicles, attack them."

"Sheikh, maybe we should make traps in the houses located in the nearby village?"

"But there are innocent people living there," the other caravan leader noted.

"That's why our troops should make traps there. They won't suspect civilian houses. It'll be to our advantage."

"We are fighting for the right reasons. This is an Afghan land. Regardless of their age and sex, everyone who lost their lives will be a martyr in God's eyes. May God forgive our sins."

"You got it, Sheikh. I'm at your service."

"Send four soldiers with him. Check the validity of his information. Inform the caravan leaders of my order and ask them to make a trap in the mountainous region. Contact Gunduz Saeid Omar. Tell him my orders. He shall watch over the fights. Let me know of the results."

The man left the cave and came back to the parked car with armed men beside.

"We need to deliver Sheikh's orders to Saeid. Radio station nearby doesn't work."

"I can take care of it if you want. I will pass the area anyway."

"OK, hurry. We have little time."

Michael Grady's battalion was heading toward Kunduz on the highway with several armored military vehicles and tanks. The heat was exhausting. Michael was in front inside the armored vehicle. He was nervous. He was trying to watch every possible suspicious spot and any movement.

They have already passed most of the road. Shining rays of the sun were tiring. Everyone was tired, hungry, and thirsty. Main goal was to complete the long distance and arrive at the U.S. military headquarters located in Kunduz.

Michael was communicating with the center and informing the condition.

The village located ahead, approximately two kilometers away, somehow made the commander suspicious. He started looking through binoculars at the houses made with mud. Seeing several armed people run into the house made him more suspicious. It looked like there were armed groups in the village. He had to inform the center about this right away.

"Captain Lieutenant, has something happened?" George Bradley asked.

"Looks like they have a surprise for us, Captain."

"Center 500, it's Eagle 320. I see suspicious movement two kilometers ahead. We are in thirty-second square."

"Center 500 is listening. Keep watching the area and take precautions. Get the battalion ready for fight and wait for the orders. Keep informing us and follow the orders."

"Boys! Be ready to fight and wait for my orders. Everyone stays in their place. No one leaves their vehicles before I say so. Prepare all guns. We will move forward. I see suspicious movement ahead. Watch your surroundings."

"What's going to happen to the innocent people in the village if we start a battle?"

"It looks quiet. Perhaps it's empty."

"Quiet is not a good sign. They probably know that we have arrived. They may have a surprise for us. We need to be very careful."

"That's what I was thinking. We shouldn't battle before we find out everything. We should approach slowly."

"Commander, we have guests," said Buster Bufford.

"I see. Cover the right flank. There is incoming."

"Center, it's Eagle 320. I see dangerous movement at the thirty-seventh square on the map. Answer!"

"Keep moving. There are civilians in the area. Be careful. Do not attack unless you are attacked. We are sending troops your way."

"Center, I hear you. I'll do so."

"Sir Captain Lieutenant, I see a large car caravan coming from the left flank. I think they are trying to flank and surround us."

"They outnumber us. Be ready and wait for my command."

"Center, it's Eagle 320. I'm reporting the situation. We are about to be surrounded. Waiting for your attack command."

"I understand. We are sending two more choppers your way. Dictate your coordination."

Michael was carefully watching his surroundings. The enemy outnumbered them, and they were approaching. The commander was waiting for them to come closer to determine the fire range correctly. Finally, when the enemy was as close as three kilometers, the commander gave the command to attack. Fierce battle began. Taliban groups were attacking from the village up ahead. Some of the bazooka bullets reached the area; the others did not. The violent sound of the bullets from tanks, guns, bazookas, and grenades mixed with the cries of the wounded and innocent people fighting for their life. It was a terrifying battle.

"They are coming right at us! Bastards! Gonna kill you all!"

"Come, come closer. I'll show you who I am!" George screamed.

"Michael, they are trying to trap us. There is a big caravan approaching from the left flank. Looks like they don't know whom they are up against."

The battle was getting more intense. New Taliban forces joined the battle. It was not good news. Michael sent two tanks and an armored vehicle toward the left flank to handle the caravan.

The Taliban were getting closer as their bazooka shots were exploding near the armored vehicles. They grew their numbers in the fight with the addition of extra forces during the fight. Grady's battalion was outnumbered at the beginning; now the battle was getting even worse as the enemy was closing in. Bullets coming from the air decided the fate of the battle; it was helicopters. The attackers pulled back after the helicopter attack as they lost plenty of men. But the fight was not over. Even though both sides had casualties, the attackers had more men injured, dead, or hostage. Among the hostages, there were the respected Gunduz Saeid Omar and the sheikh's brother. When the army arrived, the battle was already over. There were some fire shots here and there; the real danger was lying at the village up ahead. There were plenty of Taliban forces inside those homes. Michael got the report of the injured and dead. There were thirty-eight wounded; twelve special agents had died. Two armed vehicles and one tank were totaled. Michael helped the wounded to the helicopter. There were wounded among the hostages; they were treated and under supervision taken to the hospital in Kunduz.

Michael saw Buster among the injured. He could barely talk; he was really happy to see the commander. Michael tried to comfort him.

"Don't worry, man, you'll get better."

"Michael, I have a fa-vo-r to ask. If some-th-thing hap-pens to me, vi-sit my m-mom."

"Don't worry, man, you will live." Michael held his hand. Buster took out a talisman from his pocket and handed it to Michael.

"My friend, ta-ke my ad-dress. If some-thing happens to me, I want you to vi-sit my mom. Tell her to take ca-re of herself and my do-g and that I lo-ve her," and tried to smile.

"She sh-ould marry and be hap-py."

Michael couldn't stop his tears. He leaned to kiss Buster on the head.

"Be patient, man. You will survive and tell these to your mother yourself."

He was put into the helicopter. Buster was looking around at his friends in arms for the last time.

Everyone was upset because of the losses they had taken. Even tougher missions were awaiting them.

The armored vehicle caravan stopped close to the village. As the special units were entering the village smoothly, Michael noticed some armed man running into the house ahead. Michael and two soldiers went into the yard and leaned on the mud wall to take cover. The commander asked one of the soldiers to stay outside and take cover as they entered the house through the door. The house was really dark. Suddenly, there was a woman in black robe with a veil covering her face. The woman was showing the baby in her arms to Michael and saying something in Persian language. Michael was frustrated. He moved aside the woman and moved further in. Two kids were crying in the corner. A man standing with his hands held up was looking at Michael. He asked about the armed man who entered by showing his gun. The woman screamed and started begging Michael on her knees. Michael asked the man again. As soon as the man hesitantly pointed his head to the next room, Michael saw the armed man. Even though Michael shot the armed man, he and the man got hit. Michael's armored jacket protected him. The woman hugged her dead husband and screamed. When Michael was heading to the older one, the kids pulled Michael's hand to another room. The kid removed the mat on the ground and pointed to the corner of the room. Michael commanded the soldiers to open the door of the basement. They discovered a weapons warehouse. New-gen radio stations, tank blasters, handmade grenades, guns, bullet combs, and explosives.

"Bastards! It's a real war house here. I think there are more of these houses. Call the boys to clear the artillery."

The operation was over. The few remaining Taliban force members surrendered their guns. Michael headed his battalion to Kunduz. All the soldiers were exhausted after the battle and tiring road trip. When they arrived at the army base in Kunduz, Michael was called to the headquarters commander's room to report the battle. Col. Barton Coleman asked the sergeant for permission to enter the room. After hearing the report, the colonel shook the soldier's hand and praised him for his heroism.

"We had intel about the Taliban attack. Intel came from the Afghan Special Police Department. We sent the troops to the battlefield, but it was too late. The Taliban had already attacked.

We suffered greatly. If their attack was made from mountains, our fate would have been much worse. It was their mistake that benefited us. Otherwise, we have been destroyed. They usually set up traps to attack. I'm sorry for our losses. But war is war. You will have more difficult and vital missions to complete. You know how important the role of the special units during wartimes is. Good luck. From tomorrow morning, more battles await you and your battalion."

The news had saddened Sheikh. After consulting with his caravan leaders, the sheikh came to the conclusion that there was treason; someone had delivered his orders incorrectly. As a result, several caravans had been confronted by the U.S. Army and suffered greatly. The sheikh ordered to find the traitor and behead him. One of the traitors was a local police officer and the other two civilians. Two were already caught and to be beheaded by the sheikh's judgment in sharia court. The sheikh informed his caravan leaders about the rescue plan for the taken caravan leaders. The trap was a doing of the police department, and the sheikh himself had nasty plans about it.

It's noon prayer time in one of the villages located up the north of Kunduz Province. Prayer sound from the mosque was calling everybody to pray. All the town was rushing to the mosque for namaz. Mullah asked everyone to stay after the prayer for the mufti's speech. Everyone was eager to hear the mufti's words.

"People, hear and know. Our religion is at stake. Infidels have come and destroyed our land, our home. They orphan our children. This injustice cannot be tolerated. We must unite against their guns and tanks. We must not bow down to the enemy. We can win only if we unite. Every word coming out of Sheikh's mouth is an order, and we must gather around our beloved Sheikh and fulfill his orders. We lost many good men in yesterday's battle. People, pray for our fallen Muslim brothers. They are in heaven now. The rats among us are responsible for all of this. Give us those traitors—hurry—to avenge our brothers. We were going to destroy the enemy's best soldiers, but the traitor informed them about our plan, and as a result, we suffered a loss. Enemy has taken hostage two of our most respected caravan leaders, and one has died for our land and our beliefs. We are going to behead two of those traitors in front of you. Be warned, all the traitors will be beheaded by the sharia court judgment. There is no place for traitors here. Traitors must know, their families will pay for the consequences too. They will be punished properly. Pray for our fallen brothers. May God forgive their sins. They will go to heaven because they have given their lives for their beliefs and honor. Only way to retaliate is with live bombs. We can destroy more enemy forces this way. Let us destroy their armored machinery, their bulletproof clothes with our humble close-to-God bodies. This is the only way you can get revenge for your fallen husbands, fathers, and brothers. God is almighty and forgiving. Let our fallen brothers go to heaven. Everybody, come on and watch these traitors get beheaded, and that should be a warning to others. Whoever wants revenge shall visit Sheikh for his blessings after the beheading."

Early in the morning, all the soldiers are up. Michael and George went to the headquarter chief's room to receive new missions. Michael noticed an officer in the waiting room. He resembled someone. As if the officer felt Michael's looks, he turned his head. Michael and George were astonished. It was Roger Thomas. Old friends hugged, chatted a bit to catch up, and entered the office. The colonel invited them to sit after the salute.

"I hope you have had your rest. Starting today, you will be given special assignments, and we expect you to do well. After yesterday's battle, we expect that the city will be less stable. Islamic groups are going to try to take revenge using relatives of the dead ones as live bombs. You must implement various assignments while sustaining public order. During your time in Afghanistan, you will fight against terrorism by finding the location of the enemy and attacking both from air and ground on time. In addition to your normal training, you will be training Kunduz special police force members. I am sure that you all will honor your duty while you are in Afghanistan. Good luck to you, gents!"

Two months have passed since her son left for the army. His mother would sit in front of the window every day and watch the road his son would return. She prayed at the church just to have her son back safe and well. Thinking that she does not have much to live, fear of not being able to see her son again was not giving her a rest of mind. Sometimes she would open the TV and listen to the news about Afghanistan. Every news about some terror act, especially in Kunduz, where her son is, would take a toll on her life. It was not easy knowing that her son is always in danger.

She was very happy with Beth. She would always take her to her treatments, and the neighbors never left her alone. Sometimes their only daughter, Sarah, would spend the night with her, keeping company. She was fighting for her life. She just wanted to see her son come back alive and well. Then she could die happily.

She received only four letters from Michael since he left. He would say everything was OK and that there was no reason to worry. Her son sent pictures with his friends and alone to his mom, asking her to take care of herself. But his mother knew that those words are just comforting lies. She watched TV lately; she knew what was going on in Afghanistan. Despite all of this, the mother was proud of her son and what he was doing, loving the pictures he sent him. The uniform he wore looked good on him. It made him look like a brave, tall, strong, handsome knight. She was full of pride.

Every letter Beth received from Michael was like a holiday for her. She would read the letters over and over again and kiss his pictures. She wanted her lover back as soon as possible. She was unaware of the hurricane coming.

She visited Clara on her shift day. Her pain was increasing; the medicine did not seem to be helping.

"Ma'am, I think you should move back to the hospital for treatment. I'm working tonight. After taking a little rest in the morning, we can go together for a test and decide whether you stay or not."

"OK, Beth, I hope I'm not too much trouble for you."

"Don't worry, ma'am. I will always take care of you." She kissed her and returned home. Night was going to start soon. She took her work bag and got in the car. She had to hurry as the snow was already starting to cover the road. Luisa was standing near the car; she seemed angry.

"Hi, Luisa, you look worried. Are you going to work?"

"Hi, Beth. The car broke down again. I've been trying, but it won't turn on. I'm going to call a taxi. I have to be at the hospital on time."

"Don't trouble yourself. It'll take a taxi a long time to arrive. I'll take you."

"But you are going to work too. I don't want you to be late because of me. I'll just call a taxi."

"It's no problem, Luisa. I know a shortcut. We'll go from there."

"OK, don't worry," she said and got into the car with Luisa.

"Watch out, roads are slippery."

"Calm down. I know these roads. This way will be much quicker. I have to get back too."

"I'm troubling you. I'm really worried. I'm not like me before. I can't sleep at night every time I hear about some terror act in Afghanistan. I see nightmares. I think the situation in Afghanistan is not good."

"The more you talk, the more I worry."

"Believe me, I lose myself every time I hear the TV talk about the wounded and the dead. I hate this war. I wasn't like this before."

"Calm down! You need to control yourself. Don't think about it. We have an important job as well. We need to be careful."

The roads were covered with snow. It has been snowing for quite some time now. Traffic was slow. Beth noticed something was blocking the road up ahead. There were a lot of people.

"Luisa, I think there has been an accident."

"What if someone is hurt?"

"If we go further, we'll get stuck in traffic. We need to take another path. This one has stopped anyway."

"If someone is hurt there, we need to help them."

"Luisa, we have nothing but the medicine bag we have, and I can hear the ambulance sirens. It's somewhere close. The police are also trying to unblock the road. We need to get to work."

"Beth, maybe something we do will save the life of someone. Let's go. I'll help."

There were a lot of policemen in the area. They were trying to unblock and control the road for the ambulance and tow truck. They asked the drivers to take alternative routes.

"Luisa, we can't drive any further."

"Stop the car. I'll walk there."

Luisa took the bag and started walking.

"Don't rush, one of the policemen is approaching. First, we'll find out what's going on, and then we can go to help together."

"Hello, ma'am. There has been an accident. The road is blocked. I can't let you pass."

"We are nurses. We are here to help," Luisa replied.

"Ma'am, first aid has been done. The ambulance will be here very soon. You should get going. This road is blocked. I advise you to take an alternative route."

"We don't know any other route. We need to get to work as soon as possible. Please help us."

"OK, ma'am. I'll see what I can do." He called his sheriff friend.

"Carl, can you come over?"

"Coming." Carl Caster approached the car.

When Luisa saw the approaching officer, she was surprised, and she looked at Beth's reaction.

"It's the same guy that fought with Michael. He's a sheriff."

"Carl, please help the ladies out. They are nurses. They don't know any other road, and they need to get to work. Take them from the shortcut."

Carl leaned into the car and smiled.

"What a pleasant surprise! I think I know these ladies. Oh, well." He opened the car door.

"Ma'am, please move to the backseat."

Beth got out of the car with a smile on her face.

"So we are going to the hospital, right?"

Luisa did not respond.

"Yes, sir!" Beth answered with a smile on her face.

"You can call me just Carl. How come your cavaliers have let you get behind a steering wheel in these conditions?"

"They are in Afghanistan."

Carl didn't know what to think for a minute.

"My apologies, I didn't know. So I guess being separated from your boyfriends must be tough for such pretty ladies, right?"

"I think the private lives of other people should not concern you this much," Luisa answered.

"Right, of course, ma'am. That's not what I meant to say. My apologies, I'm sure you can't wait to see them again."

Luisa felt the sarcasm in Carl's words.

"They are brave and honest men fighting for a greater cause. Men like them are worth waiting for."

"I don't understand, ma'am. It's their job and duty. Everyone has a different job and a different way."

"No, don't take it the wrong way. That's not what she meant."

Luisa turned around and looked at Beth with angry eyes.

"Stop the car."

"But we are not there yet."

"I don't want it. I'll walk from here on. Please stop the car."

"Luisa, calm down."

"Bye." Luisa slammed the door and started pacing away from the car.

"Looks like I offended her. I guess I'll go. You can drive from here. The hospital is not far."

"I work at a different hospital. You can get off at the same place. I'll drive from there."

"I can't let a pretty girl like you go alone in this weather. I think I'm gonna have to change my profession tonight. Ma'am, please come to the front seat."

"Would it be a problem? You are on duty."

"Don't worry. I know a way. No one will know. I'll find some cover. There is a storm everywhere anyway."

Carl parked the car at the hospital parking lot. Beth was late for work. She said good-bye and paced toward the hospital gates in a hurry.

"Ma'am, your keys!"

"Take the car with you. I'll get off work at eight o'clock. We'll meet, and I'll take the car back."

"Thank you, Beth!"

Carl Caster was happy. This was his chance to get revenge on his enemy. Actually, he had grown some feelings for Beth since the first time they met, and those feelings came back alive when he saw her again. *Why not?* he thought. He liked Beth too.

Today's coincidence was a chance for him; he did not mean to let it pass by.

"Carl, where were you? You should have been back much sooner. You didn't answer your phone either." Brook Cletus asked.

"Roads are in terrible condition. It took a while to get back."

"You're right, but the hospital is just thirty minutes away. You came back in an hour and a half. Don't forget you are at work. Whatever. I've been waiting for you. We need to go. Drug dealers have reappeared. It's just in. You came back on time. Let's go. We're gonna be late."

They entered the car and drove away.

"Brook, I'm gonna tell you something."

"Yeah, you look like you are about to say something important. Go on."

"I recognized the girls that I just helped out. The girl driving was the girl that I danced with at the restaurant. Her friend was with her too."

"But they have boyfriends. You saw that at the restaurant, right?"

"Their boyfriends are my enemies."

"Carl, I don't think you should get your feelings involved. That's not right. You are a sheriff, they are soldiers—all of you serve your country. You might have to meet this guy again in the future. It's not nice. If she broke up, that would be OK, I guess. I mean, who would have trusted their woman behind a steering wheel at a weather like this?"

"They are in Afghanistan."

"What? That's true?"

"Yeah, girls said so. The one sitting near me was George's girlfriend. I think she's madly in love with him. Wouldn't let me say a word to her. She refused to ride the car with me."

"You probably said something mean and they reacted that way. They seem like good guys. I'd say they are happy because they found love, real love."

"No, man, you're wrong. I think Michael's girlfriend doesn't love her. She was being all chatty and flirty with me on the road."

"So that's why you are late."

"Carl, she might be cool and fun. I know what you are trying to do. That's not what a man would do. Their boyfriends are abroad."

"If a woman has feelings for me, why shouldn't I take advantage of that? I'll try to contact her. We can be secret lovers, and when her boyfriend comes back, he can have his old property back." He laughed out loud with evil.

"You're a . . . man!"

"I don't need your wisdom, man. Keep them to yourself," as he took out the gun and handcuffs and opened the door.

"Be careful! They might be armed."

"You see? They are running. Bastards! You sons of bit——s!"

Carl furiously left the car and started chasing the drug dealer, shouting at him.

"Freeze or I'll shoot!"

"Bastard, I'm here now. I'll blow your brains out."

"Carl, calm down, you are gonna kill him."

"It's OK to kill these bastards." The sheriff opened fire. One of the runners was hit. He fell onto the snow. The other fled the scene.

Carl Caster was shouting at the fugitive lying on the ground.

"Get up! Show me your hands!"

"Calm down, Carl. I think he is dying."

"Never mind, these bastards are tough," as he tried to handcuff the injured man.

"No need. It looks like he is dying anyway."

"I opened fire to the air."

"It doesn't look good, Carl. You have changed since your friend died."

"I must take revenge for him. These bastards don't die so easily. His heart is still beating."

"His pulse is getting weak. He is gonna die before the ambulance arrives. You should have opened fire to the air."

"Why do you worry so much? It's better that he dies. We'll just report that he opened fire first and we had to counterattack."

Carl checked the man's pockets and took out a few joints and put them in a sealed bag. He then reached out for the man's gun behind his belt, cleaned it with a handkerchief, and put it in the drug dealer's hand.

Ambulance sound was approaching. Brook Cletus informed the center about the situation. They have sent a forensics team to obtain more detailed information. Carl Caster explained things the way he was planning, saying that the dealer opened fire first. The doctor announced that the dealer is dead. Carl entered the police car. His hands were shaking; he couldn't control. He had trouble lighting the cigarette in his hand.

"Carl, get a hold of yourself. These things happen. It's not the first time this is happening to us. He could have shot you. We have lost two good policemen to drug dealers this month."

"I don't know. I'm not myself lately. I think I need a doctor. But I'm afraid to go to the doctor. I'm afraid they'll fire because of my psychological problems."

"No, man. Just be careful. We will go down to the center and report what happened."

"Brook, I'm gonna take a joint from the evidence. Let's keep it between us."

"Carl, you are doing drugs?"

"I have been smoking marijuana after work for the past two months. It helps me relax, takes my pain away. I still can't get Freddy's death out of my head."

"I thought something was up with you. I just didn't know how to ask. But what you are doing is wrong. I'll get in trouble for helping you too. You'll get caught sooner or later. Freddy was a friend to both of us."

"Don't worry, just keep this secret. We have been serving together so many years now."

"I can't let you willingly destroy yourself. If you don't quit soon enough, I'm gonna have to change my team."

"OK, I promise I will quit it soon enough."

There was a knock at the door. Alberto was suspicious of who might knock on the door at this time of night. He picked up his gun and asked his friend to open the door.

Brad was careful; he looked out the window.

"Don't worry, Alberto, it's the boys. They seem worried."

"Look to make sure if they have been followed or not."

"It's dark outside. I can't see anything," he said as he opened the door. They were very worried.

"What happened? What's the rush?"

"Important news. We gotta see Alberto."

"What happened again?"

"The police came. We barely ran out of there."

"Where's Chris?"

"The police started shooting at us. Chris got hit and fell down. I don't know what happened after that."

"Dumbasses, if he gets caught alive, he will rat us out. I told you to be careful."

"They caught us when we were leaving the house."

"I need to consult Arnoldo about this. Were you followed?"

"No, we hid in the dark for quite some time and made sure no one was around. We came afterward."

"Get back to the crime scene. Find out if Chris is dead or alive. I need to meet with the boss and discuss this. If he is alive, he may rat us out during investigation."

Carl Caster was in a rush to the hospital after his morning shift was over. Even though he was more than thirty minutes late, Beth was still waiting for him.

"Beth, I'm sorry, I'm late."

"Don't worry about it."

"I can go with you. Your friend is probably waiting for you. I don't want you to get lost again." He smiled.

"I told her that we could come and pick her up, but she is at home already. Let's go."

They chatted on the road. Carl was driving the car slowly on purpose. They didn't realize how the time passed until they arrived. Beth invited Carl inside, but Carl refused and gave the keys back to Beth. Before going inside home, she took some newspapers and a letter from the postbox. Carl noticed how Beth got excited after seeing the letter; it was probably a letter from Michael.

Carl walked to the highway to call a taxi. He got into the car in front of the department and headed home.

Beth took out her coat in a hurry, sat on a sofa in the kitchen, and opened the envelope with great excitement. She was happy. It has been two weeks since Michael's last letter; she was worried sick about him.

"Dear Beth, I got mesmerized from your smell on your last letter. Made me forget about everything and feel like I'm near you for a moment. Reminded me of times we spent in the woods. I miss you a lot. How have you been? My heart feels like it's about to explode every time I reread your hot love letter. When the lights go out, I put your letter under my pillow and try not to sleep. I can't wait for the day I have you in my arms again. Kisses. Sincerely, Michael."

She couldn't hold back her tears as she went into the bedroom. She pulled out the box under the wardrobe and placed the letter carefully among other letters. She lay on the bed daydreaming and fell asleep.

It was the last day of February. Even though it doesn't snow in Kunduz, it still gets very cold. It's one of those busy days in the U.S. Army headquarters. Col. Barton Coleman walked around nervously in his office. Soon, there was going to be a meeting with high-rank army officials discussing the new confidential information and future actions to be taken. Intel was that the Taliban was planning another terror attack. They have been quiet for some time now, and it looked like they have been busy.

Commander Michael Grady entered the headquarters master's office and took a seat after the salute. All the high-rank officers were there. They were eagerly waiting for the headquarters officers' words.

"Gentlemen! According to the intel we received, the Taliban is planning to strike an attack very soon. It says that a lot of artillery has been collected in a mosque located at the north of the city. A lot of Islamic groups and Taliban members have gathered around the mosque Akhund Mullah Hamid Naib. We have been told that one of Taliban leaders, Ali Zabihullah, brother of Omar Rashid Zabihullah, Taliban leader, a.k.a. Sheikh, will be there also. He is in the city with Sheikh's order. Their plan is to attack the police station to rescue two caravan leaders, kill the police, and bring the rest as hostages to be beheaded in front of people by sharia court's judgment. We have pictures of those Taliban leaders. Take a look. Local Afghans who work with or for the police are marked as traitors by Sheikh's judgment. You must attack the mosque from three sides and surround them. You must try to take them alive. It's really important. Center wants us to implement this mission flawlessly. We must respect people's beliefs and make sure that the mosque does not get harmed. You will be informed about the time of the operation. We need to make sure that we don't attack during prayer time."

The colonel looked at the map on the wall.

"East and west are the most populated regions. In the north, there are borders, not much population there, just mountains and deserts. It's not easy to get through those places. Islamic groups and Taliban troops enter the city from the desert area. The enemy is sly. A normal, harmless-looking person can be a very dangerous terrorist. You need to be careful in this operation. No civilians must be harmed. We will approach the area from three flanks. Capt. Lt. Michael Grady will lead the first team, Capt. Roger Thomas, second, and Capt. George Bradley will lead the third team. We will have five snipers located on top of the roofs of the houses near the area to watch the people going in and out of the mosque. It's obvious that the enemy is going to plant a live bomb. While sustaining the suspects, make sure no civilians and soldiers get hurt. You need to be very careful. I can't stress this enough, we must try our best to make sure innocent people do not get harmed.

"Gentlemen! Don't forget that this is a war. You may die or become disabled for the rest of your life. It can happen to every one of you. Good luck, gentlemen!"

The phone rang. A phone call at this time of night worried Anderson. The boss left his phone in the room while he was busy gambling. Anderson was high and having fun with a girl. Nonstop phone calls pissed him off. He hesitantly got up and picked up the phone. It was Alberto. At first, he didn't want to answer the phone, but then he decided to answer.

"Listening."

"Looks like my brother trusted you with his phone too."

"Yeah, what's up?"

"Give him the phone."

"A minute."

Anderson opened the door with hesitation and handed the phone to the security.

"Tell Boss it's Alberto calling. I think something has happened."

The boss was really into the game. Arlen leaned over to his boss and whispered something to his ear.

Arnoldo's facial expression changed right away. He asked the permission of his gambling buddies and went to another room where other people can't hear him.

"Hello, it's Arnoldo. You called."

"Where are you, Arnoldo? I gotta see you urgently."

"I'm at the casino."

"I'm coming there."

Arnoldo returned to the round gambling table.

"Gentlemen! I must leave you after this game. My apologies."

Arnoldo and Arlen entered the room on the second floor.

"You wait outside. I'll call you if I need you. You go downstairs and hang out there!" he shouted at the boss Arnoldo's girlfriend Elma. The boss didn't say a word until she left the room. He didn't like the way he talked.

"Anderson, you watch out. I decide who stays and who goes. You don't need to talk when I'm in the room, and don't smoke that sh——t when you are at work."

As soon as Alberto entered the room, the talk finished. Brothers met and sat on the sofa.

"Maybe we should get somewhere private. There's something I gotta tell you."

The boss looked at Anderson. Anderson left the room.

"Arnoldo, things are not good. Three of our gang members were ambushed. One got shot, and the others ran away."

"Is he dead or alive?"

"We don't know for sure yet. That's what I'm worried about. If Chris gets caught, the police will make him talk. That's not good."

"Bastards! I told them to be careful, there are cops everywhere. They have been working double since the death of the sheriff last month. I told those bastards, if you ever get caught, consider yourself dead."

"What do we do now?"

"Alberto, it's all because of your fault, your ego. This is what it got us. I keep telling you, you are too young for this. You didn't listen. You went against me. You see what happened? You hired some hobos, and this is how they work. Those you call friends will be the end of you and me one day. There is no friendship in this business. You see how everyone is afraid of me? You know why? Because they know that I will destroy them if they do me wrong, and I'll feed the body to animals, nothing left behind. That's why now there is a group of trusted men. Most of the guys came here with us. I know what they are capable of. You don't respect me. You only call me when you are in trouble, and here we are."

"What about you? When my mother died, she asked you to take care of me. But you don't care about me. You only ask the as——ole to do all of your things. You trust him more than me? As if that wasn't enough, you embarrassed me in front of him and other guys. You slapped me. Despite all of that, I wouldn't come here if I didn't love and respect you as my older brother. I have come for your wisdom." Arnoldo stroked his hair.

"Alberto, you are all I have in this life. I push you away from these things because I wanna protect you. I have nobody else except you. You know that we are on the run. We run this business under a different name. I don't need to tell you what will happen if we get caught. That's why I agreed to let you leave. If I get caught, then maybe you can escape. From now on, consult me before doing something. I will give you money. All I have is yours."

Arnoldo left the room for a moment and came back.

"I sent the guys to the area to see if he is dead or not. They'll call back."

"You see, you are not ready for these things yet. Never discuss these kinds of things over the phone. Give your boys nicknames. Let your most trusted one do all of your things. Never try to be the center of attention. Don't take photos. Find out what's going on with the help of that trusted guy. If someone gives you some important information over the phone, throw the phone in the garbage and leave the area. This is how you will have a window to escape while the others are getting arrested.

There was a knock at the door.

"Come in!"

Anderson entered the room.

"Boss, I have news."

"I'm listening."

"One of the guys from his band got shot and died at the scene."

"You can go."

"How does he know that Chris was with my guys?"

"You see now, Alberto. You had no idea that I knew everything about you and people around you with the help of this guy. Anderson is controlling all of this. He punishes the misbehavers before me. I know all of your boys. It's because of me that nobody is causing you any problems. I'm not stupid not to know who works around my little brother. What if one of them is working for the police? I know what kind of shithole they come from. I own this place. You are making business so easily. You think that's how it really works? You're wrong. You are under my wings. Now go rest. Danger is over now."

"Thank you, Arnoldo. I'll consult everything with you first from now on."

"Anderson is a good guy. Be friendly with him."

"Impossible, that's the only thing I can't do."

"All right, it's getting late. I gotta go home. Probably pretty lady is tired of waiting for me."

They both left the room and went to the first floor with a smile on their faces. A woman sitting put her cigarette in the ashtray, put her fur coat on, and approached them.

"What did I tell you? Do you see? You gotta know how to live, brother. Find a nice girl for yourself. Life is short. But always be careful. Otherwise, your hands will be cuffed forever."

"Honey, I have been waiting for so long. I'm tired of it. Let's go." Elma put her arm on his shoulder coyly.

Arnoldo smiled back at her.

"How can I say no to such a pretty girl?" He winked at Alberto. Arnoldo and Elma left the casino together and sat in the backseat of their luxurious car. The boss ordered Arlen Brooker to drive. The lights of the car made a path in the dark as they disappeared gradually.

Alberto drove his car straight to the club after his brother left. His brother's words made him think. It seems that his brother knew everyone around him with the help of Anderson. The fact that Anderson managed all of his brother's work and even supervised his boys pissed him off. He knew of Anderson's dirty works and was looking forward to proving it to his brother. To get proof of Anderson's dirty works, he had to get one of the boys near his brother. He thought of Arlen Booker; they used to be friends back in the day. He also wasn't fond of Anderson and his brother's girlfriend Elma. Sometimes he would badmouth them near Alberto. Alberto had a fight with Anderson. The fact that his brother took Anderson's side and got mad at him pissed him off badly. He gathered his boys after this and started selling illegal drugs again. Alberto had the thought that Anderson was taking advantage of his brother's fondness for girls and drugs, as he was stealing from the casino profit. Alberto had to meet with Arlen by any means necessary and explain the situation. He was there to get some evidence of Anderson's dirty work in the casino and help to get rid of Anderson. Alberto was happy about his idea; it was his only hope to get rid of Anderson. He was looking for an opening to talk to Arlen.

It has been more than three weeks since Clara Grady started getting stationary treatment at the hospital. Her illness was responding to treatments as her condition was getting worse. Sometimes she would faint and mumble Michael's name; it worried Beth. She wrote to Michael about his mother's condition, but she got no response. Beth was worried. Lately, she and Luisa were not talking to each other because of what happened with Carl. Beth was suspicious of Luisa of what was happening. She was suspicious that Luisa told George about Carl and Michael found out; maybe that's why he was not answering her letters. On the other hand, Carl's charm was attracting Beth to him even more. She would feel a step further from Michael every time she opened the postbox and found no letter. At the end, she accepted Carl's next invitation to a restaurant.

As the days passed, Beth's feelings toward Carl grew stronger. She would go to Carl's home after work every day. She didn't want Luisa to see Carl. Sometimes she would sneak into her own house to get some things and check the mailbox for letters and newspapers. No letters again. It seems Michael has already forgotten about her.

Since Beth and Luisa did not talk, Luisa didn't know why Beth wasn't coming to her home lately. It all came to understanding one day. As usual, Carl had come to the hospital to pick up Beth after work. She was running late. After waiting a few hours, Carl started to worry. When he tried to call her, she appeared at the hospital gate. She looked worried. She came close to Carl.

"Carl, I can't come today. Michael's mother, she is really bad."

"It's not your problem. You finished your shift. Let somebody else deal with it. Where are his relatives? You are tired. You should rest."

"Carl, you gotta understand. I promised Michael I would take care of her. I have written to him about this, but I can't get a response. We need to let the neighbors know. If she dies, we gotta take care of the funeral."

"I don't understand. What are you saying? Michael, Michael—I'm tired of hearing his name!"

"But you gotta understand. She has nobody else except her son. When he left, he asked me to take care of her. I promised." As she turned away to run toward the hospital gate, she saw Luisa with the neighbors at the door. She hadn't seen them coming.

"Why did you come?"

"Beth, do you have even the slightest knowledge of consciousness?"

"You have no right to blame me for anything!"

"You betrayed your love! It's your life. You will talk about the reasons with Michael. He's out there in the middle of fire worried about his mother. How can you not tell me and the neighbors about his mother's bad condition? At least I could have written Michael if I knew about it. He found out about it after the neighbors wrote to him."

"It's been two months since his last letter. I wrote to him twice to find out why he hasn't been writing back. I wrote about his mother's condition in the letter. I got no answer. What's my fault?"

"I had to go to the address George wrote in the letter to see her. The neighbors said that she is in this hospital. They came along."

"They won't let you into the resuscitation department. Wait, I'm here, I will give you the details," as she turned to Carl.

"You should go. I'll call you."

Carl angrily sat in the car, slammed shut the door, and drove off rapidly.

Luisa was waiting in the hospital hall for a while now. Beth was late. Luisa was getting worried. She approached the reception lady to ask the condition of Clara Grady. The nurse made a phone call. Luisa noticed the sudden change on the nurse's face during the phone call.

"Excuse me, are you a relative?"

"We are friends and neighbors. We have come to visit and find out about her condition."

"I'm sorry, but Clara Grady just passed away a few moments ago."

The neighbor could not hold back her tears after hearing the news despite her husband's comforting words.

Luisa was devastated. What made it worse is that her only son did not know about her death. George has always told her how much Michael loves his mother. She was thinking of ways to tell the news to Michael; at least he could be at the funeral. Luisa was starting to worry about Beth since she was nowhere to be found. Finally, Beth had come back. Her eyes were red from all the crying. She felt guilty in front of Luisa's looks and cried. The way Beth was acting was out of the ordinary for Luisa. What was happening? It was obvious that she had written to Michael about his mother. Why wasn't Michael replying to her? She told no one about Beth and Carl, not even George.

Lucas Marchelo came closer and hugged Beth.

"What can we do? You suffered a lot for her. It's fate. We have to let Michael know about this. At least he can come to her funeral and send her to her final destination."

After leaving the headquarters office, Michael drove to his unit and called George Bradley and Roger Thomas to his room.

"Both of you know about the operation. There must be no civilians at the mosque at the time of the attack."

"The enemy may attack during prayer time to make us look like the bad guys," George said.

"Roger, what do you think?"

"I think they know that we are not gonna attack during prayer time, so they will try to take advantage of that."

"It has to be a flawless operation. Scouts will give us more intel before the operation."

There was a knock at the door.

"Come in!"

"Sir Captain Lieutenant, two Afghans have come. They want to see you."

They looked at each other with Roger Thomas.

"Let them in. Don't worry, guys, these are Kunduz Police Department officers. They are going to be with us during the operation. I have special assignments for them."

Two civilian-looking men entered the room.

"Come on, guys, come sit. Tell us about the situation."

"We started watching any activity near the mosque after you ordered. There were some suspicious activities around. We mostly know the people who live there. We even noticed that some people did not come out of the mosque after prayer time was over."

"You don't know about the exact time they are planning to attack?"

"Yesterday, Sheikh gathered his caravan leaders for a meeting. He always does this when it is important. He has already blessed this terror attack."

"Where did you get this intel?"

"He is the assistant of Sheikh's favorite and most trusted caravan leader."

"Are you sure he can be trusted?"

"Of course."

"How can you be so sure?"

"His brother and a close relative work in the police. He wouldn't want them to get hurt."

"Maybe you didn't get the right information?"

They were looking at each other.

"OK, you may go."

The local police left.

"Michael, how can you trust them?" Roger asked.

"Calm down, man. We must never rely on uncertain information. We've got other plans. It's all under control. Their time for the attack soon will be known to us. You should go and rest now. Tomorrow is gonna be a tough day. George, can you stay a bit, please?"

George knew what was going on.

"I'm worried about what's happening. It's been two months since I got any letter from Beth. I was so happy to hear that I got a letter yesterday. It was from my neighbors. They wrote that Beth took her to the hospital more than two months ago. She is getting treatment there. They visited her a week ago. Everything is OK. What about you? Did Luisa tell you anything?"

"In the last letter I wrote to Luisa, I asked her about Beth. She didn't mention anything about Beth in the letter, which was weird. I wrote her your home address. I'm sure she got it."

Michael took a deep breath.

"Michael, believe me, I also am worried about these things. I don't understand." Michael looked out the window to the snowy mountains of Afghanistan.

"George, you really can't trust anyone. But there is something fishy here. I love her very much. I even asked her to take care of my mother to have peace of mind here. A soldier must not worry about his home, it's not good. I asked her to take care of my very ill mother, she promised. If something happens to my mother without me knowing, I will never forgive her."

"Calm down, Michael!"

"I'm tired of calming down. Whatever. We should rest. Tomorrow is gonna be a rough one."

He's been lying in his bed and thinking for more than an hour now. He fell asleep thinking about how to get in touch with Beth; something was not right. He wished that the war would be over quickly so he could go home and find out about everything.

He dreamed about his mother. She is stroking his hair when suddenly there is a knock at the door. Some person with his face covered comes close to Michael and explodes a grenade. Michael thinks that he died, but when he looks, he sees his mother all in blood. He screams; no one can hear him. His mother's voice whispers in his ears.

"Good-bye, my son. I love you very much. Take care of yourself."

She closes her eyes in Michael's arms. Michael is screaming for help. Beth tries to get closer to Michael with tears in her eyes. Some masked man pulls her away from Michael. Michael goes for his gun thinking it's a Taliban soldier. At this moment, Beth uncovers the man's face. It's Carl. Michael is trying to suffocate him. Out of nowhere, his father appears and saves Carl from Michael.

"Calm down, son. That bastard is not worth ruining your life, for his punishment is ready. You need to protect yourself from the dark powers around him."

His father picks up his mother all in white and starts to move away. Michael screams and tries to catch them, but he can't.

"Michael, calm down."

He saw George trying to wake him up when he opened his eyes. He quickly got up and held his head with his hands.

"I had a strange dream. I saw my mother. I think she's not well. I can't get any information. It makes me mad."

"Be patient, man. She's probably worried about you, that's why she has come to your dream. I know how you feel."

He was all sweaty. He looked at the time. It was almost morning time. He had a drink of water and then looked out the window. It was quiet outside. He thought about the dream he had; he thought it was true.

Michael's heart was pounding. Suddenly, the bell for waking up rang. He looked at his watch; it was too early for it. It had to be something serious that needed preparation. As soon as Michael was ready to go, a sergeant came in with a letter in his hand.

"Sir Captain Lieutenant, headquarter chief Barton Coleman gave this letter for you to read and implement accordingly."

Michael started reading the letter. He ordered all the battalion to get ready for the operation to prevent another terror attack from happening.

It was just an ordinary day. The sun was rising. The sound of the azan was inviting all the Muslims to come to their holy house for prayer time. Young and old, everyone was rushing to the mosque. They would take off their sandals at the door, perform an ablution, and get inside to pray. The extremist groups blend in with the population and find their way inside to implement their nasty plans. There were more people than usual at the mosque today. A Taliban member entered the mosque akhund's room and asked about the location of the guns.

"They are in a safe place." He ordered his servant to remove the carpet from the floor. The floor looked like a standard mud floor. The servant stuck his knife from the side of the mud and moved the big piece of wooden cover. A vast artillery reserve was uncovered.

"As you can see, we have enough weapons for all of our members."

"Akhund, Sheikh has great trust and hope in you. We must hurry, we don't have a lot of time. Everyone who wants to die for our belief and religion is here today."

"You are fighting for our land, for our belief, my children. God will forgive all of your sins. You are going to get revenge for your fallen brothers. All of you shall be rewarded with a spot in heaven. Amen."

"Let us hurry. No time to lose. Explosive equipped cars are in a different place. Plenty of fighters there too. They are waiting for our orders. Spread the weapons to everyone, there is plenty. We must strike before the enemy wakes up."

A man walked in screaming.

"American soldiers are coming! They entered from the bazaar side. They are approaching."

"How many are there?"

"I can count up to twenty."

"It's probably a regular checkout. Otherwise, there would be more of them."

"They are the best soldiers of America. They don't need to be that many. One of them can destroy a group of our soldiers."

"Quickly get men ready. If they know about our attack, they will surround us."

"Akhund, they are approaching the mosque from three flanks. It doesn't look good."

Akhund looked at Ahmad Naib's face.

"Perhaps we should postpone our operation? This way it won't end well. Prayer time is over. Fighters can blend in with the people and leave the mosque."

"Stupid old man, what are you saying? You want a bullet in your head? It's the best time for attack. We will have our live bombs among people, and when they are close to the American soldiers, they will blow up. Rest of the men must hide the guns until you get close to them. Kill the survivors after the explosion."

"Seems we have a traitor among us. They found out about our plan. We must hurry, namaz time is over. All of you who want to sacrifice yourself to God, come here. All of you will earn a place in heaven."

A few young men entered the room. They were all scared to death; they were miserable. They looked at Akhund and the sheikh's brother Ali Zabihullah with helpless eyes.

Akhund hugged them all.

"My children, the enemy is approaching. If we don't destroy them, they will kill us, imprison us, or even torture us. Death is much better. This is how we get revenge. When we get hit by an enemy bullet, the last thing we think will be that we could have killed more of them. You are real patriots. You will reach God by killing more of them. Revenge for your fathers and brothers."

"Enough! Enemy is near. We have no time. They will start blasting this place. You won't be able to do your jihad prayer then. Get them ready to leave with the people after prayer."

"What about other people? There are women and children among them!"

"We are sacrificing martyrs in the name of God. God will forgive us all! Allahu Akbar!"

"Allahu Akbar! Allahu Akbar!"

"Fighters, hide your weapons carefully. Don't let the enemy see it. Get among the people and approach the enemy from three sides!"

"Sir Commander, people are leaving the mosque, a lot of suspects among them."

"Looks like they know we are here. They have started moving." Commander informed the center.

"Group 1, Group 2, Group 3! All soldiers! Snipers! There may be live bombs and armed fighters among people. Open your eyes!"

"Sir Commander, there are live bombs among people coming your way."

"Other groups, report! What is going on?"

"It's not very good. Armed men are approaching, and may be a live bomb also."

"Snipers, try to take them out before they do anything."

"Attention! Commander, one of the live bombs is attempting something."

"Fire now! Make a headshot! Hurry! If he blows up, a lot of people will die!"

"Sir Captain, it's impossible! He is hiding behind people and moving forward! I can't calculate the impact point. I can hit other people!"

"Try to hit him! If he blows, many more people will die!"

The live bomb collapses with a bullet shot in the head out of nowhere. Chaos starts among people. Everyone was screaming and running. Another live bomb used this chance and got very close to the soldiers. It was a very big explosion.

Michael knew what to do in these kinds of situations. He ordered the soldiers to lie down before the explosion, but it was too late; shrapnel did the damage. The big explosion wave threw Grady on his back before he even realized what was going on. Seconds passed. He couldn't feel his body from all the ear and head pain. He couldn't hear anything. He didn't even remember what happened. He started to get back to himself eventually and moved his head with pain to see the others. Dust clouds everywhere. Screams and cries of the injured everywhere. Women screaming their hearts out.

The commander tried to pick up his rifle and get up. Pain in his back and head did not let him. He couldn't turn to his right shoulder. His uniform was bloody from his shoulder. He turned to the left with great pain. To his left side, he saw a child lying on the ground with open eyes. He assumed that he probably is dead. He crawled up to him and checked his pulse. He was still alive. The dust cloud was wearing off slowly. There were body parts and small blood lakes everywhere. Gunfire from all the weapons was deafening. He barely turned his head and saw several armed men coming from the mosque side. A second loss may mean his life. He lay on the ground and started firing at the armed men. The battle was intensifying.

After some time, the battle finished; just random shots could be heard. Ambulance cars were coming to the scene. A lot of people have come to the explosion site. Women were crying their hearts out; it was devastating. The wounded were taken to the hospital. Five soldiers from Michael's group were dead and several wounded by either shrapnel or bullet. Information about the casualties from other groups was coming in. Shrapnel hit Michael's arm, but he wasn't seriously injured. Despite the pain in his arm, he helped the injured out of the battlefield. He sent the injured kid with the first ambulance to the hospital.

Most of the mosque was destroyed.

Michael and George went to the military hospital. They asked about the condition of the wounded and the number of dead soldiers from the reception desk.

"We have eighteen wounded with either shrapnel or bullets. Five of them are in the resuscitation room, two of them are in critical condition. Eight soldiers are dead."

"The heavily wounded will definitely be transported by air to USA military hospital."

"I want to visit the wounded."

"Please, Captain, but you are wounded yourself. You need help. Let's get you to the bandage room."

"At the battlefield, they said it's not serious."

"But stationary treatment is different. It might get infection."

"You're right, Doctor!"

Even though he was wounded lightly, he needed medical treatment. After initial surgical treatment, his arm was wrapped in an aseptic bandage. He was informed to come back later again.

As he was going through the wards, visiting wounded soldiers, he couldn't hold his tears. He was shattered and devastated.

"You should control yourself. It makes them feel even worse," George said.

77

"You're right. I'm trying. Yesterday, these men were all healthy and strong. Whoever is left behind is probably going to be handicapped for the rest of their lives. Need to meet with the headquarter chief. The critical ones should be taken to a hospital in the United States."

"It's war, Michael. This is our fate. We chose this path."

"Of course."

They got in the military vehicle and asked the driver to take them to the hospital where the local wounded are being treated.

There were a lot of people in front of the hospital. People were staring at the soldiers with cynical eyes, even saying some things in Persian language.

"I think to myself, such uneducated, ignorant people. We give our lives for them to have a developed country and a better future for their kids, and this is what we get."

"Don't worry, man, they'll change."

Michael asked the nurse about the chief doctor's room. He took permission to get in and meet with the chief doctor.

"I'm Michael Grady, commander of the special unit of the U.S. Army. You are the chief doctor, if I'm not mistaken."

"Yes, sir. Please, Commander, I'm listening."

"Your English is pretty good."

"I studied medicine in England."

"I want to know the exact count of the dead and the wounded."

"More than ninety are dead. More than hundred are wounded."

"How many children?"

"They have brought only thirteen wounded children. Boys of different ages. Almost ten dead. Three of the wounded are in critical condition. They suffered several shrapnel wounds, lost a lot of blood. They are in a resuscitation room. Blood is being transferred to them. We need a lot of blood, but our reserves are running low."

"My blood is 4 plus. It's suitable for all blood groups. Can I donate?" Michael asked.

"Of course, sir."

"Soon, reserve blood, medicine, and other tools will be sent. Do everything in your power to make the wounded live. Where do I go for the blood donation?"

"I'll help you out, sir. Follow me," the nurse said to Michael.

After some time, Michael and George left the hospital and headed back to the headquarters. All the soldiers were at the headquarters ground. Everybody was waiting for the headquarter chief's next speech about the terror act that happened.

"Special units! Today, we stopped a big terror attack from happening by acting on time. There are dead and wounded among our soldiers and civilians. If it wasn't prevented, the numbers would have been much higher. It shows that we can never let our guard down. The enemy is on the move. That means there is another attack coming. Not just today, during your time here in Afghanistan, several terror attacks have been prevented. Unfortunately, we have lost good men. They died for the freedom and future of Afghanistan. We bow down to our brave soldiers who gave their lives and wish a speedy recovery for the wounded.

"The corpses of the brave men who gave their lives will be taken to their mother country by military plane. A military funeral will be held in the morning. Several of the soldiers will be given a higher reward for their exceptional services during duty.

"Special units commander Capt. Lieutenant Michael Grady will be given a leave in three days to fly and participate in the funeral ceremony of our fallen soldiers and to give a speech at a conference regarding our next six months' activity in Afghanistan. During this time, Capt. George Bradley will be the temporary commander. Always be ready to pay your duty to your country."

"Always am!"

Next day, George came to Michael's room.

"Michael, I got a favor to ask."

"Sure!"

He handed over a letter.

"It's for Luisa?" Michael smiled as he took the letter.

"When you come to my room, don't talk to me like I'm your commander. Talk to me as your friend. Sure, man, I'll give it. Don't be shy, you know how much I like you. To be honest, even though I'm going, I'm still a little worried. Feels like my legs don't want to move. I miss my mother. I dreamed about her yesterday. I think she is not good. Thank God for the neighbors. I'm very grateful for them. They always took care of my mother while I was here.

"It worries me that Beth does not write back to me. I'll probably find out this time I go."

A fast-approaching car stopped near the hillside. Several armed men were inside. The armed man sitting in front rushed out of the car and paced toward the hill. The others followed him, but they were stopped at the entrance. The first armed man went directly into the sheikh's room.

"I need to see the sheikh!"

"Wait, he is praying."

Few minutes passed.

"Sheikh, Your Holiness, caravan leader Ahmed Sarvar Saleh has brought important news from the city."

"Tell him to come."

The sheikh was mumbling prayers under his tongue and counting his beads in his hands as always. Finally, he finished the prayer.

"Amen! Ya Rasulullah, saves us from all these disasters."

"Amen! Sheikh Holiness, may God accept your prayers," .

"What happened? You worry me by coming in such a rush. I hope you have good news about the operation."

"Sheikh Holiness, I come bearing bad news. The city is a bloodbath. The Americans attacked the mosque yesterday. There are a lot of dead, injured, and hostages. It was prayer time when they attacked, that's why there are so many dead. The enemy arrested your brother. Akhund and two caravan leaders are dead. Most of the mosque was destroyed, it's unusable now."

"That's not good. What about the other group?"

"They postponed the attack because of what happened. All the military and the police are controlling the streets. Ours retreated temporarily and started waiting for your orders."

"My brother made a mistake again. It's because he doesn't listen to his older brother. I told him to make sure people don't get harmed. This is the result. You are right. This time, I will lead the operation. We will show them."

"Sheikh, the attackers were master soldiers. I wonder how they know about our plan."

"You see now, we have been betrayed again. I need to go to town. Tell everyone to be at the prayer. I have things to say after the prayer. Tell the caravan leaders about the meeting until I come back. I have important things to discuss with them."

"Yes, Your Holiness."

It was noon and time for prayer. A lot of people have gathered at the square. Since there were so many of them and no place in the mosque, they had to pray outside.

Prayer was over, but no one was leaving. They were all waiting for the sheikh's speech.

"People, disaster has struck again. They have spilled the blood of our brothers and sisters in the city. Even our children have not been spared. They have destroyed God's house. What kind of animal does this? My people, this disaster awaits us all. Kill the traitors serving them, destroy their families! Their blood is halal. We must pray for our fallen brothers' and sisters' souls. The devil's nest in the city must be destroyed soon. All the faithless traitors must be destroyed, and whoever is taken hostage must be beheaded in front of your eyes. Everyone should see a traitor's fate. If you are strong enough to hold a gun and want to get revenge for your brothers and sisters, come forward!"

All the men and teenage boys came forward. Some did it voluntarily; some did it because they were afraid.

"Good, my children. We are going to destroy the enemy with our unity. We must take revenge on our blood brothers and sisters."

After finishing the prayers, the sheikh gave orders to his assistants.

"Train all of them. Teach them how to use guns. Increase the number of live bombs."

The sheikh ordered a meeting with his caravan leaders to discuss the next attack on the police station.

The plane took off. Michael was worried for his friends in arms even though he was flying home. The next long trip was taking him back to his homeland, which he dearly missed.

He could feel that the plane was in homeland skies. The plane was about to land. He was excited, and the more excited he got, the plane got closer to the land. He was sad on one hand because he was bringing back his brothers in arms for funeral. On the other hand, he was happy to be back home after a long time with his beloved ones.

Military guards were lined up with weapons in hand. Family members of the deceased were crying as they were waiting for the coffins to be landed from the plane. Medical attendance was given to those who lost themselves. The coffins of the soldiers wrapped in USA flag were put to cars under the sounds of the military orchestra march. Tomorrow, they were going to be buried under funeral speeches and spread fire. The flag and the medals awarded will be given to the family of the deceased.

He was really upset and tired and called a taxi and headed to the hospital. It was twelve o'clock; Beth's shift was over. He asked the room number of the doctor on shift from the reception.

The doctor greeted him with respect and asked him to be seated.

"I'm listening, please go ahead."

"Doc, I'm on a temporary vacation from the army. My mother is being treated here. Please allow me to see her."

"Patient's first and last name, please."

"Clara Grady. She was in the Oncology Department."

The doctor made a phone call. Michael could not help but notice the change in the doctor's face during the phone talk.

"Mr. Michael Grady, your mother passed away three days ago. Your relatives should have told you about this. I'm sorry for your loss."

It was unexpected for Michael. It was a hard blow to him. His heart was racing. He didn't feel anything after a cold drop of sweat on his forehead. When he opened his eyes, he could see white-gowned people over his head. That's when it hit him.

"I'm sorry, Mr. Grady. I should have been more gentle with such hard news. You must be calm. You know that your mother's condition was not well."

Michael got up; his head was still spinning.

"Don't rush, your blood pressure is low. We have done first aid. Have coffee. You can leave after."

Michael lifted up his head and looked at the nurse with his teary eyes.

"You have a big heart."

He put his hand on the doctor's shoulder and left the room after saying good-bye. He went out to the hospital yard and sat on the bench to take some fresh air. He felt hopeless; he didn't know what to do now. He wanted to visit his mother's grave, but he didn't know where it was. Therefore, he had to go home and ask the neighbor. He called another taxi and went home.

After getting off the taxi in front of the house, he stared at it with sad eyes. The stairs were covered in snow. No footsteps on the snow meant that no one had opened the door for some time. He went up the stairs and looked behind the postbox. Usually, his mother would put keys there. But this time, it wasn't there.

There was a knock at the door.

"Sarah, doorbell! Who is it?"

"Mom, look who's here! Michael, welcome!" as she hugged Michael. Sarah's mother came to the door. She started to cry and hugged Michael.

"Forgive me, Michael. I'm very sorry for your mother. We couldn't take care of her until you came. Come in."

Michael gave the present in his hand to Sarah and sat on the sofa with questioning eyes.

"We were with her a week ago. She said she was OK, but her skin was really pale. Next visit we made, we heard the news. Beth was with her. She probably said her last words to her."

Michael stood up.

"You have come a long way, Michael. Sit down, rest. Lucas will arrive soon. You can go with him to the graveyard. We buried her near your father according to her will to Beth. Poor Beth, she couldn't hold back her tears. She suffered a lot for Ms. Clara. She visited her every day after her shift. She even would shop for the house and cook her favorite meals. She was so used to Beth. When she was a little late, she would miss her. Beth never left her side until her last breath. She died in her arms. She was worried about you. She asked Beth to promise to take care of you."

When Michael stood up with the keys to his house, he met with Lucas at the door. Lucas Marchelo hugged and tried to comfort Michael for his loss.

"I need to visit my mom's grave."

"Of course, my son." The neighbor and Michael headed to the graveyard at the suburb. It took them some time to arrive at the place where his mother was buried because the graveyard was very big. Clara Grady was buried side by side with her husband. It was covered in snow. He kneeled down and cleared the snow on the gravestone where his mother's name was carved.

"Mom, it's me, your son. I came to see you. I was thinking how I'm gonna put my head on your knees in our warm home in the middle of the winter during my long trip here. You would sooth my hair and sing me a lullaby, feed me with your hands with your delicious meals. But you lie in this cold ground without letting me know. My life is a dark prison without you. I had so much to say, now I can't. It's very cold here. How am I going to warm the house when you are both lying here in the cold?"

Lucas Marchelo hugged Michael.

"Let's go, son. I feel your pain. Don't hurt their souls. Life is not fair. All of us will come here one day. It's our final destination."

Michael put flowers on his mother and father's grave and left the graveyard.

He opened the door and entered the cold house. He roamed through quiet rooms. The silence was maddening him; it was as if the cold walls were coming at him. He took the white blanket on the sofa and lay there; he was tired. Everything that was happening went through his mind again; he was trying to process everything. He had to see Beth; she had to explain everything. He looked at time; it was close to the end of Beth's work shift.

He changed his clothes, called a taxi, and went to Luisa's house. Luisa would be back home soon because she was working the night shift.

When the car arrived at Luisa's house, she was already there. She felt something as she started watching the taxi arriving. It was Michael. She got excited and got closer to the taxi. Michael got off the taxi and handed flowers and a letter to Luisa. Michael could see that Luisa was very happy. They talked for a while. Luisa gave her sincere condolences to Michael for his loss. It was close to Luisa's shift, so Michael did not want to take too much time of hers. Before Michael had the chance to ask Luisa about Beth, he noticed the change on Luisa's face when she saw a car approaching. She recognized the car; it was Carl Caster's. For some reason, Beth had not been using her own car to commute to work lately.

The car stopped in front of Beth's house. Carl Caster was driving. Michael was shocked when he saw Beth getting out of the car. Even though Carl saw Michael approaching him, he acted like he didn't see him and left quickly. Beth was in shock. She felt that Michael was coming toward her. She paced directly home with her head down and locked the door.

Luisa was disappointed with what was happening. Michael looked at Luisa with questioning eyes. He was expecting an answer for this. Michael was stunned by all this. Now he knew why Beth wasn't writing letters to him. But he had to find out why. When he tried to go to Beth's house, Luisa grabbed his hand.

"Michael, that woman does not deserve you. You shouldn't waste your time on girls like this. I'll tell you everything later. I'm sorry, but I gotta go now."

Everything was clear now. Luisa had to go to work. She left with the hopes of meeting with Michael tomorrow again to talk about the matter.

Michael was angry. He wandered around in the yard for some time. He couldn't calm down. He thought about everything in his head and looked at Beth's house. He had to get an explanation for everything. He couldn't take it anymore. He paced to Beth's house and knocked on the door as hard as he could. Beth knew that Michael would do something like this. She wiped her tears, moved the curtain on the window, and looked outside. It really was Michael.

Beth screamed behind the door.

"What do you want from me! Get out of my life once and forever! It's over. There is nothing left between us."

"You betrayed me, you cheater. You played with my feelings by going out with an asshole I hate. Tell me why. You can't look me in the face, can you?"

"Knowing all of this, what do you want from me? Yes, I'm having a good time with him. I don't love you anymore. After what you have seen, isn't that enough?"

"Why did you do all of this, you dishonorable woman! You couldn't control your lust? Is that your love? You cheated on me. It's all because of that bastard, isn't it?"

"I took that step as a woman forgotten. He has no fault in this. I didn't get a single letter from you for two months. At least you should have written to me to find out about your sick mother."

"What are you talking about!? Open the door! I need to figure this out! What letter are you talking about?"

Beth was stunned after what she heard. What was happening? She wanted to open the door, but she hesitated.

Michael kicked the door as hard as he could.

"You are a worthless and dishonest person! I never should trust people like you. I came for a short time, and you and that bastard played with my feelings. You will answer for this. You were so busy whoring you forgot about dignity. You could have at least written to me about my sick mother. I asked you to take care of her. I could have been with her in her last breath. Now you won't even open the door for me. Whatever. You are dead to me! I'm leaving. We shall live and see. I'll get my answer for all of this from both of you. Bye!"

The voice was over. Beth wiped her tears and looked through the window again. Michael was walking away rapidly.

The neighbor heard the car approaching and had a sense that it was Michael coming. He was right. When Michael wanted to go to his house, he came face-to-face with the neighbor Lucas Marchelo.

"Michael, we've been waiting for you. Come, it's suppertime."

"Thank you, but I'm not hungry. I want to get some sleep."

"Michael, what are you saying? I won't let you stay alone in that cold house. As long as you are here, you will stay with us. We all will be offended if you say no."

Michael agreed to stay. Since he was hungry and tired, he didn't refuse supper either. No matter how much the neighbors insisted, Michael didn't want to stay the night there. His cold father's home was dearest to him. Without turning on the lights, he lay on the sofa and fell asleep.

He was dreaming. Dead bodies all around. George Bradley shooting nonstop and screaming at Michael for help. Suddenly, George loses conscience with a blow to the head. Two soldiers start dragging him by his arms. George screams in pain.

He woke up all of a sudden. His phone was ringing nonstop. He was worried as he got up quickly to pick up the phone.

"Capt. Lt. Michael Grady! You are expected at the military headquarters ASAP."

"Yes, Colonel."

It was past midnight. He started to worry. This sudden call from the headquarters could mean it's something serious."

Michael Grady put on his uniform and went out to the yard. He said good-bye to the neighbors and gave the house keys to them, looked at his father's house one more time, and got in the taxi to head to headquarters.

He asked permission to enter the headquarter chief's room. The colonel looked worried and angry.

"There has been a clash between the Taliban groups and the local police forces. There are a lot of dead and injured. Unfortunately, there are a lot of hostages, and among them are some special unit soldiers. We need you back in Afghanistan. Plane leaves in an hour. Get ready."

Michael directly headed to the headquarters from the airport. The road to the headquarters was passing near the police station. The aftermath of the terror attack and firefight could be seen. He arrived at the headquarters after some time. He quickly went up the stairs to the headquarter chief's room and saluted. The colonel looked worried and uneasy. He greeted Michael and started speaking.

"Situation is not good. The province police department has been attacked by the Taliban and extremist groups. It was a well-planned attack. They destroyed the walls of the police station with car bombs and then attacked. There was a battle between them and police and some special units, a lot of casualties on both sides. The enemy outnumbered them, took Afghan special unit police officers hostage, and disappeared. I regret to tell you that during this time, George Bradley and three members of XT were there to attend the training. One of our men is dead. George Bradley and two others were taken hostage. According to the information we have, Capt. George Bradley is heavily wounded. A lot of dead in this uneven battle. For some reason, the attack is postponed. There's a reason. The hostages they have taken may be killed when we attack. They are hiding in the rocky and mountainous area tunnels and caves. A lot of locals in the area. Any unplanned move may result in soldiers' and civilians' deaths. This hard task is for the special units. You will lead that group. The headquarter chief rates your skills and bravery highly. You can change the plan as the situation changes. Your mission is to get to the enemy hideout unnoticed, unchallenged, rescue the soldiers, plant explosives inside their tunnels and caves, and create a window for the air force to attack and destroy their base. You will accomplish a lot of missions in the enemy ground using your hand-to-hand combat, firearm, and military training skills. There will be special unit police officers in your diversion intelligence group. Two trusted Afghans will be with you to guide you through the rough road ahead. I'm positive that you will succeed at this mission. I have full faith in you. Good luck to you!"

The headquarter chief shook his hand and gave him a hug.

"Son, I want to see you and the other special unit soldiers back together with us. I always favor and respect you as a brave and skillful agent. Good luck! See you soon!"

He went out to the yard. A military vehicle was waiting for him. He recognized the man near the driver; it was Capt. Roger Thomas. As soon as he saw Michael, he dropped the newspaper he was holding and came to salute Michael.

"Captain Lieutenant, sir! A member of the Taliban has been arrested by soldiers. According to his words, he has been serving the Taliban for quite some time now. I wanted to meet and report to you. I think we can get some important information from him about the Taliban."

"Listen to your enemy but never believe. You never know. Let's listen to what he has to say and then we decide. We should run with the hare and hunt with the hound. I gotta see him. Tell the translator to come to my room with him."

The captain quickly obeyed the order and reported with the radio. They both sat at the backseat of the military vehicle and headed to the area designated for XT. The car arrived soon. Michael and Roger went to his room. After the order was given, the captain left the room. Surrendering Taliban members and the translator were ready at the door.

"Who are you, and why have you come here?" He looked at the Afghan and asked.

"I'm from the village near Kabul. My name is Ali Ahmad Igbal, brother of Romal Igbal. He has been taken hostage by the Taliban three days ago."

"Show me your documents."

"I don't have any. They took away all of our documents."

"OK, why did you come and surrender?"

"They have my brother. They are torturing him. He is soon to be beheaded by the orders of the sharia court. After checking his documents, they have given orders for my arrest too. I knew that as soon as they found out I'm his brother, they will order my execution. I escaped here during the night."

"But how did you know all of this?"

"Thank God to my relative, he warned me on time."

"You say the same fate awaits your family members too. They probably have them already."

"I escaped with my family through the mountains."

"You're lying. What region is it that you have escaped without getting noticed by the terrorist groups?"

"Mister, I know these places very well. I was a shepherd. I know every stone and rock in these mountains. The Taliban rarely come to those places. The area is quite difficult to pass, it's rocks everywhere. Nobody knows the secrets of these places except for shepherds like me."

"So you can help us, then?"

"Of course."

"How can I trust you?"

"You can take my family as a hostage. My wife and two little children are in coverage in a neighbor's home who lives close to here. I can show you where they are. My youngest son is five months old. I left him in a neighboring village because the mountains were cold. You have them in your hands if I end up betraying you."

"Your enemy is among you. The worm is eating the tree from inside. We have come to free your people of those worms. Unfortunately, to understand that, your people need to unite. This unity is possible if traitors would allow it. OK, I believe you. But war has its own rules. You will always be under my supervision, mistakes are not forgiven, and the punishment is fitting to war rules." There was a knock at the door. "Come in!"

"Sir, Commander! All the soldiers are ready and waiting for your orders."

Michael Grady left the room and gave orders to the sergeant standing near the door. "Prepare him quickly. He will come with us." Michael Grady came out to the yard where all the soldiers were ready and lined up, waiting for his orders.

"Special units! Domestic tension is increasing. We are lacking in numbers. That's why the regions we conquer are being taken back by the Taliban. The main roads to the city and the villages are kept under fire by them, causing trouble for civilians traveling. They even attack villagers and take men hostage later to force them to fight for them. Whoever refuses gets shot or beheaded. There are plenty of traitor police officers among us. Caves in the mountains where the Taliban are hiding have been a real problem for us. They train there. Group leaders get orders from the sheikh for their next attack plans. If their attacks succeed, we lose a lot of men. Enemy is using these hideouts perfectly to attack our forces from behind. It results in giving many dead and hostages. The scariest part is that their commanders are using those hideouts and controlling the troops easily from that position. Towns and villages nearby are controlled by them. People live in fear. If they help any of our soldiers, they will end up being beheaded. Execution is held in front of everybody. Sheikh decides how the execution will be done. There is a big town near the mountains where they do a lot of execution ceremonies like this. According to the intel we have, captured Afghan police and special units will be executed there. For some reason, the execution has been delayed by Sheikh's order. They might be thinking about hostage exchange. They are probably considering our special units. But the hostages we have are the leaders of very dangerous groups. We especially planned to capture them, and we did. Exchanging the hostages would increase their power again. Rescuing the hostages would result in our loss of manpower and artillery. This kind of attack is also dangerous for the hostages. If they see us coming, they will shoot the hostages. During this operation, we must be tactical accordingly, and alongside rescuing the hostages, we must aim to plant explosives to blow up their tunnels. The air force will take care of the rest. They will be waiting for our signal to attack. We will have helicopters for the rescued hostages. To help us in this operation, the troops will attack the controlled areas to distract them.

"The region we are headed is a mountainous region. The hostages are being held in a discreet and well-guarded place near that town. They are torturing special units to get military secrets. There is a big river nearby. The left side of the river is in the north of the town. The other side of the river is desert, rocks, and hills. The left side is usually very cold and very hard to travel. Our goal is to pass through the north mountainous region and find and destroy the tunnels under those hills. According to the intel, most of the enemy forces are based there. Even hostages are being held there. All of Taliban's main attack plans are being discussed and decided here. The main objective of the operation is to rescue the hostages and then try to destroy most, if not all, of the enemy tunnels. Afterward, we need to report the exact GPS location to the air force support. Good luck, gents!"

Both groups were headed to the targeted area. The weather was cold in these mountains. Since the moonlight was illuminating any movement on the desert sand, it was wiser to choose a path through the forest. The area looked like there has been a flood recently. As they kept moving, pebbles would make some noise and some big rock would cause difficulties to travel. The road was tiring, so every once in a while, Michael would sign his soldiers to take a rest for a few minutes and make sure that everything was quiet around them. After making sure, they kept moving. The guide was leading the way. To make sure they were still on path, Michael would check with his map frequently. They were deep in the woods. The darkness would make travel more difficult, but night vision goggles came in handy. They had to pass through a steep hill road ahead. This was a shortcut to the destination. Michael signaled his soldiers to take a rest. He took the guide and the police officer and started moving through a tight path upward. Slightest mistake would mean falling all the way down. The way the guide was moving through these paths showed that he had passed these roads before. Suddenly, the police officer slipped and started sliding down the hill. It was difficult to help him. He acted quickly to grab onto a big chunk of rock. Big and small pieces of rocks and stones started falling down. They acted quickly. They pulled the injured officer back with a rope. He was injured badly; he could barely walk. They couldn't leave him behind.

"You should keep moving, don't worry about me. I know these places well."

"There will be one person with you. Weapons and food also. If all goes well, we shall meet again."

As they kept walking down the hill, high-altitude rocks and mountains were getting replaced by flatter areas. Huge rocks made it difficult to travel, but they had to keep moving. According to the map, there was a village in the area. After the attack three days ago, the road to the village was being controlled by the Taliban. The rocky roads were too difficult to pass, so they decided to use the village road during night. Michael knew that this region is very dangerous. He had to know the situation in the village. Smallest mistake could lead to their death. They were already close to the village. Michael ordered the group to stop. He sent small groups to scout the area. He took the guide and the closest soldier to him with him to scout the village. Soldiers were approaching the village from left, right, and center. As they were approaching the village, they could feel a terrible smell in the air. They were shocked with the scene they witnessed. All the tragedy of war was flashing in front of their eyes. Dead bodies from both sides, burnt tanks, and destroyed cars were all in sight. This scene would mean that there has been a terrible clash.

"Hurry up, boys! It's not safe here."

One of the soldiers approached and informed them that there was a wounded near the burnt tank, still alive. They quickly approached the area, and the crew commander was badly wounded.

"Help me! Water, water . . ."

"Be patient, man, we'll help you now."

He was in great pain from his shoulder and leg wound. Even though he couldn't talk, he lifted his hand and pointed to the hills in the south. "They are th-ere . . . Ta-liban," as he passed out.

"Help! We don't have time. We can't leave him here like this. We will take him to the forest where we will hide before the sun comes up. A soldier should stay with him. We will inform the station. They will come and pick him up before we come back. There's no other way. Look around carefully to see if there is any more."

"No, Commander! Unfortunately, there is no more."

"Hurry up, boys! They can come back at any time. Looks like they were ambushed."

"Commander, sir! The forest may be cold and dangerous. There is a neighbor of one of the Afghan officers here. He said that if you permit him, he could ask his relative to take care of him for the night."

"OK, we have no other choice. He should take medical supplies with him too. Give him painkillers and antibiotics. If we make it back alive and if by that time our soldiers don't come and take him, we will take him back on our way back. We can't go into the village too deep. It's too dangerous. We must hurry."

The group was on the road again. What was it that was awaiting them? No one knew, but they were determined to execute the operation. They had one goal; fear was left behind. The enemy is ahead. They have to do this even if it means dying for it. Most of the road was behind; they were withstanding. They had to reach the destination in time.

Water flow could be heard ahead. It looked like they were close to the river, which means the meeting point of two groups was close. The commander ordered the soldiers to stop and rest. They have been on the road for long; they were sleepless and tired. Rest was vital. Some would sit; some would lie on the ground to rest. They put a watchman to check the surroundings. Michael took two soldiers with him to check the river ahead. When they got close, he ordered them to halt. They could hear people talking. He carefully approached the sound and hid behind a big tree to listen to them. There were two armed men. One was checking the surrounding, while the other put his gun on the ground taking water from the river. Michael signaled the soldier near him to look at the man taking water from the river. They had to act quickly. The Afghan standing suddenly felt a sharp pain in his back and turned his head to the side without moving. Michael silenced him with his hand as he threw away his weapon. The Afghan police and the other armed man were fighting for their lives. When he saw his friend shivering on the ground in pain, he understood that it's pointless to resist. The armed police cursed him in Persian and spit in his face. Michael tied his hands. They found two dead bodies and two grenade launchers in the trunk of the car nearby. This will come in handy. Michael took the weapons and quickly returned to the camp with the hostage. They interrogated the hostage. After some time, he said that there had been a big battle far from here.

"The two dead bodies are the killed caravan leaders. Sheikh ordered us to take the bodies back to the town for a proper funeral. They are waiting for them."

"How's the situation in the battlefield right now?"

"It's cease-fire at the moment. They are waiting for more Taliban forces to arrive. Your people are surrounded. Another big battle is expected."

"Will the sheikh participate in the funeral too?"

"No! The funeral will be held by Sheikh's son. Sheikh rarely leaves his place. All the caravan leaders get the orders from him there. They have their meetings and discussions there."

"If you help us catch the sheikh's son, I will let you live."

"Approximately how many Taliban forces are in the area?"

"There are a lot of different groups, that's why I can't say the exact number. They are all under Sheikh's control. He spends most of his time in the hideout. It's a small cave surrounded by hills. It's well protected. The group leaders gather here, take orders from Sheikh from time to time. Sheikh's word is an order for all the group leaders."

"Where are the main groups?"

"Most of the forces control the main areas near the city. Even though they lost a lot of men in today's battle, they still control the areas. They are waiting for more forces. Probably that's why there are less forces in the center. Most of the artillery is hidden in the tunnels in the hills. It's better for being protected from air attacks. The jail is also there. They often change their location with cars or on foot. Since they know the place very well, they put traps all over the place for your troops to fall. That's how you get ambushed every time. The village near Sheikh's hideout is the place where to implement execution of the Afghan traitors with sharia court's orders. After the mullah's blessing, they will either be hanged or beheaded in front of people."

"So that's what's expecting the special units?"

"Yes! Sheikh ordered for the Afghan special units to be brought to that village. There are nine of them. Their leader couldn't withstand the torture and died. Two are badly wounded. They will be executed today, I don't know the exact time."

"Where are you taking the bodies in the car to?"

"Since they have a high rank in Taliban, Sheikh ordered them to return their bodies for a proper funeral by sharia rules."

"How are the American soldiers?"

"I'm not sure. I heard there are three of them. One is in bad condition. They are being tortured every day."

"Captain Lieutenant, sir! Commander of the second group, Roger Thomas, ordered me to make contact with you regarding an important military intel."

"I'm listening, Captain!"

"The aftermath of a big battle in a desert area in the south is visible. Enemy caravans are approaching there. To reach our meeting point, we need to pass through that area. It's very dangerous. We are waiting for your orders!"

"Lieutenant, I will contact the station and ask them to send more troops your way. According to the intel we have, the area is very dangerous. There was a big fight between Taliban and ground troops. Some of our troops are surrounded. Make traps with whatever weapons you have left and try to save the wounded ones until the troops arrive. You should leave the area and reach the meeting point before the operation is over."

"Yes, sir." Michael Grady gave new orders to the group. "It's serious. The second group is entering a battle. It may be a while before they come to help. We are moving forward with the plan.

"Two snipers will take spots in a higher ground. They will be in an advantageous position to eliminate the enemy and keep in contact with the station through radio. The rest of us, including the hostage and me, we are headed to the hideout in the town. We should follow the river valley."

After giving orders to the snipers, Michael and his group started moving. To be recognized by each other, they tied a bandage to their arms, since they were all dressed traditionally. Two were chosen to lead as they knew the place well. The group entered the town from two sides. They all wore traditional afghan hats and head covers. Michael sat in the front seat of the car and ordered the Afghan hostage to drive the car. Some of the soldiers squeezed into the car. The rest had to walk the rest of the road. They reached the town without getting noticed by the enemy. Michael was watching the hostage. He could see that the hostage was getting more scared as they were getting closer to the destination. They reached the town center. There were armed groups all around the place. They parked the car a little bit away from there. Michael ordered Jamal to approach the sheikh's son and tell him what he was told. Jamal approached an armed man and said that he had brought the dead bodies. The man started walking toward the car. He looked at the masked soldiers with suspicious eyes and said something to Jamal. Michael saw how they looked at each other; he tried to stay calm. He looked at the bodies and asked something in Persian. When he got no answer, he quickly reached to uncover their face. When he did, he saw a gun pushing against his stomach. He was told to hold still. The rest of the group uncovered their weapons and pointed at the other Taliban members. The sheikh's son understood the situation and ordered them to cease fire. Two sides are confronting in silence waiting for a signal. Saeid ordered his soldiers to surrender the weapons. Saeid told the translator something in Persian.

"Commander, he asks your purpose in here."

"I must meet with his father. If my demands are not met, his son will be taken hostage."

Saeid told one of his men to go and tell his father the conditions. It took a while for the messenger to come back. He approached Saeid and said something.

"Mr. Michael, Sheikh wants to see you."

"We will go together. I won't leave my men behind. The hostages are coming too." The translator informed Saeid. Michael and his men tied the hostages and got seated in cars. The commander ordered the soldiers to be maximum careful.

The cars quickly arrived at the hillside. An armed man asked Michael to follow him. Michael took three men with him and started following the armed man through the tunnels until they reached a cave in the hill. A man with white hair and beard was sitting at the top. Michael guessed him to be the sheikh. After judging Michael, he started screaming.

"You have come inside our house now! I'm gonna destroy all of you! Why have you come here?"

"We want the hostages!"

"This is not how you get back your hostages. There is another reason for you to come here. None of you will leave this place alive. We are going to kill all of you!"

"I see that you are the leader here. It's important for both of us. Your every move is under supervision. One wrong move and you are all dead by my orders. But we can all do it the good way."

"You are threatening me? With death?"

"You have lived most of your life, but your son is young."

"We give martyrs in the name of God and our faith. Paradise awaits them."

"Sheikh, you talk about God and faith, but look how much innocent blood you have spilled."

"Your blood is halal."

"Sheikh, I have come here to save the captured people without spilling blood."

"Like I asked before, you have a different reason to come. You can't come all the way up here by yourself. Looks like I'm gonna have to do something about traitors. All of your blood is halal. I will destroy all of you alongside traitors serving you!"

"Sheikh, isn't what you are doing a sin? So much blood spilled. What about orphaned kids, widowed wives? Whose fault is that? You started the war! We have come here to put an end to one brother killing another brother. Is it bad that if your country develops, people become more educated, civilized, and peaceful?"

"You have come to teach me?"

"I see it's pointless to argue with you. Just release the hostages and we exchange them. Then we will go."

The sheikh looked at his son. His eyes were praying with fear. "Bring the hostages!"

Captured special units were brought quickly. Michael and his group were shocked by what they were seeing. They were unrecognizable at first. George could barely stand up with the help of the other two soldiers. He was tortured to death. They were in shock. "Take your hostages and get the hell out of here! And remember, this will cost you! I'll get back at you."

"No, Sheikh! Don't rush! I'll release your son after. First, my group and I need to get out of here alive. I give you my word. We get out of here alive, your son lives!"

The sheikh lifted his hands and asked the soldiers to cease fire. Time was passing; they had to rush. It made the sheikh angry to see them leave the cave in the opposite direction they came. He was stunned. His love for his son made him look weak in front of other members. He didn't know what to do. Surrounding Taliban members looked at him with questioning eyes, as if they were saying, "Our children are not valuable?" The sheikh angrily bowed his head; he was ashamed to look at them. Suddenly, he started to scream. "Attack! Kill these bastards!

Their blood is halal. I'm ready to sacrifice my son in the name of God! Allahu Akbar! Allahu Akbar!"

Screaming started. "Allahu Akbar! Allahu Akbar!"

The commander and his crew managed to plant plenty of explosives alongside the walls of the tunnel until the exit. Fierce battle began. The sound of firearm and explosives outside the cave could be heard. Michael took a few soldiers with himself to stay and ordered the rest to take the injured soldiers to the mountain. Fierce battle was ongoing in the tunnels. Two special units had already been deceased. The number of wounded was increasing. They had to leave the tunnel as soon as possible and blow up the explosives. All the explosives started blowing up one by one in the tunnel. The battle outside was still going strong; both sides lost a lot of men. The two snipers up the mountain and the other soldiers kept them under fire nonstop.

Suddenly, the sheikh's son and two other hostages started running, seeing how soldiers were busy with the battle. The Afghani police tried to shoot him, but it was too late. They jumped into holes in the hills. There were a lot of these holes. Grenades were thrown in through the holes. There was no time to wait and watch. The commander ordered the soldier to move up. The number of Taliban soldiers kept increasing. Now they could make contact with the station through radio. They needed air support. Several fireworks fired. Even though the enemy kept increasing in numbers. They were able to withstand the pressure as the second group had already reached the battlefield. The screams of the wounded from both sides mixed with the sounds of bullets and explosions. A firework was thrown in the air. It was a signal for the air support. Michael had thrown himself into the middle of fire. To increase the confidence and motivation in his men, he kept pushing forward to the enemy, even though their numbers were much higher than before. They needed more support.

"Cover yourself, Captain!" That was the last thing he remembered as the soldier jumped to hug and cover him. He couldn't hear a thing, as if he was deaf. He saw many dead and injured soldiers and destroyed artillery around when he opened his eyes. He felt some heavy weight over his body but did not have the power to move it. It was Elbert Ernesto. He jumped on his captain to protect him from the grenade. Surviving soldiers took Ernesto's body away. Michael tried to stand up, but he couldn't. His head was spinning. He didn't feel his legs below his knees.

"Hold on, Commander! You are badly injured," as the medic tied above his knees to slow down bleeding. They put him on a stretcher. The battle was about to be over. The air support had successfully destroyed Taliban's army, artillery, and tunnels. Michael felt like he was about to pass out. Thirst, pain, and blood loss were making him really weak. Last thing he heard were the mixed talks of the medical workers above his head. He was dreaming. His mother was on his bedside, soothing his hair.

"Mom, it hurts."

"My dear son! Look at what they have done to you." Some force pulls him away from her, tearing his body into pieces and putting everything back together again. His mother is trying to save her son from the evil forces. They are stopping her, taking him away. He screams for help.

He tried to get out of the dark tunnel, and, finally, he could see a light. He could hear voices.

"So many brave young men disabled like this."

"War never brought anyone happiness."

"They say he was a really talented commander."

"Unfortunately, he's crippled forever now. It's fate."

"Doctor, looks like the patient is waking from a coma." He opened his eyes. He understood the situation when he saw medical workers in white coats.

"How are you feeling, son?" the doctor surgeon Clayton Briam asked as he soothed Michael's head.

"Where am I?"

"You are being treated at the U.S. military hospital in Afghanistan. Rest. We will have plenty of time to talk. I ask you to be patient and calm. It's war, it has its own laws."

Everyone left the room except for the nurse taking care of him. He looked around. His left leg was gone down the knee. It was bandaged. It looked like they amputated him; he would be sent home from the army. He was shocked. His lifelong dreams were shattered in the blink of an eye. They switched him to the ward from the resuscitation room. The chief would always visit him and other soldiers. Roger Thomas was also getting treated at the hospital. He was badly wounded. Michael was mostly worried about George Bradley. He was really happy to hear that he had woken up from a coma. But after the head trauma, he would have problems in his health in the future. His treatment was going to continue in a hospital back home. The army general came to the hospital to visit the wounded soldiers. Michael Grady and many special units were given the highest military award for their exceptional services. Soon, Michael Grady would return home with his friends. George Bradley's treatment would continue in a military hospital. They were unaware of the difficult times coming for them.

Beth was on her next vacation. She spent most of her spare time at home. There was still a long time before the vacation finished. She was getting bored from loneliness. There were friends and neighbors with Luisa back then. Their relationship broke up because of Michael. Small fights happened between them. Carl never left her unattended after work hours. But, lately, she felt that Carl was distant. Sometimes he would come home and sleep all the time, saying he is tired. Beth was tired of his actions. She woke up early today. She was planning to go to the shopping mall after breakfast. She called Carl to tell him that she won't be home. But for some reason, Carl asked her to wait at home. It made Beth think. For the first time ever, Carl had gone against her wish. Some time passed before Carl Caster arrived. Beth was getting tired of waiting; she wanted to know the reason for making her wait for so long.

She looked out the window. Her neighbor Luisa was back from work. She hid behind the curtain; she didn't want Luisa to see her. She parked the car in front of the house like always and rushed into the house. As Beth was getting ready to get back to the living room, she noticed another car approaching. It was a hospital service vehicle for the disabled. The vehicle stopped in front of Luisa's house. Beth started watching people getting off the vehicle one by one. Crazy thoughts were in her mind. What was going on?

Luisa came out of the house and ran toward the hospital vehicle. She was smiling; she was happy for some reason. A man struggling to get off from the backseat was familiar to her. It was Michael. She didn't know what to do for a moment. Her heart was racing. Michael limped toward Luisa with struggle. It looked like he lost his leg in the war. He opened the door after meeting Luisa. The soldier sitting in the front seat was George Bradley. Luisa hugged him and cried her heart out. This scene went on for a while. Michael said something to Luisa as they both helped George out the car. Beth got emotional after seeing this. She couldn't hold back her tears seeing them. After a short talk, Michael and Luisa helped George into the home. Michael was the last one to go in as he felt something and turned around to look at Beth's window. She could sense that Michael had seen her even though she quickly hid behind the curtain. When she turned away, she saw Carl. She didn't notice that he had come in.

"What happened? Why are you crying?" Carl looked out the window to the yard.

"Nothing, it's just you making me wait so much pissed me off."

"I thought something bad happened. You gotta understand. I have a difficult job. I will pay you much more attention starting today."

"You are in a good mood. What happened?"

"I am on vacation for one month. I was keeping it a secret from you to make a surprise. You know how much I love you, baby. Come here, honey," as he hugged her.

"I'm tired. Can you make coffee? What do we have to eat?"

"I'll prepare something right now." She went to the kitchen after washing up in the bathroom.

"Perhaps we should go to a restaurant?"

"Very well. You drink your coffee while I get ready." Beth couldn't stop thinking about what she saw. She was distracted. Carl's vacation news was good. Finally, she will not be bored at home. She put on one of her favorite dresses and asked Carl's opinion. "How do you like this dress, honey?"

Carl switched the subject without answering. "Beth, music is coming from the neighbor. I wonder what it is."

Even though the question angered Beth, she remained calm. "I have no idea. Maybe some girlfriends came over."

"You don't know them? You have worked together for so long."

"When I looked at the garden, I didn't see anybody. I have terminated relations with her a long time ago. I don't care what happens in her house."

Carl knew why Beth was watching the car in the street because Carl had seen Michael and George coming back from the army earlier. The conditions these two officers came back in shocked him. For a moment, he felt remorse for the conflict between them and what happened in the past. He took a deep sigh and entered the house. His anger and envy toward Michael was a much stronger feeling. This talk had upset Beth, but she was trying her hardest to stay calm.

After a while, they were at the restaurant downtown. The restaurant was full. They took their seats at their reserved table and watched the dancing girls for a while. After the number, slow music started playing. Slow music was touching Beth's heart. She remembered the past, the happy days she spent with Michael. She sighed. She was saddened. She barely could hide that. She took the menu on the table and started browsing through. As she looked across the restaurant, people sitting there stole her attention. From the outside, they looked drunk. One woman and three men. Men smoked cigars, talked, and laughed loudly with no regard for the rest of the restaurant. It looked like the woman was drunk. The man sitting next to her whispered in her ear as he looked at Beth. The woman took a look at Beth and smiled. After some more drinks, the man invited her to dance. As they were dancing, the jewelry on her hands and neck were shining like a star under the lights. Beth couldn't take her eyes off the shining jewelry she was wearing. Beth sighed.

Carl could see that Beth wasn't happy, and he invited her to dance to cheer her up. They had a lot of fun at the restaurant. Suddenly, Beth started to worry. The smell of the food served made Beth nauseous. She went to the bathroom to vomit. As she went to the women's bathroom, that woman followed her in. She glanced to her through the reflection on the mirror as she approached the mirror to refresh her makeup.

"Ma'am, are you all right? You look pale. Do you need help?"

"No thanks, just have a little headache. It'll pass."

"I see since you've arrived, you look upset."

"No, no, I'm OK."

"It's probably your husband. Don't mind them, all men are like this. That's why I divorced my dumbass husband."

The woman's attitude made Beth mad, but she was calm. "Ma'am, he is my boyfriend."

The woman quickly changed the subject. "I'm sorry, miss, you looked like somebody I know. Perhaps I'm mistaken."

"Maybe you have seen me in the hospital. I'm a nurse."

"Yes, I was thinking to myself, *How do I know this pretty girl?* I'm Elma. Pleasure to know you."

"I'm Beth. Thank you."

"I was watching you. You look upset. I don't like seeing girls upset. You should dance and laugh." As Elma kept talking, Beth couldn't take her eyes off of her jewelry covering her neck and chest. The woman could feel her looks. It looked like she has found Beth's weakness. "It's very nice to meet you. This is my phone number. You can call me anytime you want. I am free all day anyway. Come on, honey, men are waiting."

"Yes, OK."

"Who is that woman that came out with you?"

"I don't know exactly how, but she says she knows me. From the looks, she looks rich. She is a nice and friendly woman. She wants to be friends with me. She even gave me her number."

"She doesn't look like the decent type."

"That's what you think about all the women you meet. I don't care about her personal life. The important thing is that she is happy as a woman. That necklace was amazing. She has got a boyfriend that takes care of her well. What else does a woman need in life?"

"I see you have learned the bio of someone you don't know in a very short time. So you are saying that happiness is jewels and wealth? Do you even know who they are?"

"Ah, Carl, I'm tired of these words!"

"All right, let's not spoil our appetite. I want to take some fresh air near the sea. Let's go."

It was late when they returned home. They both were tired. Beth had a headache. She threw up in the bathroom. She was getting suspicious. She even refused when Carl wanted to call an ambulance. It looked like she was pregnant. Her suspicions were right. The test results were positive. Beth was really happy about it. She woke up early. She was feeling nauseous and dizzy. She had to go to the doctor for a checkup today. She had to make sure she was pregnant before telling Carl about it. She was worried; she didn't know how Carl would react to this news. An endless phone call disrupted her from her thoughts. At first, she didn't want to answer the unknown number but then decided to answer.

"Hello! Who is this?"

"You didn't recognize me? It's me, Elma."

"I'm sorry, I've never heard your voice on the telephone before, I didn't recognize."

"How are you feeling? Are you still tired from the night out?"

"Yeah, a little bit."

"Looks like you are alone in the house like me. Tell you what, I'll give you my address. Come over. I would love to have you as my guest."

"I'm sorry, ma'am. I'm not feeling well today. I think I'm gonna go to a doctor. I will call you later."

"No problem, honey. I got worried for you. You'll tell me the results later?"

"OK, ma'am. You are very kind. Thank you."

When she arrived at the hospital, there was a waiting line for the doctor. Dr. Guliana Barner confirmed that she was five weeks pregnant and the health of both mother and the child was good. It was close to noon when she arrived home. When she entered the house, she saw Carl in the kitchen.

"Hi."

"Where were you? You should tell me when you go somewhere. Why didn't you answer your phone?"

"Carl, I had a doctor's appointment today. I have good news!"

"I'm listening."

"I'm gonna be a mother. I have been feeling nauseous since yesterday. This is the test result, and Dr. Barner confirmed that

I am five weeks pregnant. There is no problem with health." It disappointed Beth that Carl wouldn't even look at the paper.

"Beth, we are not ready to have a family yet. You should have asked my opinion on the matter too."

"What do you mean! I have been waiting for this day to happen. I thought you would be happy to hear this. But looks like I'm wrong."

"Yes, I wanna be a father. I wanna have a beautiful wife and children greet me when I come home. We live in a civil country. Both of us should agree to have a family and a child. You give me such news and expect me to be happy about it? We are just going out. Getting married is serious. We are not ready for that."

"So all of these years you have just been playing with me just to satisfy your needs? You haven't loved me!"

"What I have seen all these years is a woman acting like she loves me but inside still madly in love with another. Don't scream, nobody forced you to do anything!"

"If that's what you were thinking, then why did you play with my feelings?"

"I have never said no to any of your wishes to this day. You gotta understand. I'm not ready to be a father."

"You say deep down I love someone else! That's how you always treat me. Yes, I loved Michael, but he didn't stand behind his word. I still don't know why. He is not that kind of person. You are saying that I should refuse this baby, is that it? If it was Michael's child, he would have never done this."

"It's your right to have a child, I can't deny you of that right. But, yes, I don't want to have this child."

"You are such a jerk."

"Control yourself, dumb bitch. Since seeing that son of a bitch, you are acting all different. I saw the way you were feeling yesterday. Don't treat me like I'm stupid. You still love him."

"I hate you, asshole. How can you say that? I can't abort my child. I'm gonna bring it to the world."

"It's up to you." Carl stood up, picked up his jacket, and left the house angrily. Beth fell down on her knees crying her heart out.

It's been a week since the last time Carl called Beth. Her pregnancy was not going well. She was vomiting several times a day. She got bored at home. She would Carl call sometimes, but he never answered. Elma, on the other side, has managed to create a bond with Beth, keeping her company with phone calls over time. She was sick of being alone. She needed a girlfriend. Finally, they decided on a date for a meeting.

Her new girlfriend arrived at the address. She invited her in, but she asked to put a rain check on that. They had good food and good fun at the restaurant. Elma has won Beth's heart with her sincere attitude toward her. She would talk about her life to Beth, all of her hard times, how her husband mistreated her, and how she had miscarried her baby. She went into depression after the doctor's report. She would never be able to be a mother. After losing all her life dreams, she even tried to kill herself. The psychological rehabilitation did her good; she gained her love and will to live. She met her boyfriend two years ago. She excitedly talked about how Arnoldo Carmelo was a rich businessman. He would take care of her and buy her expensive gifts. Elma took her new girlfriend out and bought her presents. Beth was embarrassed, and she didn't know how to thank Elma.

Arnoldo Carmelo was happy. Elma has successfully done her part. But there was a lot more to do. He was looking for ways to get to the sheriff. He had plenty of information on Carl Caster, but he had never met him in person. He had heard he was a mean and strict police. The sheriff's area was very suitable for drug dealing; a lot of money could be made. After Anderson pointed Carl to him, he has been thinking of ways to get closer to him. It was a chance for him to realize his future plans. It had been several days since their fight.

She hadn't heard from Carl since then, but she was not alone. She bonded with Elma during these times. She would always ask for Elma's advice on things. Thanksgiving holiday was just around the corner. Elma's next visit to Beth's house was during holiday times. All the nation was getting ready for the holiday. Elma was going to ask Beth and Carl to come to the holiday party the boss was holding. Her offer made Beth very happy; she happily accepted the invitation. Beth invited Elma for lunch. Elma noticed the changes in Beth's behavior.

"Are you feeling all right?"

"Yeah, I get headaches and nausea."

"Maybe we should call an ambulance."

"No need for now. I have been to the doctor's. He said it's all temporary."

"Are you pregnant?"

"Yes."

"Congratulations, honey. So happy to hear that."

"It's six weeks now. But when I told Carl, he got very angry."

"I remember you saying that you are not married."

"Yeah. We have been together for a long time now. It's my first pregnancy. I don't want to abort the baby. I have been waiting for this moment. He doesn't accept my marriage proposal."

"You should talk to him again about this. Maybe he will change his mind."

"He doesn't want a child. He left after he found out that I'm pregnant. He doesn't even answer my calls."

"Some people just have no honor. No offense, darling, you are in a tough position. Girl, are you crazy? It's never a good idea to have a child without a father. What if he never comes back? You want to lose your boyfriend over a child? On the other hand, there is some truth in what he is saying. You should better your financial condition. I'll help you. Don't push him away from yourself."

"That's what I should do?"

"Of course, you silly. You know how much I like you. I'm ready to help you whenever."

"No, I need to think about it first. I'll tell you my decision. I'm having difficulty deciding."

"It's up to you. You are young and pretty. Enjoy your youth. You'll have time for being a mother."

"Thanks for listening and advice. I will tell you my decision later."

Carl was still mad at Beth. He didn't call or visit her for the last several days. He even deleted her phone number from his phone, but he could feel for Beth. It wasn't easy for her either. He felt bad about the way he responded to Beth. He would spend some time at home or go out to clubs and bars for a drink with his friend Brook after his work hours. Brook could feel the difference in Carl; he was always mad at something.

"What's up with you, man? You look so angry. Are you gonna tell me what's bothering you? Perhaps you are tired of vacation?"

Carl told everything to Brook. "Look, man. I have been married three years with Bella. Having a child is a great gift, but we could not have one. The doctor's report says that I'm the problem. She asked me many times to do an artificial insemination, but I didn't agree. Time is passing. She wants to be a mother. I don't want to go against her wish anymore. God has given you a gift, and all you want to do is deprive a woman from her motherhood rights and kill the child she is bearing. You shouldn't think like that. This woman loves you and wants to have your child. Go buy some flowers, surprise her, ask her to marry you. Let your child have a mother and a father."

"You are right, man. I think you are right. There is a time for everything. You're a good friend. You will be the godfather of the child. Thank you for your advice."

When she opened his eyes, she was in the ward. She was feeling pain in her lower stomach. Elma was sitting nearby. It was over and done with. She felt hopeless as her dreams shattered. Elma tried to comfort her, but she couldn't stop her tears. She lay to rest when they arrived home; she was in pain. Elma went to the kitchen to prepare some food and coffee. She didn't realize when the door opened. She heard screams from Beth's room. She quietly approached the room Beth was resting in and started listening in to the conversation. She recognized the voice; she couldn't see his face, but the voice was definitely Carl Caster. He was shouting at Beth.

"Why did you do it without asking me!"

"You already gave your answer to this. It's all done, no point in fighting about it."

"It's that bitch, isn't it? She convinced you to do it. I'm not gonna forget this."

"Talk quietly, she is in the kitchen. What if she hears? It's not nice. Don't get her involved in this. I told you I had a bleeding and Elma helped me get to the hospital. You should thank her. The doctor said the fetus had stopped growing. There is no need to continue the treatment."

"Do you have the doctor's phone number? I'll call myself and find out the truth."

"Carl, what's the point? It's all over now."

Beth quickly returned to kitchen. Carl threw the flowers on the bed and went into the kitchen. He looked at Elma with judgmental eyes.

"Is that right?"

"What is?"

"Don't act like you don't know. Don't stick your nose into other people's business. You'll regret it!" He smashed the door hard, leaving the house. The sound of the car driving away meant that he was already gone. Elma whispered something as she watched him drive away.

"Stupid, we will see about that." As she turned to take the coffee to Beth, she was standing there.

"My god! I'm so sorry. I apologize for him."

"Don't worry about it, it's nothing. I'm used to it. You see? All men are like this. Don't worry, I'll fix you up so good, he will come running to you." Elma noticed the safe door in the kitchen when she was talking to Beth. "Beth, why do you have a safe door here?"

"This door opens to the first floor. My father was rich back then. He owned the biggest casino in the city. He kept all of his money and gold on the first floor. To make it safer, he put a lock door here."

"Your father's alive?"

"No. He died young. After losing all of his wealth in gambling, he went bankrupt and started drinking. He died in a car accident. A year after that, my mother got ill and died shortly after. Ugh, whatever."

"I'm so sorry."

"Don't worry, honey."

They got back together shortly after their fight. The cold tension between them was gone. Changes in Beth's behavior and looks did not go unnoticed by Carl. The sheriff was getting suspicious. She was too capricious. She was nothing like Beth before. She wore expensive dresses, jewelry, and perfume. She was more attractive than ever. She and Elma would go to clubs and restaurants every night. She got fired from the hospital because of her irresponsibility and incompetence at work.

Carl was getting worried about her. After all the changes in Beth, Carl was getting more and more attracted to her. She was a real sexually pleasing woman in bed now. Carl was getting jealous. Carl didn't approve of Beth and Elma's friendship. He tried hard to break them apart, with no success.

For some reason, he came home earlier than usual today. Beth was preparing to leave.

"Where are you going now?"

"Elma's boyfriend is holding a holiday party today. We are also invited."

"Why haven't you told me? Who's gonna be there?"

"Closest friends. They asked me to come with you, but I know that you don't wanna go. So I didn't even ask you."

"How do you know that I'm not gonna go? I'm still on vacation."

"You're coming? Good, get ready. We don't have much time. I don't wanna be late to the party."

The party had already begun when they arrived at the restaurant. Carl had never seen such festivity in his life. It was really expensive holding a party in such a luxurious restaurant.

The party was going well. Beth was too happy. She danced with everyone near their table despite Carl. Elma was not holding back either. Good food, good music, and good service kept everyone satisfied. The boss had the feeling that Carl was getting bored. It was the right time to approach him. He took a wineglass and stood up to a speech. Everyone was listening to him.

"My dear friends! It's one of the most beautiful days in my life. The whole nation is celebrating. I'm so happy and grateful that I get to spend this day with my friends and closest to me. There is a valuable person here today. Most of you don't know him. It's Sheriff Carl Caster. It is a great honor to have him here at this party today. I thank you for accepting my invitation, Mr. Carl. Welcome, dear friend. I toast this to you."

He approached Carl with a drink in his hand. Carl stood up lifting his glass. Arnoldo put his hand on Carl's shoulder and chugged the glass and asked Carl to do the same. People slowly started clapping. He drank the shot. Everyone got up and started cheering. Arnoldo hugged Carl. "We consider friends as brothers. Alberto, come closer. As of today, Carl I are both your brothers."

Alberto took a seat after giving Carl a hug. Even though Carl didn't understand the sympathy shown to him, he was starting to enjoy it.

He had fun, like everybody else. The alcohol was starting to make him drunk; he was getting dizzy.

Arnoldo stood up. "Gentlemen! Tonight's my night. I invited all of my friends to my private yacht. There's no sleeping tonight. Nobody's going home."

As soon as Carl approached him to say something, he said, "I know you are thinking about leaving. If you say one more word, I'll get offended. We are gonna have fun together at the sea with you. That's it."

"Darling, what are we gonna do at home?" she hugged him.

"Watching the stars in such a beautiful woman's embrace must be every man's dream. Is it not so, my friend?"

Carl smiled and agreed. "There you go. Now I know you are my real friend."

The party in the yacht continued until morning. Arnoldo invited everyone for a game of poker. It was difficult to breathe with all the smoke from cigars and cigarettes. Carl was offered one; he didn't refuse. Every puff from the cigarette would relax him even more. Beth's loving embrace and the winnings from the game made Carl feel like he was on top of the world.

For a moment, he didn't recognize the place when he opened his eyes. Beth was lying naked next to him. He woke up and sat on the bed.

"What's wrong, honey? You scared me."

"Get up, we are leaving."

"Don't rush, Carl. Let's wait for everyone to wake up. We'll have breakfast and then we will go."

Carl put on his clothes. He noticed a bunch of bills on the table and asked Beth, "What's with the money?"

Beth laughed out loud. "They are yours. You forgot the game from last night? You won that money yesterday, silly. I didn't know you were so good at poker."

Carl smiled. He went to the bathroom to take a shower. After shower, he went out to get some fresh air into his lungs. He watched the waves hit waves and seagulls flying. The sun was rising. Soft breeze was creating small waves in the sea.

He reimagined everything that had happened yesterday. It was all very strange for him. He hadn't gambled for a long time. Was he really that good, or was there some other reason for him to win so much yesterday? He thought about trying his luck again if asked.

They had breakfast with the boss shortly after. The boss invited Carl to the casino after seeing his gambling abilities.

Their friendship was bonding stronger. The boss has managed to show himself as a wealthy man in front of Carl. Sometimes he would even invite him over without Beth. Carl would have a good time with the girls around the boss. Carl was addicted to gambling. Sometimes he would win; sometimes he would lose. But he still had plenty of money left from the past victories. He started doing drugs in parties. Sometimes he would blame himself for getting involved in such things. But then he would comfort himself, thinking that his vacation will be over soon and he will have to go back to work.

Few days until the end of vacation. He had met with Brook only twice in a cafe during this period. Brook could feel the changes in Carl. He couldn't get an answer from Carl when asked about it. At first, Brook thought that Carl had some health issues. But some of Carl's actions convinced Brook that he was doing drugs again.

The boss was happy. He had Carl by the weak spot. He was using his addiction to drugs and money masterfully. He knew that he was on vacation. This short time was important. He called Carl to parties every night and paid for everything. Carl even started having a relationship with one of the girls from the casino. Carl and Beth met seldom lately. Beth could feel something strange from Carl's actions, but she had no idea. The boss was always very discreet in his business plans. He even changed his phone number to get away from Elma. He made sure all the calls went through Anderson first. His new number was given only to closest friends.

Carl would have parties with drinks and drugs at the boss's expense. He would spend the nights in the blonde's embrace. His addiction was making him worry.

At first, Beth tried to ignore the changes in Carl, but she couldn't take it any longer. She was tired of this lifestyle.

Finally, it was the moment Arnoldo had been waiting for. Carl was asking for money from him, not a small sum either. He didn't want to explain why he needed the money, but the boss knew everything. He wanted to buy an expensive present for his new girlfriend. It was all a part of the boss's plan.

The gift was ready. He put it in his jacket pocket. They will meet tomorrow. He turned off his phone with the excuse to spend all day with Beth to make sure she doesn't get suspicious.

Early in the morning, the doorbell rang. Beth woke up hurriedly and worried. Who could it be at this time? She put on a coat and opened the door. Beth got angry seeing Carl come so early. "Good morning, baby!"

As Beth went to the kitchen to make coffee without saying a word, Carl hugged her from behind. "Darling, you are right. But you gotta understand, the boss invited his friends for a poker night. He invited me too. How could I say no? Look at how much I have won?" He threw the dollar bills on the table.

The more Carl kept talking, the more Beth got suspicious. "Carl, you are still doing drugs. You will start working in a couple of days."

"It's a light thing. It's not even a drug. It just cheers you up a bit, that's it. You can try if you want. It eases all of your pain." He threw the joint on the table.

"You will like it. I can bring more."

"Carl, I don't need this shit. I don't need this in my life. I don't want anything from you. Let's break up friendly. I'm begging you, please, don't bother me again."

"Is that so? I used to come to your place whenever I wanted, and you never said a thing! You have changed since you saw that bastard! Am I not right? Answer me! He ruined my life. If a Taliban bullet won't kill him, I will get rid of him myself. I will get him out of the way, no one will know! That's what you want? I will take care of this matter today. Only if I knew where he lived, I would show him. I got an unfinished business with him anyway."

"I'm tired of hearing these things again! Michael! Michael! I don't understand what's the problem between you and him! What's the meaning of bringing up the old stories? Don't get me involved in your conflict. My life is destroyed. Don't pull me into your personal problems!" She smash closed the door and went to another room.

Carl felt bad about the things he said. He washed up his face in the bathroom. When he saw his reflection in the mirror, he noticed changes in his looks. He had blacks under his eyes. After finishing his coffee, he entered Beth's room and soothed her hair, sitting next to her. "I'm sorry. I didn't mean to hurt you."

"Carl, I'm still here after all you have done. But you gotta understand me, quit talking about the past. It hurts me every time you bring that up. It's ruining my life, I can't take it anymore. I don't care what happened between you two! It's as if you are getting your revenge from me. You have done enough. All you have done, isn't that enough?"

"Fine. Quit it. We will never talk about this again. I haven't slept all night. I wanna sleep. I'm getting a headache."

It was lunchtime. Beth went into the room to wake up Carl. Suddenly, she noticed a box-shaped object in Carl's jacket pocket. She opened the box. It was an expensive ring. She was suspicious. A car stopped. Beth looked out the window; it was Elma. Beth quickly went and opened the door, careful not to make noise.

"Hi! Are you going somewhere?"

"No! Carl's at home. He is sleeping."

"I wouldn't have come if I knew. I should go. I don't wanna meet him."

"Oh, no, honey. Don't worry. Come inside. I have things to say to you."

"Tell me, tell me! I can't wait."

"Elma, my birthday is in two days. I found this ring in Carl's pocket. I wonder if it's for me."

Elma looked at the ring carefully. It's beautiful. "Of course, it's for you. Put it back before he finds out. I bet he wants to surprise you."

Beth quickly returned the ring back to its place.

Carl was already up. He heard them talk and acted like he was still asleep. Elma's words changed his attitude toward her. She partly saved Carl from a problematic situation.

The diamond ring was beautiful. Beth was really happy. She was feeling bad about the way she treated Carl in the morning. She went near Elma. "Why are you standing here? Come in!"

"I'm going. I don't wanna meet him. Thank you, maybe next time."

Carl knew the reason for Beth to be happy was the ring. She hugged and kissed him all the way on the road. It was obvious. Carl had to find a way to get out of it.

A phone call. It was the boss. "Hello, my friend. How are you?"

"Hello, Mr. Arnoldo."

"Are you with someone?"

"I'm with Beth."

"I heard about her upcoming birthday from Elma just now. Come to the restaurant with Beth tomorrow. Don't worry, I won't say a thing. Elma has told me everything. Don't tell her about the ring yet."

"OK, Mr. Arnoldo."

"What were you talking about, honey?"

"Arnoldo wants to surprise us tomorrow."

"I wonder why."

"I don't know either. He wouldn't tell me."

"It's probably a party. We're going, right?"

"Of course."

"I love you so much." She hugged Carl.

It was a festive party as always. Arnoldo was keeping the reason for this party a secret from everybody. He wanted to make a surprise. At last, he stood up with a drink in hand and started his speech. "My dear friends! We are all gathered here today because today is the birthday of our lovely Beth. All of your friends are happy to be here to share this moment with you. I have finally found a worthy present for you. It is my pleasure to present to you the keys to your new car."

Arnoldo kissed her hand after presenting the keys.

Carl wanted to give his gift too, but the ring was small for her. The ring was tight, but Beth tried not to spoil the moment. She was over the moon with happiness.

For a moment, Elma didn't know what to do. She couldn't get over it. She couldn't understand the treatment Beth was getting. Deep inside, she started feeling jealousy toward Beth. Everyone was congratulating Beth. Even though Elma was not happy with this, she started acting like she was also happy and gave her a hug and kiss.

Carl did not expect such an expensive gift from Arnoldo. On one hand, he thought that the reason for all of this was that the boss was trying to help him out of a difficult situation; on the other hand, he started thinking about paying back the boss. It was a big amount. He thought he was screwed, but he played along.

They came to the casino after the birthday party. Many took their spots behind the gambling table. Anderson followed the boss to his room and couldn't hold himself anymore. He had to say something to the boss about the expensive gift.

"Boss, you know that I never stick my nose into your business, I have no right. But I can't wrap my head around the way you treat the sheriff and his girlfriend with expensive gifts and presents. Can I ask why? The boys are feeling the same as me."

"I don't have to explain my actions to anyone. But there are some things you should know. Alberto is my brother, but I can't trust him."

"My apologies for intruding with your plans, boss."

"There is truth in your words, but I know what I'm doing. It will all be paid back with interest. The main goal is to lure him into a trap. He is getting closer." He laughed out loud.

"We gotta be careful. The prey is a very dangerous cadet. He can destroy us before we catch him."

"You are right, our prey is dangerous, but I know how to lure him in. We gotta be on standby. If he doesn't fall for the trap, we must destroy him. Don't worry, we got him now. Both of them are important for our future plans. Safe in Beth's house is gonna come in handy. Elma has made a great discovery."

"I am hearing about this safe just now."

"Elma told me about it a few days ago. That place is very suitable for hiding the jewelry we will obtain."

"That's a good find. After the operation, we can hide the goods there. No one will be suspicious of that house because of the sheriff. We can even bring the drugs here to hide that we will import with the money made from the jewelry. You're a genius, boss."

There was a knock at the door. The security informed the boss that Carl had come. Carl entered the room with the boss's permission.

"Take a seat, Carl."

"I came to say thank you for the present, Mr. Arnoldo. But it's a very expensive gift, maybe . . ."

"Don't say a word. I bought the car. It's all paid for. It's my present to Beth."

"I don't know how to thank you for your generosity. but currently Beth is unemployed. Driving such an expensive car will draw suspicions."

"It's a gift. Whatever happens, it's up to me. How about the ring? Did she like it? I did that for you. I saved you from a difficult situation and you got a present for her birthday."

"The ring is too small for her. Perhaps I should sell the ring and pay back some of the car's money."

"Don't trouble yourself. Change the ring and buy one that fits properly. Don't hesitate to ask if you need extra money. We will start playing soon. You can come if you want. A lot of wealthy people are in the casino today. I have seen how good you are. Maybe you should try your luck."

"Boss, Mr. Adrian Darvin is a very dangerous player. I wouldn't want Carl sitting face-to-face with him behind the table and risk everything."

"I guess, he heard you."

"Thank you. I think you can't win anything if you never take risks. I'll play."

Carl was happy. He was confident. If he won today, he could pay the money back to the boss.

Beth was really happy. For the first time ever in her life, she was given many expensive things. She went to the casino with her new car. Unlike her, Carl was very nervous and angry. He was worried about the game tonight. If he lost, it could all get even worse.

The game began. A lot of money at stake. Carl entered the game with the money he borrowed from the boss. At first, the boss didn't want to participate in the game, but Carl insisted on playing. It was actually Arnoldo's wish to see him play. It surprised Carl that the boss himself did not play.

The first few hands were lucky for Carl, but later in the night, he lost everything. He was shaking with anger. It was the tipping point of the biggest mistake he had ever made in his life.

He was frustrated, angry, and disappointed. Even if he sold his house, he wouldn't be able to pay his debt back. Time was running out. He could not think of a single solution.

Finally, Anderson called him to the boss's room. Carl was just standing, his eyes looking to the ground and waiting for his boss to speak. "But I told you they are good players. You see, I didn't play, because I know who they are. You insisted. Now we gotta find a way to pay them back. I know these people. They are very dangerous. If you don't pay them back on time, they may kill you. Don't worry. We will talk about this. Go home. I won't let my friend down. Take this. It'll help you sleep. Come find me in the morning. I'll tell you about the decision."

It was past midnight when Carl arrived home. His hands were shaking. He had a headache. He couldn't sleep. He started walking around in the house. He was running out of breath. He tried to get out to the balcony and take some fresh, but it didn't help. He needed drugs; maybe then he could relax. He sat on the sofa and took out the small bag from his pocket. He spread the white powder and sniffed it through his both nose holes with great excitement. Suddenly, he felt a great relaxation. As if nothing bad happened, he fell asleep right there on the sofa.

Arnoldo was happy. He had trapped Carl; his hands were tied. The main thing was the one condition he would present to Carl. At this point, Carl probably would agree to anything.

He called Alberto to his room. "Alberto, I wanna thank you for doing your part in this thing. You will get your share. You have done most of the things necessary for my future plans. I will present him my conditions tomorrow. He will definitely accept."

"What if he doesn't? What if he gives everyone away? What happens then?"

"True. That's why you should take your boys and move to the house in the woods. It's safer there. He will come here in the morning regarding this matter. We must watch his every move. Slightest mistake he makes, we finish him."

"He will go back to work in a few days. Maybe he is an undercover agent sent to get information on us. I think you are taking a big risk."

"You can't win anything without risking. My plan is to rob the jewelry store. There are a lot of expensive pieces. We are going to use the money for our bank robbery. We decide so with Anderson. I need your help in this. I only need the most trusted men in this. Anderson is very careful with this."

"You always preferred Anderson over me anyway. I'm your brother, but you only listen to him."

"You gotta understand. We are not legal here. Police can get on to us at any moment. My goal is to have Carl under my wings, so that I have information whenever the police are going to raid my area. He will be very useful. I want unity among the men. We need to realize these plans and get out of the country as soon as possible. We need to put aside our conflicts and fights. I'm tired of these talks!"

"OK, brother. Everything I say pisses you off. You and Anderson can decide everything, I am just the servant. I'll do whatever you say, and don't worry about the boys. I hope everything goes well."

"Just do as I say and do nothing else!"

Alberto smashed closed the door and left. Arnoldo was left in anger. He called for Anderson. Anderson knew that the reason the boss was mad is Alberto and his spoiled behavior. "My brother is very arrogant. We can't trust him. I trust you more than Alberto. With whom I do what, I know very well. I'm meeting with Carl in the morning. I will tell him my condition. If he doesn't agree, finish him and his girlfriend."

Carl Caster woke up early. He still had a headache. When he started remembering the night before, he started to worry again. He washed up, changed clothes, and went straight to the casino.

He quickly ran up to the second floor and asked the guard. Before the guard answered, the boss opened the door to let Carl in. Arnoldo looked at Carl with a strict face. "I spend the night in my office to find a solution for your problem and you have the nerve to come here smashing my door?"

It was the first time Arnoldo was treating Carl in such an aggressive manner. He was shocked to see this. "I talked with them for hours. You have gotten me and yourself in trouble. I paid some of the money. They gave us time. They are very dangerous people. If we don't pay in time, they will kill you and hurt me and the boys. Women, even worse. They have seen them both."

"Please, I'm asking you, help me. I can't lose my job over this. I promise I will sell the house and give some of the money back."

Arnoldo laughed out loud. "Your house value is just a bit of the sum. We must find a different way."

"Show me the way. I'll do anything."

"Only way out is drugs. He has street business in these areas, you can help them. Maybe it'll work."

"Boss, if we agree with what I say, the best way is to deal the drugs ourselves. We will ask them for some time. During this time, we can gather a lot of men and sell the drugs in the streets. That way we can make money and pay them back."

"I'm ready to help in any way I can."

Arnoldo acted like he didn't know. "What part of the city do you watch over?"

Carl explained his area. "There are dealers in this area. If you somehow get me their names and places, I can take them all out in one-night raid. Then the area is all free for you. How does that sound?"

"I think it's a good idea, boss."

"You are wrong. Those dealers in the area are their people. If they ever find out that we are behind this, it won't be good for us—for both of us, you know that, right? We have to cooperate. You will keep the area under control, no surprise raids. Other problematic sheriffs are for us to handle. You will just give us information about any future raid plans to the area. We will take care of it."

"Can we pay them back on time this way?"

"Good thinking. Let some time pass first. We'll find out. We'll think about it when the time comes. When do you go back to work?" he asked Carl.

"The vacation is over in two days."

"How are you planning to get in touch with me? Important members of the group need to get together from time to time."

"Boss, I think we can discuss this later, and I can inform Carl about it."

"Carl, I'm a very loyal friend, but I never forgive betrayal. Whoever betrays me regrets it later on. Think about that. I'm gonna help you out of this mess. All I want you to do is do your own part. We need to know before the police raid the area. You need to inform us in time of their operation plans. Beth must not know about this. I am keeping Elma away too. From now on,

Anderson will receive all the phone calls. He will transfer me the details. You will be informed with time and place for a meeting. You hear me?"

"Yes, sir. I am ready to pay you back for all you have done for me. Don't you worry about my side." Carl left the room.

It was twelve o'clock/ Arnoldo was still asleep. He came late from the casino and just fell asleep on the sofa with clothes on.

A phone call woke him up. His head was still spinning. He had a headache. He was still under influence.

He picked up the phone to look at the number. It was Alberto; he recalled him. Alberto wanted to meet with him. He knew it wasn't just a random phone call.

After some time, there was a knock at the door. "Come in."

"Sir, Alberto has come! Should I let him in?"

"Dumbass, since when do you ask for permission to let my brother in? What's that now?"

"Boss Anderson asked us to do so. For your security, he even asked everyone, including him, to check before entering your room."

"Is that something new? Let him in."

Alberto entered the room in anger. "Do you see what that bastard is doing to keep you away from me? Now I need to get permission to get near my brother. Do you know why he's doing this?

"He's trying to look like the good guy, but he's putting barriers between us. As if he is taking care of you. He's trying to make me look bad in front of you, and you are just letting it all happen!"

"Alberto, you really are acting like a child. I love you. I would never put anyone ahead of you. You got your own bad, I didn't say a thing. You know why? See, you don't know. The police are onto us. They can get us at any moment. I want you to stay alive if something happens to me. Mother asked me to take care of you. I have to fulfill that promise. Anderson's job is to protect both of us. I pay him for it."

"I don't need a bodyguard. I have plenty of my friends and men around to protect me. They would never let Anderson protect me."

"Don't trust them so much. One of them gets caught, he will sell you in a minute."

"You're my older brother, but you're wrong. They are brave men and ready to give their life for me at any moment."

"All right! We shall wait and see. OK, Alberto, enough. Tell me, why have you come?"

"Arnoldo, your sheriff, what's he good for?"

"Oh, he is useful. He has no choice. He's addicted to drugs. He has debts. He says he is thankful to me till the end of his life for helping him. If he makes a single mistake, it will not be good for him. I have information on him that will get him fired for sure. I have plenty of intel to put him down for good. Don't you think that your brother is letting everyone a pass. I told him I will pay some part of the debt. He has to pay everything back."

Alberto laughed.

"He creates an area for us to deal drugs. He never visits the area during his shift. Sometimes he brings his partner sheriff with him to the restaurant before checking the area. That's a signal. Our men in the restaurant warn others about a possible raid. We need to be careful. He is still a police. He might give us away."

"If he wasn't drug addicted, I would have worried about it. I don't think we need to worry now."

"Arnoldo, there's a reason for my visit. They are gonna find out about his drug addiction in the department and put him in rehabilitation anyway. He's not gonna be useful to us too much anyway. We need to use him as much as we can. The jewelry near the restaurant for example. Do you know how much value there is?"

"How did you come up with this idea?"

"We are being wanted by the police. They will arrest us at any chance, that's why we need to rob the jewelry and get out of the country with as much money as we can."

Arnoldo laughed. "Alberto, where did you get this idea from? Few days ago, we talked with the ex-owner of the shop about this. It's a good idea. But! It's not so easy."

"Just try to do what I say. There's good money in this."

"How can we rob the place? There're cameras and safe doors everywhere. The shop has good security. It's not possible."

"Think about it. You probably have seen how many expensive pieces there are when you are shopping for your girlfriend. The jeweler was the owner of the shop. He can tell you a lot about the place. Invite him to your place, talk about it."

"Is it your idea or the people around you?"

"I've been thinking about it for some time now. I haven't told anyone about it."

"You did good. No one must know about this except the trusted members of the group. Arlen! Call Anderson."

"You're gonna discuss this with that jerk? Your brother is not enough for you?"

"Alberto, it's not that easy. OK, your offer was good, but now we need to discuss things."

"Talk to the jeweler first, get his opinion on it."

"I'll handle that. You protect yourself. Don't get your name involved in anything."

"All right! I'll do what you say. I guess I'll go. I will come tomorrow to find out what happened."

"Alberto, don't call me. Get one of your boys to get in touch with me. If I have something important to say, I'll send Arlen. Only a few people will get involved in this. Meeting here would be suspicious. We will be in hiding. You will be informed of the meeting place."

"Thanks, Arnoldo."

"Take care."

Alberto's suggestion was good. But he had already talked to Carlos Darrick about this a few days ago. Entering the shop wasn't an easy task; it needed concrete planning and precision.

The ex-owner of the shop met this offer gratefully. He didn't get along with the owner anyway. The owner has given him time until he finishes the last job he has in his hands. The order Carlos received needed precision and time to complete. The set of necklace and earrings to be fitted with expensive stones was an order from a businessman from another state. That person is aware of Carlos's skills and experience, that's why he had faith that Carlos can create such a masterpiece. It's because of those jewels that Carlos was working day and night to finish and get out of the place once and for all.

Carlos agreed to help the boss in this however he can. His main goal was to hit a blow to the owner and get behind the jewel masterpiece he was working on. It meant millions, which means he also had a share in it. He had already told Arnoldo about the jewel set. He needed the money. He had to sell his restaurant after losing everything in gambling and going bankrupt. His wife left him because of his drinking and gambling problem. Because of money problems, he had to sell the jewel shop and the workshop. With what's left behind, he wanted to open a small cafe. With the income from the cafe, he could pay for his daily expenses. The offer made by his ex-client excited him. He agreed to do all in his power to help the boss.

Carlos informed everything to the boss, the location of the goods, the safe doors, security cameras, lighting, etc. According to the plan, the jewels need to be hidden safely for some time after the robbery. The plan was to wait for a while and let Carlos rework the pieces and then sell it slowly. Carlos was promised a share in the profit for his work.

Anderson did everything that was asked of him and gathered a group of ten most trusted members. Arnoldo wanted to keep Alberto away from the dangerous side of this operation. Anderson was also feeling the same way. If Alberto knew, people around him might also find out. That would put the secrecy of the operation in danger.

Since Arnoldo was counting on Anderson to keep his crew together, he also gave him the task of gathering trusted men.

They decided on a meeting in a discreet location. The crew would meet in an abandoned hunter cabin in the woods. It was located on a mountain hill, covered with thick trees. The back side was also covered by trees. There was the only entrance to the place. Hunters used to come back then. During rainy, snowy, and stormy days, hunters could stay here for a day or two. It has been abandoned long ago; it's not much of a use anymore. The cabin was falling apart, the wood rotten, holes on the roof, rainwater dripping from the holes. This abandoned cabin was the perfect spot for the crew meeting. Women were told nothing about the meeting; they did not need to know.

All the members of the crew including the boss were at the meeting location. To avoid drawing attention, they all arrived at different times. Everyone was given their tasks in the operation, but they had to decide the time for the robbery. Only the sheriff was missing from the meeting; he was already given his tasks. Only a few apart from the boss and Anderson knew about Sheriff Caster's involvement in the operation.

Alberto was waiting for news about the offer he made to his brother, but Arnoldo didn't say anything. He came to the casino to find out. Arlen was happy to see Alberto at this time of the day in the casino. Seeing Arlen in the casino made Alberto suspicious.

He went up to the room and called Arlen over. "Where is Arnoldo?"

"I don't know. He went on a vacation I think."

"Why didn't he take me, then?"

"He asked me to be around here. You know I can't ask them anything. He probably went to the sea with his yacht."

"It's strange. With whom?"

"You know who, like always."

"The girl was with them?"

"I didn't see her."

The door opened; it was Elma. "Hello, Alberto. How are you, dear?"

"You didn't go with Arnoldo?"

"Where were we supposed to go? Nobody told me anything."

"OK, you can go."

"Arlen, you must know where they have gone. Don't worry, I would never tell them it was you. Come on, you can tell me."

"Alberto, the boss liked your offer. They are gonna meet today to discuss the operation."

"Why are they hiding it from me?"

"Honestly, your brother is trying to protect you."

"He is not protecting me. He just doesn't trust me. It's all because of that bastard."

"Alberto, you know I see you as my friend. He is not an honest person. I serve the boss. If I do something wrong, the boss can punish me, but he sticks his nose into my work too. He screams at me near the boss. Acts like he loves your brother. It's all fake, everyone can see through that. Elma is working for him, that's why she is here. He probably asked her to watch over while they are gone."

"He probably chose the crew for the robbery also, right?"

"Yeah."

"You'll see, my brother will lose everything in the end. That bastard will take the money from the robbery and escape with his men, and my brother will either get shot or spend the rest of his days behind bars. Arlen, you are a good guy. If you help me in some matters, you will become my loyal friend and consultant. Just help prove everyone who that bastard really is. I need to explain to my brother that his sweet words and actions are not to be fooled by. I know he saved his life, and he will always be grateful for that, but it doesn't mean that Anderson should get all the control and push aside his little brother. I know my brother loves me, but he doesn't trust me."

"Alberto, he finds out everything about the boss's plans."

"What do you mean?"

"I think maybe Elma. It has to be between us, OK? Your brother has been doing too much drugs and drinking lately. When he is high or drunk, he becomes very generous, showering Elma with money and talking about his future plans. Elma informs Anderson of everything.

"It was more obvious during your last visit. Boss was gambling downstairs that night. He asked to call Anderson over. I went upstairs and opened the door. I heard two of them talking about your meeting with your brother. Anderson quickly tried to strike me, but she stopped him. She insulted me."

"So you didn't say anything to Arnoldo?"

"I'm scared, Alberto."

"This is how it is. That slut was out in the streets, my brother took her in, dressed in expensive clothing as his girlfriend, and this is how she repays. Arnoldo deserved this."

"Alberto, I need to go. Elma is downstairs. She will get suspicious if we talk for too long."

"She saw you anyway. If what you are saying is true, then she will tell everything to Anderson. What kind of people is my brother with? What can we do? All right, listen to me carefully.

Arnoldo is my brother and your boss. He gave you a job. We must protect him. Drugs are killing him. We can't let that bastard take advantage of him and steal everything from him."

"Alberto, your words are an order to me. I will let you know as soon as I get new information on them."

Hunter's cabin in the woods. Everyone was in place for the meeting. Two were appointed as guards. The boss explained the reason for the meeting and let Carlos have his words. Carlos informed everything regarding ins and outs of the restaurant and the workshop, all the security measurements, etc. The staff dressing room of the restaurant was connected to the store with a thin wall. It was the best entrance option. According to Carlos's information, the building was totally owned by himself back then. Only a door was between the restaurant and the store. But after some time, Carlos had to sell the restaurant, and the door in between was replaced by a two-layer thin brick wall. From the side it wasn't noticeable, but Carlos knew well where the wall was. Carlos knew the danger of this operation and warned everybody to act exactly as planned.

Every member of the group had to do their parts correctly. After entering the store and the safe room, a skilled member of the group will unlock the door. The restaurant was adjacent to the store and was one of the popular restaurants in the city. Since it was always packed full, there were workers working even at nighttime.

First, three members of the group were elected to apply for a job in the restaurant. One of them was to be a cook, another waiter, and the other courier. For this, they needed fake documents.

At last, the robbery plan was complete. Everybody has to get to work starting tomorrow. Arnoldo asked everyone in the meeting to keep it a secret from other members of the group.

Three members of the group applied for a job at the restaurant at separate times. Applicants asked that because of their studies during the daytime, their shift has to be put at night. They will work at the restaurant for a trial period of one month, and in the end, the head chef will test them to their abilities and decide who stays, who goes. Most of the clientele of the restaurant were Chinese; that's why the restaurant needed a chef who is a master in Chinese cuisine. The application of the Chinese workers was right on point.

The head chef noticed the ability of both workers; they were both very skilled. They earned the respect of everyone as sincere and hardworking in a short time. As a result, they were accepted to the job two weeks earlier.

Michael Grady was getting bored at home; he was unemployed. He is used to being on the move at all times; this condition was not something he was used to. It was playing with his nerves. Only thing that could calm him down was alcohol. Without even paying attention to it, he was drinking more and more every day. His leg would still hurt and mostly during cold times. Sometimes he would go to the hospital because of his leg pain. Leg prosthesis was already ordered for him.

Neighbor Lucas Marchelo was worried about Michael. He would try to keep him company at most times, sometimes take him out for a walk. Michael had a strong bond with this family, and they loved Michael as their own son.

There was a big happiness in the family this year—Sarah was accepted to university. Michael was also happy; he loved Sarah like his sister.

Michael noticed that Sarah is usually not at home during nighttime; he worried. Her father said that she had started working at the restaurant during nighttime. Michael did not like what was happening; it was not safe for Sarah. Lucas tried to explain that Sarah wants to help raise the money for her education fee.

Arnoldo headed out to the casino to get an update on the operation. He went up to his room and asked for Anderson. Tom Anderson entered the room directly, regardless of the security near the door.

"Hello, boss."

"Hi, sit. You probably know why I called you."

"Yes. Everything is going according to the plan. The guys are working at the restaurant. We are working on getting the necessary equipment and tools."

"Anyone else working with them during their night shift?"

"Only one student girl. She works the night shift."

"She may be a problem for us on the operation. We need to do something about her. Try to get her shift changed for that day. She shouldn't be there."

"We don't know the exact day yet. Weather conditions are important for that too, and we need to make sure that same security guy is working that day. He orders food from the restaurant a couple of times a day."

"OK, think about it. This girl can cause us problems. We need to think about the medicine. They can't be bought from the pharmacy without a doctor's prescription. Police are probably going to investigate every pharmacy where these ingredients can be bought. They will get on to us."

"Don't worry, Carl solved that problem with the help of Beth. He has insomnia problems, and Beth bought the medicine by her own prescription recipe from the pharmacy. Arlen already collected the meds from Carl."

"By the way, when we were gone, Alberto came. They had a long talk with Arlen in the room."

"Really? How do you know that?"

"Boss, I have my eyes everywhere. My men bring me all the information I need."

"Arlen, come inside. Alberto came?"

"Yes."

"When?"

"You went somewhere that day."

"Why didn't you tell me? Answer!"

"Boss, Anderson knows about this, that's why I didn't say anything."

"You fool! I told you to never hide anything from me, not even the smallest thing!" He quickly stood up and slapped Arlen very hard.

"Last time, you son of a bitch! I could chop your body into pieces, no one would find you. Get the hell out of here!" Because of the blow to the head, Arlen was feeling dizzy. He somehow managed to get out of the room. Elma was there in front of him. She noticed him barely walking out of the room and smiled at it. Arlen was shaking in anger. "What do you need?"

"I need to get in."

"Not allowed. Go downstairs!"

"Get outta here, bastard!"

Arlen grabbed Elma by the collar. "Listen, bitch! Stop spying around, or I'll choke you with my own hands!"

"Bitch is your slutty mother, bastard!"

"I told you many times, never say her name again!" As he tried to slap Elma, Anderson grabbed and stopped his arm.

"You try to hit her again, you're dead."

Elma understood what was going on right away and quickly went down to the first floor.

Hearing all this noise, Arnoldo Columbus came out to see what was happening and looked at Arlen with menacing eyes. He yelled at Anderson. "You can't control them?"

"Don't get angry, boss. These fools are not worth your trouble. I will take care of this." They went back into the room.

"Alberto is my brother. I didn't want to get him involved in this. I don't trust the kids around him."

"But he already knows something is up. If he finds out late, he can do something drastic."

"He can't do shit. I'm in between, but he is my brother and he has given this offer. I'll explain everything to him. I'll tell him that I am gonna need him on the operation day only and to keep it discreet."

The new workers were appointed to the night shift at the restaurant. It was good news for them. The other member had already started working the delivery. New workers managed to gain the respect of the head chef in a short time.

Most of the robbery plan was completed, but the girl who works the night could be a trouble for them. Something needed to be done. For some reason, she refused the offer to switch the night shift. Anderson went to see the boss about this issue.

Arnoldo was lying on the sofa, as always. "Hello, boss."

"Sit, you look like you have something to say."

"Boss, we got a problem. Everything is going good at the restaurant. But I wanna talk to you about the girl working there at night. I think her name is Sarah. She is a student. I told you about her. For some reason, she refuses to switch her work shift."

"So she's a student. It's probably because her family is not doing very good financially."

Arnoldo walked around the room, thinking. "Alberto can take care of this. He's a young man. He should go out there, ask her out, take her out to nice places, buy her nice things. I need to talk to him about something else too. Call him over. I'll talk to him myself."

Anderson didn't like it, but he did not react.

Alberto arrived in a short time. Anderson left the room with an excuse; he just didn't want to come face-to-face with Alberto. Alberto and Arnoldo talked for a long time. Arlen was standing right in front of the door. Anderson was mad; if Arlen wasn't standing there, he could have listened to their chat. Alberto left.

The fact that Arnoldo kept Alberto's mission a secret from him made him angry, but he saved his face.

Class finished. Sarah quickly started to get ready to get home as her classmate Brandon Randel approached. "Sarah, what's the rush? I thought maybe we could study for the exams together, like before!"

"Brandon, you're my friend. Please don't tell anyone else. To help my family financially, I work at the restaurant a few nights a week, and tonight I have a shift. That's why I'm in a hurry."

"But it'll be so hard for you."

"Guys working at the restaurant are cool. They like me. They're nice and friendly. You should come visit someday. I'll introduce you to the guys. When there isn't much work, they let me study."

"You make it sound so nice. All right, I'll come visit one day for sure."

"Of course."

After dinner, Sarah took her books for tomorrow's classes and went out to go to the restaurant. Michael was just getting off the taxi when he saw Sarah. He asked the driver to wait. He knew she was in a hurry. "Hi, Michael."

"Hi, Sarah. Aren't you late for work?"

"I am. The owner yells when I'm late."

"Get in the taxi. I'm going to the restaurant with you."

Sarah smiled. "I'm pretty hungry. Perhaps you guest me in your precious restaurant."

"All right. Let's go." Sarah was happy.

He had never been to this restaurant before. He was really hungry. He took a seat and looked through the menu quickly and put it back. Sarah was the host; she knew what to do. Not so many people in the restaurant. A man sitting alone in the corner got Michael's attention. He looked very arrogant and self-righteous. He put his leg over his other leg and smoked cigarettes regardless of others. For some reason, the restaurant staff did not say anything to this man. He was looking around constantly; he was waiting for someone. The waiter approached to take orders.

"May I take your order, Mister?"

"I'm waiting for my friend. When he arrives, we will order together."

"I'm sorry. I'll come back in a while." Sarah walked toward Michael with a smile on her face. "Here you go, sir. I have brought your order. I hope you like it."

Michael laughed. "Miss, I'll eat anything you bring."

"Then go ahead please, Mr. Michael." She put the plate and the drink on the table.

"Thank you."

"You're welcome."

"Ma'am, I would like to order."

"Just a moment." Sarah approached the client sitting in front.

"Ma'am, bring me some coffee, please."

Sarah returned shortly after. "Here you go."

"What is your name?"

"Sarah Marchelo. Why do you ask?"

"You have a very beautiful name, just like yourself."

"Thank you. Would you like anything else?"

"I would like you to sit and chat with me. I feel mesmerized looking at your beauty."

"Unfortunately, I'm at work. This is a public place."

"You shouldn't have to work in places like this."

"Why does my place of employment interest you so much? I don't need anyone's opinion on where I work."

"Don't get mad, cutie. Can you sit near me?"

"I'm at work, and this is not a bar for you."

"You don't know me. If I say sit, you sit." He grabbed Sarah's arm and tried to pull himself. Sarah managed to control her body and keep herself away from him. Suddenly, a Michael grabbed his arm and tossed him. Even after Michael had let go of his arm, he was still shivering in pain on the ground. Michael reacted quickly when he got up and tried to reach for his gun. He disarmed the man and put him on the ground.

"You stupid! Do you even know whom you're messing with? You're gonna pay for this." He took his jacket and left the restaurant. Sarah was shocked; she didn't know what to do.

"Don't worry. Go get your things. You don't need to work here. Continue with your studies until I get a job. I'm gonna help you with the university."

"Michael, I took a loan from the owner because I couldn't pay some of the education fee. To pay that back, I have to work here."

"That asshole can come again. If something happens, call me and the cops. Don't worry about the money. I will try to pay them back as soon as possible. After that, you will only focus on your studies. Your father, mother, and I will work to pay the bills."

"Thank you, Michael. I'm worried for them."

"Don't worry about it. There are plenty of jerks around like him. Don't ever think that you are alone. I'm also alone. Your brother Michael is always there for you. Never forget that."

Michael Grady took some money out his pocket and put it on the table. "This is for the food. Keep the change."

"But you didn't even eat."

"Don't worry about me. Forget everything that happened."

Alberto was in shock. If his friends or his brother knew about this, it wouldn't be good for his reputation. He had to know who that man was; he had to get his revenge. A way to get to him was the girl. It was obvious that there is some kind of connection between the girl and the man. After figuring who the man is, he would be able to execute his evil plan to get revenge.

Arnoldo got the news of Alberto a day after the incident. One of the members working in the restaurant told him everything about it. He managed to find out the name of the man in the restaurant through Sarah. Arnoldo hesitated for a moment when he learned that the same man is Sarah's neighbor, an ex-Special Forces. He told Anderson to arrange a meeting with Carl Caster right away. At first, he couldn't accept the fact that his brother was put to shame by someone, but later when he found out that the man is an ex-Special Force, he changed his mind and called Alberto to his room. He knew that Alberto is not very stable; he might do something stupid. On the other hand, he lectured Alberto about his careless behavior at the restaurant. It looked like Alberto wasn't ready for these things after all. He asked Alberto to be patient and very careful with this girl. The result is out there.

Michael arrived at home. He was angry. He thought about what happened. That man was acting that way for a reason. It's not a coincidence. Michael had to find out the identity of that man. This rude attitude toward Sarah seemed like a preplanned act. He sat down to take off his prosthesis. Thoughts were spinning in his mind.

His leg was hurting. Three days ago when the new prosthesis arrived, he had to walk around the hospital for two hours to get used to the prosthesis. He was happy because he didn't have to use the walking stick anymore. Now he could drive a car and even find a stable job. He felt like the old Michael with the new leg. He was advised not to be on foot too much until he's used to it. Today he had walked more than he was supposed, therefore he had to take off his prosthesis. The amputated part of his leg was red and swollen. He applied the gel to the swollen area. Suddenly, he thought of something and stood up using his walking stick. He took a bottle from the fridge to drink, but then he changed his mind. He put back the whiskey bottle. He opened the wardrobe, controlled his gun, and counted the bullets. He went back to his bed and put the gun under his pillow. He took a painkiller and went to sleep.

Carl Caster found out about what happened in his meeting with the boss. He thought of something. He knew the guys who worked at the restaurant. If what they are saying is true, it might have been Michael. The next day, he went home early without telling Beth and took one of her old photos with Michael.

Guys at the restaurant approved that this man was at the restaurant that day when Alberto got beaten up. This man was Michael Grady, dismissed from the army because of his injury, an ex-Special Force.

It was Carl's chance to get rid of Michael once and for all. His plan was to make the boss mad about him beating up his little brother. Carl talked to the boss about it and tried to convince him to get revenge on him. He talked to Arnoldo; he agreed with hesitance. Arnoldo knew well that killing an ex-XT officer is not an easy task, and the news of it could be big. It would get everyone's attention. Eventually, he avoided the idea of killing an ex-Special Force.

Alberto was angry about everything that happened. Alberto, who didn't agree with his older brother's offer, was making a plan trying to avoid the allusive attitude of his gang members. His plan was using gunfire to get revenge on him. For the girl, he had other plans.

Michael was already driving a car with no difficulty. Sometimes he would take Sarah from university or take her to work. When he told about the unfortunate incident at the restaurant, he asked Lucas to be more careful. He said that when he gets paid, he will give money to Lucas Marchelo to pay some of the debt back and she would quit after that.

He needed to go to the hospital today. He woke up early, took a shower, got ready, and went out to the yard. He was going to take Sarah to work today. It snowed all night; the roads were covered in snow. Michael headed directly to the neighbor's house. Suddenly, he noticed footsteps on the snow. It had been snowing nonstop since last night, so the footsteps meant that somebody either at night or close to morning circled around the house. The footsteps lead to the back side of the house and returned back the same path. Michael got suspicious; perhaps it was the neighbor himself.

"Good morning, neighbor!"

"Good morning, Michael. Come inside."

"I was going to the hospital. I thought maybe I could take Sarah to class on my way."

"The school is closed because of snow today. Her friend will arrive soon. They are gonna study for the exams. Come on in, Michael."

"Lucas, I have something important to tell you."

"Michael, you worry me. Did something happen?"

"I saw footsteps in your yard. Someone went to the back of the house and then came back. It worries me."

"Now you got me curious. No one has come here. Let's go check it out together. I wanna see."

"OK, let's go."

"The footsteps are big. It's probably someone with big feet. To be honest, Michael, I'm a little worried now. Looks like someone was scouting around the house."

"I think so too. We can't be too careful. You got a gun?"

"I got an old revolver."

"I don't need one. But it looks like I need to expand my gun reserve, and you need to get a new one."

"Michael, guns are expensive now, and one more thing— who would have anything to do with us, huh? I don't think it's worth worrying."

"Perhaps we should continue this talk on the road. Don't take it so easy."

"Of course, Michael. I also am worried."

Lucas Marchelo spoke out to his wife.

"Close the door. I'll be back soon." They headed to the car. "Maybe I should drive."

"No, don't worry. I need to get used to driving with this leg. Looks like there are a lot of surprises for me." It was a long way to the gun shop. Michael told everything that happened to Lucas. "It's something serious. But we don't have any enemies. I get that what happened at the restaurant. It's just some rich spoiled kid acting out, but the footsteps got me worried. I haven't seen anything like this. He is probably gonna try to do something to you. We really need to be careful here. Maybe we should call the police."

"We just need to be careful for now. Maybe we are just overreacting. Let's just wait and see. If we see anything suspicious, we will call the police. There is something fishy about this."

Anderson reported to Arnoldo. Everything was ready for the robbery plan. The date needed to be decided. Arnoldo had the final decision. Carl Caster was on the night shift that day. Weather conditions and the security guard shift were important. They needed their guy on the shift that night. He usually orders several times from the restaurant during his shift. Finally, the day has come. This weather was ideal for the robbery. Two days of stormy and snowy weather have caused damages in some streets. Citizens were advised not to leave their homes unless it's something necessary for some time. But the main establishments in the city kept on working despite conditions. Arnoldo was worried that the weather would change for the better soon. Security guard came to work; it was their guy. *It's time to get work. Tonight's the night,* Arnoldo thought to himself.

"Don't you just hate this weather?" Brook Cletus asked.

"Yeah, I do. I don't wanna leave the home in a weather like this. I am cold. A hot tea or a coffee would be nice."

"I know a cafe nearby. Maybe we should go there?"

"I think we should go to the city center. Criminals become more active at times like this. First, we can go to a restaurant to grab something to eat and check out the area."

"All right. Sounds good. Let's go."

Sheriff Carl Caster parked the car near the restaurant. They went inside and sat on an available table. "I'm starving."

"I'm not that hungry. I will just take some snacks," Brook Cletus replied.

Waiter of Chinese origin approached to take their order. Shortly after, the delivery man entered to take the next bag of orders and went out to deliver. "Looks like they need the money real bad. Otherwise, why would they work at this weather?"

"They are young. It's their time to earn some money."

"You are right, man. It's better than sitting at home and doing nothing. But it's still dangerous to go out in a weather like this. Look, there is not even one customer at the restaurant."

"Yeah, it's true we have to work, but everyone should be extra careful during times like these."

Shortly after, the waiter arrived with the food. "I come here often, but I have never seen that waiter here." Brook expressed his curiosity.

"Me too. He is probably new here."

"This place is usually packed with customers. I guess it's because of the terrible weather condition, it's empty."

"It'll get back to normal when the weather changes."

"Talking about the weather, Carl, we need to be extra careful today. Criminals tend to act up during bad weather."

"You're right. Let's finish eating and go to check out all the main establishments in the area."

Suddenly, Brook Cletus started feeling uncomfortable. He was feeling dizzy, sleepy, and tired. He barely could keep his eyes open. "What happened, man? Sleeping already?"

"I think I ate too much, Carl. What about you?"

"Yeah, I'm uncomfortable too. The warmth of the car makes me sleepy. Let's go check out the jeweler and other stores around, and then maybe we can park somewhere quiet, take turns sleeping. No one's gonna look for us in this weather."

"No, no. That's not right. I'll get out of the car, walk around a little bit. That'll wake me up. Criminals are not sleeping, neither should we."

After looking around for a while, they arrived near the jewel store. "You stay in the car. I'll go check it out," Carl told his partner and approached the store.

When the security guard noticed Carl, he slowly started walking to the door. "How are you, my friend? How are things going? Is everything all right?"

"I'm good, Sheriff, thank you. How long do you think it's gonna keep snowing?"

"Don't know. Call me if anything happens. We are in the area. Do you need something ordered? Coffee or tea maybe?"

"Thanks, man. Guys brought my order from the restaurant just a moment ago. Sleeping at home in weather like this would have been so nice. That's the thing about this job—the more you sit, the sleepier you become."

"What're you gonna do? This is our job. All right, you take care. Your job is more important."

"Of course. Sheriff, come visit more often."

"All right, man. See you."

Carl got back in the car. "What did he say?"

"Just talking about the weather."

"He could barely walk to the door. I thought he was sick or something."

"No, he's not sick. He just eats too much."

"Let's go, we need to check out the areas too."

When Michael found out that George wasn't doing well, he went straight to his home. It has been a long time since he visited his old friend. He didn't want to meet Beth there.

Luisa and George were very happy to see Michael. Two friends talked for a long time. Lately, he has been getting severe headaches because of his high blood pressure. The doctor wrote some medicine and put him on a diet, but it wasn't helping much. His head was feeling numb. He definitely needed stationary treatment.

After dinner with George and Luisa, Michael headed home. Because of heavy snow, he arrived home late. Before getting inside, he walked around the house for a while. The neighbor Lucas heard the car sound and came outside. He knew it was Michael.

"Good evening, Michael. How are things?"

"Thank you. I went to visit George. He's not feeling well. I just came back."

"Wanna come in for tea or coffee?"

"Thanks, but no thanks."

As Michael talked, he noticed tire trails on the ground. "You had guests?"

"Sarah's friend. Sometimes he drives his father's car here. They left a little while ago. Their house is close to the restaurant."

"Sarah was supposed to work today?"

"You are right. She switched her shift because one of the other workers is Chinese and has to travel back to his country in a couple of days. At first, she didn't want to do it, but considering the weather today, she agreed. There won't be so many customers. Soon her exams will start. They have been studying since morning. I saw how hard they work. I think they should go and rest a little."

"This weather is dangerous. You shouldn't have done so."

"Don't worry. Come on in. They will be back soon."

"Thank you. I'm a little tired, maybe next time. Have a good night."

A car parked in front of the restaurant. "I think they are not working."

"They are. It's just that nobody came because of the weather."

"Storm is slowing down. It's gonna be sunny tomorrow."

"It's not so bad right now either. Wanna play snowball fight?"

Sarah smiled. "You are serious?"

"No, just kidding. Are you sure the restaurant is open in this weather?"

"Of course, I had a shift tonight."

"Why didn't you go to work, then?"

"One of the Chinese guys is gonna go back to his country for vacation in three days. He kindly asked me to switch, and I accepted. The exams start in two days anyway. Since there wasn't much time left, I agreed. Why not?"

Brandon lowered his door window. "Sarah, the restaurant is closed. The sign on the door says so."

"It can't be. Maybe the wind blew the sign over."

"Perhaps, but I don't see anyone inside."

"I don't get it. Wait for me. I'll be back now."

"Maybe you shouldn't. We can come back tomorrow."

"I'm coming, wait."

Sarah started walking toward the restaurant door. The door was really closed. She rang the bell and looked inside through the window. Suddenly, she saw her Chinese colleague inside. She was happy. He heard the bell and turned around; Sarah was behind the window. Sarah waved hello to him and asked him to open the door. For some reason, he didn't open the door as he headed straight back to the kitchen. Sarah got upset and thought about heading back to the car. She decided to stay and look through the window. When she saw her colleague coming to the door, she changed her mind happily.

"Hi, Tian. Why's the door locked?"

"Sarah, come in. It's cold outside."

"My friend's in the car."

"We closed the door because we are preparing for tomorrow's party."

"They hold parties here? I didn't know that. I should go, then. Don't wanna be any trouble to you guys. We will come back tomorrow."

"No, Sarah, what are you saying? You work here. It's not nice, you have a friend with you. What do you need?"

Sarah was happy to hear this. "We came to eat sushi. If you are busy, I can do it myself quickly and I just take it and we can eat it at home. You do your thing." She went into the kitchen without waiting for a response from her colleague.

The waiter was expecting this. He looked out the window and checked out the car out front. He flipped the door sign back. As Sarah headed to the kitchen in a rush, she got really scared when she saw two strangers in the kitchen. She turned back to run away. The man from the restaurant who harassed her was standing right in front of her. Sarah understood that she was in trouble.

"Guys, I think there has been a misunderstanding. I better leave. My friend is waiting for me."

"What a nice coincidence. We meet again. Which friend have you come here with this time?" said Alberto, touching Sarah's hair and laughing.

"Guys, I haven't seen anything. Believe me, I won't tell anyone about this. Let me go, please. I'm begging you. They are waiting for me at home."

"Stupid girl. You can't go anywhere. Scream if you want to. No one would hear you. No one's coming to help you, not even your officer. I will teach him a lesson myself." He slapped Sarah with great power. Sarah fell down from the blow; her head was spinning.

Branden was starting to get worried. Sarah has been gone a long time now. He got out of the car and started walking toward the restaurant. The door was locked again. As soon as he looked inside through the window, he started shaking in fear. Two men with knives in their hands were pacing to the door. Braden understood the situation and started pacing to the car. But it was too late. He didn't have the time to get in the car and turn it on; they would reach him before that. He decided to run toward the woods ahead. Heavy snow was blocking his view. He didn't know these areas very well. He couldn't be sure which direction to go.

He was exhausted. He wanted to stop and return. But it was too late.

The security guard was long asleep. The police were not around. So it was going to be easy for them. The gang entered the safe room of the store through the wall they smashed down. They broke into the safe room and took all the jewelry, anything that's worth money. They also stole ten gold ingots and a vast amount of cash from the owner's private safe in his office. Shortly after, the gang members collected all the jewels, gold, and cash. A lot of cash. They headed to the preplanned destination.

The destination was an old house in the woods that no one lived in. They rented the place for a long time. It was suitable for hiding the jewels temporarily.

Carl Caster was worried. He kept on checking his watch. Time was passing by. He was eagerly waiting for the Ford truck to come; it was the gang's truck.

Only a few of the gang members knew that Carl was involved in this. The stolen jewels and the money had to be kept in this house for some time, but they have to change the location after for safety reasons. Only the sheriff, the boss, and Anderson would know the next location.

Carl Caster was anxious. Time was passing by and still no truck. He looked at the time. According to the plan, he was supposed to park his car somewhere near the woods. Brook Cletus was still sleeping. Carl was worried for him. He may be overdosing with all the medicine given to him. It could result badly.

Finally, a car passed the parked police car. It means the job was done.

Sheriff Caster turned on the ignition and drove to the station. On the way, he tried to wake his partner up. "You have slept plenty, my friend. You need to wake up. We are going to the station." He acted in a hurry.

Brook Cletus barely opened his eyes and lay in the backseat. Suddenly, he realized that he was still at work and got up. He looked out the window. He tried to get a hold of himself.

"What time is it?"

"You slept more than two hours. Didn't get much sleep last night?"

"Carl, I told you to wake me up sooner. I don't know what happened. I feel weird."

"I was just like you, I was getting drowsy. So I kept on moving. Visited a couple of spots while you were sleeping. It's normal in a weather like this."

"Stop the car. I want to get to the front seat. I don't what happened to me today. Someone from the Department of Control could have seen me sleeping on duty. It would be a disaster for me. You shouldn't have let me sleep for that long."

"This is what I get for trying to help you. We have worked together for so long. It was quiet all night. I just didn't wanna bother you, that's all."

"OK, sorry. Drive to the center. We need to revisit some places."

"Don't worry, we just did that. Everything is OK."

"All right, let's just hope it stays that way."

Carl Caster drove in front of the jewel store on purpose. As they approached the store, what Brook Cletus saw was agitating for him. "Wait a minute. Why are the lights off at the jewel store?"

"Calm down! We'll go and check it out. Storm probably broke some of the electricity cables."

"Unlikely, the storm is not so strong now."

"Maybe a tree fell on the cables or something."

"The guard would have called us. Something happened here."

Brook Cletus took out his gun and started pacing toward the store. He checked if the door was open or not. It was locked. It was dark inside; he couldn't see a thing. He flashed his light toward the big window of the store. It was terrifying. The guard was sleeping on his seat. Brook called his phone, but he wasn't even budging. Things did not look good.

"Call an ambulance and the department! Looks like something big happened. I'm gonna go to the restaurant and see what's going on. Come there after contacting the department."

Brook Cletus ran to the back side of the building with a gun and a flashlight in his hands. The door was open. He entered the restaurant and checked into the kitchen. It was all obvious. Thieves entered the store safe room from the restaurant's kitchen and swiped everything valuable.

Police, ambulance, and the feds were at the crime scene shortly after. Brook Cletus couldn't just shake it off. For some reason, Carl was very calm; it drew his attention. The most suspicious part is that the guard was also asleep. It might have been a planned thing. *They probably drugged the food,* he thought to himself. He understood the situation but remained shut. He had some business with Carl himself, some matters to dissolve.

The guard was in critical condition. The doctor said that he had fallen into a coma. After first aid, he was taken to the hospital for treatment.

A car approaching fast drew everyone's attention. "It's the feds. They got the news already."

"Those sons of bitches stick their nose into everything!" Carl complained.

"Carl, it's their job to do so. Crime has happened here."

"Since when do you take their side? Are we not smart or skilled enough to solve this ourselves?"

"It's not a small casual crime, Carl."

Car stopped near the crime scene. The man sitting in the front seat got out of the car and approached the police officers and showed his badge. "Federal agent Darren Edmond. I want the officers who were on shift in this area to give me detailed information on what had happened here."

"Agent Darren Edmond, let's get inside. I will explain everything you need to know about the scene," Brook Cletus replied.

"I need both of you to speak."

"We haven't had the time to investigate yet. Investigation is still ongoing."

"Mr. Carl Caster, please explain it to me. A big jewel store is being robbed in your area during shift, and yet you have no idea what happened. How so? Give me what you got so far. What about the murder?"

"Guys, we are all on the same boat here. We serve the same purpose. You can't solve anything with anger. So we need to stop fighting and complaining so much and concentrate on solving this crime together. Mr. Edmond, it's a big area. Because of the stormy weather, transportation becomes difficult. It takes a long time to visit all the establishments. We all need to calm down and decide what to do next. This report says that there are two different tire trails."

"What if the trail was just a client coming to the restaurant?"

"That I can't say for sure, but we found an abandoned car not far from here. Tire trail indicates that the driver came here and then drove to the roadside, and there is the abandoned car."

"Approximately at what time both of you were in this area?"

Brook Cletus looked at Carl. "Approximately two hours ago. Everything was fine."

"When did you arrive at the scene?"

"Don't know for sure."

"They tore down a thick brick wall and entered the store and stole everything of value in just two hours. If the times you say are correct, it's a planned robbery."

"One of the cars that was in front of the restaurant is found near the highway."

"A thief wouldn't leave something that belongs to him or her behind. It's not their car. They just probably wanted to get rid of the car. They thought the storm would cover the trails, but it stopped snowing, so we have tire trails now."

"What about the people inside the car?"

"They have identified the owner of the car. Police are on the way to the address. It's strange. Such coordinated and skilled robbers would never leave their privately owned vehicles behind. There's something else in this. Maybe they just got rid of the passengers in the car. Any news on the owner of the vehicle?" the federal agent asked.

"They will inform us as soon as they arrive at the destination."

A phone call. Brook answered the call. "The owner of the car was at home. He said that he lent his car to his son for the night."

There was a knock at the door. Michael suddenly woke up and looked at time. It was past midnight. He got his walking stick and gun and walked to the door. "Who is it!"

"Michael, it's me. Open the door! I wanna talk to you about something important."

Michael looked to the yard through the window. It was Lucas Marchelo and his wife with him. He started to worry. His wife was crying.

"Good evening, Michael."

"What's going on? Why is she crying? Did something bad happen?"

"Michael, we don't even know what's going on. Brandon's father called. Police came to his house. His car was found near the highway. They interrogated him because he is the owner of the car. He said that he lent the car to his son, but the kids are gone. Police took him to the station. I can't reach Sarah's phone."

"But you said they went together."

"After our chat with you, I worried. I called Sarah. She said that they went to the restaurant with Brandon. I got a little mad, but I thought it's not that far. They should be OK. They are young kids. I didn't want to disturb them. But later Sarah's phone was turned off and Brandon didn't answer the calls. I thought of calling Brandon's father, but his father called before me, saying that the police came to his house. On the TV, they are talking about a big robbery in the city. The jewel store adjacent to the restaurant where the kids are has been robbed clean."

"We need to go to the crime scene right away."

The police noticed a car approaching. Carl Caster recognized the car right away. He asked the driver to park the car on the side and present driver's documents. "It's forbidden to enter the area. What do you need? What's the purpose of your visit?"

"This citizen is my neighbor. His daughter came here with her friend, left the house approximately at 2300, and headed here. The girl's phone is offline, and the boy doesn't answer the phone."

"The police are in the area. Investigation has begun. They are searching for clues."

"The car they were in was his father's car. It's the same car that's found near the highway, but they are missing. They took Brandon's father to the station."

"We know all of that. They will clear out everything at the department. Why have you come here?"

"This is where the kids disappeared. Maybe there's some news about their location. He is the parent."

"Only the parent can come. You stay in the car."

Lucas Marchelo and the sheriff approached the police at the scene. Michael Grady got out of the car and looked around. The footsteps leading to the woods nearby drew his attention. It was suspicious. The intervals between footsteps and sliding trails indicated that the owners of the footsteps were running.

Michael Grady thought to himself for a moment, and he picked up his phone and called the number that Lucas Marchelo gave him earlier. The weather was windy. He barely could hear a distant phone call. It was ringing. Michael followed the footsteps trail without stepping on them. The brightness of the snow was illuminating the night. A black spot up ahead drew Michael's attention; there was something. He paced toward the silhouette and pointed the flashlight. Dead body of a young man. His phone was in the snow, near his dead body. He returned to the car without touching anything. He was agitated.

"Did I not tell you not to come closer? Can't you hear?"

People around heard the screaming and looked at them. "There is a dead body in the snow."

"You were told to stay in your place!" the sheriff shouted.

"Mr. Officer, he is with me."

"Move aside, let the man come through. Maybe he knows something." Darren Edmond started walking toward the man.

"Please, Mister, present yourself."

"My name is Michael Grady. There is a dead body. I just came to inform you."

"Who said you can go there without asking us?"

"I know the laws. I called the boy's phone. When I heard a distant phone call sound, I approached it carefully. I didn't touch the body or the phone. Lost kids are citizens of this country and children of a mother and a father."

Darren Edmond interrupted. "Mister, calm your nerves. We must be thankful to anyone who can be helpful in solving this crime regardless of their profession or identity. Please show us the area, Mr. Grady."

Brandon's corpse was taken to the hospital approximately thirty minutes later for further forensics examination. The sharp object that was used to kill him was not found. The police searched the area for two days; there was no trace of Sarah. She was announced missing, and search for her was ordered.

A tragedy has struck both families. Lucas Marchelo could not accept the fact that Sarah was lost. Sarah was very dear to Michael. He thought that there is a connection between Sarah missing and the robbery at the store. One of the workers asked to switch the shift with Sarah; it might have something to do with it.

Since Sarah's phone was not found, they couldn't find whom she had contacted last. The phone needed to be investigated. The numbers obtained were not to be reached. Perhaps the workers at the restaurant were a part of the thieves' gang.

Michael tried to remember the faces of the workers and the guy who harassed her. It looked like Brandon and Sarah went to the restaurant that night, and since they were witnesses to the crime, they had to be taken care of. They killed Brandon; what about Sarah? No trace of her death or life were found after a prolonged search. Michael's intuition was that Sarah is still alive. Another thing bugging Michael was the police. He noticed Carl's face change when the body was found; his allusive looks. Michael remembered something from the restaurant. When that man was harassing Sarah, none of Sarah's colleagues reacted in any way. It looked like Sarah was just a brick on the road for them. That's why the man came and tried to scare Sarah away from the restaurant.

A phone call. Federal agent Darren Edmond asked Michael to come to the department to answer some questions regarding the ongoing investigation. Michael arrived at the department shortly after. He was told to wait at the hall. After some time, the door opened. Sheriff Carl Caster came out of the room. He looked at Michael with sinister eyes and left.

"Please come in, Mr. Grady."

"Good morning. Your call worried me. Any news about Sarah?"

"Unfortunately, there is no news. I invited you here because I need you to answer a few questions for me."

"I'm listening."

"I want to clear out the information we have received."

"Am I a suspect?"

"I received contradictory answers from both police officers when I questioned them. According to what Sheriff Caster said, you calling the victim from your own phone and getting involved in a fight at the restaurant because of the girl does raise some suspicion. What the sheriff is trying to prove is that the robbery has nothing to do with murder and the missing girl."

"I don't understand. What is this about?"

"According to the sheriff, you have a romantic relationship with the girl and it all happened because of that."

"It's all bullshit. I don't pay attention to unjustified rumors. What he says is not true."

"Mr. Michael Grady, I know all about your past, but I need to put an end to suspicion. A murder needs to be resolved. Lives of two young people depend on it. I am authorized as FBI agent in the field to lead this investigation and solve the murder case. Love is a sacred feeling, maybe some jealousy in between."

"Mr. Darren Edmond, I think these allegations are the result of Sheriff Carl Caster's pursuit of conflict with me over the years. It's a long story to remember everything that happened between us in the past. I have loved one woman all my life. I have lost all my faith in love after that. I love Sarah like my little sister. I would die for her. No matter what, I'm gonna continue looking for her, even if I die doing it. Many brave men died in my arms. Maybe God let me survive through all of that for this day. Just ask the sheriff a question and try to get an answer. When did he find out about the conflict at the restaurant, and why didn't he do anything about it? When that boy harassed Sarah that day, none of the waiters reacted or tried to help her. I couldn't just let it happen. I'm sure you would have done the same. But they overlooked this matter, and the police were not informed of the incident. But today I see that Sheriff Carl Caster remembers the incident, isn't it suspicious?"

"Maybe he arrived at the restaurant at the restaurant and the workers told everything. Please, can you try to remember the physical appearance of that man and the waiters? Their height, weight, color of the skin, etc."

"I will tell you everything I know about them. You are probably gonna compare them with the sheriff's description. I think the timing of the information is important."

"Of course. We are going to thoroughly investigate everything. What would you say about the phone call to the victim's phone?"

"You already know if we talked on the phone or not. I'm sure the FBI and the police have it figured out."

"We know all of that, Mr. Grady, but sometimes you get a different answer when you ask it face-to-face."

"I get it. Psychology is a vital science, and you need to analyze things psychologically too."

"Thank you, Mr. Michael. The investigation will continue. By the way, from your talks, I see that you have a personal matter with Officer Carl Caster, am I right?"

"That's another matter." He said his good-bye and left the room.

He met Lucas Marchelo and Brandon's father at the department's yard. When Lucas Marchelo asked Michael the reason for his visit to the department, Michael changed the subject and asked about the latest information. Forensics results show that Brandon died because of internal bleeding to death with a knife from a knife wound. Michael gave his deepest condolences to Brandon's father for his grave loss.

Carl Caster came home very tired. He put his gun on the table and lay down on the sofa. He tried to concentrate and remember the things that happened. He could feel that Brook Cletus was on to him. He had to be extra careful from now on. Even though they both testified, Carl never asked Brook about what he said to the FBI. It would be more suspicious. He thought that if later on Brook decides to admit being asleep on duty, they might use it against him. On the other hand, if Brook had already done that, he would be at interrogation right now.

Carl Caster was angry. He was suffering for all that happened. Death of the security guard and the boy on one side and the missing girl Sarah's fate on the side—his conscience was tormenting him. He looked at his gun. Fed up with everything for a moment, he thought of killing himself. Suddenly, he had a change of heart, stood up, washed up in the bathroom, and got an alcoholic drink from the fridge and sat on the sofa. He was tired, sleepless. With all the thoughts in his head, he wouldn't be able to sleep. He checked his stash spot; it was finished. His hands started to shake. He panicked around the house. He smashed the whisky bottle to the wall. He was down; he needed drugs. He took a seat on the sofa; he didn't know what to do. The doorbell distracted him. It was strange and suspicious to Carl. He took his gun and approached the door. He stood for a moment when he saw Anderson at the door.

"What are you doing here?"

"I came to visit. Boss said that perhaps you have forgotten your debt to him and cut all the connections!"

"It's not safe now. You shouldn't have come here. It's too dangerous. There is an investigation going on. I have a feeling that the feds are suspecting us. They can come here at any moment. I was gonna contact you. Get inside. Anybody see you come?"

"Don't worry, I've got this place under control since last night. If I suspect something, I wouldn't come here. I don't have much time. How are you doing?"

"Like I said, be careful. They haven't found anything yet. They called the ex-army to the department for interrogation, same guy that hassled Alberto."

"Why him?"

"The girl is Michael's neighbor. They are like a family. He came to the crime scene with the girl's father. He somehow knew to call the boy's phone. It's like he had a feeling that the body was nearby, and today I saw him at the fed's room door. They probably called him over to get more information from him. It doesn't look good. You should've listened to me and taken care of him. He is gonna give a description about Alberto and the other guys working at the restaurant for sure."

"Alberto went to his place with the boys to get rid of him, but for some reason, it didn't happen. One of the boys let me know."

"They changed their plan for some reason. I would've helped if they asked me about it. For now, Alberto and the boys at the restaurant should stay hidden. If they get to them through Michael's description, they will sell out the rest of the gang."

"I need to get this to the boss quickly. They have already interrogated the restaurant owner and the workers about the Chinese workers. About Alberto, only Michael can say something. Thankfully there is no camera installed around and inside the restaurant. Long story short, Alberto's life is in danger. He should change his looks and stay home for a while. If he gets caught, they will identify him. That son of a bitch needs to be dead."

"I'll take care of this very soon. Boss sent me here because of the goods actually. It's not safe keeping the gold and jewels there. We need to hide them in Beth's basement. That's why we are here."

"How do you know about the safe room there?"

"Elma told the boss about it."

"We need to be maximum careful while loading the jewels to the basement. Beth's neighbor lives close by. He is Michael's friend and an army veteran. Your appearance at the address may raise suspicion. They were Special Forces. They will inform the police at the slightest suspicion."

"It's as if this son of a bitch is following us everywhere. Looks like I need to take care of them both. Think of something. Help us with this. I don't know what or how you do it, it's up to you. I'm guessing it's not hard for you to figure out where the keys to the safe room are. Try to get the keys to the house too."

Carl Caster thought of something. "I'm going to Beth's place. Beth will be working tonight. She'll probably leave the keys out for me. I'll turn the lights off. Approach the area from the back side. You will see a parking lot there. The kitchen door opens to the back. There is a fence. I will be in the kitchen."

"You will have a pair of keys too. You need to watch it."

"How come?"

"Carl, that's what the boss said. He trusts you. No one must know the location of the jewels except for the three of us. Boss is even hiding it from Alberto. He is not to be trusted. We are taking the jewels from the place that he rented. Boss told him that he would be informed later of the new location of the jewels. I am sure he will be looking for answers. There are people around me working for him. That's why we are gonna hide in Beth's basement and you will have the keys. Beth shouldn't know where you hide the keys."

"I'm worried for Beth. She might ask why I closed the basement door."

"Just think of something in case she asks. She is friends with Elma. Elma can't be trusted. Alberto is gonna want to know where the gold is. He can use Elma. We will keep changing the location of the goods. If she asks, just say some bullshit lie. You are good at it."

Police and federals were working together to find the criminals, but the searches showed no results. Looking at pharmacy stores all around, all their sale records, they have been sold to citizens only with a doctor's prescription.

He was tired when he returned home. As usual, he took a shower and went into the bedroom. He did his usual security routine. He examined the things happening in his head. It has been five days since Sarah's gone missing and still no news of her.

Where could she be? Who was that man at the restaurant? Maybe he has something to do with Sarah missing. He had an idea—starting tomorrow, he was going to start looking for this man in all the bars, clubs, cafes, and restaurants of the city. He fell asleep thinking about it.

He was dreaming. Sarah is trying to run to Michael, but dark powers pull her back into the fire. Sarah screams for help. No matter how hard Michael tries to reach, he can't. His mother comes to his dream.

"Son, you are uncovered. The door is open. You will get cold."

"Mom, where are you going?"

"Get up! Close the door! It's cold. I'm leaving"

He woke up suddenly. It was dark and quiet. He tried to listen to the silence without moving. He really was feeling cold. It was a freezing night. Moonlight was illuminating parts of the room from the window. Looking at the window, he kept listening. When he tried to reach for his walking stick, he heard a noise. He reached for his gun under his pillow. He aimed the gun at the door and waited. He was regretting taking off his prosthesis before sleeping. He carefully slid down from the bed to the floor and started watching the door. A gunshot spooked him. It was coming from Lucas Marchelo's house. Second gunshot heard. It continued several times and then silence. Michael waited at the door for a moment. When he went outside, he saw Lucas Marchelo shouting and coming toward Michael.

"Sons of bitches! Trying to get into my house! The door was open."

"Should we call the police?"

"I don't think so. They will be here soon."

Approaching police sirens could be heard. "It was probably a robbery attempt."

"Maybe."

The boss was spending most of his days doing drugs and having sex parties.

He was distant to Elma lately. Sometimes he would send her some money, but it wasn't enough to pay her needs. Beth, on the other hand, had a new car. She even left her job. It looked like Carl was supporting her properly. When Elma found out that the stolen jewelry was hidden at Beth's house, she hated Beth even more, but she tried to hide her feelings. Beth liked her very much. She would always consult with Elma and help her when she needed some money; Beth would just give it to her, never asking for the money. That's what hurt Elma the most. She didn't want to depend on anyone. Loneliness was pushing her to depression. She would close herself in, get mad at every little thing. Arnoldo's indifference toward her was unacceptable. She wanted something new in her life.

She needed money; she wanted to sell her remaining gold. The most valuable one was the one with a diamond ring; it was the boss's gift to her. This ring was bought from a very expensive store, which has been robbed clean recently.

She used to be a client at this store. The boss loved her very much. Once during her birthday, the boss brought her to this store, and the ex-owner of the place invited them to his own room; they had coffee there. All the expensive rings were exhibited before her eyes. She was free to choose whichever she wanted. The one she chose was the jeweler's handwork. The jeweler showed all the pieces one by one and showed their price tags.

The boss invited his friend to all the gatherings.

He could feel the jeweler's attention toward Elma. The jeweler invited Elma to dance at the boss's birthday party and called her to the store the next day. Elma happily accepted the invitation and went to the store as she was asked. The owner greeted and invited her to his own room. He showed her his next unfinished expensive jewels set that he was working on. It was beautiful. This jewel piece was ordered by the owner for one of his clients. The jeweler didn't hesitate to kiss Elma and give her a gift. The boss's visit to the store was either by luck or on purpose. In any case, Carlos found a way out of this awkward situation. As if as a sign of respect to the boss, he invited his girlfriend to give her a present. After this incident, the boss's attitude toward Elma changed drastically.

She put on the ring and watched it. It really was beautiful. But she didn't know the price. They could have cheated during the sale. That's why she called Carlos to meet. She knew his phone number, but she hesitated to call. She planned to go to his house. She went to his house as guests with the boss before, so she knew the exact address.

There was a knock at the door. Carlos was having headaches because of heavy drinking. He was planning to lie to sleep early. Gun in hand, he was looking out the window. He recognized the woman; it was Elma. It was strange that she would come to his house at this time. He opened the door.

"Good evening, Carlos."

He couldn't believe his eyes. Elma has changed so much. "Welcome, my dear. What a surprise. Please come in."

Elma noticed Carlos checking out the surroundings. "Don't worry, Carlos. No one has followed me. I don't think anyone cares where I am."

"Don't misunderstand me. If Arnoldo sees us, it won't be good for the both of us."

"I understand you. Looks like you were getting ready to sleep. I'm sorry to disturb you."

"No need to apologize, I'm a single man."

"Why? Where is Julia?"

"Julia left me forever. I've been living alone for a while now. We are getting divorced."

"I'm so sorry."

"Sit, you have been standing since you arrived. Sorry for the mess."

"I understand your condition."

"Tea or coffee?"

"Do you have alcohol?"

"I got the best one for you. Are you hungry? Sorry, I order food from the restaurant."

"Thank you, Carlos, I'm not hungry."

"Does anyone know that you came here?"

"No, Carlos. Nobody needs me anymore."

When Elma told the real reason for her visit, Carlos went into deep thoughts. "This ring is very expensive. I wouldn't want you to sell this, but I see that you need the money. All the men are like this. As soon as they start making money, the number of women in their lives increase alongside their bad habits. Why didn't you come earlier?"

"To be honest, I was hesitant. I thought that you worked for him. If he found out that I want to sell the ring, he wouldn't be mad, but he would feel sorry for me."

"No, you're wrong. I always stay away from chaos and nonsense. Friendship is friendship, but I'm still careful about meeting with him. He asked so. He finds the people when he needs them. Just be patient, I will give you some money. Don't sell the ring yet."

"It's late. I should go."

"I think you should stay." He suddenly soothed her hair and started kissing her.

Elma was expecting this from Carlos. They spent the night together.

She was happy. The hot relationship between them was still going strong. They were keeping their relationship a secret from everyone. Sometimes Carlos would spend the night at her place; sometimes Elma would spend the night at Carlos's home. They avoided using telephones by arranging a meeting date beforehand. Next meeting was going to be on Carlos's birthday. They were going to spend it together.

On Carlos's birthday, they both had a good time. They ate good food, had some drinks, and danced to the music all night. Even though it was long past midnight, they had long, sincere conversations about Carlos's passion and skills for his work, his art.

Carlos told Elma about the jewel set he showed before. It was his most expensive and last work. "This jewel is probably gonna be some rich man's wife or lover's favorite gift."

"No, he prepaid some of the money legally for the order, and when the job is finished, he would pay the rest. After the new owner bought the jewel store and the workshop, most of the workers left. Because the new owner decreased the wages and he didn't even pay on time, workers were not happy. I sold all of my gold and jewels to him, but I asked for some time at the workshop because I want to finish the rich man's order. During the robbery, it was stolen alongside others.

"Me and the owner declared the price of the jewel lower to avoid the high tax, and I was keeping most of the money from the deal here at home. Boss knew that I had some money. He asked me for that money, saying he is going to return it as soon as he can. He has been giving excuses every time. He says he's not doing well financially and that he had spent the money on drug deals. I am afraid to ask back for my money.

"My wife thought that I had lost all the money gambling. That's why she left me. If I knew that it would be stolen, I would have taken that piece away. It's very valuable. I wish I had it."

"What would you do?"

"I'm a master at this. I can take away all the stones and rework them into different shapes and sell them for good money."

"Carlos, I'm gonna tell you a secret. I know who stole the jewels."

Carlos pretended to not know what she was talking about. "Really?"

"Yeah, I even know where it's hidden."

Elma told everything she knew about the jewels robbery to Carlos. "They kept it a secret from me and Beth. They thought it would be a good idea to hide stolen jewels in Beth's home because her boyfriend Carl is a police officer—they wouldn't suspect a thing. We both were unaware that they were hiding the jewels there. Beth told me about it. Carl can't take the keys with him. After searching for a long time in the house, we finally found the keys. Safe door to the basement was locked, and it looked like someone had hidden something in there. Carl's frequent visits to the basement was suspicious. Beth noticed him, and one day, she followed him to see the jewels they were hiding.

"It was her father's safe room. He used to own a big casino, hiding most of his money and other valuable belongings here. He specifically ordered the safe door for the basement. After losing all of his money in gambling, he became an alcoholic. He died in a car crash after some time. Beth told me all of this."

"Can we trust Beth?"

"Of course."

"How can I meet with her?"

"For what?"

"What if she doesn't believe you? She will tell the sheriff, and you know what will happen then."

"She doesn't know you. Leave it up to me. Let me talk to her first and get her opinion. Then we can decide on a secure place for a meeting."

"Good idea. Talking on the phone is dangerous. One of the main things is to get the password for the safe. Otherwise, it's all meaningless. You know what to do. I will be waiting to hear from you."

Elma took a deep breath. It was a dangerous game she started playing. Backing off now is even more dangerous. Carlos could get suspicious and kill her; he had told all of his secrets. The jeweler obtained some information about the jewels too. He had to act fast.

"Hello, Beth. How are you?"

"Hi, Elma, how are you?"

"Thanks. I just wanted to call and check up on you, to see how you are doing. I'm bored at home. Wanna go somewhere?"

"Elma, I don't feel like going out. Come to my house, I'm alone."

"OK, I'm coming."

She was happy for the invitation; she was waiting for it. She got dressed quickly and headed to Beth's address.

Elma complained about her financial state and saying how much she needs money.

"Looks like your fate awaits me too. I am tired of living like this. He doesn't accept my marriage proposal, and he has been so distant to me lately. He comes with an excuse every time I bring up the topic of marriage. I'm afraid he is gonna finish the relationship with me one day. That's when I won't forgive him for all that he has done to me."

"I don't understand, Beth. Did he harm you in any way?"

"Harm is nothing compared to this. He ruined my life. He broke me apart from the person I love. Ugh, whatever. I don't know what to do!"

"Beth, I got a proposition to make. If it happens to go well, we could both profit from it."

"What proposition is that?"

"I'm kinda afraid to say."

"Don't worry about me. You know how much I like you. Go on, say it. If I like what you are offering, I will accept. But, please, the things I told about Carl, we need to keep it a secret."

"No worries, girl. I have a great proposition about the jewels."

"What is it?"

Elma quickly explained the situation to Beth.

"Are you crazy? They will kill us!"

"Beth, all you need to do is just agree. I will take care of the rest. You don't need to worry about anything."

"Tell me the details first. I wanna know what you are planning."

Elma told everything to Beth about the plan they made with Carlos, the jeweler. "Every couple of days, Carl goes down to the basement and checks all the jewelry by the list, and I don't know the password to the safe door. He can change the location of the keys any time.

"We are not alone in this. The man helping us can be trusted. You don't know him, but if you want, I can introduce him to you. It might be better to hear our plan from his mouth. He is a master jeweler. If we manage to get a hold of the keys for some time, he can make a copy quickly. Your first job is to get the password. Beth, you gotta understand. They are busy with girls and drugs right now. They are being careful with the goods for now. It's our window of opportunity to get to the jewels and switch them with fake ones. We can make a lot of money."

"Have you lost your mind? Police are searching everywhere. Just a slightest misstep and we will become suspects. They can catch us easily."

"Beth, all I am asking you is to get the password to the safe and get to jewels. Leave the rest to me. We calculated everything. These people are safe. We can trust them."

"Take me to meet them. I wanna hear it from them."

"It's possible, but they are being very careful. You just need to get a small piece of jewel from the basement. This way you can prove to them that you know the password to the safe door and they can replicate that piece to prove you that they can do the job well."

"Elma, I need time to think about it."

"You gotta hurry. We don't have much time. They can change their mind anytime about the goods. It'll be too late."

Beth thought about Elma's offer thoroughly. If they managed to pull this off, they could make a lot of money. Getting to the password was not going to be easy. Thinking about all of this, she had an idea.

"Hello. Hi, honey."

"Hi, Beth. Can't talk right now. I'll call you back."

"OK, I'll wait."

Soon after, Carl called. "Beth, you got me worried. What is it you have to say? You know I'm at work. I am not always available to talk on the phone."

"Carl, I thought maybe we could have dinner together tomorrow night. I'll cook delicious food for us."

"How come? All right. Will you have guests?"

"No, honey. No guests. Just the two of us."

"OK, I won't say no to that. Tomorrow is my day off anyway. I will be there."

"You get the wine."

"Of course, I'll get the one you love."

"OK. Seeyou."

She suddenly decided to check into the first aid box. Only three sleeping pills left. These are drugs Beth bought from the pharmacy with the doctor's prescription Carl asked her. Carl took some of it for himself, but there's still some left.

Two pills were enough for her plan to succeed. She was cautious about overdosing.

Carl was very tired when he returned home from work. After resting on the sofa, he was planning to go to Beth's place. The phone rang. It was Anderson. He didn't like it.

"Are you at home?"

"Yeah."

"Can I come?"

"Come."

There was a knock at the door. He was calling from nearby. "Hi. I hope I'm not disturbing you. Boss asked me to come and pay you a visit to find out how things are going."

The sheriff was mad; he had to stay calm. "I'm tired, just came back from work. Perhaps I should talk to him myself about how things are going. What would you like to drink? Coffee, alcohol?"

"No need for anything. You meeting the boss is not a wise move right now. You know it better than I do. So how does it look? Boss is worried."

"Investigation continues. We need to be maximum careful. Pictures of the stolen items have been given to all the jewel stores and to anyone who has anything to do with dealing jewels. Owner of the restaurant is detained for tax evasion, breach of labor contracts, and defects in recruitment. Those are the cases.

"Sarah, the girl working at the restaurant that night. Parents complained. Police are still searching for her. There is information that she had a shift at the restaurant that night. But she didn't come to work for some reason. She came to the restaurant at night with some guy during the robbery. You killed the guy, and the girl is missing. They announced her missing. Her pictures are posted all around the city restaurants, pubs, and establishments. Security guard is still in a coma despite everything they tried. The sheriff whom I was with that night, I think he suspects something."

"Tell me his living address. If you allow, I will ask the boys to take care of him tonight."

"Don't even think about it. Are you crazy or what? Killing a police is a very serious matter. They search and find whoever is responsible for killing a police, they will catch us all in a minute. All of us."

"This is why I keep telling my boss not to trust the people around him. I know what kind of shithole each one of them came from. They would do anything for money and drugs. Let the things dissolve first. I have my own plans."

"Boys are bringing profit from drug dealing. Most of them participated in the robbery. They know each other very well. It's thanks to them we finished the debt. What are you planning about them now?"

"This doesn't include everyone. Boss's brother has his own gang. He doesn't care much for Arnoldo's word. It's because of me, he says, that the boss doesn't listen to him because I am the one that changes the boss's mind about his ideas. Actually, the boss himself has gathered fools around him, like his brother.

Anything is possible with them. I have told my boss we need to clear the group from useless trash. I am at their target anyway."

"So the second gang working in the area is Arnoldo's own brother's. These conflicts are enough to get us all caught. Looks like I'm gonna have to meet with the boss sooner about these problems."

"Don't tell anything to the boss about this yet. In reality, his brother is still afraid of Arnoldo—he's got the ropes. He just has useless junk gathered around himself."

"His brother won't do anything because of Arnoldo, but you watch out for the rest of them. Don't tell anyone your foolish ideas. They may speak and give everything away. It'll be the end for the boss and his brother, including you."

"All right, let's talk about those later. What do you know about the girl that went missing on the robbery night?"

Anderson was thinking of something. "There's a reason you are not speaking."

"I'm being cautious. What I'm about to tell you, you didn't hear it from me."

"Don't worry."

"Boss's brother Alberto is keeping her in a house in the woods he rented. He doesn't stay at his own house. After the incident, the boss asked him to move out to a discreet location. They have turned the house into a party house with his gang. The owner doesn't live there. Sarah is there with them. He turned her into his sex toy. She's a drug addict now."

"How did that happen?"

"Sarah had a shift that night. She's a student. She was working at the restaurant for some extra money. Boys came up with an excuse to change her shift for that day. One of our Chinese guys convinced her that he will be going back to his home country after a few days, therefore asked her to change with him. She agreed. But for some reason, she came to the restaurant that night with her friend. She arrived in the middle of the operation. The sign at the restaurant was closed. It would be suspicious if she came and saw the closed sign. We had to let her in. Zed Richardo opened the door. She came in. Zed said that they are preparing for the banquet party tomorrow and that's why the sign was showing closed. He asked the reason for her visit. She said that she came to eat some sushi with her friend as she quickly entered the kitchen. She saw us. We didn't know what to do. As soon as Alberto saw her, he started harassing her. She was scared. She could feel the danger. She started begging.

"'Guys, don't worry about me, if anyone asks, I'll say I wasn't at work.' She wanted to escape.

"But after Alberto's slap, she fell to the ground. We duct-taped her mouth to make sure she doesn't make noise. We tied her arms and legs. Two of the men went after the boy and killed him in the forest. After the operation, we took Sarah with us. Despite Boss's intentions, Alberto refused to kill the girl. Arnoldo asked him many times, but he won't do it."

"That bastard! Why does he need the girl? She is being searched for. If they find her, it's over for all of us. You need to talk to the boss about it."

"You think his brother doesn't tell these words? He does these things on purpose, to go against his brother. He thinks that his brother decides everything important with me and doesn't care about his opinion. That's why he always goes against his brother's will. He doesn't understand the reason why the location of the jewelry is being kept a secret from him. I think he may have his own plans for the jewels. We need to be careful with him."

"I'll talk to the boss about this when I see him."

"The boss asked me to inform you about the meeting at the woods one of these days. You will be informed. I need to write down your off-work days. I think he wants to leave the country. Your opinion on this is important."

"It's important that I see him. There's a lot to discuss. But it needs to be just the two of us. I told him that I will help you in any way I can. All I ask in return is that, except for the ones who already know me, nobody else from the gang should know my involvement in this. It's important for you and me."

"I'll deliver your message to the boss. He asked about the goods."

"It's all under my control. Every now and then I check them according to the list."

"Be careful with Beth. You keeping the door to the basement shut may raise suspicion from her side. Does she ask about it?"

"Of course. I come up with some bullshit every time. But I think it would be easier if she just knew about it. She would be more careful. She won't do anything. She's a coward."

"You may be right, but women can't be trusted. Your lately distant attitude toward her may lead her to cheat on you and find a new lover."

"She doesn't have the guts to do it. Don't worry about it."

"OK, I should go. I never trusted women, and I suggest you do so too. If she does something wrong, the boss will take care of her with or without you. I'll tell the boss everything you said. I'll try to arrange a meeting for you. You came from work, you must be tired. I better get going. Take care!"

"Good-bye."

Carl was not happy about Anderson's visit. He usually spent most of his time at Beth's place; he would stay here seldom, and he kept the address of the house a secret from everyone. He had to meet the boss soon and complain to him about Anderson's late visits. He was going to put his terms. The meeting had to take place where both of them decided on. The decisions need to be taken by two of them. He looked at his watch. It was time to go. He took out the small bag from his pocket and put the cocaine on the table. He snorted a line through each nose hole and got ready to leave for Beth's house.

Beth greeted Carl very cheerfully. It was suspicious to Carl, but he didn't spoil it. She had cooked many of Carl's favorite foods. They ate, drank, and had fun together. Carl was already losing his self-control after all the drinks and drugs. Beth's embrace was hollowing his mind. He soothed her hair, saying romantic words to her. "I love you. I'm gonna make you one lucky woman. You will have a . . . lot of je-wels."

Beth was happy, and it looked like it was time to act on her plan. She started flirting with Carl. "I'm not that lucky."

"No, honey, that's where you are wrong. They are here, at . . . your ho-use. It's all g-onna be yo-urs."

Beth laughed out loud. "Perhaps there's a treasure in this house that I don't know about?"

"Yes, the-re is. I can p-rove it. No-body else kn-ows this. Keep it be-tween us, or the-y'll kill . . . you."

Beth noticed changes in Carl's behavior. He was probably doing drugs again, she suspected. Sleeping pills were starting to kick in. Beth was worried for Carl; she didn't want to overdose him. On the other hand, Carl's last words were worrying Beth. She tried not to look scared.

"I wanna see the jewel, Carl. You bought me an expensive gift?" She hugged Carl.

"Come, I'll show you. Come, see," as Carl tried to stand up, but he stumbled back to the sofa.

"No, darling. You gotta show them to me. Maybe you were lying. But you don't look like it." She grabbed his arm to help him get up.

"Of course," Carl replied. They got to the basement.

"Look at this, look how much gold there is. There are millions here." He put in the password and opened the safe door.

"They are so beautiful. Where did you get them, honey?"

"You will know when the time comes. But you gotta promise to keep it between us. They will kill you if they find out."

"OK, Carl, enough! You don't wanna fall asleep here. Come on, let's go upstairs. I see you are tired and drunk. Go to sleep. We can talk about it tomorrow."

"Of course, h-oney."

Carl fell asleep in Beth's bed. Beth started to worry. She sat on the sofa thinking. Having this much stolen jewel in her house could be dangerous; her life could be at risk. She thought about Elma's plan and went into the bedroom. Carl was sleeping tight. She checked his pulse and then reached out for the keys from his pocket. She knew the password now. She took a ring with a big diamond stone; it was probably as expensive as the one Carl showed earlier. She left the house quickly. It was late, but Elma was just falling asleep. Overthinking everything had kept her awake. The sound of a car on the street distracted her. It stopped in front of her house. She wondered, *Who could it be at this time?* She put on her nightgown and looked out the window. It was Beth. It was strange of her to visit at this time. Beth paced to the door quickly as Elma opened to greet her.

"Hi, Elma. Can I come in?"

"Of course, honey. What's the rush? What's the reason for your late night visit?"

"Give me a glass of water, please."

"What happened, Beth? You look very excited."

"Elma, I got the password."

"Beth! Really? I'm so happy to hear that. Good job. Tell me, how did you get it?"

"Why does it matter? Important thing is that we have the safe now. I even brought an expensive ring. I have the keys too. Carl is sleeping at home. We need to make a copy of the keys tonight."

"Quick, show me!"

"Wait a minute."

"Beth, well done. It's so beautiful. Ugh, Beth, wish it was ours."

"Don't live in foolish dreams. We don't have much time. Where is your famous jeweler?"

"Patience, honey. I will go to his house soon."

"Not just you, both of us. I want to see him too. I wanna hear everything from his mouth too. Carl is sleeping at home. He can wake up at any time. I need to get back quick."

"OK, as you say. But we shouldn't go there together. It's better this way. First, you need to go to a false address. Check around to see if it's OK to come to the real address. I will come after."

"OK, see you." She left Elma's house.

Elma did this just in case someone followed her here. She was being cautious. She arrived at the address Elma said. She rang the bell. She waited. A middle-aged man opened the door.

"Who are you looking for, ma'am?"

"I'm Beth, Elma's girlfriend."

"I don't understand. Who is Beth? Who is Elma?" He looked out the window to check.

"Maybe you have the wrong address."

"Sir, don't worry. I understand your concerns."

He turned to the sound. "Excuse me, sir. She is my friend. She has the right address." She continued speaking.

"There's a man called Carlos that lives here. He gave me the address."

"Don't worry, ma'am. Come inside. I rented him the house. He'll be back soon."

"We are in a hurry. We have to see him."

"Maybe we are at the wrong address, Elma?"

"Don't be afraid. This is Carlos's new address," as she entered. The owner invited them to sit. Elma could see that Beth was really scared. She was shaking.

"Why isn't he coming? I need to go."

"Calm down, girl. If he said he will come, that means he will come. Have patience."

Suddenly, Carlos entered the room. The girls were surprised. He was in the house the whole time. He was just being extra careful. Elma introduced Beth to Carlos and gave him the keys. The owner took the keys and quickly went to another room. Beth was terrified. Time was flying. They talked about the jewels. Carlos gave them assignments to protect the security. He even managed to sneak a note with his phone number into Beth's bag. Beth took out the ring and showed it to Carlos.

"It's a very valuable ring. The diamond is worked perfectly. High carat." He gave his opinion.

"I brought this for now. The stones need to be changed as soon as possible. Carl checks the jewels by their attributes and lists every few days."

"We don't have time, we must hurry. I need to get going, then. It needs to be done quickly. Wait to hear from me, I'll find you. Soon the keys to the safe room door will be copied. You know the password, right?"

"Yes, I do. But it can change any moment."

"He is not gonna be able to remember the password numbers. He is going to take it as a note somewhere. Watch his actions. Don't worry about the keys. The owner is a master at this. We talked already. He's an old friend. We can trust him."

The owner came in from the other room with keys in his hand and gave them to Beth. "Farewell, girls. Unfortunately, I need to go. Have a sit if you like."

"No, Carlos! We better get going our different paths."

"Good idea! Beth is in a hurry. She should go first. We don't have much time. Beth, you go. You did good. This is just the beginning. We are gonna get rich at the end of this and get out of this place. Those bastards can't be trusted. Be maximum careful. You will see who your real friends are at the end."

Beth said good-bye and headed home.

Carlos sent her out and came back to the house. "Things are going well for us now. We got the password and the keys to the safe room. The main problem is the password. If he doesn't change the password anytime soon, things will end well for us. I'm gonna increase her share from the sale of the ring to get her more into this. Arnoldo can change the location of the goods at any time. We need to act quickly. We need to make another plan and go for the gold before it's too late."

"What are you thinking?" Elma asked.

"They can collect the gold from the basement anytime now. We need to act before them. Only way is to get to gold before them and leave the country as fast as possible. We can't trust them. They will leave us behind as soon as they are done with us. We need to gain Beth's trust. If we manage to change the stone of the ring, we should give most of the money to her. She loves money."

"That's a smart idea. But it's not gonna be easy to get the gold. It's very dangerous."

The owner of the house entered the conversation.

"You're right, my friend, but you can't win anything if you don't risk anything. I'm the one who helped them, but I'm already forgotten. Arnoldo even took all the money I had. He doesn't even think about paying back his debt. He comes up with an excuse every time. This much wealth is worth risking for. I'm gonna meet with Beth to offer this plan and try to get the password from her. Try to get her more excited about this deal. If she refuses, we will make her talk and then get rid of her."

"I talked to my friend. I'm gonna meet with him about the ring in the morning. After that matter is taken care of, I will return and we'll discuss the later steps of our plan."

It was almost lunchtime when he woke up. He had a terrible headache. Beth was trying her hardest to make him feel better, but for some reason, Carl was still feeling bad. "When did I sleep last night? I don't remember a thing."

Beth hugged Carl with a smile on her face. "I think it's the wine. I was so drunk last night, I don't even know when I fell asleep, just like you. I woke up an hour ago."

Carl Caster approached the window and checked the street. It was strange. He remembered that Beth's car was parked a little further down the street, but now it was in front of the house. "Beth, when did you wake up?"

Beth knew right away why Carl asked that question. "Honey, I'm up an hour already. I went to the store to get some groceries for the house."

Carl thought of something. Before washing up his face, he went straight to the room upstairs and then went down to the basement. He opened the safe door and checked the jewelry, had breakfast, gave Beth a kiss, and went to work.

Carl was trying to remember what happened last night. He couldn't remember a thing. Something was going on, something suspicious, he thought to himself.

As always, Alvaro was very tired when he returned home from work. The medicine he took because of his illness was not helping anymore; his pains were getting stronger. Doctor's report showed that the lung cancer cells had metastasized, which meant the medicine was not working. Most of the money in his insurance account was used for the treatment, and the rest of the insurance money was not enough for the medicine necessary. The new owner of the workshop always paid his salary on time and even helped him extra because of his illness. Even though the workshop belonged to his son, he often would come to the workshop and personally supervise the shop. The owner's son is an ex-army. After getting wounded really bad, he was released from the army. With his father, he returned back to his old profession and took control of the workshop. The owner has given many years of his life to this profession; he has made plenty of money over the years. He was wealthy now. He wanted his only son to continue his profession and taught him all the secrets of this art of a profession. Later on, Roger Thomas decided to go to the army with his friends. But after getting wounded at the army, he returned home and decided to continue his father's legacy. Buster Thomas brought in his son and trusted him with the management of some workshops and stores. Since Buster's will was changed to leave everything to his son, Roger became rich in a matter of instant. Roger loved and respected his parents. His father's word was a law for him. The new owner had earned everybody's respect with generosity. Everyone, including Alvaro, loved and respected him.

It has been a long since he returned from the army. He hasn't seen his brothers in arms who were also released from the army because of their injuries for a long time now. Roger Thomas missed his friends from the army. Since he didn't have their phone numbers, he hasn't been able to get in touch with his friends. He made a plan to go to the neighboring state to find his friends.

Alvaro was impatient to meet his old friend. It's been a long time since the last time they met. They had a sincere friendship. After Carlos sold his own workshop, most of the workers quit, mainly because the new owner was always rude to the workers and the salaries were never on time. Alvaro also quit and returned to his home state. They were apart for a long time, but they kept in touch by telephone.

This last phone call was strange. His friend called and said that he needed to see him for something important but didn't explain what.

Carlos ordered a taxi, and after a long trip, he arrived at the biggest in the state. It was not hard to find Alvaro's address. He showed it to the taxi driver, and the driver took care of the rest. He asked the taxi driver to approach the workshop and ask for Alvaro while he remained seated in the car. The security guard said that he had gone home early today and gave his home address. Soon after, he was at the address.

Alvaro was very happy to see him. He even prepared some food for his visit. His wife prepared delicious home food and opened a big dining table. They reminisced, talked and laughed, and had some drinks. Carlos talked about how his wife left him after he went bankrupt and that he lives alone now. He even lied about having a divorce court in the near future. Alvaro worried about his friend and advised him to stay and find a job there.

Finally, it was the moment he had been waiting for. Carlos Darrick showed the ring to his friend as an explanation of his sudden visit. He said that the ring belongs to his wife and just wants to switch the stone and sell it. He explained it too. He said that it was his gift to her, but the ring will be taken by his wife at the court. He just wanted to switch the stone to a cheaper one, and with the money he made, he could pay back his debts. He said that he knows how well a master Alvaro is, and he can take care of it with ease. He even promised some of the money to him. Alvaro was ready to help his friend in need without a charge, but he needed the money too, so he agreed to his offer and decided to get to work as soon as possible. Thinking about the sale of the stone, Alvaro came up with an idea. He was sure that the new owner would buy this piece. He knew the time was short; he had to do it quickly.

He came to work early that day. He explained to the security guard the reason for his early arrival. Highly demanding work and not enough time, he needed the money. He came early to finish early to go to a doctor's appointment.

He knew that the owner usually comes to work later. He had to get everything done before lunchtime and give it back to his friend.

Michael didn't go to his friend's house for some time. Beth and George's house were close to each other; there was only a narrow road between them. He didn't want to risk meeting Beth by going there. He didn't want to see her. He knew that one day they would sort everything out, but not now. It had to be the right time and place.

Michael called George every day about his health. Lately his friend has been having some discomforts in his health. Because of this, Michael decided to visit his friend. He had to see him face-to-face.

George complained about his weakened senses in his hands and legs and high blood pressure. He was nervous and angry. He said that he was tired of taking medicine.

"Be patient, my friend. You should control your anger. It's not good for you. You need to listen to me. You need to take some stationary treatment at the hospital. You will feel better after that."

"No way! I'm not leaving Luisa alone."

"You don't need to worry about Luisa. Wasn't she alone when we were in Afghanistan? She is a brave woman. She's not afraid of anything. I'm sure she asked you to do the same about your health situation."

"Of course, but I can't leave her alone now, not right now."

"Why?"

"I'm gonna be a father."

Michael was very happy to hear this news. "I'm so happy to hear that. Congratulations."

"Thank you, man. I love kids. It was my biggest dream to become a father. Looks like it's happening."

"It was both our wish."

"Forget about the past, man. That woman did not deserve you. You need to find the right woman to get married. Hurry up, man, time is going."

Michael stopped to think for a moment. "George, the girl I got to know and loved was the clean and pure Beth. I'm gonna find out who stole her from me and dragged her into this mess. I'm never gonna forgive them for what they have done to me."

"We have lost plenty. You deserve to live, my friend. I don't wanna lose a friend like you. She chose the wrong path. The Beth you have in your heart is gone. She is a woman who's gotten into dirt and that can't be cleared. Forget her!"

"It's difficult for me, man. I need to know why she cheated on me."

George tried to distract Michael. "I can't go to a stationary treatment at the hospital. Luisa has some problems with her pregnancy. She gets pains. Doctors suggested that she sleep at the hospital. For now, she keeps going to work because her medications are working, but soon she will be back from her shift.

"When she arrives, we will decide this together. We are gonna go to the hospital together. I need to get examined too. Pain in my leg increases after walking a little bit. Then we can go to a restaurant to celebrate the good news."

The doorbell rang. It was Luisa. "Hello. Welcome, Michael. It's so nice to see you. How have you been?"

"Thank you, Luisa. How are you?"

"Thanks, Michael." She entered the room.

"I'm good. If George doesn't complain too much, we both would be fine." She leaned to kiss him.

"When I see you and your smile at home, all of my pain goes away."

"Congratulations, Luisa. I heard the news. I'm happy for you."

"Thanks, Michael. Looks like George already told everything to you."

"Michael is gonna be the godfather of the baby."

"Of course. Now, tell me, where are we going to celebrate this good news?" Michael asked.

"I will cook something beautiful and we can stay at home."

"No, you need rest. Don't trouble yourself. We should go to a restaurant."

"Of course. Luisa, take a little rest until we come back from the checkup at the hospital."

"OK, boys, as you wish."

Michael heard the sound of an approaching car. As if he felt something, he looked out the window. Luisa and George looked at each other; they knew whose car it was. It was Beth. Michael was staring at the woman inside the car. He was looking with anger, but in the depth of his heart, he still had feelings for her.

"Michael, I think she is on the wrong path. Who could have bought her this expensive car? Even if it was leased, the sheriff's salary still can't cover that."

"There's something behind this, and Carl knows about it," George replied.

"Whatever. Are we celebrating or not?" Michael moved away from the window.

"Of course, Michael," Luisa replied.

"I'm going to the hospital with George. You should rest until we come back."

Beth was nervous. She was tired of staying at home. After Carl left, she went to the mall to buy things necessary for the house. Since that night, she was still nervous. She entered a dangerous game willingly. She had a strange fear in her heart. The more she stayed at home, the more nervous she became. She planned to go on a holiday, as always. She called and talked to Elma about this. They could go out to have fun, and maybe she could get some news from Elma. Beth was going to pick her up from her home.

They drove downtown and bought some clothing and perfume from expensive boutique stores. They were hungry and decided to go to one of their favorite restaurants. They found a table, ordered food, and some drinks. They partied and had fun until late.

Beth took a seat to rest. She was exhausted from all the dancing. Suddenly, she noticed some people up ahead. She recognized two of them. They were George and Luisa. The third person was looking the other way, so she only saw the back of his head. But it looked familiar. *It is Michael,* she thought to herself. They found a table on the other side of the restaurant facing Beth and Elma's table. Beth knew that Michael is back from the army. She saw him not far ago in front of Luisa's house while he was getting out of the car. Long time has passed since then. The man she didn't recognize looked at her all of a sudden. It was Michael for sure. It was the first time Beth saw him up close since they have been separated. She panicked; she did not know what to do. Her heart was pacing, and her face was already red. He has changed so much; he was young, but his hair was already turning to white. She didn't know how to react; trying to avoid eye contact with him, she put her head down. Elma noticed the sudden change in her behavior.

"What happened to you, girl? You look nervous."

"Elma, I don't know. I'm not feeling well. Maybe we should head back."

"Who was that staring at you? Do you know him?"

"No."

"Then why are you upset?"

Beth didn't say a word. "Honey, I couldn't help but notice that since they arrived, you are uncomfortable. You look pale. Calm down. You are scaring me. You can't see yourself," as she quickly stood up and hugged Beth, who was about faint. The waiter helped Elma to take Beth to a room where she could lie down and rest. She was cold sweating.

"Ma'am, should I call an ambulance?"

"No, don't worry, it'll pass. Beth, how are you feeling?"

Beth opened her eyes. She looked at Elma and said, "Take me to get some fresh air."

They took a seat at a bench in the park close by. Beth was crying her heart out. No matter what Elma tried, she couldn't calm Beth down. Finally, she managed to calm Beth down. Elma insisted on asking what happened. Beth didn't say a word about it and asked Elma not to tell Carl about it too.

Elma thought a lot about what happened. There was some connection between the people at the other table and her. Beth didn't admit anything, but Elma was determined to find the truth and use it to implement her evil plan.

Michael was nervous. George and Luisa insisted on him staying, but he apologized and refused and went straight home. He wasn't angry. He had a few glasses of wine on an empty stomach. He lay on the sofa. He couldn't stop thinking. He could feel the sadness in Beth's eyes, and, suddenly, the volcano of feelings deep down his heart sparkled. Beth still loved him. But what happened? It looked like Carl tricked her. It was obvious from her looks that she was unhappy. Michael promised himself he would get to the bottom of this. He was going to find out the truth.

"Roger, wake up, son. It's time. Your father is angry again. You are always late to work."

"OK, Mom, one minute."

"Breakfast is ready."

"Where's Dad?"

"He had to leave early for work. He'll be back in a few hours."

"OK, I better get going."

"But you didn't eat anything!"

"Just for you, I'll have a coffee."

"I just want to see you get married. Roger, your father and I are old now. We just want to play with and feel the love of a grandchild."

"Don't you worry, Mom. I'll fulfill your dream soon enough. But I have to invite my friends to my wedding. I can't find the time to go and meet them."

"Decide on a date for the wedding and invite them."

"I don't know their phone numbers. I must go to the state and find them. I haven't seen them since Afghanistan. I miss them."

"I think you were going to meet the last time, weren't you?"

"I knew Michael's address, so I headed there first. His door was locked, so I asked the neighbor. He said that he hasn't been home for a couple of days now. He asked who I was, but I didn't say my name. I want it to be a surprise. Since I don't know anyone there, I decided to return home. I don't know George's address. He is my other friend. I know that he suffered a heavy head trauma and was getting treatment at the hospital, I don't know what happened to him after that. It's gonna be OK, Mom. Be patient. See you at lunch." He kissed his mother and left.

He entered the room and turned on the computer, like he always does. He looked through the security camera records. The man who approached the workshop door and talked to the security guard was familiar. He looked at the time. It was half past five. He zoomed in the video record and looked closely. He couldn't believe his eyes. This was Alvaro. His early arrival was suspicious to Roger. The night shift guard was already gone. He tried to call.

"Mr. Roger, Alvaro is here. He wants to see you."

"Let him in."

"Hello, Mr. Roger. Sorry to disturb you."

"Please, Alvaro, no trouble. What is it?"

"Mr. Roger, it's not good. I need money for my treatment. My wife returned the ring I gave her years ago to sell. It's an expensive ring. She said she was OK if the stone in her ring was just a simple one—that we should sell it to pay for my treatment. At first, I didn't accept, but I had to. You are my last hope."

"Alvaro, this is a really expensive stone. True masterwork."

"It's my own work."

"I worry for you. If you are doing this for your treatment, what can I say? I guess I'll buy your ring. You want it cash?"

"Yes, if it's possible."

"But you gotta be careful."

"Of course. If you'll allow it, I would like to leave early. I came to work early to work on my last project. I have done quite a lot. I have a doctor's appointment."

"Of course, you can go."

"OK."

After Alvaro left, Roger examined the stone he just purchased. It was a beautiful and valuable work. It was a masterpiece. He stopped to think for a moment. Alvaro was living a modest life; it was strange that he would end up with such an expensive ring. He put the ring on the table and went back to watch the videos. He suddenly stood up and left the house in a rush. He headed straight to the workshop.

All the employees were at their place. Since Alvaro's room door was locked, he asked the security guard to bring the keys. The guard said that he didn't leave the keys when Alvaro left. Roger got angry at the guard.

"Mr. Roger, we will call him right now."

"He's a sick man, don't bother him. Perhaps he forgot. He must be at the doctor's now. I don't know why you weren't paying attention. Never let it happen again."

"But to me he said that he's having guests and is in a rush to get home. Maybe that's why he forgot to give the keys."

Roger stopped to think. *Everybody needs to be careful.* He walked around the workshop and watched over the workers.

A phone call. "Roger, where are you? Come to the room, quick."

"OK, Dad. Right away."

When Roger entered the room, he saw his father sitting in his chair, and the safe door was open and there were some pictures in there. His father was holding a diamond stone in his hand. He looked angry. "Dad, I'm sorry. I was in such a rush to get to the workshop, I forgot the stone on the table. I know it's a very valuable stone."

"Roger, answer me. Where did you buy this?"

"Dad, I bought it from our worker. It's his own handwork. The stone belonged to his family. He had to sell it to pay for his treatment. Why do you ask? Is it not a good stone?"

"Roger, I can't believe you made such a big mistake." He took the photos from the safe and spread them on the table.

"Look closely. I can't believe my ex-Special Force son made such a big mistake. What if I didn't come here today? There is an ongoing police investigation of the robbery. This is evidence. It's enough to get you arrested. Including this ring's stone, they have stolen our most expensive jewel set."

Roger could not believe his eyes. Did his trusted employee really sell him a stone from a stolen ring? He crazed around the room. He couldn't believe this was happening. "I'm calling the police now. We should have our stories straight. You bought the stone because you suspected and then informed me. I had the keys to the safe where the pictures were, and the employee left unnoticed. We opened the safe, compared the pictures to the stone to make sure, and we called the police after. We didn't want to make Alvaro suspicious. Our stories need to match. Otherwise, you are gonna get arrested as the main suspect."

"But I took money from the safe—meaning, I bought it."

"Listen to me carefully. You are gonna say you bought the ring because you suspected something. If you didn't pay the money, he wouldn't have given you the stone and that you wouldn't be able to prove anything."

Roger Thomas thought of something. He called the security guard. "How did you know that Alvaro is having guests?"

"Sir, after he left yesterday, someone came by in a taxi. The passenger stayed in the car. The driver approached and asked about Alvaro. Alvaro was long gone already."

"Did you see the passenger's face?"

"No."

"Give me the taxi's plate number."

"I don't know, sir."

"You see? It's all because of your negligence." His father refuted Roger.

Roger quickly opened the computer and checked yesterday's security records and found the taxi's plate number. He zoomed into the face of the passenger.

"OK, Dad, call the police the way you consider best. I need to go somewhere real quick."

"Where are you going? The police will be here soon."

"I'll be back soon."

"Take your gun. Be careful."

Roger went out to the street and got in the car. He headed to Alvaro's address. He parked the car a little further from Alvaro's house and walked there, checking and controlling the surroundings. Alvaro's car was parked in front of the house, and nearby there was the taxi from yesterday. The taxi driver was snoozing behind the wheel. Soon after, he recognized the two men coming out of the house. It was the same man from the video footage that was sitting in the car. The man hugged Alvaro good-bye and sat in the car. At first, Roger wanted to go to Alvaro's house, but then he changed his mind to follow the car the man got in.

The car left the city and got onto the highway. It was a one-way road going to the neighboring state. Roger checked his gun and decided to follow the taxi. He got stressed when he saw his phone ringing. It was his father calling.

"Roger, where are you? The police are here. They want to talk to you."

"Don't worry, Dad. Give them your explanation and tell them that I will visit the station myself and explain everything. I've got an important thing to do now. I'll call you back."

"Mr. Roger Thomas, this is FBI agent Darren Edmond you are speaking to. What you are doing is against the law. You need to be at the police station as soon as possible. Otherwise, charges will be pressed against you."

"I'm following that taxi. I'm gonna lose him."

"The police have the plate number and the model of the taxi car. They are doing their part of the job."

Roger had no choice but to stop the pursuit. It was pointless to continue the chase. If they had to stop him, it wouldn't result good for him. He had to return back. The taxi that he was chasing was no more visual. Police sirens were approaching. Roger got out of the car and lit a cigarette. His hands were shaking from anger. "All right, you son of a bitch, you'll get caught soon. You escaped from me today, but I'll catch you one day. I'm not gonna leave it like this!" He got back in the car and headed to the police station.

Buster Thomas was walking around the hall angrily when Roger arrived. He explained everything to his father. The traffic police have been notified. "Your actions are against the law. Write everything as I tell you. I just gave my explanation."

Police surrounded the area quickly on an intel. The night shift guard was called to the station to get his side of the story, and with that information, a warrant was given to search Alvaro's house.

The taxi was on the road within the speed limit. At first, the taxi driver didn't understand the police car's order to stop the car. "Did I hear it right? Did the police ask me to pull over?" the driver asked Carlos.

"What did you say? We are being followed?" He quickly turned back and saw police cars approaching them fast. When the police ordered them to pull over the car again, Carlos understood the situation.

"Carlos, they are asking us to pull over! It's not good!" As the driver turned his head to look at his friend's face, he saw a gun pointed at them from the police car flanking them from the right side. That's when he realized how serious the situation is.

"Drive faster! Don't you dare pull over! Try to lose them! Hurry!"

"But they are gonna shoot. We're gonna get killed. Maybe we should stop the car!"

"If you say one more word, I'm gonna shoot at them. Then it's gonna be worse! I said drive faster!"

"OK, but there's a police post up ahead! They can try to shoot us from front. They can kill us easily!"

"Increase the speed! Find some turn to enter. We need to get away from them!"

"What if they have been following us for some time?"

"Hurry! Cover your side! Don't let them get ahead of you! Don't let them block the road!"

"Carlos! Third car joined the chase! I have kids, man!"

"Just listen to me! Try to get away from them! There's an intersection up ahead! Go into the woods from there. Lose them! You'll stop where I tell you!"

"Driver! You have been warned to stop! Obey the law! You are causing disturbance! If you do not comply, you will be shot at!"

One of the police cars took the right side of the road trying to get ahead of the taxi. He probably tried to block the fugitive's car from the front. Carlos saw this right away and acted quickly. He grabbed the steering wheel and pulled to the right, smashing the police car flanking them. The police car rolled to the roadside spinning several times as smoke started coming out from the car.

"You son of a bitch! What are you doing? They are gonna shoot at us. I don't wanna die!"

"If you say one more word, I'll put a bullet in your head! I said go faster!"

"There's a police post up front! They're gonna put chain blocks on the road! We are both gonna die. Is that what you want? You bastard!"

"They need us alive. They're not gonna kill us! Calm down. Turn to the woods from there!"

The driver was driving fast through the woods, but the fuel was about to be finished. The police were still chasing them, but they did manage to get ahead further. Suddenly, the driver saw a car coming from the opposite side. The taxi driver managed to pull the car to the left side of the road to avoid clashing with the other car at the last second, but he lost control of the car, and the car kept moving on the rocky roadside until it crashed to a tree, coming to a full stop. Carlos's head was spinning from the blow. He turned his head to his motionless friend; the driver was bleeding in his head. He opened the car door with great difficulty and managed the get out of the car. His head and arms were hurting. He gathered his energy and started running toward the woods. Shortly after, he disappeared in the depth of the woods. Police sirens approaching meant that they were close.

Soon after, the police arrived at the scene. The taxi went off the road and hit a tree. The driver was critically injured, and the passenger managed to escape.

"Son of a bitch! He's gone. Call an ambulance, quick! The driver's condition looks critical. We need him alive. We need to continue the pursuit until the search group arrives. We can't lose his trail."

"His pulse is very low. If we get him to the hospital quickly, he might make it."

After the security guard's phone call, Alvaro understood the severity of the situation. It looked like his friend tricked him into a crime. He was nervous; he was in panic. He didn't know what to do next. He was feeling guilty for lying to the owner and his wife all because of his friend of many years. Because of his illness, Alvaro was used to living the hard life expecting death any day, and his friend has gone and gotten him involved in crime. How can someone stoop so low for money? There was no more reason for him to be alive. On the other hand, he was certain that he did not want to spend the rest of his life in jail.

"Calm down, Alvaro! You did nothing wrong. How could you have known that that bastard has given you a stolen stone?"

"I trusted him. He was an honest man! Looks like something had rolled him into crime."

"What am I supposed to tell the police now? Give him away? My mistake has caused problems to people who have been so good to me. They already called Mr. Roger Thomas for interrogation. How am I going to look him in the face after this? How am I gonna face my coworkers? I am causing serious trouble to innocent people. As of today, there's no meaning in me living. You must forgive me, darling. I love you very much."

Edna couldn't hold back her tears. She hugged her husband and cried her heart out. "Don't talk that way, you are scaring me. Calm down, Alvaro! Do you even hear what you are saying? Do you even think about me? What would I do without you?"

There was a knock at the door. Edna looked at Alvaro. "Go and open the door. It's the police."

Edna stood up, wiped her tears, calmed down, and walked to the door.

Alvaro reached for the drawer and pulled it open. He put the piece of paper that he took from the drawer on the table and pointed his gun to his own temple.

"Hello, ma'am. Is this Alvaro Columbus's residence?"

"Yes, sir."

"I'm Darren Edmond, FBI agent." He showed his badge to the scared and devastated woman.

"We have a warrant for your husband's arrest and house search." As he said that, men behind him walked in without waiting for an answer and saw an unexpected scene. Alvaro was sitting with the gun pointed at his own head.

"Alvaro, don't do it! I swear to God! Think about me!" She was begging Alvaro.

"Mister, put the gun down! Surrender! I give you my word, I will protect you. You are just going to answer some questions regarding the investigation."

"Don't come closer, Edna! Forgive me. I love you." He looked at his wife's face for the last time and pulled the trigger.

With the bullet shot to his head, he fell on the floor. Edna hugged his bleeding body, crying, asking for help. Darren Edmond checked his pulse. "Call an ambulance quickly!" as he picked up the gun with the gloves he was wearing and put them in the evidence bag. He passed the bag to his colleague. It was difficult to pull Edna away from her husband's dead and cold body. The body was sent to forensics.

All of this was shocking for Darren Edmond. He was stunned, and all of a sudden, he noticed a piece of paper on the table. He picked it up and started reading.

"I lived my life with honor. In my time of grave illness, I have been hit the second time by someone dear to me. I consider myself guilty in front of my wife, who has always been there for me through good and bad, and in front my boss, Roger Thomas, who always supported me with my illness financially and mentally. It's unacceptable that Mr. Roger Thomas has been called to interrogation because of me. I can't bear this weight, that's why I have decided to end it. He did not deserve any of this. I do not forgive the bastard who did this to me. I hope he will get his punishment in life. Forgive me, Mr. Roger Thomas. I trust you will take care of my family. I hope you'll never stop caring for Edna. Good-bye!"

Darren Edmond was touched. Alvaro's clotted bloodstains on the floor and his wife's tears were too much for him. He went out of the house to get some fresh air.

Phone call. He was called to the station. Darren Edmond got into a car and drove off. Shortly after, he was at the station.

"Mr. Darren Edmond, ex-Special Forces military Mr. Roger Thomas is here. He is waiting for you," the police chief said.

When he entered the room, he saw a man who looked uncomfortable physically. He looked angry and disturbed.

"Hello."

"Hello. Are you Roger Thomas?"

"Yes."

"Sit down, please. I'm FBI agent Darren Edmond. I'm sure you already know what is going and why you are here."

"Yes."

"Do you admit your wrongs?"

"I would like to know what wrongs we are talking about."

"I can explain. You have probably seen the news about a big robbery that happened in our town. It's all over the news."

"Yes, I have."

"Thieves were masters—they knew what they were doing. They have stolen millions of dollars' worth jewelry, and in the process, not just the owner of the store but also citizens got hurt, innocent people died, and one person is missing. Despite investigating and searching, we have been unable to find any clue to solving this crime. What happened today was our first lead in a long time, but you ruined it by not obeying the orders and following the taxi."

"I'm guessing my father already gave his written explanation. We are both witnesses. I can approve that in my explanation."

"We will have your explanation, that's for sure. But I need you to tell me about, before your father got involved, how you bought the stone. If you called us as soon as Alvaro left your room, we could have been there right away."

"I needed to make sure it's the same stone. My father had the keys to the safe."

"So you are the owner of the store, but your father still has the keys to the safe. Does he not trust you?

"Answer my second question, then, please. Were you not aware of the photos inside the safe until that moment?"

"Of course, I knew about them."

"So you had the keys to the safe too. Why do you keep the photos that could have been very helpful in solving this investigation in the safe and not on the table? Do you really not care at all for this crime as a law-abiding citizen and an ex-Special Force soldier?"

"I love my country and my people. It's not right that you are trying to make me look guilty."

"You and your father's written statements match for the most parts. But some information given looks suspicious. After calling the police, you have left your work and went somewhere. Why did you not wait for the federals to arrive?"

"After leaving my room, Alvaro left work without telling anyone. I thought maybe I could follow him to his house before he escapes into hiding."

"Is he a good employee?"

"He's a clean, honest, and a loyal family man who loves his job."

"A person with such good qualities sold you a stolen jewelry and left work without permission."

"Looks like I have made a mistake about him."

"But why did such a good and humble person get into crime?"

"I think someone tricked him and he just fell for it."

"If you understood all of this, why didn't you call the police or the federals about it right away?"

"Like I said in my statement, I was suspicious of the stone at first, but I had to make sure, so I waited for my father to arrive. We matched the stone and the photo."

"Like you said, you bought the stone because you suspected. If it is so, why didn't you keep Alvaro under supervision? At least the security should have informed you about Alvaro's unauthorized leave from work. What if they are working together?

"The guard's explanation was that Alvaro had informed you about his early leave."

"He told me that he has a doctor's appointment."

"So he did ask you."

"Yes."

"Were you in a hurry to go somewhere?"

"To Alvaro's house."

"You confronted him. What did you say to him? Did you offend him in any physical or mental matter?"

"I saw him, but I changed my mind before approaching him."

"Why did you go to his residence?"

"I went there in a hurry because of Alvaro's lies. As soon as I found out the truth about the stone, I called Alvaro's doctor. The doctor said that he has not contacted him for any reason. It meant that there was a reason for him to go home early that day. I decided to go to his house directly and shed a light on the matter. I was sure there's a reason behind Alvaro's early leave. I bet he was in a hurry to deliver the money to someone. Men who came to the workshop last night and asked about Alvaro made me more suspicious. I thought that they were here for something regarding the stone. After I knew that Alvaro had lied to me, I went there to catch them."

"By the way, you said that the safe was closed and your father had the keys to it. One may ask, where did you get all the money to pay for the stone?"

"Mr. Roger Thomas, looks like you have outplayed yourself. You just proved that you were lying. What happened after that?"

"I kept Alvaro's house under watch. That man was in Alvaro's house. He said his good-bye and got back in the taxi car that was waiting for him outside, the same taxi. I managed to follow them until they got on the highway to another state. I couldn't keep following him because of nonstop phone calls to my phone."

"Do you think that you were doing the right thing?"

"Yes, of course."

"Mr. Roger Thomas, this is not Afghanistan and you are not a soldier fighting the Taliban. That person is a legal citizen. You have no evidence of his guiltiness. Maybe the people you were following were just ordinary citizens. Did you have a gun?"

"No."

"You are lying again. The camera footage shows getting out of the building and sitting into a car. You put your gun on the passenger seat. It's all visible from the angle of the camera."

Roger put his head down without saying a word.

Phone call. After listening to the caller for a few minutes, Darren Edmond turned to Roger. "Mr. Roger Thomas, there are discrepancies between your statement and what happened in reality. You must admit your negligent actions and admit that you made a mistake. This unpleasant situation is the result of your negligence toward your employee," as he took out an envelope from the folder and gave it to Roger.

"If you suspected and reported on time, these people would have been alive now."

"Who are you talking about?"

"Read, Mr. Rogers. You will know."

Roger started reading the letter. As he kept on reading, the agent was watching Roger's facial expressions. His hands were shaking; he was looking pale all of a sudden. He started walking around the room in worry.

"Colonel, is it OK if I smoke?"

"I understand you, Roger. You can smoke. This letter shows that you were not suspicious about the stone. You are just the victim of your own negligence and humbleness. You bought the stone because you wanted to help your employee with his illness and you could make good profit from the sale of the stone. Alvaro's tragedy is not the end of it. Because of your mistake, one of the police cars chasing the taxi rolled over and a police officer died. The other sheriff's condition is critical. He's at the hospital. The fugitive fled to the forest and shot and injured one of the policemen chasing him. He managed to escape."

"I'm ready to pay for my mistake."

"Mr. Roger, does punishing you make everything right? No, it doesn't. Everything needs to be handled by law. I am well aware of your honorable service in Afghanistan. I know that you are a law-abiding citizen. There's a big criminal group active in the country. They are being searched for criminal activities such a robbery, drug dealing, murder, and some missing people. They are professionals. They know what they are doing. They never leave a trace behind."

"Then let me make up for my mistakes."

"Like you did today? It's our and the police's work to solve a crime, Mr. Roger."

Those words hit Roger hard like a bullet. He was stunned. He got a hold of himself with difficulty. "Mr. Darren Edmond, to be honest, when I realized that I made a mistake, I tried to fix it by going after the enemy alone. If I wasn't held back, I would have brought that bastard to you alive by now, if I managed to survive, of course. At least I wouldn't have to carry this conscience if I died."

The door opened. "Mr. Darren Edmond, Mr. Roger Thomas's lawyer is here."

The federal agent stood up and left the room. He came back shortly after and asked Roger Thomas another question. "Mr. Roger Thomas, when were you demobilized from the army?"

"About six months ago."

"You are being released temporarily. I'm sure we will meet again, Capt. Roger Thomas."

"True, in this life or the other."

"Of course. Try to not lose your ex-Special Force qualities even if you are demobilized from the army. The medal you received for your honorable service to the country is very valuable and important. The department chief said something very important during a meeting regarding the murder in the neighboring state. He said, 'Regardless of our duty or our profession, we must obey the laws. If we broke the law, we must accept our punishment.'"

She woke up to a noise in the middle of the night; she tried to listen to it. After some silence, she heard it again. Someone was knocking on the door very softly. She got nervous. *Who could it be at this time?* She got up and put on her robe to approach the door. She thought something as she stopped to look out the window. When she saw Carlos looking exhausted and devastated, her hands started to shake. She opened the door quickly.

"What happened, Carlos?"

Carlos went inside the home pushing her aside. Elma checked the surroundings and closed the door. Carlos's clothes were all wet and dirty.

"Carlos, what happened?"

"I'm too tired to speak. Try not to sleep. I'm really tired and sleepless. If you feel any danger, wake me up. I need to leave early. I'll explain everything later," as he took off his dirty clothes and lay down on Elma's bed. He fell asleep right away.

For some reason, Beth was really happy today. She planned to call Elma and maybe go to a club together.

Elma suggested that they go to an expensive boutique to do some shopping first and later to the club. They had a lot of fun at the club. She did not let meeting Michael coincidentally spoil her fun; at least she tried to act that way. Michael hadn't seen Beth in a long time. It was the perfect time to get answers to some questions. He went outside. He waited in the car for a long time. After some time, two women came out of the club and got in the car. Beth noticed the car following them. But she didn't pay much attention to it. After driving for some time, Elma noticed that Beth keeps looking at the mirror. She looked back and saw the car following them. She got nervous.

"Beth, a car is following us. Do you see it?"

"That's what I have been looking at all of this time."

"Do you know him?"

"No."

"Let's call the police, then. What if he wants to murder us? I saw him at the club earlier. He was staring at us for some reason, and now he is behind us. He didn't look like the normal type." She took her phone to make a phone call.

"Girl, I told you, don't worry about it."

"So you know him, then. Why did you hide it?"

"Elma, he is following because of something to do with me. I'm not in the mood to give you an explanation. I'm angry anyway." The car stopped in front of the building.

"We never had secrets between us!" She got out and slammed shut the door. She started walking toward her home.

Beth got out of the car in the same manner and followed Elma. She returned shortly after, and when she did, she saw Michael standing next to his car. She didn't stop and started pacing to her car until she saw Michael walking to her. She quickly turned back.

"What do you need? Why are you following me? Our relationship ended long ago. I love someone else now. We talked about this. What's the point in bringing up the past again?"

"Yes. There's a lot to be sorted out between us. You closed the door to my face. I couldn't come face-to-face with you and get answers. I don't want to miss that chance today. I need you to look me in the eye and say the truth about what happened. No need to run from me. Get in the car." He grabbed her arm and pulled her into the driver's seat. He sat next to her.

"There are some things I need to ask you. It's the last time you will ever see me. You're gonna answer me honestly, and I will get out of your life once and for all. You'll never see me again!"

"I'm listening."

"When we split, you promised that you will wait for me till the end of your life, even if I died. You didn't even bother to answer my letters. Is your love not stronger than your urges?"

These words hit Beth really hard. "Ask that question to yourself, not me. I got only five letters from you after you left. You didn't write to me once for three months! But I was holding on despite everything. There's a limit to my patience."

"You are lying! You were the first person I wrote to during my free time. I wanted to know about my mother's condition. George kept getting answers to his letters from his girlfriend, but not me. There's no chance I wrote the address wrong.

"There's only one reason for betrayal. You couldn't wait because you didn't love me. You played with my love just to satisfy your needs. Sometimes I think it's for the better. At least I got to know the real you, what you are inside, and hated it. Because you don't deserve that love. Your conscience is not clear. That's why you became a love toy for some people. That's where people like you belong."

"He loves me. He doesn't play with my feelings like you did!"

"It's a lie. Love ends. If he really loved you, he would already have chosen you as the mother of his children! He is just having fun with you! That's all! Good-bye! You are dead to me. I will try not to get in your way ever again!" He got out of the car and slammed the door shut.

Beth was shocked; she didn't know what to do. It looked like the letters were being stolen from the postbox before she could get to them. It could only be Carl. Beth started crying, her head between her hands.

After leaving Beth, Michael went to the nearby park and took a seat in one of the benches facing the sea. He was mad. No matter what he tried, he couldn't control his feelings. He thought of the conversation he just had with Beth. Even though he was still angry, he felt bad for treating Beth so harshly; he cursed the war. It was getting dark. He stood up. His leg pain has been getting worse; it was affecting his nerves. He went to the nearby cafe. He took a seat near the window and ordered some food and drink. Soothing music was making him emotional. He thought of all the good days he had spent in Beth's loving embrace. He had a few glasses of wine.

"Sir, you don't look so well. Are you feeling OK? Do you need help?"

"What?" he said as he stood up. His head was spinning. He held to the table for stability and paid the waiter.

"Can you call a cab for me?"

"Of course, sir. Just a moment! You can have a seat and wait here."

"OK."

Five minutes passed. The waiter and the taxi driver helped Michael into the car.

When Michael arrived at the house, he barely could open the door. He put the keys on the table and fell deep asleep on the sofa.

He was dreaming . . . It's summertime. The smell of the green grass was everywhere. Beth is in a white bride's dress. They are walking to the tree near the lake while holding hands. They are very happy. Michael wants to refresh their name's capital letter engravings on the tree. He sees that the engravings are gone. Some force hits him hard in the arm, and the knife falls from his hand and stabs Beth in the heart. Beth is calling him for help; she's bleeding all over. Suddenly, dark clouds appear in the sky. Heavy rain, flood. Big flood wave takes Beth away from him. No matter how hard he tries, he can't save her. He screams, but no one can hear him. He hears Beth's voice in his head. "I loved you!"

He woke up screaming. He was sweating too much. He had a strong headache. He sat on the sofa, his head between his hands. What he dreamed worried him for some reason. He stood up. It was two o'clock. He tried to call George, but the number could not be reached. *He is probably asleep,* he thought to himself. He thought of contacting Luisa, but he changed his mind. He didn't want to disturb her because she was pregnant. He didn't want to get her worried. He lay back on the sofa again. Suddenly, he had a change of mind as he stood up quickly, grabbed the car keys, and went outside. He was planning to go to George's place.

He thought of various things during his trip. George never left his calls without an answer. What if something happened to him?

Elma was worried about the plan she had made with Beth. If the boss found out about this, he would kill them both. Even though she and Beth made a lot of money with the sale of the stone from the ring by switching the stone with the jeweler, she had other plans for the jewel set. She didn't like the fact that Beth hid the password from her. The only way left was to get the password from her one or the other and get rid of her. That way she could get the most expensive piece from the basement. Beth would be blamed for the missing piece. Only Carlos could be helpful to her in this. First, she needed to make the group members believe her lies about Beth. Getting Carl to believe the exaggerated version of Beth and Michael's meeting was the first step of her evil plan. This way she could put an end to the warm relations between Carl and Beth. She knew that the man at the club was Beth's ex and that he and Carl have had a dispute between them since long ago.

She called Carl. "Hello, Carl. How are you?"

"Hi, Elma. I'm good, as always."

"Carl, I'm sorry to bother you, but there's something important I got to tell you."

"Something serious?"

"It's very important for the situation we are in. It's about Beth. But it has to be a secret between us."

"Of course."

"Carl, Beth is seeing someone. His name is Michael."

"What do you mean? Are you sure?"

"Of course! You can check if you want."

"But she wouldn't dare to do something like that."

"To be honest, I was feeling something between them lately, but I had to make sure before telling you. What I witnessed today put an end to my suspicions, and I felt that I have to tell you about it. We were sitting at a cafe. He was there too. During our time there, they didn't take their eyes off of each other. After leaving the cafe, we headed home. He was following us with his car. I kept asking her who the man following us was, but she wouldn't say a thing. After insisting for a while, she admitted that she knew the man. It was Michael, her ex-boyfriend. After we arrived, I went into the house and watched from the dark room's window. Michael got into Beth's car. They talked for some time and drove away together. I never expected such a thing from her. That man could be a threat to us. You need to get them away from each other."

"Thank you, Elma. You are a real friend. I will talk to her about this as soon as possible. Don't worry, I'll make sure she doesn't suspect you."

Elma took a deep breath. All the lies got her nervous. Her heart was racing. It was a scary game she entered. It was the beginning. She had to act for the second step of the plan.

She thought about meeting with the boss. Where and when? She was afraid of going to his home. Anderson forbade her to call the boss's private number. He took care of everything regarding the boss. She had to meet with Anderson. He is usually at the casino.

She got off the taxi in front of the casino. They let her into the casino no questions asked, since they knew her. She hesitated to go to Anderson's room at first. She decided to take a seat at one of the tables and have a drink. She lit her cigarette. She recognized the man coming down from upstairs. It was Arlen. He approached her.

"Anderson wants to see you."

Elma hesitated. "Don't worry. Just follow me."

It looked like they were watching her from the security camera. Perhaps even the boss was in the room. Elma followed Arlen to the second floor. He opened the door. "You may go in."

The air in the room was heavy and filled with smoke. All the smoke and smell made her dizzy. Anderson was sitting on the sofa with two girls near him. As he saw Elma, he blew the smoke of the cigar toward her. Elma didn't like the way Anderson was acting, but she didn't say anything about it. Anderson changed lately.

"Where's the other pretty little thing?"

"For the moment, I don't know. Perhaps she is with her new lover now."

"How come? All women are the same. As soon as you have a little trouble in between, you start gossiping about each other."

"I thought it's important and the boss should know about it."

"I have told you a thousand times, and I'm saying it again. Boss asked me to take care of everything. You need to inform me about everything and consult with me. I'm listening." He pointed with his gun to the girls to leave the room.

Elma understood that arguing with Anderson was meaningless as she played along. "Tell me! What's this important thing you need to talk about?"

"This lady had a boyfriend called Michael back in the day. He is an ex-Special Force. He served in Afghanistan. After getting badly injured, he returned from the army. Beth has been meeting with him secretly."

"Just look at what that bitch is doing. How dare she? Does Carl know about it? I had a strange feeling about her from the beginning. Are you totally sure about this? This is not something small! What if she said something about us to him?"

"You can expect anything from her."

"I need to inform the boss about this right away. I don't have the time to discuss with Carl. Go to her house today. Carl is on shift today. Try to be friendly. Order some food. Don't forget to buy drinks."

"What are you thinking?"

"It's none of your business. Do as you are told. There's no time."

Elma was getting more nervous by the minute. It won't be good for her if they find out about her lies. On the other hand, Anderson's plan for Beth could be dangerous for her too.

What to do? Time is short. She had to decide quickly.

She came home, got her gun, and put it in the purse. She wanted to meet and talk to Carlos. His number could not be reached. She thought about what Anderson assigned her to do. She wondered what they were planning to do with Beth. Maybe they wanted to kill her?

After killing Beth, they could decide to get rid of her too, since she knew everything. She had to meet with Carlos.

After returning to the state, Carlos was temporarily living in his friend's house and was using his old mobile phone. The phone number was registered to his friend's name, and only Beth and Elma knew his number. He didn't want to stay too long at his friends. He packed his things and left.

Beth was still shaken after her chat with Michael. She was stressed. She drank some alcohol to calm her nerves. She wasn't doing good.

There was a knock at the door. It was Carl. She opened the door unwillingly and went back into the room without waiting for him to enter the house. Carl noticed her attitude but didn't say anything.

He approached her from behind, trying to hug her, but Beth pushed his hand away. "What happened, darling?"

No reply. "I'm talking to you! Why are you acting this way?"

"You know what, we either get married or end our relationship."

Hearing this, Carl laughed out loud. "And here I thought something bad happened. Of course, darling, but you know how it is now. Need to be patient. After all of this is over, we will take care of that."

"No! We gotta do it today!"

"What else do you need? Are you not living well enough?"

"To hell with you and your friends. Get out of my life, I don't want anything from you."

"So that's what you are saying now. You are spoiled. You can't get rid of me that easily. You ruined my normal life. You introduced me to those bastards. You pushed me into a world of crime. I put the nation's holy uniform on and betray its honor. I'm gonna pay for this. I didn't need this. It's all because of you. And now you meet with your old lover and you want to break up with me. You think I don't know about that? You can't lie to me. Looks like you are pretty satisfied after yesterday's meeting."

"It's none of your business!"

"You really have no honor! You can't control your urges. Do you even know whom you are dealing with? You fool, they will kill you! Don't cause problems to yourself and me! After this is done, we can break up peacefully."

"You're a bastard! You played with my feelings. You ripped the letters from the person I love and made me into your lover! I hate you!"

Carl slapped Beth with all his might. "I see that being nice to you doesn't get me anywhere! Stupid cunt!"

"I'm gonna destroy you! You are gonna pay for what you said!"

"I will kill you and get rid of the body. No one will ever find out what happened to you!"

Beth was crying as she went into the bedroom and locked the door.

Carl was really angry; he didn't know what to do. Beth may tell everything to Michael to get back at him. He stood up and walked around the room in anger and frustration. He knocked on the bedroom door. After getting no reply, he came back to the living room, took his phone, and left the house.

Beth came out of the room after Carl left. She was still angry. To calm her nerves, she smoked and drank a lot. She was certain. She calmed down and started thinking about the jeweler's proposition. She had to get away from this place.

She went down to the first floor. She had the copy of the keys and she knew the password. She was in a hurry. She took the expensive necklace and earrings from the safe. It was the most expensive set among the stolen goods.

She called the jeweler. "Hello, this is Beth."

Even though Carlos recognized her voice, he acted like he didn't know her. "Hello, ma'am. Do we know each other?"

"Of course, sir! Elma's friend, Beth. Don't you remember? You gave me your phone number that day we met."

"I don't seem to remember. Go on, I'm listening."

"You probably remember, we talked about something important. I'm ready to meet with you regarding that issue."

"I don't understand what you are talking about, ma'am. Perhaps you have the wrong number!"

"Can we meet? If it's possible for you, I will be at the address we talked about."

There was no answer on the other side of the line. "Sir, I understand. I think we should meet. It's really important. I'm gonna give you the address. I will be waiting for you. We don't have much time. It's important that we meet."

She waited for an answer. Even though the man didn't answer, she knew for sure that it was the jeweler. She recognized his voice, and the number was correct. He was being cautious about talking on the phone about it. Time was running out; Beth was in a hurry. She was invited to a birthday party that night. She put the jewel in her bag and got in the car and drove off to the address she gave on the phone. She parked the car near the address and took out the small bag from her purse and put it in the glove box. She started waiting for the jeweler. She was very nervous. Suddenly, she noticed police sirens approaching from her rearview mirror. She started shaking. What is going on? Were they after her? She thought of turning on the ignition and getting away from there, but she changed her mind. She decided to wait and see how it goes and rolled down the window.

A car obeying the sheriff's order to stop stopped the vehicle close to Beth's car.

The sheriff stepped out of the police car and approached. "Your license and registration, please."

"May I know why you pulled me over?"

"You were going over the speed limit and created a serious accident situation during overtaking, and your documents aren't in order. I'm gonna have to ask you to come to the police station with us."

"Of course, Sheriff."

"Step out of the vehicle, please. You will be handcuffed and taken to the police station in the police car. Sheriff will drive your car to the station."

Beth took a deep breath. Her heart was racing. She looked at the time. Carlos was late for some reason. What if he wasn't going to come at all? What if something happened to him? She tried to calm down. She thought about going back home, but she was drunk. If she got pulled over, she would be taken to a test lab and her car would get searched. They would find the jewel.

The birthday party she was invited to was nearby. Going there would be the best idea. The jeweler would call her for sure.

His phone was ringing. Carlos knew that it was Beth calling. He was well aware that he needs to be maximum careful at a moment like this. Even though he didn't admit to knowing Beth, he headed to the address she gave. Repetitive calls angered him. "Stupid woman, just wait. I'm coming." But it was Elma calling.

"Hello, Carlos! I need to see you right away. It's urgent."

"I'm almost there. I'm in a taxi."

"You are going home?"

Suddenly, the taxi crashed into the car in front. "What home? I'll call you back. You rushed me, and this is what happened!"

"You just don't know how to drive a car. Good-bye." Carlos got out of the car and slammed the door shut. He called Elma. "No, I'm not going home. Beth gave me some other address."

"What? Beth? What address? Where are you?"

"Like I said, I'm going to meet with Beth. Aren't you together?"

"Carlos, give me your location and don't go anywhere. I'm coming. Beth didn't tell me anything about meeting with you."

"OK!" He gave the address and threw the phone into a trash bin nearby. Elma was angry. Beth acted behind her. She made her decision. As soon as she went out of the house, her phone rang. It was Carl.

"Hello! Good evening! How are you? I hope I'm not disturbing you."

"I'm fine, Carl."

"Were you going somewhere?"

"No, I'm at home."

"Elma, I need to ask you a favor. We had a fight with Beth. She is mad at me, she drank a lot, and she is gonna go to a birthday party. I'm afraid she is gonna drive. I'm worried for her. Please, can you visit her? Maybe you can go together."

"OK, Carl."

Elma was in a taxi and approaching the address Carlos gave. She was watching around. Suddenly, she noticed a man with a hat pacing. She recognized him; it was Carlos. She asked the driver to stop and got out of the car after paying. She ran after the man trying to catch up with him.

"Hi, Carlos! It's me, Elma. What happened? The address you gave is far away from here."

"There were suspicious people in the area. I think we are being followed. Quick, what is it you wanna talk about? I told you that I will get in touch with you."

"Believe me, I wasn't aware of that fool's actions. I wonder, why did she want to meet with you? You should have met with her."

"There were suspicious people around. I didn't risk it."

"Maybe she wanted to meet with you about the jewel."

Carlos answered this question with another question. "You got something important to do with me?"

Elma told Carlos everything that had happened. "I need your advice."

"It's very crucial right now. I'm not living at my home at the moment. Circumstances demand it. The house I'm living in belongs to my friend. He will be out of town for some time. Only you will know the address. Don't tell anyone. Go to Beth's residence. I think there's a reason she wants to meet me. I think it's got something to do with the jewel. Find an excuse, try to get her home as quickly as possible. If she doesn't play along, find another way. Anderson's visit to the place is not a good sign. He is gonna take the jewels tonight. He's on to something."

"Looks like she wanted to run away with you."

"Perhaps. We need to act before Anderson. We will get the password from Beth somehow. We can take several expensive pieces from the safe. If we can't convince her, we will just have to kill her to get the goods and get out of there."

"But the police will search for me. They have seen me at the birthday party. There are witnesses. Arnoldo's men will search for me too. It's too dangerous."

"We will leave the country very quickly. So don't worry about that part. Make sure Beth gets really drunk today at the party. When you come home, leave the kitchen door open. Take her upstairs. Make some coffee—don't forget to put the sleeping pills. Check her bag. There may be a piece of paper or a notebook with the password. I'm gonna be watching around outside the kitchen door. If anyone comes, I'll know. If you manage to succeed, come downstairs and give me the password with the keys. I'll take some expensive pieces from the safe. Anderson is smart and sinister. He will cross-check the goods with the list. When things don't match up, all the suspicion will be centered on Beth. They are gonna think she is in it either with her ex-lover or the sheriff. Carl will be the suspect for giving away the password."

"What happens if we don't succeed? What if Anderson comes earlier?"

"That's why you need to hurry. We need to act before him. At least we should get to the jewels. They won't kill you for now. The boss needs you."

"What happens after?"

"Anderson asked you to leave the kitchen door open. When you return home with Beth, tell them that the door was open. That way, everybody will suspect Beth for the missing jewels. Only Carl had the keys and the password to the safe. He only could have told Beth."

"What are we going to do if it doesn't go according to the plan?"

"In that case, we are gonna have to do with the piece that Beth has."

"Your plan is reasonable."

"Time is running out. We must hurry. Call her, make sure she is at the party."

"Hello! Beth, where are you?"

"What's it to you?"

"I'm coming to your place."

"Don't, I'm not at home." She hung up on her.

"Stupid! She is at the party."

"Do you know the address?"

"I've been there once with Beth before."

"Hurry, we don't have much time!"

Because of her health condition, Luisa did not go to work for several days. After the stationary treatment, her health condition was improving. Sometimes Luisa and George would go out for a walk near the sea or at the park. She missed her friends and colleagues. She was happy about her friend Ella's phone call. She invited her to a birthday party. George didn't want her to go.

"I think you shouldn't go. Just give me a reason. I'm worried for you."

"George, honey! What are you so worried about? I'm feeling much better now. I will be going back to work in a couple of days. I don't get to go to many parties because I work the night shift."

"I'll take you myself. I can't let you drive in this condition. Call me after the party. I'll come pick you up."

Luisa hugged and kissed her husband. "Don't worry, darling! I'll call Bella. If she is also invited, we can go together."

"Who is Bella? Do I know her?"

"She is my colleague. You remember her, we went to their wedding. Her husband is a sheriff. According to what she says, he works together with Beth's boyfriend.

"Oh, yeah! I remember now. He is partnered with Sergeant Caster. Looks like an honest man."

"I made your favorite food. Call Michael over, have dinner together. I'll try to get back early. Take care."

Phone call. "Luisa, I'm waiting for you."

"OK, honey. I gotta go." She took her bag and went outside. She went to the birthday party with Bella.

The party had already begun. There were a lot of women at the party, as it was a women-only party. "Welcome, girls! Why so late?" Ella greeted and invited them in. "Other guests are already here. Never mind, don't lose time. Get inside."

It was very loud inside. Some were dancing, some were having drinks and snacks near the bar, and some were standing around and chatting. Luisa and Bella took their assigned seats. Luisa was looking around as if she was looking for someone.

"Luisa, waiting for someone?"

"I don't see Beth. Have you seen her?"

"Yeah, it's weird. I wonder why she didn't come. She never misses parties. You are neighbors with her. Don't you see her?"

"I haven't seen her in a long time. We don't see each other anymore. There are reasons for it. She would never miss a party like this. She is probably late. I think she'll come," Luisa replied.

"Why are you so interested in her, then?"

"I heard she has changed a lot since she left her work at the hospital."

"Yeah, I have heard that too."

Luisa was feeling uncomfortable. The smell of the food and cigarette smoke made the air in the room unbearable for her. She went out to the balcony. "Girl, what happened to you? You look pale."

"No, don't worry. Just a little tired. It'll pass."

"You crazy, are you pregnant?"

"Yeah, these are the first months of pregnancy."

"I'm so happy to hear that. Congratulations, honey. Don't worry, these things happen during the first few months. It'll pass. Let's get inside, I will serve you myself."

"Thank you, Bella. You're a real friend. I was having difficulties in the beginning, that's why I took a leave from work. I used to have pains. I haven't had any pains for five days now."

"You need to be careful. I'm sure George is really happy, isn't he?"

"Yeah, he is. At first, he didn't want me to come, but then he allowed me to come because of you."

"Of course! Starting today, I will take care of you personally. But you should have listened to George. Places like this are not good for you. Whatever, it's water under the bridge now. You need to protect yourself. Let's go and sit inside. If you feel bad again, I'll take you home."

A car stopped at the street, and a woman came out of the car. "Bella, look! Isn't that Beth?"

Bella could not hide her curiosity. "Looks like she is drunk."

"Yeah, she does. Let's get inside. I don't want her to see us."

The party was continuing. Luisa was sitting at the side and watching people dance. She noticed Beth was behaving at the party. She looked nervous for some reason. She was keeping her purse tight close with one hand and drinking with the other hand. They invited her to dance, but she refused. Luisa was watching everything that was going on. Beth started to look around the house. She tried to act happy when she noticed Luisa and Bella. She stood up and walked toward them. She was struggling to stand straight. She can't even stand up straight.

"Be quiet, I think she is coming this way."

"Hi, girls! How are you?"

"Thanks, Beth. How are you?" Bella replied.

"I'm great. I see you are chatting. I hope I'm not disturbing you."

"Of course not! You look very pretty today."

Beth laughed out loud. "A woman should be beautiful and attractive, unlike some . . . Most are jealous of me. I'm happy to leave people like that behind before it was too late. I'm very happy. I live my life. Living a life with a sick husband is not for me."

Beth's words shocked Luisa; Bella could feel it. "Beauty and happiness need to come from within first, dear Beth. The person you are trying to ridicule has all of those qualities. Expensive clothes and presents, however you obtain them, that's not all. You wouldn't know what real woman happiness is . . ."

Before she could finish talking, the house owner approached Beth and told her that some woman was looking for her. Beth's facial reaction changed in a heartbeat. A blonde woman standing near the entrance door was waiting for her. She looked angry.

"Luisa, do you know her?" Bella asked with curiosity. "I have never seen her before."

Luisa was quiet. Bella looked at her girlfriend's face. Her reaction was shocking; she looked angry. "She is an unworthy and dishonorable woman. That is all that can be said about her." Bella complained about Beth.

The blonde woman pulled Beth from her arm near the window and said something in her ear. After Beth's aggressive reaction, she kept on insisting on what she was saying. Beth pulled her angrily to the side of the table and sat down. The blonde woman's phone rang, and she went outside for a few minutes to talk in private. After returning, she held Beth by the arm and said something to the homeowner. The owner showed them to another room.

Bella was following all of this. Luisa was feeling uncomfortable. She asked Bella for a glass of water. Bella was happy to hear that. This way she could see what was going on between that woman and Beth while she was going to the kitchen to get a glass of water for Luisa. As she was returning with a glass of water, the door to the room was not fully closed, therefore Bella saw Beth and the blonde woman arguing. Suddenly, she slapped Beth. Beth fell unconscious on the bed. The blonde woman took out a piece of jewelry from Beth's purse and started yelling at her. "You bitch! So you had a plan, huh? You will pay for this." As if she had a feeling, she turned around and saw Bella peeking from the kitchen. She quickly put the jewel in her bag and yelled at Bella.

"Don't you see she passed out? How can she drink that much shit? Come, help me get her to the car."

Bella approached quickly and grabbed Beth by the arm. They took her to the car. Everyone was worried for Beth. The blonde woman apologized to everyone for her drunk friend's behavior at the party.

Bella returned back to bring Luisa her water. "Looks like all of this made you feel uncomfortable. You don't look very good. You wanna lie down?"

"Yeah, I think that would be good. I'm feeling dizzy. I'm feeling pain in my stomach. I should have listened to George."

"Don't worry, honey. These things happen during pregnancy. I'll call an ambulance right away. Should I call George?"

"No, no! He can't know about this. He will overreact. He worries too much. He shouldn't worry too much. Please, I'm asking you."

"No worries, darling! After medical aid, we will go home together. You also shouldn't worry too much. Forget about the chat with Beth. What can you expect from a person who doesn't respect herself?"

The ambulance arrived shortly after. The doctor's report after examining Beth stated a drop in arterial pressure and a risk of miscarriage; she had to be taken to the hospital for treatment.

Beth was complaining and screaming at Elma during the car ride. She didn't hesitate to insult Elma. "I'm talking to you! Answer me! So since the boss doesn't care about you, now you are into Carl? What have you told him about the chat between me and Michael? Tell me! What are you trying to do? I'm gonna destroy both of you because of this, as you have ruined my life."

"Stupid woman! You have lost your mind! Get a hold of yourself! You don't know what you are talking about! Think about it, don't false blame anyone."

"You slut! Now you are telling me what to do. Are all of these lies?"

Elma pulled over the car. She slapped Beth. She grabbed her by the neck and pulled closer. "Know your place! I'm losing my patience with you. I didn't come after you to hear your insults. I could kill you right now. No one would find a piece of you." She let go of her neck.

Beth was crying her heart out. Her nose was bleeding. Seeing this, Elma felt bad; she handed her a towel. "All right. That's enough. Calm down. We are all women. Instead of supporting each other, we are insulting one another for no reason. Trust me, I had no idea about that. Be patient, everything will fall into its place. I'm always near you." She kept on driving.

They arrived home. Beth could barely stand up. Elma helped her get upstairs. She put Beth's bag on the sofa in the living room and took her up to her bedroom. She excused herself to make some coffee and discreetly took out the jewel from Beth's bag and went downstairs. She knew that Carlos was going to come. The light at the corridor was turned off for some reason. Elma started shaking with fear. She tried to get into the kitchen to turn the light on.

When she noticed the silhouette of a man standing in the dark, she was really scared. She was shaking. Even though she couldn't see his face, he didn't look like Carlos or Anderson.

"Who are you?"

"Shut up! Password and the keys to the safe, where are they? Hurry up, if you wanna live!"

The man's voice was familiar to Elma from somewhere. "Did Anderson send you? But he was supposed to come. Who are you?"

The headlights of the car approaching illuminated the street. "You got lucky!" he said and took the jewel out of Elma's hand and escaped through the kitchen door.

Several minutes later, Anderson arrived in the kitchen. Elma was shaking in fear.

"What happened? Calm down. Is she awake?"

"No, she's drunk. She is in the bedroom upstairs. She's probably asleep by now."

"She went over the line. If we don't kill this bitch now, we all will get caught because of her. We will just choke her to death quietly and get out of here. That's it. Where is jewel?"

"Who's there? Elma, can you hear me? Who came?"

There was no answer. "Why don't you answer me?"

Elma did not respond. Beth stood up with difficulty. Her head was spinning. When she went out to the corridor, she noticed her open bag in the living room. She quickly came to check inside the bag. The jewel was gone. She searched her other bag. She took a gun and tried to get downstairs to the kitchen. She could barely stand up.

"Who gave you the permission to dig through my bag? Give them back to me right now! Bitch, where are they?" She pointed the gun toward Elma.

Elma was shocked and scared. She didn't know what to do while staring at a gun Beth was pointing at her.

Anderson, standing behind the door, pulled Beth's arm that was holding the gun. A shot fired from the gun hit the window. Right at this moment, Anderson started stabbing Beth several times in her body. She screamed and fell down after several knife blows. She was bleeding out and dying on the floor of the kitchen. Elma was in shock. She didn't know what to do; she was scared for her own life. He could kill her too. She squeezed to the corner of the room crying, waiting for what's to come.

"What are you waiting for? You stupid cunt! We don't have much time. Where is the jewel?" He took off his bloody gloves.

"The man inside took them from me and ran away."

"What? What are you talking about? You stupid woman!"

"Anderson, I swear to God. The room was dark. There was a man. He took it from me and ran away."

"You will tell your theories yourself!" Anderson quickly went downstairs to the basement, opened the safe door, and collected all the jewels from there. He came back upstairs. "Hurry! Police are gonna be here any moment. They probably heard the gunshot." He grabbed Elma by the arm, and they went outside. When Anderson looked around the street, he noticed a man peeking through in darkness from the house on the other side of the street.

"We need to get out of here right now."

He was quite angry. He had a night shift that day. He thought about what happened, a lot. He didn't know what to do next. He wanted to go and apologize to her after work. *But it is meaningless for now,* he thought to himself. He wanted to meet with his partner and friend before their shift somewhere quiet and discuss this with him. He tried to calm his nerves. He called Brook Cletus to tell him that he was waiting for him at the cafe.

Sheriff Cletus noticed Carl's anger right away. "I was getting out of the house when you called. I was thinking about coming to work early too. Bella was getting ready for a birthday party. I get bored alone at home. What's up, man? You look upset."

"It's nothing, just a little pissed off."

"Can I know why?"

"I had a fight with Beth again. I lost control for a moment and I hit her. I can't calm down. I feel really bad for it."

"You used to be so happy before."

"It all happened after her ex-boyfriend came back from Afghanistan. According to the information I got, they met yesterday, had a very friendly chat. He was very distant and rude to me today. I think I'm gonna have to face him again."

"You are a police officer. Get a hold of yourself. Double-check the information. Go apologize tomorrow and just ask her to marry you. Get married."

"That's what she keeps saying. That's the problem. I don't love her, never did. She's not the Beth she used to be. She has changed a lot. When I refused her marriage idea, she insulted me by admitting that she still loves Michael. That's when I hit her. I told her that I will meet with Michael and put an end to all of this. She said something about revenging me."

"You've made a big mistake. You should apologize to her and make things right. Ask her to marry you, get married. For how long are you just gonna hang around?"

"I tried to make it right, I apologized, but it was no use. I was running late to work, that's why I had to leave."

"What if she does something to herself? Call her, keep in touch—you're a police officer—before it's too late."

"Yeah, you are right, I better call her. I should apologize. I have ruined her life anyway. I will go in the morning to make this right. Maybe the given information is wrong."

"Good idea! Call, check everything yourself."

He stepped out of the car to make a phone call to Beth. He got no reply; he started to worry. He came back to the car. "For some reason, she doesn't answer the phone. She usually answers when I call."

"She's probably asleep or at the birthday party and she can't hear the phone ring."

"I'm really worried. What if something happened to her?"

"Calm down. Shift is about to begin. It's better I drive the car."

More than two hours later, carl was still worried sick. "Maybe you should call her? Or maybe find out from someone you know if she went to the party or not."

Carl had an idea. He quietly stepped out of the vehicle and walked away to make a phone call. He then changed his mind and came back to the car. He called Beth again. He waited for her to pick up, yet there was no answer. "She's probably sleeping or at the party. It's probably loud there, so she can't hear it. Do you know any of her friends? Maybe you can call and ask them?"

Carl thought of someone. He stepped out of the car again and called a different number this time. He returned to the car, satisfied from the phone call.

"Did you talk to her? Where is she?"

"I talked to her girlfriend. I asked her to go and find Beth. She said OK. She'll call back soon. Elma will be with her soon. I'll find the time to talk to her."

"I see that you worry too much. Let's go and check out the area. We need to control the checkpoints. Drug dealers have become very active lately. We need the suspicions to be controlled."

"Don't put your life on the line, my friend. You know how dangerous that area is. Do you wanna die at this young age because of some drug addict or some gangster?"

"What are you talking about? This is our job!"

"Of course! Tom got killed there last time. He was young. Now his two kids have no father."

"Carl, I never expected such words from you. We chose this road and took an oath. You have changed, man."

"I'm just tired of this shit."

"It's the anger talking this way, I know it. You are worried for Beth. Let's roam around the area for a few hours. Then we'll drive by her house. You will see her yourself."

"Wait a minute, man! Let me call again. Be back." He stepped out of the car to make a phone call. Brook noticed this strange behavior.

"You were talking to her friend again? What does she say?"

Carl was quiet for a moment. "Yeah, yeah. She's still at home. She said she'll go soon."

Brook Cletus was aware that Carl was lying, but he said nothing about it. For some reason, Carl made a phone call from a different device. The sheriff felt suspicious. "It's very quiet tonight. Let's go check out the area and you can check her house too."

George went out to the yard with a flashlight and a gun in hand. He walked toward Beth's house. He was really nervous. He didn't realize how he arrived in front of the door with various thoughts in his mind. The door was closed; he went back behind the house. He became more nervous when he noticed that the kitchen door was open. He slowly entered the house. It was dark inside; he turned on his flashlight. What he witnessed at that moment was shocking. Beth was lying in the lake of her own blood on the floor. He checked her pulse; it wasn't beating. A bloody footstep trail inside the house was leading to the basement. A shiny object under the kitchen table drew his attention. He reached out to pick it up; it was a diamond earring set. Suddenly, he changed his mind as he threw the jewel on the floor. He was getting more and more nervous. He was in a hurry. He went downstairs and looked around with his flashlight. He noticed the safe door was open and the bloody trail was leading toward the safe. It looked like something was taken from the safe; it meant that the burglars did it. George realized that it was dangerous to stay there. He went back upstairs and left the crime scene.

He hesitated to call the police because he was drunk. He thought of calling Michael and consulting with him, but then he changed his mind. He looked at his watch. He was worried for Luisa. She should have been back by now. He called her phone. It was strange that her friend Bella answered her phone. "Luisa was taken to a hospital because of her condition and she will have to stay there for a while," Bella said on the phone.

He planned to go to the hospital. The sound of a car approaching drew his attention. He looked through the window to see. It was the police. He wondered whether they knew about the incident or it was just a random visit. George recognized the sheriff walking toward Beth's home. It was Carl Caster. The other sheriff standing near the police car was looking around. As if he felt something, he looked at the house George was in. Their eyes met for a moment.

George quickly moved away from the window, but the sheriff had already seen him. Leaving the house at a moment like this would raise more suspicions.

There was a knock at the door. It was the police knocking. He was getting more and more nervous. He tried to calm himself down.

"Who is it?"

"It's Sheriff Carl Caster. Open the door, please!"

"I'm listening."

He recognized both officers standing at his door. Sheriff Brook Cletus showed his badge and introduced himself.

"We are sorry to disturb you. There has been a murder in the neighborhood. A woman called Beth has been viciously murdered at her house. Have you seen anyone or anything suspicious around? Perhaps you heard some noise?"

"My wife is not home, so I had a little drink and fell asleep on the sofa. Around an hour ago, I thought I heard someone scream. I couldn't tell if I was dreaming or if it was real. I got up and looked out the window without turning the lights on in the room, but I saw no one."

Caster walked in. "Are you alone at home?" Brook Cletus asked. Even though the sheriff noticed George's muddy shoes, he kept quiet about it.

"Like I said!"

Sheriff Caster entered the dark room through the hallway and quickly returned back. "You have no right to enter my home without permission. Have you forgotten the laws?"

Caster replied to his question with a question. "Since what time are you at home today, or have you gone anywhere during the day?"

George understood his suspicions right away. "I went out for a short while and returned home."

"You are dressed. Going somewhere?"

"Yes. My wife has been taken to a hospital because of her condition. I was going there. I had returned back because I had forgotten something.

"You questioning me and treating me like this is against the law. I am gonna have to talk to my lawyer about this."

"You will be called for interrogation anyway," Carl said and started walking to the police car with his partner.

"Carl, he is right. What you did there is against the law."

"I suspect his friend Michael in the murder. I thought maybe he was inside."

Ambulance and police sirens were approaching from afar. George furiously got in the car and headed to the hospital.

He was going to arrive at the hospital soon. He thought about what happened while driving. They were going to interrogate him anyway. *They would just ask a few questions and that would be it,* he thought to himself. Terrible things came to his mind for a moment. Coming eye to eye with the sheriff through the dark room's window could make him a suspect. But there's no proof. He tried to ease his mind. He kept thinking again, why did sheriff Caster enter the house when they were talking at the door? He knew Carl well. He knew about Caster's conflict with Michael before they went to war in Afghanistan, and Carl knew that he is Michael's best friend. *This conflict has been ongoing since their school times. What if Carl had something to do with Beth's murder?*

Suddenly, he changed his mind about going to the hospital. He turned back home in a hurry. He had to put an end to suspicions. He parked the car near the house and quickly went inside the house. There were police and ambulance cars in the street. Several officers were talking outside the crime scene.

George Bradley was not mistaken in his suspicions. He noticed a shiny object behind the armchair. He picked it up; it was the same piece of jewelry that he saw at Beth's house. He started shaking with anger and frustration. He was shocked. It was obvious what was going on.

He went up to the second floor and looked around; he was looking for a place to hide the earrings. He opened the window facing the back of the house and threw earrings into the bushes. He went out of the house and headed to the hospital.

It looked like Carl was trying to plant an evidence in his house in an attempt to get George arrested for the murder of Beth. It was his revenge plan for all the past years. Considering his condition, the police would assume that he would be unable to commit this crime alone. Therefore his best friend Michael would be the only person that could help him. Considering Michael and Beth's relationship in the past, Carl would try to convince the police that Michael had committed this crime on the grounds of jealousy and robbery. They would become prime suspects. He was aware that Michael should know about what was going on, but talking on the phone would be too dangerous. He wanted to see Michael in person.

Luisa's condition was getting better, but the doctors advised her to stay for stationary treatment for a little longer. George was happy about this. He was hiding everything from her; he didn't want her to stress over it. Luisa felt that something was bothering George, but in her mind, she just blamed it on his mental condition.

George returned home after some time. It looked like what he was fearing in his mind was happening in real life. He parked his car and headed home. As soon as he entered the house, there was a knock at the door. He opened the door. Several policemen were standing at the door.

"Are you Mr. George Bradley?"

"Yes."

"This house belongs to your wife?"

"Correct."

"We have a search warrant to your house in our hands."

"May I know why?"

"Mister, you are being involved in the criminal investigation of your neighbor Beth's murder. You can appeal against it at the department."

"I'm gonna have to call my lawyer."

"That's your right."

"If you'll allow me, I would like to inform my close friend Michael about it."

"No. Please sit down quietly and don't interrupt the search."

"May I know what you are searching for in my house?"

"Soon you will know."

After searching thoroughly, the police were unable to find any evidence. "Am I still being pulled into investigation? I'm sure the results convinced you."

"We are taking your shoes especially. You will come with us. If it's not proven that you were at the crime scene, you will give a statement and you are free to go."

Arnoldo was furiously pacing around the room, waiting for Anderson. There was a knock at the door. Arnoldo pointed his gun at the door and asked Arlen to open it. Anderson and Elma entered the room in a rush.

"Everything is OK, boss!"

"You weren't followed, were you?"

"No."

"Are you sure?"

"Of course, chief!"

"Bring the goods. Everything's in its place?"

"I took everything in the safe. I didn't have time to check."

"Everybody, leave the room except you." Arnoldo checked the jewels with the list. Everything seemed in order except for one diamond set.

"Where's the diamond set?" he asked Anderson angrily.

"Ask her yourself." He called Elma in.

"Where's the diamond set?"

"Believe me, I'm telling the truth. After I called Anderson and told him everything I saw, we came back home together with her. As he said, I left the kitchen door open. When I took the set and went downstairs, it was dark in the hallway and kitchen. When I entered the kitchen quietly, I saw a silhouette of a man. For a moment, I thought it was Anderson. But he didn't look like Anderson much. He had a gun. He wanted the keys first, but he heard the cars approaching. He just took the set from me and escaped from the kitchen door."

"You're lying!" Arnoldo slapped Elma as hard as he could. Elma was bleeding.

"I swear to everything I hold holy. She took the diamond set on purpose. When I arrived at the party, she was having a sweet chat with two women. According to what the house owner said, one of them was Sheriff Brook Cletus's wife, and the other was Beth's neighbor. She probably wanted to hand over the set to someone. Maybe that man followed us from there and entered from the kitchen door."

"How did he look physically?"

"He was tall, but I didn't see his face."

"Maybe he was that bitch's ex-boyfriend?"

"His height and body shape resembled him, but he didn't limp."

"Boss, I will say it again. I don't trust Carl. He gave the keys and the password to the safe to her. What was his plan? We need to ask him. Perhaps he sent that man there."

"Be patient. Don't rush into decision-making. We can't blame him for this until we are certain. We really need him. Maybe he was high on drugs and that bitch did something to him. Carl is gonna answer to me for that. What were you planning to do taking the set downstairs?"

"I knew that Anderson was coming. I was gonna give it to Anderson before Beth hid it somewhere."

"I don't trust your words. I will check the information you gave, and if I find out that something is up, you are both dead. Where's the gun?"

"Here you go." Anderson handed the gun to the boss.

Arnoldo's hands were shaking from anger. "Boss, I swear. He even fired at Elma with that gun. If I wasn't there, he would have killed her."

"Why did he shoot!"

"He wanted to take the diamond from Elma," Anderson replied.

The boss was angry. He was calculating the risks, thinking what to do. "Sheriff has got something to do with this. Let's call and ask him before it's too late."

"Stupid woman! He is working tonight! Don't forget, I can do you just like I did that other bitch. I forgive only because you helped. Try to make up for your mistakes. That diamond set needs to be found!"

He looked at Anderson. "Don't tell the boys anything yet. I'm gonna meet with that jerk in the morning. Find her a place to stay as soon as possible. She can't leave anywhere without my order. Change her appearance. If she doesn't wanna end up like that other bitch, she should obey. You must know about where she goes, and she must have your permission."

"Maybe we should take her to Alberto's place. He doesn't live there anyway."

"Send Arlen, find out what he says to that."

"OK, Boss." Anderson went out of the room with Arlen and Elma, and shortly after, he returned.

"Boss, your brother did not agree to your offer about Elma staying at his place."

"I'll talk to him myself. Elma might have something to do with the diamond set getting stolen. I need to find out the truth."

"Allow her to stay at the casino for now. All of her actions can be under my supervision."

"All right."

As he was approaching his friend's house, police cars near the street drew his attention. He started to worry. *What was happening?* The sheriff approached his car and asked him to pull over.

"Where are you headed, Mister? It's not allowed to enter. Please pull over and present your documents."

"What happened? I was going to my friend's house."

"Who's your friend?"

"George Bradley. He lives nearby." He pointed to George's house.

"Present your documents, sir."

Michael handed over his documents. He was getting nervous. It looked like something really had happened.

"Can I go to my friend's house?"

"Wait here, sir."

The sheriff walked to the officer standing near George's house and showed him the documents. They both looked at Michael and said something to each other. The same sheriff approached Michael again and asked him to get out of the car and approach the officer.

"Hello."

"Hello. Michael Grady?"

"Yes."

"Mr. Michael, you say that you have come to visit your friend."

"Correct."

"Let's get inside. I need to ask you a few questions."

Michael entered the house with the sheriff. There were other police officers inside George's house. Looking at the mess in the house, it was obvious that a thorough search had been done at the house.

"Mr. Michael, please sit down. I'm guessing you already know about the murder."

"What murder? Who has been killed? Where's George? Where's his wife? What's going on!" Michael stood up with frustration.

"Mister, sit down. Get a hold of yourself. Your friend George is fine, but he is at the department. His neighbor Beth was murdered mercilessly at night."

Michael was stunned. He didn't know how to react. "It can't be! It can't be!" His head was between his hands. The news was unexpected. He stood up angrily and smashed his hand to the table.

"Be quiet! Did you know the victim? Why are you so worried?"

"Her lover. As if you don't know what happened? Otherwise, why is he here in the middle of the night?"

He recognized the voice. He turned back, and it was Sheriff Carl Caster. "Am I not right? You are both involved in this!"

"Son of a bitch, you destroyed her life and now trying to put it on me!" Michael screamed and attacked Carl Caster. But he was stopped. He shivered in pain after the police officers hit him with a rubber baton to his arm and leg. The police handcuffed Michael and took him outside.

"Bastard! You ruined her! You're gonna answer for everything!"

"She was happy with me until you came and ruined everything."

The police put Michael in the patrol car and took him to the department.

This was big news. Media and television were shedding a light to this and informing people with the distorted version of the truth.

Federal agent Darren Edmond parked his car in front of the department and entered the building in a hurry. The meeting had already begun.

"Gentlemen!" Department chief Mr. Jonas Nilford started speaking.

"Vicious crime has happened. Mrs. Beth Francesco has been murdered in cold blood. All the witnesses and suspects sustained have been questioned. FBI has assigned agent Mr. Darren Edmond especially for this case. The jewel store robbery that happened not long ago, which created a big resonance not just statewide but nationwide, still remains undisclosed. But I think tonight's crime is going to give us plenty of evidence. Few hours before being murdered, the victim had an expensive piece of jewelry in her bag. Unfortunately, the jewel was not found during search at the house, and an open safe was uncovered at the basement. We can only assume that there was a lot of jewelry or money. We don't have evidence to back that up. It's very strange, how did Ms. Francesco get her hands to such jewelry? What was in the safe in the basement? Looking at the bloody footsteps, the killer either knew the password or got it from her before killing her and came downstairs to open the safe door. Either the victim was a member of some criminal group or she was followed by someone for the jewelry. But if it was for just one piece of jewelry, the killer would have just killed her before she arrived at the house, or even if so, the killer would have just left after taking the jewelry. Blonde woman that was with her would have been in trouble too. She was probably involved in this. Even though George Bradley did not say this in his first statement, later on he admitted seeing two people leaving Beth's house in a hurry in the dark. The open safe means that it was an organized crime, and even the victim might have been in it. They knew about the safe before they entered the house. We couldn't find the victim's cell phone. Looks like the criminals knew what they were doing.

"According to witness statements, the victim was at a birthday party earlier that day. A blonde woman was with her. The owner of the house said that the blonde woman arrived later on. That woman was a guest with Beth at the owner's house once before. She presented herself as Clara. They argued at the party. Beth was really drunk.

"Another eyewitness said that she saw the blonde woman hitting and insulting Beth and taking a piece of jewelry from her handbag. She was drunk. She passed out after her slap. The blonde woman put the jewel in her handbag and called the witness over for help. The blonde woman gave an excuse that this happens to her all the time, and they took her to the car. The house owner insisted on calling an ambulance, but the blonde woman refused. Beth was already conscious when they left. We have conducted a search for a woman with that name and similar appearance. We have no results yet.

"Two men detained as suspects and witnesses are former Special Force soldiers. They have been arrested based on what Sheriff Carl Caster stated. Carl Caster and his partner were the first to arrive at the crime scene. With Carl Caster's statement, the victim's neighbor, ex-Special Force war veteran George Bradley has been detained. He was at the crime scene—there's evidence. That night, George's close friend and the victim's ex-boyfriend Michael Grady has been detained on the basis of hooliganism. He arrived at the crime scene and tried to attack on-duty officer Carl Caster. Fortunately, he was neutralized by other officers and arrested. He's being interrogated. They both served in Afghanistan. They have been sent home because of their injuries. Their service has been rewarded at highest order. It's surprising to see such veterans' names get involved in such a crime. There are a lot of dark areas. Nonetheless, there are laws, and everyone has a liability regardless of their service to this nation or their job. If they are not proven guilty, they will be set free. Regarding Mr. Darren Edmond's complaints, we do not arrest innocent people without having valid proof and evidence.

"The search continues. Fingerprints found the night of crime indicate that there was someone else besides George Bradley. We took Michael Grady's fingerprints as one of the prime suspects, but they did not match the ones at the crime scene. Search was conducted at Mr. George Bradley's house, but no solid evidence of the crime was found.

"We will keep researching. Unfortunately, there are a lot of mismatches among statements given. Sheriff Caster's statement is mostly based on the grounds of slander and revenge. Both ex-military officers have filed a complaint against unjust investigation against them. Because of their complaint, an FBI special agent has been assigned here. He will be in charge of this investigation from now on. I sincerely hope that your investigations will bring the criminal to justice as soon as possible. I, Special Agent Darren Edmond, by the authority given to me, will personally get involved and lead the reinterrogation of the witnesses and suspects. According to the intel I have, there are many suspicious matters in this investigation. I'm gonna try to shed a light on these matters. Our cooperation is vital. I believe that it will be the key in solving this murder case, which can lead us to the robbery and murder cases happened a while ago at the state. There's one thing that drew my attention. It's strange that Sheriff Caster often goes to that house and yet he doesn't know the people around her. Criminals are on the run, and they will do anything to lose their trail. This means new innocent victims. We must be mobilized and united in the fight against crime. I am certain that by uniting in this fight against crime, by working together as a team, we will successfully accomplish this hard and honorable mission."

Carl Caster was waiting in the hallway. He was angry. He was drawn into investigation for the murder of Beth Francesco.

The sheriff entered the room and greeted the agent and took a seat. He took out his napkin from his pocket and wiped the sweat from his forehead. The agent noticed that he was very nervous.

"Sergeant, how long have you known Beth Francesco?"

"Approximately two years."

"Do you know anything about why she left work?"

"I have no idea."

"She was fired because of negligence and incompetence at work. As an officer of the law, did you ever show any interest in finding the reason for that?"

"I did, but she came up with excuses whenever I asked, so I never asked her again."

"What can you say about her luxurious lifestyle of late? How can an unemployed woman afford such an expensive car?"

"She said that she leased it."

"According to the information we have, the car was purchased by someone with cash and registered into her name. That person is wanted."

"She borrowed some money from me. We've been having arguments over it lately. I asked her to pay me back."

"When she asked you for money, did you know that she wants the money to buy the car?"

"She never said anything about a car when she asked for the money. I'm guessing she took money from people around me too."

"A car is bought to someone else's name with borrowed money, and you didn't care to look into it, is that right? You have been in a relationship with this woman for two years, and you never bothered to get to know the people around her?"

"As you know, I have a hard job. We didn't meet very often. I didn't know about her contacts. I've had several women like her in my life."

"Who did you know from the people around her? Describe them to me."

"No, I don't know anyone. Because I never asked about her personal life."

"So this murdered woman has been your mistress for two years, and you, as a police officer, never showed the slightest sign of interest in her life after so many things that happened to her."

"We weren't so close lately."

"Do you know Michael?"

"Yes."

"How do you know him?"

"He's an ex-military. I was confronted with him several times during hand-to-hand combat training before he went to war. He was really good—he beat everyone. We had a fight once with him on a personal basis. I had to be hospitalized several times after his strike."

"Did you file a complaint?"

"No."

"Why?"

"I can't say."

"Because he loved her. You had feelings for the same woman. They had a very intimate love relationship. He defeated you many times, and this is how you wanted to get revenge, is that it?"

"It's something else."

"Refreshment in Michael and Beth's relationship was the reason for cold air between you and her, as you say?"

"I think so too. Perhaps Michael bought her the expensive car."

"Did you know that she had expensive jewelry?"

"Only after the incident."

"What about the hidden safe in the basement of the house?"

"I didn't know about that."

"Mr. Sergeant, this accusation is very serious. Ms. Bella's description of the jewel she saw in Beth's handbag is quite similar to one of the pieces from the robbery that took place a few months ago. As a police officer, what do you think about that?"

"Ms. Luisa was at the birthday party too. She's the neighbor and a former friend of Beth. Her husband is Michael's best friend."

"So what you are suspecting is that the people you mentioned are responsible for Beth's murder. What kind of evidence do you have to support that?"

"There are a lot of suspicions."

"Sheriff Carl Caster, that night, she returned home with a blonde woman. Do you know who she is?"

"No."

"During your two-year relationship with this woman, was it the first time that you two were having trouble?"

"Like I said, we were having arguments over the money she borrowed."

"Did you know that she went to the hospital for her pregnancy? Did you make her abort the child?"

"No. She only proposed to get married. But I wasn't ready to get married."

"So she just wrote a statement to kill her future child in tears?"

"She told me that she was having some problems with her pregnancy and that the fetus was not growing properly. That's why she had to abort."

"You called that Elma woman and asked her to go to the birthday party with Beth because she was drunk."

"I have not seen her. She just made a phone call from my cell phone to her once. That's how I knew her number."

"So you just happened to save that number?"

"Yes."

"What happened between you and her ex?"

"We had some conflicts on a personal level."

"Did you call her friend again about Beth?"

"I did, but she didn't answer the phone."

"Can you describe Elma to me?"

"Like I said, I have never seen her."

"OK. According to your partner Brook Cletus's statement, you discovered the crime while you and your partner visited her house. What was the purpose of your visit?"

"I kept calling her, but she didn't answer the phone."

"Were you suspicious of something?"

"I had a fight with her that day because she had met with Michael. I asked her to marry me, but she refused. I got angry and left the house. I called her at night to see how she was doing, but when she didn't answer the calls, I got worried for her."

"Is it the first time that she doesn't answer your call?

"What made you think that she had met with Michael?"

"From her attitude."

"But you just said that she was an easy woman. Seeing her with another man has upset you, and you asked her to marry you. Am I correct?

"A day before the incident, her friend Elma calls you and tells you about her meeting with Michael. Looks like her friend had your phone number too.

"Mr. Carl Caster, the investigation continues. We will work hard to make sure that the investigation is done correctly and solve this crime while it is still hot. We may need to meet again while the investigation progresses. We are done for now. You may leave. Mr. George, where were you at the night of murder?"

"My wife was at a birthday party with her friend that night. I was alone. I got bored, had something to drink, and fell asleep on the sofa. It was pretty late when I woke up. The lights in the room were off. I was sleepy."

"What happened after?"

"I thought I heard a scream and a gunshot in my dream. I sat down quietly and listened to noises. I didn't hear anything. As I approached the window and peeked behind the curtain to the street, for some reason, it was really dark. Beth usually left the front light on even when she was not at home. I got suspicious, especially after seeing two people get out of her house rushing out of her house and disappearing in the darkness."

"Why didn't you call the police right away?"

"I hesitated. I wanted to make sure."

"Go on."

"I decided to check out the area. I was being careful. That's why I took my gun and my flashlight. The front door was locked. When I wanted to get behind the house, I saw Beth's car in the parking lot. The door to the kitchen facing the backyard was open. I was getting more and more suspicious. When I entered the kitchen, I saw Beth on the floor, blood all over the floor. She was already dead."

"You should have called the police and an ambulance right away."

"I didn't have my phone on me. I didn't want to use her phone, so I returned home quickly."

"Did you see her phone at the crime scene?"

"To be honest, no."

"You have kept crime information from the police on purpose. You are liable for this, did you know that?"

"I know the law and respect it. I needed to think. I came home and looked at the time. My wife should have been back by that time. I started to worry. I wanted to call her when I heard a car sound on the street. I looked out the window. It was the police."

"Who is Michael?"

"A hero and a real friend."

"I'm sure, as Michael's friend, you knew about his relationship with Beth. Perhaps she was murdered because of jealousy."

"Michael is a law-abiding citizen. He knows how to hate but not to kill."

"But he killed plenty during the war."

"Like you said, 'war.'"

The federal agent stood for a moment. "My apologies, Mr. George. Have you filed a complaint against the police for their unlawful actions against you?"

"Yes. Sheriff Caster has obtained a search warrant for my house with groundless accusations. I was taken to the department, where I demanded to speak to my lawyer."

"That is your right. The reason you were taken to the department and a search has been conducted at your house was the blood sample taken from your shoe matches the blood of the victim."

"I didn't hide that I was at the crime scene. The reason for my complaint is the illegal entrance of Sheriff Caster into my residence and the arrest of my innocent friend."

"But the police had a warrant for search."

"Caster's illegal entrance to my home happened when they arrived at the crime scene."

"The reason for your friend's arrest is that he refused to cooperate with law enforcement officers while they were trying to do their job. We will look into that. Fingerprints have been taken from the door handle. They belong to someone else. A former Special Force soldier would not make such a mistake. Looks like someone else was at the crime scene besides you. What was in the safe? Who stole the jewel set from Beth's bag? It either was you or someone else. Before the police arrived at the scene, there was someone else in there with you, perhaps more than one person, and she was murdered. Despite all of these, you still consider that police conducting a search at your house is illegal? Perhaps you have grouped with some people and committed this crime. Where is the jewelry?"

"When I went down to the basement, the safe was already empty."

"Mr. George, you probably have heard about the news of the robbery. It was big news a few months ago."

"Yes."

"It's possible that the goods from that robbery were stored there. What can you say about the people that visited Beth's house?"

"I can't say much about it. When it comes to jewelry and wealth, I lost many good friends in life. Brave young men died in front of my eyes. I can't get the images of their faces and the tragedies of the war off my mind. My beloved wife, dearest friend, and my future child are the only things that keep me going."

"Mr. Roger, investigation continues. I am sure the accuracy of your statement will be decisive in the enlightenment of this crime. Any incorrect information given can and will be used against you.

"Mr. Michael, you have been arrested because of your hooliganism acts against an officer on duty and intended to use force on him. Do you consider yourself guilty?"

"No!"

"Witnesses' statements can back it up. This fact has been added to your interrogation process. What was the purpose of your hooliganism? Can you explain?

"I'm gonna ask you several questions. Are you ready?"

"Yes."

"What was the purpose of your visit that day to the crime scene area?"

"I tried to get in touch with my friend. He didn't pick up the phone, so I got worried for him. He has a health condition. I wanted to come and check on him myself."

"Why did you have a gun with you?"

"Security."

"From whom and what are you protecting yourself? Do you have any particular enemy or some people that might want to harm you?"

"There have always been people like that and always will be."

"Understood. How long have you known Beth?"

"She was the woman I loved. It was two years ago. I don't forgive cheating. Even though she was out of my life once and for all, in my heart I still had feelings for her. I met her the day before the incident. I was waiting for that moment. I was a little drunk, so it was a good time to tell her my thoughts that were the result of my hatred toward her."

"So you had an argument with her the other day?"

"Yes."

"Perhaps there's a connection between your argument and her death the next day. Was she alone that day?"

"No, she was with some blonde woman."

"Was it the first time you were seeing her? How did she look?"

"It was the second time I saw Beth with her. She was a blonde middle-aged woman. I don't remember much else about her appearance."

"Using other witnesses' statements, we have come up with a robot photo of the woman who was at the birthday party with Beth. Look at the picture. Do you see any resemblance?"

"It's the same woman."

"Are you sure?"

"Yes."

"Sheriff Caster's statement indicates that the relationship between you and Beth had rekindled and somehow you knew about her extravagant lifestyle. Is it true?"

"I already gave an answer to that question."

"It's strange. Neither you nor Sheriff Caster is unaware of the surroundings of the woman of whom you have known for many years."

"The Beth I knew two years ago was a pure and naive Beth who had only one friend."

"Interrogation reports show that she wasn't living the ordinary life. The attributes of the diamond set she was using were quite similar to the one that was stolen a few months ago. Did you know about the jewelry?"

"After I returned from Afghanistan, it was the first and last time I saw her."

"Can you explain your aggressive behavior toward a police officer on duty?"

"The terrible news, arrest of my friend, and Caster's nasty accusations were too much to handle."

"Any negativity that comes along is handled by law. There's a higher law of the state, and we are liable. Mr. Michael, I have plenty of information about you. I know that you are an honorable and an honest man. You are a war hero. I would not want such a man's name to be involved in something like this. Looks like someone is trying to push you into this investigation as a decoy and hide the real criminals. I have a feeling that you will have a personal interest in solving this case. To say the least, it is understandable that you are still angry about the dirty games that got the woman you loved and still have feelings for killed. Investigation continues. I'm sure that you will do your best to help us in solving this case as a former hero soldier and a brave officer. I sincerely hope that this chat we had between us will not leave this room. Investigation against you is considered unlawful and has been dropped. It's the FBI's decision."

"Thank you!" He greeted the detective and left the department.

He came out of the department building and sat in his car. He was feeling some comfort at last. Even though he felt like he was abandoned by the love of his life and he was useless for his job and nobody needed him, this made him realize he made a mistake in his feelings. He was still needed as an honorable citizen. He was happy to see that there are still plenty of people who value honor, honesty, and consciousness.

He went to the graveyard. He finally managed to find Beth's grave after searching for quite some time. He couldn't hold in his feelings anymore. His tears were falling to his cheeks. "Rest in peace. As long as I'm alive, I won't stop until I find your killer."

He spread the flowers over Beth's grave. He cleared the gravestone where her first and last name was engraved and left the graveyard with great sadness.

Officer Carl Caster came out of the chef's room. He was feeling nervous after all that happened. He didn't know what to do. It was too dangerous to meet with the boss. The case of the blonde woman was worrying him too. If she got caught, she might give away everyone. After the feds got involved, the situation grew worse for him. All the witnesses who saw Beth were questioned about the blonde woman. She may get caught at any moment.

He went out to the yard, sat on the bench, and lit a cigarette. He wanted to think in silence. The fact that George had gone into Beth's house on the night of the murder was a mistake to Carl's benefit. On the other hand, if the jewel he planted at George's house was found, then it sure would have proved George's guilt. But they found nothing of the earrings during the search. Michael and George were released by the lack of solid evidence that links them to the crime. Only evidence was the sample from George's muddy shoes matching Beth's blood, but George brought an explanation to this in his official statement. He was temporarily released considering his health condition, with no permission to leave the state until next interrogation. Michael, on the other hand, was the real danger. Carl knew Michael very well. He was certain that Michael would go after the killer.

Caster decided to meet with the boss no matter what happens. Michael was the biggest threat at the moment. He was certain that Michael would go after this matter. That's why he wanted to get rid of both former officers once and for all to leave no trace behind. Probably George found the jewelry that he planted at his house. Carl wanted the news of the ring investigation that was going on in another state. The boss was going to be suspicious of him anyway. Only they knew the password. This ring investigation would make things more complicated.

He got back in the car and headed home. He kept looking at his rearview mirror during his drive home. He was checking to see if he was being followed or not. Finally, he arrived home. The door was unlocked. Carl got nervous, took out his gun, and entered the house quietly. He was shocked when he saw the boss sitting there and waiting for him.

"Did I scare you?" Arnoldo asked.

Anderson, standing next to the boss, had a smirk on his face. "What if someone was following me? How can you be so careless?" Carl complained.

"You see, he is teaching me how to be careful. This is the result of how careful you are. This is how careful you are. You and your slut have caused me plenty of problems, and now you are trying to come on top of things."

"Beth's murder, it's your doing, isn't it?"

"Let's say it is. What do you have to say to that?"

"We agreed that we are gonna decide on everything together."

"Anderson, do you see? This is how he thanks us." Arnoldo turned to Anderson.

"So what you are saying is that we should have waited until that bitch got everyone caught, including you and me. Answer me! Tell me, how did that bitch know about the password to the safe?"

"How can you ask me that question, Arnoldo!"

"You see, Boss? He acts like he doesn't know what we are talking about." Anderson spoke out.

"When I trusted you with the goods, I thought it would be safer at her house. That's why we decided that only two of us know the password to the safe and you keep the key copies with you. You insisted on that. I agreed because I trusted you the most. You knew about this woman's past. Why weren't you careful? Are you really that stupid that you didn't know about this woman's ex-lover named Michael?"

"Do you really think I would do something that stupid? How could it happen?"

"It's obvious, you told her. It's that simple. Don't act stupid."

"Son of a bitch! I'll kill you." He stood up and shouted. He quickly grabbed Anderson by the collar and tried to punch him.

"Stop!" The boss pushed Carl aside. Anderson left the room with anger.

"We need to find a way out. As soon as possible!"

"Where's Elma?" Carl asked.

"Don't worry about her."

"What about the goods?"

"They are at a safe place. Thanks to Anderson and Elma, we were able to relocate them before it was too late. But the piece in your bitch's handbag is nowhere to be found. According to what Elma said, she left the kitchen door open like she was told and helped Beth to the second floor. Later, she came down with the piece. That's when she saw that the kitchen lights were off and there was a man standing in the dark. At first, she thought that it was Anderson. That man took the piece from Elma by force and ran away. Five minutes later, Anderson arrived. Beth heard the noise and came downstairs. She made a shot from her firearm, but Anderson was able to neutralize her before she did any harm. Did you know that she has a gun?"

"No. Where's the gun?"

"We have the gun. What are they doing about this at the department?"

The sheriff told everything that happened after Beth's murder. "Arnoldo, you must believe me. I have been maximum careful about everything."

The boss went to deep thoughts. "Who else was there at George's house when you planted the earrings?"

"Brook Cletus was with me at the night shift. He was standing at the door."

"If it wasn't found where you planted it during search, that could only mean someone took it. Maybe when George returned home that day, he found the earrings and got rid of them. Maybe it was Michael at Beth's house?"

"Michael limps when he walks."

"Maybe she hid the jewel in her handbag to give it to Michael. Maybe they were planning to run away together, and Elma hindered their plan. Maybe he sent someone else not to be recognized. The boys will take care of the George matter today," he said and stood up.

"I will meet Michael myself after some time."

"Boss, looks like we have guests." Anderson came into the room nervously.

The boss looked at Michael in anger. "Go and check who it is." He picked up the gun from the table.

"Quick, get downstairs." Caster approached the door.

It was Sheriff Brook Cletus. His visit was strange to Carl.

"Hi. Can I come in?"

"Hi. Did something happen?"

"No. I just wanted to come and talk to you in private about some things."

"It's boring at home. How about we sit at the porch? A drink, coffee? What would you like?"

"No, man. Thanks, no need for anything. I just wanna talk to you in quiet about some things that have been bugging me. It's true at your insistence we both gave our written statements to our own benefit, saying that we were at the area at 2:00 a.m. prior to the burglary, but I was asleep at that time. I have no idea what happened. It's true, the criminals drugged and overdosed the security with sleeping pills and then got to work. Doctors couldn't get the guard off the coma. But I was also sleepy!"

"So what you are saying is that we have been drugged with sleeping pills too?"

"You weren't asleep or sleepy before the robbery. Admit the truth. I had a feeling. You are the only one I told these thoughts.

It was the first time that I was having such a sleeping problem, and I had plenty of sleep the night before at home."

"So the same thing should have happened to you too? Is that right? Are you suspecting me in all of this? What are you waiting for? Get up, go and tell everything at the department, tell them that we were having sweet dreams in a duty car at the night of the robbery, that's why we had no idea about what happened there that night. Just sign your resignation. They will just fire you right away. Me too. Then an investigation will open up against us. We won't just lose our jobs—e will go to jail."

"It doesn't look good anyways. Whatever, I'm tired. I'll get going. We will talk about it again sometime." Brook stood up and left the house in frustration.

The man sent after Carlos returned and said that Carlos was not at his home. Arnoldo looked at Anderson with suspicion. "Carlos is a very careful man. He probably changed his place for safety reasons."

"Why didn't he say anything about it to us? It's strange. I need him urgently. Find him however you can, but don't call him."

"I know his close friend. They are usually together."

"You have until nighttime."

"OK, Boss." Anderson left the room.

Approximately, Carlos was near the boss. "I didn't expect this from you. Where were you?"

"Boss, I rented a house somewhere else."

"Why did you move? There's something fishy about that. Why didn't you tell me your new place?"

"It's a family matter. I got divorced. I needed the money. That's why I rented my own house. I'm living in a single-bedroom apartment now."

"I understand. I will return your money piece by piece. I'm bothering you for something else, though." He explained everything to Carlos.

"I really need to know who took the jewel. Yeah, there are some suspects, but I don't want to create problems with the wrong people at a time like this. There's a reason I called you over. It's about that jewel set. Why did she want to give that specific piece to someone? How could she have known that that piece was the most expensive one?"

"I understand you perfectly. I'm sure I have already told you about that piece back then. You rushed into killing her. Why didn't you question her about the piece before killing her?"

"Good question. But according to the information I was given, she was seeing someone else at that time, a former Special Force officer. Beth was at the birthday party with Elma that night and she had the jewel in her handbag. Elma went to the party for Beth. When she entered the house, she saw Beth with two other women having a sincere chat. Later on, we found out that one of them was Sheriff Brook Cletus's wife and the other one was George Bradley's wife. It looks like Beth and those women knew each other well. When Elma informed Anderson that Beth went to the birthday party with the jewel set in her handbag, I decided quickly. We had to get rid of the witness. She even fired at Elma. Elma said that when she went downstairs, she saw the kitchen lights switched off. The man in the dark kitchen took the jewel from Elma's hands and escaped. At first, she thought it was Anderson. But Anderson arrived quickly after he got rid of Beth, and they both left the house in a hurry after taking all the goods. Elma didn't see the man's face, but she did say that the physique of the man was similar to this former Special Force named Michael. In that case, a question comes up. If this man loved Beth, why didn't he try to protect her? One more thing, Michael lost his leg at the war. This man did not limp while walking—Michael does."

"Perhaps to avoid getting recognized, he quickly grabbed the jewelry and fled. In any scenario, that man came there knowing what to look for."

"It's very strange. There are a lot of people that I suspect. When I find out who's behind all of this, no matter who it is, I will punish him myself."

After Carlos left, Arnoldo called Arlen over and took the car keys from him and gave it to Anderson and asked him to follow him.

He sat in the backseat of the car and smashed closed the door.

"Boss, where are we going?" Anderson asked.

"I need to see Alberto right away. Need to discuss some things with him."

"What things?"

"Just drive. You'll know soon enough."

"It's your decision. I don't trust this sheriff. He didn't answer your question about the password. Maybe he gave the password to Beth for some reason. We don't know why. If it was up to me, I would have shot him dead right then and there."

"Doing that is not very difficult. We must not rush into decisions. We need someone from the inside of the investigation that would keep informing us. I just want all of this to be over good. Don't you see what we are facing because of that bitch? The sheriff is important to us right now. I will find out the truth about the password and the jewelry. Be patient."

Around thirty minutes later, they arrived at his brother's rented house. Alberto was still sleepy. The others were playing around.

"Alberto, get up! Your brother's here."

Alberto started complaining angrily. "What now? Won't let me relax a bit. It's so early in the morning."

"I told you many times don't use that shit so much. You've lost track of time."

He didn't expect his brother to come into his room. He quickly got up. "What am I supposed to do? You don't let me leave the house." He couldn't control himself. He was pissed.

"Did you take care of the girl?"

"No."

"I told you many times, take care of this. She's gonna cause us problems. Are you really after some girl? We don't need this right now."

"Is that why you came?"

"There's something important I need to talk to you about. I need two good and trusted men from the gang. Choose two of the closest and trustworthy guys from your gang. I need them to do something for me tonight."

"What is it? I'm curious. You usually let Anderson handle these matters and push me aside."

"As you can see, I haven't forgotten about you. It's a very important matter, and I can only trust you in this. You must get it done. Otherwise, everything might end up terribly for us. Anderson got some of the tasks done yesterday." He explained the rest of the situation to his brother. They both have their hands in the jewelry stolen.

"Brother, you know how much I love you. But you show no trust in me. You let Anderson handle everything. That's why I'm always angry with you."

"I trust you, silly. But you gotta understand, I'm doing this to protect you from all the dangers. We are the heirs to our family. If something happens to me, you will be the leader. I want you to get married soon. I didn't get married, and now I regret that decision. Someone should continue our heritage. Whatever, we will talk about this later. Call the guys over. I need to explain to them thoroughly the details of their mission."

After half an hour of discussions, the boss ordered the final mission. "Get this done well and quickly. Leave no trace behind. I will get in touch with you to find out the result. It's not safe during daytime around the house. Tell them to be there at night. The sheriff who controls the area has a night shift today. He will leave after checking the area. They can do it easily and quietly. His wife's at the hospital. He's alone."

"Trust me with these kinds of things. You'll see what your brother can do."

"Alberto, I don't want you there. Let your boys handle it. He's an ex-Special Force who has been in a war. He is the friend of the guy who beat you at the restaurant."

"Is that so? Don't worry, Arnoldo."

"Take care! You are all I have. Be safe." He left the place after hugging his little brother.

After Alberto left, Arnoldo picked up his gun and started mumbling angrily. "You think I'm afraid of him. I will take care of it myself tonight."

Even though it was springtime, the weather still was chilly. Michael was not feeling well. He decided to stay at home. His days would pass by watching TV on the sofa, walking around in the house thinking. He was getting bored. He opened the room window and looked outside. The front of the house was illuminated, but further down the street was impossible to see. He took a drink from the fridge and took a seat. He thought about calling George. He decided that it was inappropriate to make a phone call at this time. He planned about meeting with George face-to-face.

The police returned everything they took from his car when he was being detained. He checked among his belongings for his gun and counted the bullets. He was exhausted. He went to the bedroom. Lack of sleep was causing severe headaches. He couldn't fall asleep. He kept asking questions to himself about everything that was happening—questions he could not answer. He thought about the sheriff's false accusations against him. But he had met with Beth only once since he came back from war in Afghanistan, and he had never seen the blonde woman with her before. "It probably was her who told Sheriff Caster about me and Beth. I thought I saw someone peeking from the window, but I didn't pay attention." He talked to himself. It was getting serious. It seems like it was the same blonde woman who was with Beth at the birthday party—the reason the feds were asking questions for. This woman was quite mysterious. "How and when did she inform the sheriff? She's wanted since the day of the crime, but not a single clue about her. Understood!" He took a deep breath. "There's a connection between the sheriff and this woman, and he knows her well too. In his statement, he denied the fact of knowing her as Beth's friend." He had to find that woman. He was thinking of a possible connection between Beth's murder and the blonde woman. Some time passed. His thoughts wouldn't let him fall asleep. He took another drink from the fridge and approached the window. The only source of light was the lights in front his house; the rest of the street was dark. For some reason, his neighbors lights were also on. It was strange; they usually go to sleep early. He hesitated for a moment. They haven't had a good day since Sarah's disappearance. Lucas Marchelo had to undergo treatment twice at the hospital because of his heart condition. But he was still hurting and crying for his only daughter. He went to church every day, praying for her soul. Michael was worried for him. He planned to go to the neighbor's house and went out to the hall. The doorbell rang. It was George; he looked nervous. His visit at this time of the night was very strange to Michael.

"Good evening. Can I come in?"

"Of course, come on in."

Michael checked the street and closed the door. "You look nervous man. What happened? Calm down."

"Michael, I came without calling, but there's a reason for it. It's better this way. After what happened, I feel like I'm being followed. I'm worried for myself and Luisa. I didn't want to bother you at this time. I wanted to meet with you tomorrow. But later I couldn't just sit and wait. Some suspicious things were happening. I think someone wants to kill me!"

"How's Luisa?"

"She's better now. After returning home from the hospital, she even plans to return to work after some time. She doesn't know about the things happening. She knows about Beth's murder, but that's it, nothing else. I told her I won't be home for another two days and asked her to stay a little longer at the hospital."

"What are you suspicious of?"

George told Michael everything that happened about the diamond earrings. When he wanted to call the police to inform about the murder, there was a knock at the door. It was Sergeant Carl Caster. He explained his visit's purpose and wanted to get some information about the crime. "I explained everything I knew. I know what time it was, but the police and ambulance arrived much later. It seemed like the information was not given on time. They took my statement at the department, and I specifically pointed out the exact time when I talked to the police. For some reason, Officer Caster was half an hour late to inform the department. I was looking for the jewel in the backyard when I noticed some strange men near the factory. I went straight to the car and drove here."

"If you hadn't just been to the crime scene, we would have had nothing to worry about."

"Should I turn in the jewel to the feds?"

"Never. They will use it as evidence against you. The sheriff planted the jewel in your house on purpose."

Michael was thinking. "I understand your concern, man. Don't worry, you're not alone in this. I'm always by your side."

"I have to go. Take this!" as he handed the diamond jewelry.

Michael hesitated for a moment before taking the earring. "Perhaps you should stay. Luisa is at the hospital anyway."

"No, I better get going," he said and walked to the door. Suddenly, he stopped and turned back.

"Tonight, both officers came to the area. Sheriff Caster knocked on the door. He asked to check if I was OK and if I was alone or not. His question was strange. He said that he has come here to protect me because of the crime. When Sheriff Caster went over to Beth's house to check, his partner approached me and told me that he wants to meet with you in person. I think he was hiding something from his partner. He didn't say why."

"What does he want from me?"

"I think you should see him. Michael, take care for now."

"Do you have your gun with you? If not, take my pistol."

"No worries. It's in the car. See you."

"Take care!"

Michael went inside and looked out the window after closing the door. George got in the car and drove away. Michael was still looking out the window. The lights of the car approaching distracted him. The car was coming toward the house. Michael quickly hid behind the window and watched the car. The man sitting in the front passenger seat was staring at the house when he said something to the driver. Their coat collars were lifted up; it was difficult to see their faces. Perhaps these were the men following George.

What to do? Time is passing. Michael went inside, got his pistol, and paced outside. There was a taxi parked up front, and the driver was helping the customer with the bags. He paced toward the taxi and got inside. The keys were on the ignition. He drove off with the taxi car. The driver ran and screamed after his stolen cab. The road was a one-way road. Since there was no traffic, he could speed up easily. The road to the town where George lives passed through the forest. It's rare to see a car on this road at night. There was a railroad ahead. He increased the speed, but the railroad traffic lights turned red and the barrier was coming down. It could only mean one thing—the train was near. Michael was able to stop the car; otherwise, he would have been smashed under the train. The rear lights of the car he was following started to disappear in the darkness. Michael hit the steering wheel; he had to wait.

After George passes through the forest, he would have almost two kilometers left to his town. Headlights in his rearview mirror drew his attention. At first, he didn't pay much attention, but it was approaching fast. It looked like he was being followed. What to do? Only way out was to drive faster, he thought. But it didn't work; the other car passed him, turned the car, and blocked his road. George barely managed to stop the car. He tried to reach for the gun in his glove box, but it was too late. A man got out of the car and started walking toward George as he opened fire. George got hit on the shoulder. He tried to get down and hide from the bullets. Suddenly, everything changed. A car ran over the man with the gun and smashed into the car blocking the road. A man got out of the car and started beating the other man from the roadblock car. He took away his gun and smashed closed the car door at him. The driver took a big hit. He tried to resist the other man, but it was no use.

"Don't shoot. I have nothing to do with this." The driver was begging.

Michael pointed the gun to the driver's head. "Talk, you son of a bitch! Who sent you?"

"Nobody."

"You're lying!" Michael hit him in the head.

"They will kill you."

"Who are they?"

"Boss and his gang. There's a sheriff among them."

"Who's the boss? Give me his address! Answer me!" Michael shot him in the leg.

"In the forest . . . old hunter's cabin . . ." The driver passed out from the pain.

Michael let go of the driver's collar and started approaching George's car. "You are badly wounded. How are you feeling?" as he took out his shirt and attended to the wound. "Don't worry, it's not serious." He took out the first aid bag and bandaged George's wound.

"Michael, look out!" George screamed as Michael quickly turned back and managed to shoot the criminal before he was able to pull the trigger. The man fell down. After making sure that he was dead, Michael returned to George.

"I took away that asshole's weapon. I guess he had one more in the car."

"Michael, I owe you my life. If you came just a little later, I would have been dead by now."

"This is a very dangerous gang."

"Perhaps you should talk to the police."

"No, I can't. They have someone inside the department. We don't know how many of them are there. They are going to take you to the hospital. We need to be careful. I will definitely meet with Brook. I'll ask him to help you rent a house somewhere else. Your house is no longer safe after this. Make sure Luisa doesn't go to work. Use her condition as an excuse. They may follow her home or, worse, kill her. My life is also in danger. I'll hide out for some time. I'll deal with these bastards. Take care, my friend."

"Pick up your phone. Call the police and ambulance. You don't know the man who helped you."

Michael wiped the gun he used and threw it on the dead body.

He had to walk a lot of distance through the woods to reach the train station. His leg pain was making it much more difficult to walk. He was getting closer to the station. He decided to take a break to rest and plan his next steps. He decided to go to the place George told him about to meet with Sheriff Cletus.

He was exhausted. He decided to spend the night in the forest. He took out his jacket to make a pillow and slept in the woods until morning.

With the information given, Sheriff Caster and Cletus headed to the forest road. Feds and the ambulance arrived at the scene earlier. The wounded were taken to the hospital. Consecutive murders happening in the state alarmed both the police and the federals. Sheriff Caster parked the car on the side of the road and walked to the crime scene. The two deceased looked of Hispanic heritage. It was impossible to identify the dead because they didn't have any kind of document of identification on them. But Caster definitely recognized one of them. It was the boss's brother, Alberto. He passed away from the crash. The wounded citizen was known. Sheriff Caster analyzed all three cars, pointing his flashlight. Something was strange.

"I wonder, where was our hero coming from in the middle of the night?"

He approached and pointed the flashlight at the plate number of the car. "It really is his car. I guess they had some kind of problem between them. I've said it before, these ex-Special Forces are up to something. Another crime, and yet they don't believe me. It's strange. What was he doing here at that time?"

"I'm sure he will have something to say in his statement," Sheriff Cletus replied.

"Do you know the owner of the taxi?" Caster asked the sheriff.

"It's one of the cabs working in the area. I know the owner."

"Then where's the driver? Also at the hospital?"

"No, the taxi driver escaped the scene. There's no update on whether he is dead or alive."

"It's very strange. We need to get him to the department to interrogate."

"The taxi driver is at the station. He gave a written statement about his taxicab being stolen." Darren Edmond spoke out.

"After checking the corpses, send them to forensics. Identify them. Present all the guns and shells used to the forensics. Anything you can find."

Carl Caster was shocked. He tried to hide his surprise. He stayed calm, but he was really nervous. What was going on? The boss said that he will take care of George and Michael. It looked like the boys from the gang couldn't take care of the business. Most probably Michael was involved. George could not have done this alone. The man who stole the taxi cab had helped George and fled the scene. It had to be Michael. But the owner of the taxi couldn't describe the man in any way; it drove Carl mad.

Darren Edmond headed to the hospital regarding the crime incident that happened. He entered the wounded ward with the doctor.

"Mr. George Bradley, the special agent, is going to ask you a few questions about the incident. Are you ready?"

"Yes."

"Hello, Mr. George. Such a short time has passed and yet we meet again. How are you feeling?"

"Feeling better. Still got some pain. I'll be better in no time. According to the doctor, my wound is not very serious."

"Mr. George, where were you driving to when the incident happened?"

"Since I'm alone most of the time at home, I get bored. Sometimes I drive off to the seaside park, relax, and take some fresh air. That's what I was doing yesterday. It all happened when I was driving back home."

"Do you know the men who died?"

"No."

"Why would these men follow you? Perhaps there's a connection between the latest murder and these."

"I have no personal conflict with anyone. That's why I don't believe that someone would follow and want to kill me, and I don't know those men. Perhaps they had something between them."

"Did you see anyone suspicious at the park? Maybe they followed you from the park? Did you get into any trouble with anyone at the park?"

"No."

"What can you say about the car that followed you?"

"I knew something was up when I saw that car approaching really fast."

"The car passed you and blocked your road. What did you think?"

"Maybe he saw the taxi car following him and tried to take a good position to take a shot."

"What you are saying is that you certainly know that they were not following you?"

"I think so."

"Did you see the man who drove the stolen taxi?"

"I couldn't catch a look. It was all dark."

"What about the killed men?"

"Them also. I waited in my car until the ambulance and the feds arrived. Only after that you insisted that I look at the corpses, and I didn't recognize any of them."

"The stolen cab owner's description of the thief is that he is tall, thin-haired, and a with brown jacket. He limps."

"It is kind of resembling, but that man had a bracket on his head."

"The man you saw, did he limp?"

"I think not."

"If it was some kind of conflict between them, the killer would have killed you as well to get rid of any eyewitness. Can you tell me why that did not happen?"

"I can't."

"Who helped you?"

"As a former Special Force who has participated in war, I know the first medical treatment."

"It's you who called the police and the ambulance, right?"

"Of course."

"If it was their beef, why did they fire at you?"

"Maybe he was shooting at the other guy and one of the bullets got me by accident."

"You had a gun. Why didn't you fire back for self-defense?"

"At first, I didn't understand what was going on, and when I did, it was too late. After the trauma I had in the army, my hands shake, I can't aim straight."

"Did any of your friends visit you after your short arrest?"

"No. Nobody came to visit after what happened, and my wife's at the hospital."

"But after Ms. Beth's murder, Michael was arrested for resisting Sheriff Caster somewhere near your house. He said that he was coming to visit you. When did you see him last time?"

"Unfortunately, I haven't seen Michael in a long time."

"Mr. George, taxi driver's description of the thief is quite similar to Michael's characteristics. You, on the other hand, are stating the opposite."

"Maybe. I just don't get why would Michael be there at that time of the night."

"I think I should talk to Mr. Michael myself to find out answers to these questions. Mr. Bradley, it's our duty to protect you. Call me if anything disturbing or suspicious happens." He left his card and left the ward.

The agent suspected that it was Michael at the scene, but he decided to meet him before calling him to the department. He went to Michael's address of residence but couldn't find him there. He tried calling; the number was out of reach.

It was past midnight. There was no news from the two men sent to kill George. The boss was worried and nervous. Time was passing. Soon it was going to be morning. At first, he wanted to send some men after them, but then he changed his mind and decided to wait and see.

The gang members who watched TV news were hesitant to tell the boss the bad news. The news did not identify their names but showed a photograph of the two young men who were murdered. They asked the citizens to inform the police if anyone knows anything about them. Their names will be kept a secret to protect their rights. Anderson decided that it was time to tell the boss; he had no other choice.

The news was shocking to the boss. After Anderson told him that his little brother was murdered, Arnoldo was devastated. He locked himself into the room for two days, didn't let anyone come, and didn't eat anything. He regretted giving this mission to Alberto; he was blaming himself. Alberto was the youngest in the family. He took care of his young brother after they were orphaned. Arnoldo made a lot of money in a short time after they crossed the U.S. border with a small group. He was dealing drugs. By increasing his manpower, he was increasing his turf. He loved his brother dearly; always tried to protect him from harm, always made sure that the difficult and dangerous task was done by someone else. Alberto was never happy about that.

Alberto was always a misbehaving child and always stood out among others. He never listened to his brother's orders and was always thinking about getting together his own gang. He had finally done it. After forming his gang, he started going against his brother's rules even more and frequently got involved in criminal activities. Anderson was an opposition to him. Arnoldo always discussed the most important matters with Anderson. Alberto thought that either his brother thought he was useless or he didn't trust his brother enough to get him involved. Alberto's only goal was to make a lot of money and show that he is better than everyone else. He didn't want to depend on Arnoldo anymore.

The boss was still shaken. He blamed himself for the loss of his brother. It was a mistake; it was his mistake. He couldn't accept the fact that his little brother was gone. He should've taken care of it by himself. It was supposed to be an easy job; he did not expect this outcome. It didn't make sense that Alberto was killed on the forest road. Maybe they followed George and this happened. But how did it happen? How did they kill him? How did George survive? They said that he can't use a gun after the injury. Arnoldo kept asking questions by himself, trying to come up with answers. Considering that George was wounded lightly, someone must have helped him. Who is that? He wanted to find that person and end his life with his own hands—get revenge for his brother. Anderson was starting to worry for the boss. His health condition kept getting worse. At a moment like this, it's even scary to call a doctor.

The police hung the photos of the victims all around the town in restaurants, cafes, bars, and all public places, trying to identify the dead, especially among younger citizens. None of them seem to know them. The ones who did know them were too scared to talk. The boss called Anderson over. Anderson was shocked when he noticed drastic changes that happened to Arnoldo in such a short time. His hair was significantly grayer than before; his waist was bent.

"Find a way to send one of the boys to meet with Carl and get me detailed information. How did it happen? How did that bastard survive? Who helped him? I need to know everything. Go and find out where they are going to bury the kids. It probably will be the graveyard for the unknown. Which one is it going to be? I need to know. Tell the sheriff I want to meet him. Tell him I need an answer. He can choose the time and place for a meeting. I can go to our usual spot too. I don't need to remind you every time to be careful. I give you full control for now under my supervision. Meet with Alberto's gang and tell them what I told you. They will obey my orders from now on. Any mistake or betrayal will cost them their lives. They will act according to my plans. If someone doesn't cooperate, you can finish them without asking me. Soon enough, I will go and see them."

Michael spent his time in various places. It wasn't safe to go back home during daytime. He was planning his next moves. He thought about the cabin in the woods and planned his way and timing. It was logical that they meet during daytime; any kind of light during the night could draw attention. Having such a discreet meeting place could only mean that there will be members from different gangs. The reason for their sudden gathering at the cabin could be for planning their next moves, and they weren't going to be there too long. It was serious. The incident from last night was not to be taken lightly. If the taxi driver saw him from behind, he could give some kind of description to the police. He was sure that George's statement would be that he doesn't know the man who helped him. On the other hand, he had to put an end to his suspicions about Beth's involvement in the gang. He was certain that Sheriff Caster was involved in all of this, but he had to keep quiet since he had no solid evidence to prove his thought. The planted diamond earring was Caster's plan, but it didn't work out. Now the enemy would go into different measures to fulfill his plan. Last night's incident is an example. Michael was worried for George and Luisa. How is George doing? If he's at the hospital, he will be safe for now. He wished that George would stay a little longer at the hospital and get treated. What about Luisa? He decided to meet with her and clear some things out.

There had to be someone helping him in all of this. He decided to finally meet with the sheriff George talked about. He would go and visit Sarah's parents afterward.

It was late in the night. Michael was exhausted, but he had to keep going. He forgot his pain medication but decided not to return home for it.

He managed to reach the area where he would meet the sheriff. He was really tired. It was dark, cold, and quiet in the forest. He lay on one of the benches to rest. Lack of sleep was troubling for him. He kept closing his eyes for short periods and walking around not to fall asleep and lying back on the bench.

"Mr. Michael."

He woke up quickly and sat straight up. His hand was inside his jacket, holding on to his gun.

"There's no reason to worry, Mr. Michael."

"Who are you?" He pretended to not know the officer.

"We have met. I guess you didn't recognize me without the uniform. I believe that Mr. George informed you about my wish to meet with you."

"State your name."

"Sheriff Brook Cletus. You look really tired."

"I'm sick, I'm angry. What else is there? You wanted to see me. Here you go, I'm listening."

"My goal is to clear some unsolved matters and by cooperating with each other to get out of this mess altogether."

"You are a police officer and I'm just an ordinary citizen. We trust you with our own safety and security."

"That's correct, but sometimes there are matters that designated citizens can be helpful to the law enforcement. A person with the set of skills like you should not feel unwanted and unappreciated. We need help from people like you."

"There are plenty of people like me."

"We are both involved in things that are happening. Somebody is trying to realize their dirty plans and make us look bad in all of this mess."

Michael pretended to now know what the sheriff was talking about. "Whom do you suspect and on what basis? From the way you are talking, I think you, too, are in the center of attention. Do you know that? They can take you in right away as a suspect."

"Of course. But I'm being cautious. I watch every move of Caster until I get a solid evidence of his crime. To be honest, I went to his house as his old-time partner trying to find answers to some questions. But his reaction made me suspect him even more." Brook Cletus talked about what happened between him and his partner.

"How did he greet you when you went to his house? Did you think that it was strange of him not to invite you in?"

"I suspected something, but I didn't want to push my chances too much. I pretended to not care about that. There was a smoke smell in the room, and I saw a cigar butt on the ashtray. I knew that there were strangers there. Carl never smokes cigars."

"Don't take your enemies for a fool. It's the number-one rule for Special Forces. You are on their blacklist now. Watch your back from now on. Purpose of your visit was just to clear some things as a friend and partner, but they see you as a potential threat to their plans. They will try to get rid of you. You need to be very careful! There's a woman inside the gang. Her address is known, but it's doubtful that she will stay there after the incident. There's no information whether that house belongs to her or not. They will hide the woman after the incident, for sure, or maybe kill her."

"You know everything that happened. There are a lot of dark corners in this crime. We are against an organized criminal gang." The sheriff reminded Michael of the seriousness of this case.

"We need to prove that Caster is involved in this. I don't know if that woman is still alive or not. For now, I don't believe that she is dead. If they wanted her dead, they would have killed her alongside Beth. Perhaps this woman was helping with Beth's murder and gained the gang's vote of trust. But where and how? You can't keep the rabbit in the bag forever. Sooner or later, the rabbit will come out. But when and where? She will probably change her appearance. I am a little familiar with her facial characteristics. This woman is very mysterious. It's going to take time for me to find her. I need you to do one thing for me. Protect George and his family. He is ill. He can't even use a gun straight anymore. Find them a good place to live. His wife's pregnant. We can only meet at night at the designated place after all the caution measures have been taken. I have plenty of trusted friends. I have my own plans about this. Unfortunately, that plan belongs to me, and I'm not going to share it with you. We can only meet when there is something that needs our help to each other and cooperate on some issues. Take care of yourself. It's an honor to win such a friend like you."

"I will find them a temporary place to stay. I think George will stay at the hospital a few more days."

"Why?"

"You don't know what happened yesterday?"

"No. What happened to him?"

"He's wounded, but don't worry. He's doing good now." When Sheriff Cletus told Michael the brief story of what happened yesterday, he noticed the facial changes on Michael.

"You go and talk to him. Tell him everything, that I'm not gonna be able to see him for some time. Can't risk being at the center of attention. I talked to him about this. Remind him what I said. He knows. I will find him after all of this is left behind. You should be careful too. We need to be patient and cautious while dealing with this enemy. Let's try and make our friendship last."

"Thank you."

"Thank you. We shall meet again soon."

"Of course. Good-bye."

After the sheriff left, Michael headed to one of the restaurants close by. He was happy that he had his wallet with him; he was starving. After eating out, Michael called a taxi, planning to go to Sarah's. He could talk to the neighbor, discuss some things, and take necessary things from the house while protecting. Going home was dangerous right now. If Sheriff Caster is involved in this, he would know that the man helping George was Michael. Just like they did with George, they could send some men to his house.

He gave the taxi driver wrong directions on purpose. He got out of the cab somewhere near his neighbor's house and walked the rest of the road while checking the dark street corners. He approached the back door to the house and rang the doorbell.

"Who is it?"

"It's me, Michael."

The door opened. "Welcome, son. You surprised me with your visit."

"I'm sorry to disturb you at this time, but there's a reason for my visit."

"Please come in. I was worried sick for you. I called your home several times. The lights were turned off at your house. It got me worried."

"I wasn't home. Is it quiet there?"

"I always watch your house."

"Michael, welcome. How have you been? I haven't seen you in a long time. I was worried for you."

"Thank you, ma'am. How are you?"

"Not good. We haven't heard any news about Sarah for some time now. We keep waiting for something. I feel like she will come through that door at any moment and give me a hug. They called in to the department yesterday. They asked questions about her behavior and actions. They even reached out to the college she attended and got information about her from her mates and teachers. They were probably trying to see if she had any bad habits. Everyone said only positive things about her. The words of the officer at the department shocked me. I still can't get it out of my mind."

Michael looked at Lucas. "What was his name?"

"Officer Carl Caster."

"Be patient. Justice will be served very soon. There will always be people with no honor and self-respect. It's terrible that until they are proven guilty, innocent people will keep suffering."

"We were very worried for you after not seeing you for so long. We went to your house, called your number. You weren't there."

Michael didn't want to talk about that, so he changed the subject to something else. "Girls usually tell their secrets to their mothers."

"True, but she never had any secret from me. Her friend was a nice kid too. Everyone liked and respected her at the restaurant where she worked. I don't know if she had a boyfriend or was involved in anything bad. She never kept secrets from me." The mother started crying.

Michael hugged his crying neighbor. "Be patient, ma'am. I'm very sorry for what happened. She was very close and dear to me, just like you are. I have been looking for her ever since. Starting today, the first thing I do will be giving you some new information about your daughter Sarah. I hope that it will be good news.

"I need a recent photo of Sarah and your help. We must work together to get some things done."

"Thank you, Michael. I believe in you."

The neighbor noticed that Michael kept checking the outside from the window during their talk. He had a feeling that Michael was worried about something much more serious but decided that since he doesn't want to talk about it, there is no need to bring it up. It was probably better that way. He loved Michael as if he was his own, and his behavior was worrisome. Lucas Marchelo could see that Michael has not slept or rested in a long time. He asked Stella to prepare something to eat.

"So you will be staying at home tonight?"

"No. I have got some things to do first."

"Michael, what is so important to do in the middle of the night? I can see that you are really tired. If there's a problem about you spending the night at your place, you can stay the night here with us. Michael, I'm starting to worry for you. I think something is troubling you."

"You are right. I've come to some serious obstacles. It might cost me my life. Without even realizing, I found myself struggling in a swamp of trouble. There's one thing everybody is afraid of—it's being accused of something you have not done. You find the wrongs and try to make them right, only then you realize that the evil's power is much greater than you predicted. They have eyes and hands everywhere. If you slip for just one moment, they will get you in the blink of an eye."

"Michael, there's a reason you are hiding things from me. You shouldn't try to do everything by yourself. Don't risk everything."

"It's something that I have to take care of alone. If I need, I will ask a friend for help. For now, it's better this way. If someone asks, you haven't seen me. We are just neighbors, that's it. I won't be home from now on. If I ever come, I'll spend the night here at your place. If something dangerous or suspicious happens, remove the flower from the door and keep the kitchen lights on. Give me some old clothes and a coat. Watch over my house secretly. If you see something fishy happening around the house, call me and immediately delete my number from your phone. I won't bother you often. When it's safe and secure, I will come home. I will try to bring you some information about Sarah."

"Michael, I almost forgot to mention. Yesterday someone was looking for you. He kept on ringing the doorbell. He looked like a wealthy person."

"What did he look like?"

"Tall, handsome man. He arrived in an expensive car. He said he has a business in the neighboring state."

"He didn't give his name?"

"I asked. He said, 'Let it be a surprise.' He had a gift in his hand."

"It's strange. I wonder who it is. Maybe it's someone who served in the army with me."

"He said that he will come again. If he does, I will take his phone number."

"Let me know about it."

After Michael left, Lucas Marchelo sat in the kitchen thinking about what Michael had asked him to do and how to do it. He had to be careful. He checked his gun and bullets. He checked all the entrances and exits of the house. Everything seemed quiet. He wanted to sleep, but with all the thoughts in his mind, it was not easy.

Michael entered the house from the back door with a pistol in his hand. It was quiet. He went into his room and grabbed his phone on the table. It was turned off. Since he didn't have much time, he only took the most necessary items he needed and left the house.

It was his second night in a row that he was spending the night outside. Days were warm and the nights were cold. It was one o'clock. He wandered around. Today was Sheriff Brook Cletus's day off. He wanted to meet with the sheriff. He came to a park near the cafe they agreed to meet in and kept the restaurant on watch. Several hours passed. According to their agreement, he and Cletus needed to decide the time and place for their next meeting with the condition that each one of them had to be there on time. He noticed Brook coming. Since it was late, there were not many customers left at the restaurant.

The sheriff took a seat near the window and observed the surroundings. A little sparkle of flashlight from the park on the opposite side of the road drew his attention. The signal and the time was matching. It must be him.

"How's it going?"

"I want to ask you something about the last murder that happened. Do you have anything to do with that?"

"What do you mean? What murder are you talking about?"

"The night that George got wounded."

"You are not following the rules."

"Two men were murdered yesterday. George is at the hospital. In his statement, he said that he has nothing to do with the killings. He didn't see the killer either. Sheriff Caster is very angry. We haven't been able to ID the dead bodies yet and the killer."

"How's George doing?"

"He's OK. I think they will send him home soon."

"I wanted to meet with you for two things. The girl you see in this picture is very dear to me. She was at the restaurant when the robbery happened. Her friend was killed. Well, you know the rest."

"Of course! I knew her. That day she was working the night shift at the restaurant near the jewelry store. The restaurant has been shut down and the owner arrested—for illegal activity. Most of the workers at the restaurant were illegal immigrants. Restaurant management was not even able to present an accurate list of staff. Search for her is still on. I think she had a shift there that night."

"Do you have any information about her disappearance?"

"Considering the fact that Sarah and her friend were at the restaurant that night, she is either dead or kidnapped. Search goes on."

"I think so too. Did you talk to George?"

"Yes. I even found them a new place to stay."

"Thank you, my friend."

"Looking forward to seeing you again. Take care of yourself and never hesitate to call in for help."

It was nighttime. The moonlight illuminated the streets lightly. It was possible to see movements. He was near his own house, making sure it was OK to get inside and pick up a few important items. He approached the back door to check the floor mat. He always put little sign traps for himself in both door locks and floor mats; that way he would be aware of intrusion. The floor mat was moved; someone had been here. He suspected that they are still inside and reached for his gun. He got hit in the head and lost his consciousness.

He opened his eyes with difficulty. He had a severe headache. He tried to look around and saw three men standing on the side and talking to each other. It wasn't easy, but he could sense that they were talking about him. His hands were tied to the heat pipe. He tried moving his legs; they were tied up too. One of the men came closer.

"I told you that I would see you again. Here I am. Son of a bitch, are you so tough now?"

He punched Michael as hard as he could. Michael was shivering in pain. "Does it hurt? I feel you. It hurts losing a brother. You scarred me for life."

"Who are you? What do you want?"

"I'm Alberto's brother, the man you killed. You thought I can't find you? I know every house in this city. I hate myself for making this mistake. You killed him, you killed me. You destroyed my dreams and wishes. It's over. The same fate awaits your George too."

"Let's solve this like men, face-to-face."

"You have already done your part. It's my turn now. A bullet in the head would have been too easy for you. I'm gonna burn you alive in your own house."

"Boss, we are running out of time."

He hit Michael one more time, and Michal passed out again. "Burn down his house. I want him to suffer before he dies. Let this house be his grave. Make sure everything burns down to the ground before anyone is here to help."

The news that came into the department was a terrifying crime. Darren Edmond was in shock after what he heard. It was unbelievable.

The federals, police, fire truck, and ambulance arrived as quickly as possible, but the house was burned down to the ground. The owner of the was known, but nothing remained of the dead body, all ash.

This was big news in the city. After forensic investigation, it was proven that the house was set on fire on purpose, but there was not a single sample of evidence to prove that the owner, Michael Grady, did die burning in his house. The neighbor Lucas Marchelo said that he hadn't seen him in a long time. He was the one to call in about the fire. He reacted a little late because he was asleep.

There was something strange about the way this whole mess happened. Perhaps he had enemies and they wanted to get revenge by burning his house. But where's the owner? According to his neighbor's statement, he had been living the homeless life lately and came home very seldom. That was the general idea. It was important to know if he was alive or not. Search was conducted for citizen and ex-military Michael Grady. Darren Edmond had a mysterious feeling about Michael's disappearance.

He was in severe pain after getting burned on several parts of his body. The neighbors insisted that he go to the hospital to get treated, but Michael refused. Marchelo agreed to his terms, but he was really worried for Michael. It didn't take Michael too long to get better; the neighbors were taking good care of him. Michael owed them his life. He wasn't surprised when he heard that a search had been conducted to find him. This would help Michael implement his plans easier.

The owner walked into the room in a hurry.

"Michael, it's the same man. He's standing in front of your door."

"Go talk to him. Find out who he is!"

The man standing in front of Michael's house recognized the old man approaching.

"Hello."

"Hello, we have met before, right?"

"Yes. How could this happen?" The unknown man could not stop himself from crying. "A hero who survived a heavy war, how could this happen to him? I can't get out of shock since the moment I heard what happened."

"Excuse me, how did you know him? Is he a close relative?"

"He was more than a brother to me. We served together in the army. It's been a long time since I saw him. Last time, I drove a long way to get to this state to meet Michael and my other friend. I shouldn't have returned without seeing him. Is this an accident, or was he killed by someone? I wish I knew who his enemies were. I would kill them with my own hands."

"You are right. The reason why is unknown."

"There's no grave of his that I could visit either. Investigation is still on? Is it approved that he burned to death?"

"Calm down, son. Perhaps you should come over to my house, be my guest. You can go after you rest a bit."

"Thank you, Mister. I better get going. I see your hands and arms are burned as well. You were injured in this fire too? You were probably fighting the fire."

"Yes, it was a big fire, terrifying. Everything burned to the ground until the fire truck and the ambulance arrived, no matter what I tried. I'm getting treatment."

"Thank you. You did all you could. It seems it was his fate. Whatever, I should go." He started walking to his car. He got back in the car, looked at Michael's burnt house one last time, and suddenly had a change of heart. He reached into the glove box and took some money out. With money in his hand, he started walking toward the neighbor's door. He could not believe his eyes when he lifted his head up. It was Michael standing in front of him with the help of the old man and a stick. He had a light smile on his face.

"My friend, you are alive!"

The two old friends meet after a long time; such a scene that made everyone cry. It was a moment where two brave souls who survived the terrifying times of war together and had been separated from one another reunited. A true friendship scenery.

Roger Thomas's visit was like a holiday in the house. The homeowners showed their greatest hospitality as if he was their closest relative. Mrs. Marchelo put together a wonderful feast, and Roger was being very helpful to them. Michael was touched. After seeing his dear friend, he forgot all about his pain. After eating, Michael and Roger went downstairs together. They talked until midnight. Roger talked about himself first, how he decided to continue his father's business and develop his own business and even open a shop. He was doing good. Roger Thomas talked about the robbery that happened in the state and that the people responsible for that are hiding in this city. By explaining his purpose of visit, Roger wanted to ask his friend to help him with this matter. Michael gave him information about the crimes happening in the city. He talked about Beth's unknown murder, Sheriff Carl Caster's very suspicious behavior, and his and George's false arrest, and the gang that tried to lose any trail by burning everything to the ground, with Michael inside.

Now everyone, except for Roger and the neighbor, thought that Michael is dead; it was announced on the TV. Michael understood that all of this could be a part of federal agent Darren Edmond's plan to find new clues leading to the real criminals. He knew well that Michael was alive. He spread the false information to get the real killers relaxed. Michael already knew the boss and the rest of his gang who has been working in the city for a long time now; he saw them during their last incident. That's why he decided to go against them alone; it was too dangerous to get anyone else involved. He asked his friend to be careful. He talked about the mysterious woman who was involved in Beth's murder. Getting to her could reveal many secrets. She's nowhere to be found. Probably the criminals killed her or kept her as hostage. She could not have hidden for too long on her own. She will probably change her appearance as well. Michael described her physical attributes, facial lines, and every piece of detail that could be useful, and asked his friend to make contact with Lucas if he ever does come across her. Maybe these murders have another kind of connection between them. Roger was well informed about everything now.

"What are you going to do now?" Roger asked his friend.

"An important test awaits me. I have a lot to do. If I make it alive, I'll start a new life. That's when I'll need your help."

"I plan on giving you that helping hand right now. Do you really think that I would rather think about money and business after all that happened? Michael, don't ask me to stay aside in something like this. I'm with you at this dark moment."

The friends hugged. "Thank you, Roger. You are a true friend. I trust you."

"Starting today, we move and act together. We're together on good and bad days."

Roger was decisive. Alvaro's death was difficult to accept; he blamed himself for it. Roger went to his friend's house, gave her his condolences, and visited his grave. He asked his father to give Alvaro's wife a job at the factory. He printed out the picture of the criminal. At home, he said that he has some important matters and asked to leave for a couple of days. He returned to the neighboring state with a fake ID to follow his own plan.

He made changes to his appearance every day in order not to get recognized. He was spending some time at the city's clubs, restaurants, and casinos, but he found nothing useful. At last, he decided to go to the most famous casino in the city. It was the place where the rich people of the city go. He took a seat and ordered a whisky. He started watching around. A man who came in with a bodyguard and went up to the second floor drew his attention. The moment that man walked in, the casino became alive. After spending some time at the casino, the man left. It looked like this man was the owner of the casino. After a while, another younger man came down from the second floor and started giving orders to employees. It seems that he is in charge. Later on, he found out that this man was Anderson and he was actually managing the place. But who was the man that came in with a bodyguard? Why did that man let this person take care of the business? These are the types of things that raise questions and suspicions that could lead to solving many mysteries. Time and patience were needed for that. Alek wanted to realize his plans in this casino. It was possible that the criminal he was looking for would come to this place as a customer sooner or later. Having a good connection with the place owner could be useful. He started implementing his next steps toward that plan. He needed help from his close friends.

An expensive car pulled up in front of the casino. The driver approached the gate.

"Stop! Who are you?"

"I'm Mr. Alek Castello's driver. He wishes to meet with the owner of the casino. He's expecting Mr. Castello."

"Wait here!"

The casino worker approached the car and opened the back passenger door. He got out of the car and entered the establishment. The bodyguard standing at the door, who looked like a bodybuilder, went up to the second floor with Mr. Castello. The driver had to wait downstairs. The security guard opened the door, and Mr. Castello entered the location on the second floor. The man sitting on the sofa with two girls blew the cigar smoke at Mr. Castello when he saw him come in.

"I manage the casino. I have never seen you here before. Am I right to assume that you have come here to gamble? This is a serious establishment. It's not like other places for many reasons. We are pleased to see that you have chosen our establishment for gambling. You will be informed of our gaming rules. Beautiful ladies will be at your service as well. Extra services will cost you money. If you obey the rules, you are always welcome here."

"My pleasure to know you. I have my own rules about gambling. There are a lot of people who lost to me by these rules. I believe my opponents will regret facing me on the table."

"It's just a game. Losing and winning are part of the game. The rules are strict, and the punishments for those who break rules are severe. You look like a fine gentleman. I am looking forward to witnessing your gambling abilities."

The door opened. A woman entered the room.

"What do you want? Arlen, you son of a bitch, I told you not to let anyone in without my permission."

"Darling, I thought maybe you should let me go out for half an hour."

"Not allowed!"

Arlen grabbed the woman's arm and tried to take her outside. When the woman wanted to slap him, the bodyguard held her by the hand. "Consider yourself dead if you ever touch me like that again." The woman pulled back her arm and left the room.

"I told them a thousand times to lay off of that shit! My apologies, Mister, there's been a misunderstanding. She is in control of our girls, and she only drinks this much at night."

"I need to get going. Looking forward to meeting with you again." The client stood up.

"You didn't present yourself."

"Alek Castello."

"So you are from the same region as us. Nice to meet you, Alek. See you soon."

As soon as the new client left the room, Anderson mimicked Arlen to close the door. "Let two of the boys follow him. I need information about his identity and his address. I have a suspicious feeling about him."

After leaving the casino, he headed to one of the expensive restaurants at the city. He took a seat and ordered some food. After finishing his food, he went out of the restaurant and approached the homeless beggar on the street, gave him some money, and handed the takeaway food to him that he ordered at the restaurant.

"Thank you. You are very generous." The homeless man showed his gratitude to the generous man and started eating the food he just received. The homeless man finished his food and threw the food packaging to his side and opened his hands to continue begging for money. The homeless man watched around for a bit and took the same takeaway food package and put it into his own bag of belongings. He left the area right after.

It was past midnight. There was a knock at the door.

"Come in, Michael. We were worried for you."

"I'm sorry to disturb you. Please excuse me." He came down, changed his clothes, and took a seat at the table. He took out a piece of paper among his belongings and started reading the notes carefully.

There is a little resemblance. Perhaps they made changes to her appearance to avoid recognition, he thought. He decided that he has to keep the casino under control and find out more about that woman, including her address.

Michael kept watching the casino his friend mentioned. Several days of watching the area, there was no result. Nothing useful came out of it. Even though he changed his looks to a homeless beggar, he was still hesitant to get closer to the casino. They may recognize him. That's why he was not able to identify the people coming in and out of the casino. He needed a better, closer look. On the other hand, staying at that place for too long could draw unwanted attention to him. He had to find another way.

Alek came to the casino every day. He would gamble. Sometimes he won, sometimes he lost, but he made sure that he spent plenty of money at the place to become a regular customer. Anderson came downstairs every day to check and control the gambling tables, gave some orders to workers, and went back to his office room on the second floor. It was obvious from his behavior that he had become a heavy drug user. Alek had earned respect at the casino by regularly gambling and spending a lot of money at the establishment. The man named Carlos, whom he was looking for, was nowhere to be seen. He showed a photo of him to Michael as well.

Roger, known as Alek, presented himself as a rich customer who is into gambling. Two ex-Special Force soldiers were up against the same criminal, drug-dealing gang separately without knowing about each other's actions.

Confidential information entered the federal bureau. The information was about the man who came to Alvaro's house and presented himself as a relative. He gave his condolences to Alvaro's wife and asked about the incident, about the owner of the workshop's age and appearance, and where Alvaro worked. He also stated that the workshop owner is involved in Alvaro's murder, and as his relative, he swore to get revenge. Alvaro's wife knew the owner well, but she said nothing of note to the relative and called the police right away. There were some questions, though. Perhaps, for some reason, the criminal has started to show interest in Roger. He had to inform Roger Thomas about this as soon as possible and ask him to watch out for anything.

Roger Thomas was called regarding this matter. For some reason, he did not answer the phone call. He wasn't at home either. His father said that Roger had left for some important business for a few days and that he had been unable to get in touch with him ever since. The old owner was worried for his son. Roger Thomas's disappearance was surprising to his family and relatives, but Agent Edmond had an idea about where Roger could be. Perhaps the former officer had put his own life at risk despite the laws that prohibit him from doing so.

Nighttime came. He left his house. His plan was to dress up as a homeless man and go to one of the most popular streets for drug dealing and do what is necessary. He walked around the streets for a while. It was a really dangerous place; danger around every corner. He was already tired and hungry. He took a seat on the sidewalk to rest. Two homeless men across the street were staring at him, looking like he was in their turf.

"Hey, man! You don't know the rules in the street?"

"I took a seat to rest. I'm tired."

"Go sit somewhere else. This place isn't free."

"How much?"

"You got money? What's your name?"

"Frank."

"I'm Fidel, and this is my friend Aldo. Looks like you were lucky today. Me and my friend are starving. Come on, man, buy us some dinner."

Michael quietly stood up and walked into the cafe nearby.

"What do you want?" The employee of the cafe stopped him from entering in a rude manner.

"I'm gonna buy some food. I got money." The homeless man showed the dirty and wrinkled money bills and coins in his hand.

"OK, go and buy whatever you want. But you are not sitting inside."

The homeless man approached the counter and asked for a pizza and cola drinks for a party of three. People in the cafe kept their distance from the homeless man. Michael took the food and the drinks and returned back.

"Hey, man! Look, he is back!"

"Yeah, he has food in his hands!"

"Looks like he did it, man. He paid for dinner."

"Here you go, guys. I was lucky today. A nice and generous man gave me a twenty-dollar bill today. He asked me for an address, and I helped. That's it. And now, you guys are my guests."

"Thanks, man. You look like a nice guy. We are friends now. If you want, you can stay here with us. It's not safe here at all."

"Your friend doesn't talk?"

"He is usually quiet. He's a drug addict. Anything he makes during the day, he spends it on drugs and alcohol. He used to be rich, but his cheater friends ruined him. They were going to kill his friend because of his gambling debt. Aldo paid all of his friend's debt. Later on, his friend became rich by selling illegal drugs and got Aldo hooked up on it to keep him depending. He used to supply him with drugs before. He stopped doing that also. He's getting more aggressive because he can't afford to buy drugs today. He's a different person when he's not using."

"I also do drugs."

Aldo turned to Michael as soon as he heard him say those words. "What? Don't worry, man, I got you. But I don't know where to get them."

"There are some dealers around the corner. They have the good stuff, but they only sell to the people they know. Their boss ordered them to do so. Everybody is afraid of the boss. They have their regular customers. We are the only bums that they sell to."

"What do I say? We can buy from the people you know. We can go now if you want."

"That place is just two blocks away, but it's not safe going there during the day. We should go at night."

"All right, let's wait for nighttime."

"I don't mind, but they won't let you in. We'll tell them you are a friend and you have cash."

"OK, I don't mind."

There was a knock at the door.

"Who is it?"

"It's the usual bums." A loud laughter was heard, ordering to open the door.

"These guys make good money. If the people giving you tips knew that you spend their charity money on drugs, they would lose their minds," the same man replied and laughed out loud.

"You need to keep these bums under control. You have been warned to be maximum careful with these kinds of people."

"These are regulars. They know how we work. They are afraid of us. They won't dare to do anything wrong."

"Don't rush to give them the goods right away. Go and check out the surroundings first. Make them wait."

"Don't be afraid. They are regular customers."

Three people entered the room.

"Who's this asshole? I told you before, no strangers allowed!"

"Tom, this is our new friend. We didn't make much money today. He is buying today. He has cash."

"I have never seen him before. Eddie, have you seen this guy?"

"No, I haven't seen him before."

"You dumbasses, I told you many times not to bring any stranger in here!" Tom yelled at them.

"Don't worry, guys, I will be with them from now on. I will pay your money up front, no debt."

"We don't sell drugs. Get out!"

"He doesn't look like an addict."

"Show me his arms." Tom pointed at Michael and asked two men near him to roll up Michael's sleeves and show his arms.

"Guys, no need for that. I will show you my arms." With a sudden maneuver, he grabbed the man on his right and twisted his neck. He then reached Tom and pulled him closer, trying to punch him. A shot fired at Michael hit Eddie on the chest. In the blink of an eye, Michael dropped the gun from Tom's hand with a swift kick. Michael kicked Tom in the head. He fell down to the floor. Michael picked up the gun from the floor and pointed at Tom's head.

"Who are you? What do you want? Son of a bitch, do you even know whom you are dealing with? They will chop you into small pieces."

"I know damn well whom I am dealing with. If you wanna live, you will give me their names and address. You don't have much time."

"Fuck you! Bastard!"

A shot fired. Michael shot Tom in the leg, Tom was shivering in pain. "What are you talking about? I don't know what you want? God damn you to hell!"

"You know that you don't have much time. You tell me the truth, I will leave you. If you don't, I'm gonna have to shoot you. Tell me, where's your boss? Where is he hiding that bitch?"

"I'm scared if I tell you, they'll kill me!"

"That is, if I don't kill you first. You can still have a chance to run away and hide. Where's Elma? Where are they keeping Sarah?"

"Elma is at Alberto's place. They kept the girl at the place where Alberto used to rent. I don't know where she is now. She must be at that house, if she is still alive. What else do you want to know?"

"Who's your boss?"

"Answer me! Who's your boss?"

"I don't know his real name. Everybody calls him the boss."

"Where's his hideout?"

"I swear to God I know nothing about that!"

"Tell me the address where Sarah is!"

"I don't know exactly, but it's in the suburbs, the woods area."

"That's enough for now, my friend. I'm not gonna kill you. But think about your future."

As Michael, with a gun in his hand, turned around to leave the room, as if he felt something, he quickly turned back and stopped Tom's knife-holding hand from striking. Michael twisted Tom's hand. The knife fell on the floor. Aldo quickly grabbed the knife and stuck it to Tom's back. Tom gave his life right there on the floor in agonizing pain. Michael looked at the homeless men.

"Guys, I will help you with money. Get away from these places for some time. Make changes to your appearance. Don't let anyone recognize you. It's better that way. If you want to survive, you will do as I say. Don't be seen anywhere for some time. If I make it, I will come and find you. This is serious."

"Thank you, man. You took revenge from these assholes for me too. Don't worry for us, it's not safe for us to stay here anyway. Good luck to you, my friend." The two homeless guys disappeared into the darkness.

Michael took the drug dealers' phones and Tom's gun and got out of there.

When Carl Caster and his partner heard about the incident, they drove to the crime scene, but the feds were already there. Even some media members were there too. The police department chief looked really angry. Seeing two of his officers on duty arrive at the scene after the federals was not a good sign. He was not happy about it.

Special Agent Darren Edmond was thinking about what happened. According to witness statements, the man who did this limped when walking. He looked like a homeless guy, but it was obvious that he was good at what he was doing. He left no trace behind. The gun used was not found either. The reason for him to kill these guys and take the weapon was a mystery. Bullet shells taken from the crime scene gave plenty of information about the owner of the gun. The gun belonged to a citizen who died a year ago. The gun was first fired by one of the three dead. It means the gun belonged to one of them. No kind of ID was found on the bodies of the deceased. None of the witnesses recognized the man who killed them. Perhaps some of them did recognize him but were too afraid to admit anything. At last, information came in that the deceased were indeed drug dealers, but the reason why they were killed remained unknown.

Darren Edmond was waiting for the forensics results; it was vital in solving this case. But he was also aware that just the forensics report alone would not be enough to conclude this crime case. It seemed that an organized crime gang was still active in the state. There's another reason why they are still not found.

"Boss, I think the time you gave to the sheriff is up. He was supposed to give information about the password and the person who took the diamond set. There's nothing from him yet. I think he forgot about it completely. He is too calm at all times. It's suspicious to me. I just hope that we don't see police at the door one day when we open it. It's time to have a serious talk with him."

"You are right. We agreed on a time and place to meet, but there's time for that."

"He will be at his home tomorrow night. We can go there at night."

"Deal. Don't forget to make sure it's safe. Send someone over and watch over the house during the day. We need to make sure it's totally safe before going there."

There was a knock at the door. It was one of the gang members. He said something to Anderson's ear in a hurry.

"Are you sure it's our guys?"

"Of course."

"What happened? Inform me now!"

Anderson approached Arnoldo with the other gang member. "Boss, it doesn't look good. Three of our guys are dead. One of them is shot, the other's neck broken, and Tom is stabbed."

"What does it mean? Who did this?" Arnoldo smashed his hand to the table. "Speak clearly. What happened?"

"Mister, there were three of them. Two of them were the usual bums we see around there. We know them. Our man in the area saw them, but he had never seen the third one. The police and the feds are at the crime scene now."

Arnoldo looked at Anderson in frustration.

"Somebody's after us, boss. We need to do something about it, and quickly."

"How did that man look?"

"He was just another homeless guy. He limped."

"The killer is not just some guy. The description is very similar to Michael's appearance."

"You are talking foolishly. We killed that man!"

"A single man cannot do so much damage to three men. There's something else behind this. Perhaps these junkies did it all together to get their hands on the drugs."

"You fool! How can the three junkies deal with three armed men? At least one of them could have been dead."

"Those two junkies probably took the third one to them for money."

"Boss, maybe they had some problem between them during trade?"

The boss gave a mean look to Anderson. "How did he look? Tell me again!" the boss yelled at the gang member.

"He was tall, had sparse hair, and had a beard. Tall man limped when he walked."

"These signs are very similar to Michael, whom we killed and burned his house to the ground. Anyone seen him in the area before this?"

"We asked the kids on the street, the junkies, and even the prostitutes. They said that a man with these attributes lived as a junkie for some time in a different region. Nobody saw him in this area before this. He probably kept changing his spots."

"Tell the boys to watch out for all the bums of the city. If they see someone matching these attributes, bring him to me at all costs. Find the other two bums, make them talk everything, and make sure to kill them at the end. Maybe those junkies know that jerk's place. Hurry up!"

Just like his friend asked, he hid the jewelry. After his death, he was the only one who knew the place of the jewelry. He was ecstatic about the fact that now he has such a piece of jewelry. It was in a safe place. He kept quiet and watched everything that was going on. He was protecting himself while waiting for things to dissolve. He was not happy about hearing that Elma is being kept at Alberto's house. But she wasn't always home. Sometimes he visited the house and checked to make sure that the jewel is still safe. He was nervous about it. He had the key copies and he hid it somewhere near the house to keep it safe.

Sheriff Carl Caster was facing a difficult situation. The chief used slanderous words toward him because of his negligence at work; he was tired of it. On the other hand, he had to give out written statements several times during Agent Darren Edmond's investigation. It looked like he was a suspect; he could feel it. The time given by the boss to find out about the password and the stolen jewelry was about to be finished. Another thing worrying the sheriff was the cell phones of the deceased could be found at the crime scene. He was relieved to hear that no phones were found at the scene.

Carl Caster was really tired when he arrived at home, as usual. He was still angry. The boss was going to want to meet with him regarding the incident that happened at night and about the stolen jewelry set. He promised Arnoldo that he would give some information about the password, but he had nothing to show for. They gave him time, and if he didn't have anything to tell them, he might become a suspect; they might kill him. The sheriff had to be prepared for what might happen. He had the official duty gun on him, but he decided to take, as an extra caution step, his father's old rifle and bullets and hid it under the table in a secret compartment. He took the whisky from the fridge and took a seat on the sofa. Remembering what happened, he kept asking questions to himself and trying to come up with answers with a clear and quiet mind.

He overheard when the officers at the department were talking about what happened at the birthday and whom Agent Darren Edmond interrogated. Sheriff Caster found out that a woman at the party named Bella saw a woman taking jewelry from Beth's handbag as she stated in her statement to the FBI. If it was so, then Sheriff Cletus knew about this for sure because Bella is Brook's wife. Bella was able to accurately explain what happened at the party and the woman's facial and physique attributes to the feds. Carl talked to Cletus about this, but his partner denied knowing anything about it. The relationship between Carl and Brook was not like it used to be. He applied to work the day shifts because of problems with his health. It was mentally hard for Carl and even got him worried about it. Carl had an approximate idea about why Brook was trying to get away from him. It seemed Brook suspected something about him. After a week, he saw Brook Cletus working the night shift with another officer. It was alarming. He had to meet with Elma and get some answers before it's too late. He already knew that she lives at Alberto's place.

The sheriff decided to meet with Elma. It was about time they meet and discuss some important matters. This woman still had plenty of mystery in her. There was a possibility that she was involved in the murder of Beth. On the other hand, she was wanted. If she got caught and talked, all of their plans could be unveiled before the cops. If he didn't act on time, it would end well neither for the gang members nor for him. By getting rid of Elma, they could put an end to all of their worries. He was going to propose it to the boss tonight. He thought if it wasn't for the missing piece of jewelry, Anderson would have done her the same way he did with Beth. That day, who knew that Beth had the jewelry? Elma; the sheriff's wife, Bella, who was at the party; Anderson, whom she informed; and the boss. According to what Elma said, a man in the kitchen darkness took the jewel from her and ran away. Who was that man? Why didn't that man cause any harm to Elma? Beth was murdered, and yet Elma lives. Why didn't they kill her? He had to see Elma. He planned to pressure her to talk and then kill her. This woman had something to do with the missing jewelry and the stolen password. He was going to go to Alberto's house to find Elma. He was anxious for nighttime to come so that he could go and find her.

He looked at the time. It was getting late; she was probably home by now. He pulled his car over far from the house. He wanted to continue the rest of the road on foot. The house was dark; it seemed that she wasn't home yet, or maybe she was asleep already. In any case, the streetlights should have been left on.

He slowly approached the house. When he wanted to ring the doorbell, a quick flashlight reflection appeared on the window. It looked like someone was home. He tried to peek in through the window. He saw someone coming downstairs with a flashlight in hand. It was suspicious that this person was walking around in the dark with a flashlight. "This person is either a thief or from the gang. What the hell is he doing? If he was from the gang, he would know that after Boss's brother Alberto died, only Elma is allowed to stay here." The sheriff was becoming more nervous. Time was short; he had to act quickly. He took out his duty weapon and tried to hide and wait, but it was too late. The door opened. Caster recognized the man immediately.

"Good evening."

"What are you doing here?"

"I need to see Elma about something."

"Chief doesn't allow her to see anyone."

"Is she at home or not?"

"She won't be here today. What is it? I can deliver a message if you want."

"Why are you here?"

He replied to the question with another question. "How long have you been here?"

"I just arrived."

"So did I. I had something to do. Wanna get in?"

"No, it's not right. I'm tired anyway."

"OK, where's your car? I'm on foot."

"I can drop you off somewhere."

"All right."

"I hope you won't be going around and telling everyone that you saw me here. I told everyone that I am going out with my girlfriend. Boss won't like it if he knows I was here."

"Don't worry about it. I'm gonna ask you a favor too. Get me a meeting with Elma tomorrow."

"I know you wanted to see her. Sometimes she sleeps here. I will bring her tomorrow. What time will you come? Maybe she won't open the door for you and call the boss. I know where the spare keys are. I'll tell you. Weren't you supposed to meet with the boss today?"

"I see that you are a smart guy. I like you. I will value your friendship if you help me with this. I will ask for one more day from the boss. I have to talk to Elma about some important things."

"I have a lot of secrets."

"Really?"

"Of course."

"About what?"

"More like about whom—about that slut, of course. I'm gonna let you in on a secret, but you gotta pay me share up front. I'm not gonna give you all the information at first. This'll be a secret between us. I want some of the money for now. I have an unfinished business with that bitch."

"I'm in. Wanna go to my place?"

"OK. You got good wine?"

"I got just the one for you."

"Let's go, man."

He found out about the terrible incident that happened in the other state from his friend. His friend Alvaro's death was shocking to Carlos. He didn't even imagine that things would turn out this tragically. Carlos knew that they were after him. He frequently changed his appearance and the places he lived. It was all because of the owner, Carlos thought to himself. The information he got was that the owner called the police about the diamond stone, and an arrest warrant for Alvaro was given right away. It looked like Alvaro chose to put an end to his own life instead of selling out his friend.

The police were after Carlos, but arrest operations were unsuccessful. Carlos knew well what to expect if he got caught. His plan was to get revenge from the owner and escape the country once and for all. The police were after him already; the court's decision was not going to go easy on him. He had to do it while he still had his freedom. Carlos sent his friend to the neighboring state to find out about the owner, but the owner wasn't there. Where could he be? There's mystery behind the owner's disappearance. First thing that came to Carlos' mind was, what if the owner was looking for him too? What if he came after Carlos to this state? Maybe. He knew the owner was an ex-Special Force soldier. Information about his physical attributes was vital; his friend was the one to get Carlos that information. The most significant attribute was the scar on Roger Thomas's face. He had to act quick and do what's necessary at a moment like this. Get it done.

Michael was exhausted. He left the area in a hurry and got away as far as he could. Eyewitnesses from the scene were going to describe him to the police. A man matching those descriptions was being searched by the police, federals, and gang members.

He found a quiet and safe spot to sit, took out his phone, and started writing down the contact numbers on his notepad. Most of the contacts did not have names but rather signs or signals. After writing down the numbers, he took out the SIM cards from all three of his phones, put them in a bag, and hid the bag in the small pocket created by the tree's two big connecting branches. He needed the gun. He checked the bullets; only five left. If Sarah was still alive, they could kill her as a witness to the incident. Considering how big the area and the number of houses is, he had to scout the whole place first.

He walked around in the dark parts of the park for some time. Going there by car or even walking on the sidewalk was too dangerous; it's better he stayed hidden. He was really tired and sat on one of the benches nearby. Exhaustion and hunger were getting to his nerves. He needed sleep and food. He took out the sandwich from the bag, which he bought earlier, and ate it, and finished the drink too. He got comfortable on the bench as he covered his head and neck with his hat and a scarf.

He fell asleep right then and there. He was having nightmares. He couldn't give a meaning to what was happening. He is being choked, tortured. He screams in pain. Someone's trying to calm him down. He wakes up to a sound.

"Sir, you can't sleep here. Get up!"

The woman cleaning the park streets was calling him. "I don't understand why these youngsters are ruining their lives like this."

"I'm sorry, ma'am."

"You were screaming in your sleep. I felt bad for you, that's why I woke you up. You are a young man, why are you throwing away your life with such an idle lifestyle?"

"I have no place to stay, ma'am. Don't worry for me. I'll get out of here now."

"How can I not worry, son? You are young. Why do you destroy your future with such a miserable life? You are probably as old as my son."

"What can I do? No house, no job, no family."

"I feel bad for you. My life is not any better than yours. I have a house, so what? War took away my only son. Now I live alone among four walls. It stresses me so much that I don't even wanna go home. Your clothes don't look very warm to me. Let's go home, it's close by."

He was happy to hear her offer. They arrived at the woman's home after a short walk together in the twilight of the morning. The three-room house was neat and clean and had a little yard up front. Lots of pictures were hung on the walls.

The woman prepared a breakfast table in the kitchen. As she came into the living room, she noticed how much interested the man was in the pictures on the wall.

"This was my husband. We were married for a year. His family always pressured him because he married a black girl, but he loved me. Then our son was born. Shortly after, my husband died in a car accident. I raised my son alone, and this is how it ended. Come, son. Come eat. I didn't even ask you your name." As she turned to Michael, she noticed tears falling down his eyes. Her guest was staring at her son's picture; he was crying.

"You are worrying me. Why are you crying? Did you know my son? Tell me the truth, did you?"

"No, ma'am. Your son's tragic death in the war saddened me."

"Have you been in the army?"

"No."

"Then what's wrong with your walking?"

"A car accident."

"I need to get to work. Make yourself at home. Take a shower. I will put a towel and some clothes in the bathroom. My son's clothes, you can wear them if you want. You are not like other junkies. You are different. All right, I'll get going." The woman left the house to return to work.

They arrived home at night. Caster opened the door and entered the house with the uninvited guest. He kept his duty gun on himself, just in case. He showed the guest to the living room and went to the kitchen to get some food and drink. He was hungry and tired. He opened the fridge door. Before he was able to reach into the fridge, he was hit in the head with an object and passed out.

He had a terrible headache when he woke up. He was lying on the floor, his hands and legs tied. He barely could move his body. As he moved slowly, he saw a man sitting on the sofa with Carl's pistol in his hand.

"You really are stupid, dumbass. You think I'm as stupid as you? Tell me, why did you go to that house? That bitch told you something, didn't she? Tell me!"

"You gotta believe that's not why I was there. I just needed to ask Elma a few questions about the jewelry. I think this has nothing to do with you. Don't worry, I'm not interested in what you do. I'm just trying to do my own thing. Things have not been good lately for me. I feel that the feds and police are suspecting me, Arnoldo also. Look, man, I will give you some money, good money. If you want, I can even help you get out of the country. I'll help you. Go and get yourself a business there. I promise."

"OK, I guess. First, tell me where the money is. I wanna know how much you are going to give me. I heard the cops make good money."

"My salary is in my card. The money I have at home is the part of my share from the robbery. Arnoldo gave it to me. It's all there. I haven't spent much from my share. Take it, man. It can all be yours."

"Bastards! You have taken everyone for a fool. We risked our lives to make it happen, and you two just share the money between each other and spend it the way you like, just using the rest of us like we are morons. I'm gonna destroy all of you. You will answer for everything, same goes for that bitch too. So tell me, it's she who told you to come over to the house and search for it, didn't she? Your plan was to kill Beth and take the jewelry with her, right? Since your plan didn't work out, you two tried to trap me. Yes? I guess that's why that bitch was asking for permission from Arnoldo. She wanted to meet with you and plan your next move against me. You are the one helping her."

"I have nothing to do with her. You are lying. If you want, we can have all the gold and jewelry. We can kill all of them tonight, and when everything sorts out, we can have the jewels. I know where it's hidden."

"Don't take me for a stupid. I already took my share. If I'm alive, it will be enough for me till the end of my days. I'm sorry, my friend. See you in heaven, if we ever make it there." He shot Carl Caster in the chest, where his heart is. The sheriff passed away right then and there. He took a towel and cleaned the pistol for fingerprints and left the house.

Brook Cletus was at the bureau again. Agent Darren Edmond asked him some additional questions regarding the investigation going for Beth's murder and the robbery. After interrogation, Cletus returned to the police department. He looked upset. He had to see Carl. They were probably going to ask the same questions to Carl too, therefore he had to see Carl before that. It was strange that Caster didn't show up to work. He asked the officers in the department; no one had seen him yet. Brook Cletus called Carl's phone several times, but there was no answer. After several unanswered phone calls, Brook got more suspicious and decided to head to Carl's home, where he witnessed a tragic scene.

The killer or killers were professionals; they killed the sheriff with his own gun. Forensics report showed head trauma— meaning, Carl was hit in the head with a blunt object before he was shot. Whether the killer was alone or not remained unknown. Drug stash was found in his house and heroin in his blood; the sheriff was a drug user. It looked like someone hit him in the head and then shot him; it must have been a conflict of some sort. Time was passing, and more murder news kept coming in from the area. Unfortunately, the killer or killers did not leave a single trail behind. The victims were either someone doing or selling drugs in the streets, or someone who was attacking some ordinary innocent citizen. The police and the feds did not have much lead to follow; all they knew was that the killer was a professional and unknown. Who was this? What was he trying to do? Sheriff Carl got killed with his own duty gun, and an ex-Special Force's house was burned down as he disappeared; that was the only lead they had, which they couldn't follow. After questioning the eyewitnesses, Agent Darren Edmond had an idea about who might be the homeless cripple killer, and he was right in his instincts.

It was nighttime when the boss heard the news. As soon as the man he sent up to Carl's house to murder him gave the news,

Arnoldo called Anderson, gave orders, and changed his place of residence. Anderson ordered everyone in the gang to pause working for now and leave the area as soon as possible.

No lead came out of detaining two prime suspects about the last two incidents. There was nothing on the homeless killer guy either. When asking around, either people had never seen him or they have seen him in the past few days. The cleaning lady was asked the same questions; she had not seen anyone. After hearing the news, the woman rushed home to her guest, but he was gone.

He left the house before lunchtime. He changed his appearance drastically. He cut his hair short but still covered his face with the hat and a scarf. He avoided densely populated areas and walked near the beach until nighttime.

The address he was going to was located in the suburb. It was very far from where he was at the moment. He needed some kind of transport to get there. He took a taxi ride not directly to the address. He got out of the car somewhere near the intended address and walked the rest of the road. He noticed a house in the woods covered by trees. All the signs matched; it was the house. He hid behind an old tree and watched the house. He tried to follow the people coming in and out of the place to guess the number of people inside the house. Only two vehicles were parked outside. Probably the vehicles belonged to the people coming to the house or to the people who rented the place. He approached the cars in darkness and slashed both cars' front tires.

It was past midnight. He tried to enter the house from the back door. When he saw the headlights of the car approaching, he turned back and hid behind a tree again. The car stopped near the house. Two men came out of the car. Someone from the inside greeted them at the door, and they entered the house together. Michael hid behind the car in darkness and started waiting.

Few hours passed. The lights facing the front of the house switched off, and two people came out of the house. They were carrying a big bag into the trunk of the car. The two men stopped for a moment to check the surrounding. As they headed toward the front end of the car, suddenly, a man appeared from the darkness and shot one of them down quickly. Before the other was able to react, he got hit in the head and fell down. Michael quickly picked up the phone on the ground, got in the car, turned on the ignition, and left the area as quickly as he could. When the criminals got out of the house, the car was already far away and the two men were lying dead on the ground.

He got away really fast. He pulled over the car after making sure that he wasn't being followed. He opened the trunk to look into the bag. He was shocked when he opened the bag. He saw Sarah's face in there. She was barely breathing, her skin was pale, and her eyelids were very dark. He checked her pulse. Her heart was slowing down, bubbles coming out her mouth. It was obvious that she was given a very high dose of drugs. It looked like the criminals planned to drug her, and until they reach their destination, she would die of overdose. They could bury her and get out of the area. Time is flying; if Sarah doesn't receive medical treatment very soon, she could die.

Michael got back in the car and headed to the main highway as fast as he could. He was receiving phone calls constantly. When he reached the intersection, he called the ambulance and informed the person who is in need of medical assistance. It was not safe to enter the highway; the police were on the watch. He received another phone call.

"Bastard! I'm gonna find you! Consider yourself a dead man. Son of a bitch, I'm gonna kill you! You are gonna pay for everything you did!"

Michael switched off the phone and threw the SIM card into the bush. He took out Sarah from the trunk and laid her on the grass on the road side. He wiped her mouth. Her pulse was becoming slower. Michael started giving Sarah a heart massage using his both hands. She was sweating. Soon she started throwing up constantly. She was crying as she was staring at Michael. He was very worried for her. Ambulance and police sirens were approaching. He leaned over to kiss Sarah's forehead. "Good-bye! The ambulance is close by. They will take you to the hospital. I'm gonna get those bastards soon. If we make it, we will meet again." He left her there with tears in his eyes.

Arnoldo got the news of the murder on the same night. The boss and Anderson discussed everything for a long time in the room. The men killed were very handy and useful members of the gang. Anderson was in shock about all of this. If Alberto had listened to Arnoldo and got rid of the girl on the night of the robbery, all of this would not have happened. The boss wondered whether it was the same killer. The killer was either killing the gang members one by one on purpose, or it was just a random act of killing, which seemed unlikely. The killer was a master at what he was doing. But who was this man? How did he know about Alberto's rented place? Why did he save that girl? According to witnesses, that man's physical characteristics and limp leg made Arnoldo more suspicious. All the descriptions given were similar to Michael Grady. What if he was still alive? How could it be? How could a man whose hands and legs are tied and unconscious escape such a big fire? There has got to be something else in this. Arnoldo remembered what happened between Michael and Alberto at the restaurant before the robbery took place. It looked like what Anderson said about Michael had some share of truth in it. The news of his tragic death was on the TV news. Perhaps it was part of a plan by the federals against the criminals. Something needed to be done as soon as possible if he was still alive, because Michael was the only person that had seen them.

The boss ordered Elma to stay at Alberto's house. Elma had made a lot of changes to her appearance; she was now impossible to recognize. She worked at the casino during the night. Arnoldo had given Anderson the management of the casino. Anderson was always rude to Elma. He would yell at her at any chance he gets. The boss gave instructions that Alan Booker would take Elma home after work. Her every move was being watched by someone. Arnoldo suspected Elma about the expensive diamond set that was lost and therefore asked Anderson and Arlen to watch over her.

The boss suspected the sheriff too. He blamed the sheriff for telling the password to Beth. Only he knew the password and had the keys to the place. It's because of him that Beth was able to get her hands on the diamond set. Carl was given a period to come back with answers, but he was killed out of nowhere. It was strange and suspicious to the boss. Maybe it was Carl and Elma's plan to get rid of Beth together. But the man who took the jewel from Elma did not look like Carl. He had a shift with Brook Cletus that night. Brook is an honest sheriff. Carl would not have had the chance to go to Beth's house to steal the jewelry without Cletus noticing it. It was important to know who was the man in the kitchen. Maybe Elma was with someone from the gang, and when the sheriff found out about their plan, they killed him. Carl promised the boss that he would find out the truth soon. Things were getting more and more complicated.

As usual, Elma returned home from work very tired. Arlen parked the car and followed Elma home. It was strange. He went up to the second floor and checked all the rooms. Elma hesitated to ask.

"You are scaring me. Why are you checking the rooms? Are you suspecting something?"

"It's better this way. It's for your own good."

"I didn't expect that. Since when do you care about my well-being?"

"Boss asked me to do so."

"He is doing this because he wants to protect me, or . . . ?"

"The second option seems more logical. If any strange man enters this house, it won't be good for you."

"Bastard! You told him that, that's why he has that opinion."

"Stupid woman! I'm tired of your insults. Believe me, you will pay dearly for everything you said! Forget the past! You are nothing to the boss now!"

"Have you gotten so rabid, you son of a bitch!" She lifted her arm to slap Arlen.

Arlen stopped her arm and squeezed. "Stupid bitch, I'm not like Alberto. Because of you, two brothers separated from each other. You and Anderson sent Arnoldo to his brother to kill that man. You knew that Alberto was a little crazy, and to get rid of him, you convinced Arnoldo to involve his little brother. Caster told everyone how skillful that ex-military was and how he protected his friend."

"Let go off my hand, you jerk! You are hurting me! You just wait, I will tell all of this tomorrow to Anderson and the boss."

"You can't. Because they won't believe you."

"Why wouldn't they?"

"Because I'm gonna tell them that I saw you with another man in the house. They think that you are the one who stole the jewelry anyway. Arnoldo will never forgive you if he finds out that you have been having an affair with someone in his dead brother's house. Stop the way you are acting with me and get silly thoughts out of your mind. You don't want to make me angry. You hear me? I can kill you with my bare hands right now if I want and feed you to the birds. Not even a finger will be left behind."

Elma started screaming and crying. "God damn you! You bastard!"

"We are all damned by God anyway. Soon, that invisible being will give all of us the punishment we deserve." He closed the door and left.

"All right, jerk! You will answer for everything!"

She sat on the sofa and lit up a cigarette in anger. Her hands were shaking. She couldn't calm herself down. She grabbed the whisky bottle and poured into a glass. She had several glasses of whisky and went to bed. She couldn't sleep. She kept thinking about why Arlen went upstairs to check the rooms. What was it? Suddenly, she remembered something. That man at Beth's house in the kitchen who took the jewelry from her looks like Arlen. It can't be. Not possible. Arlen is at the casino every day. Why would he come to Beth's house that night? Arlen used to be so quiet and naive. He was always scared of Anderson. Changes in his behavior suspected her. It was strange that he was so protective of Alberto. Was there anything between them?

She was starting to feel drunk, but her thoughts won't let her fall asleep. She was the main witness and a participant in what happened to Beth. There were only two people she was most afraid of: Michael Grady and Sheriff Carl Caster. Both of them were murdered; it was good news for her, but she still was in fear. News on TV said that he burned to death in his house. What if the information given by the officials was wrong? The boss, Arlen, Anderson, and two other men were there that night of the incident. She heard about the murder of Michael from the boss himself. He was high and drunk, talking about how he got revenge for his brother. Michael was the only person who had seen them up close and could recognize them in the future. That's why his livelihood is important to the police and the federals. The news of his death could be fake. Elma had a feeling that Michael is still alive, and one of these days, he's going to walk in and question her about Beth's death.

The sheriff's killer remained unknown to everyone, but she hoped that it was Carlos and wanted to meet with him soon.

Sometimes when she's in the casino, she looks around hoping to see Carlos, but every night ends in disappointment for her. It would not be smart to go to Carlos's house, since her every move was being watched. Besides, Carlos was being extra careful; he kept changing his address very often. After she left the birthday party, Carlos was supposed to come after her. What happened then? Who was the man in the darkness? If the corridor lights were on when she came downstairs, she could at least recognize the facial lines of the man. His voice was familiar, but she was too scared to recognize. Maybe Carlos sent that man? She finally made up her mind. No matter what, she had to find an excuse to ask for permission from Anderson and go to see Carlos. She fell asleep with all these thoughts in her mind.

It was lunchtime when she woke up. She had a terrible headache. She didn't want to leave her bed and decided to wait until nighttime. There was a knock at the door. Arlen had come after her. She got dressed and headed to the casino.

For some reason, Anderson was very angry today. He didn't leave his room, and whoever got into his room was yelled at. She didn't want to come face-to-face with him at a moment like this. She sat on the side and smoked a cigarette while watching people inside the casino. Alek was not around. He is usually at the casino every day. She kept watching people inside the casino. A man sitting near the window smoking a cigar and looking out the window drew his attention. At first, she could not recognize the man because he had a hat and sunglasses on, but he resembled Alek. Changes in his appearance were strange. Alek called over the waiter and ordered a drink. Elma thought about approaching him, but she changed her mind. Perhaps he was waiting for someone.

A lot of customers were at the casino already. She was busy working, that's why she didn't notice it when Carlos entered the place. He approached the waiter and asked something. The man talking to the waiter drew Elma's attention. At first, she didn't recognize him, but later on she realized that it was Carlos. He had made a lot of changes to his facial appearance; even the way he dresses has changed. He got rid of his long moustache and changed his hair color to brown. Elma hesitated to approach him and decided to follow his movements. After talking to the waiter, Carlos went up to the second floor. He returned a moment after and got back to his table near the window. He continued to smoke his cigar and watch the people inside the casino. He looked angrier this time. Maybe he had an argument with Anderson and came back downstairs to wait for something. Elma got nervous. What was going on? Perhaps Carlos wanted to see the boss and was waiting for him. She was getting more and more nervous. Carlos could feel that Elma was watching her, but he pretended to not see her. Considering the situation, Elma understood why he was acting that way, but she didn't like it anyway. If Carlos really wanted to, he would have found a way to meet with her, but he didn't.

Elma didn't notice when Alek left the casino. Carlos, too, went out of the casino after some time. His inconsiderate behavior toward Elma pissed her off. She needed to meet with Carlos face-to-face today. She was going to find an excuse to go to his house and get answers.

She went up to the second floor, and without asking Arlen for permission, she entered Anderson's room. Anderson was still mad, and the way Elma entered his room made him ferociously angry.

"Stupid woman! How many times have I got to tell you not to enter my room without permission?"

"Anderson, I apologize. I need to ask you something important."

"What do you want?"

"I have a close relative who is very sick. I would like to leave work early today to pay a visit to my relative before going home."

"Where was this relative until now?"

"I used to meet with him here. But lately he has not been able to come because of his health condition. I'm worried for him. I haven't seen him in a long time."

"You may leave after an hour. One of the boys will take you. If you have anything to say, you will say it to the security from now on. Don't come inside. I hate your face! You should all be killed one by one. You and people like you should be sent after her. We should clean our surroundings from trash like you. Get out of my sight, whore!"

His insults hurt her feelings deeply, but she did not respond and left the room quietly. Arlen's mocking looks at her could only mean that he could also hear the words Anderson used against her. "What are you looking at, dumbass! It's what you have always been doing, listening behind the doors!"

Arlen didn't respond; he was used to this kind of insults. He was happy on the other hand. Elma used to get information about other gang members and give them to Anderson. Many times, Anderson and even the boss slapped and insulted Elma for betrayal without questioning. Anderson always hated her.

Elma cried all the way home. She was questioning her own life choices. She was getting closer to Carlos's address. She tried to calm down. She was full of fate toward Anderson. She had to meet with Carlos and discuss some important matters. If the man in the kitchen that night was sent by Carlos, she had a share in that expensive diamond set. Carlos did not have a choice but to agree. Otherwise, it won't be good for any of them. Elma did not want to give up on her last chance in life, but she was faced with a difficult situation. If the driver decides to follow her to the house, he could see Carlos. Elma knew the danger, therefore the talk with Carlos had to be short. She just wanted to tell him her new address and ask him to come over whenever he finds it suitable. They had to discuss everything that's happening.

"You know how he is. He is angry. Say what you got to say to me!" Freddie complained.

"Thank you, Freddie. You always know how to take care of me. I like you very much. May the Holy Mother bless you."

"All right, is this your relative's house?"

"Yes."

"Maybe I should come too."

"Of course. Just wait a moment, I can't reach his phone. I'm gonna go to his address. If he is there, I will call you."

"OK, go. I'll be waiting for your call. If Anderson knew that I let you go there alone, he would have me stuffed."

"Freddie, honey, you know how much I like you. I would not want you to get in trouble because of me." She got out of the car and entered the building.

Elma was shaking nervously. She got near the door and rang the bell with pauses in between. It was dead quiet. She waited for a while. Nobody was at home. He wasn't home, or maybe he just moved to another address. Elma returned to Freddie angrily.

"What happened? Is he not home?"

"No. I guess he went to the hospital."

"Call him. We'll go wherever he is."

"But I told you before, I can't reach his number."

"Give me the number. Maybe he will answer my call."

Elma gave him Carlos's number. It really was out of reach. "You thought I'm lying?"

"Honey, looks like your relative has passed away. All right, then, where shall we go? Home or the casino? Say something, I'm running out of gas. We need to refill somewhere and continue."

"Take me home. I'm not in the mood anyway."

"Whatever you say."

George and Luisa temporarily moved to the house Sheriff Brook Cletus rented for them. Luisa was feeling well so would go to work every once in a while, despite George not wanting her to. She would feel homesick sometimes, but she understood the difficulty of the situation. She was twenty-two weeks pregnant now. George was not feeling well, that's why Luisa decided to go to work late. Her girlfriend was going to replace her for a few hours.

Freddie pulled in at one of the gas stations nearby and went inside to get a cashier's check. At this moment, a car came in from behind and parked near the station in front of them. A woman driver got out of the car to refill her tank. At first, Elma didn't recognize the woman, but then her face was familiar. She finally recognized her; it was the same woman from the birthday party. The house owner told Elma that the two women talking to Beth are her friends. Elma was happy, as if she had found a treasure.

"Freddie, I need to ask you something serious. It's important for all of us. I'll explain to you later. That woman you see is Beth's friend. We have been looking for her. We must follow her. We can't let her go."

"Are you sure it's the same woman?"

"Yes, of course. I saw her at the birthday party. That night I presented myself to the house owner as Beth's friend, that's when she said that the people Beth were talking to were her friends. I don't know any of those women, but I remember their faces. Beth told me about Luisa before, her neighbor and friend. She is one of them."

"So what? Why do we need to follow her?"

"This is very serious. I will explain everything to you later. Just do as I say now. If we don't follow and find out her address, the boss won't forgive us. Through this woman, we can get to the other woman too. It is connected to something really important. We need to follow her home. The boss will decide what to do with the information. Hurry, drive faster. Don't let her out of sight."

"OK."

The car they were following pulled into the hospital parking lot. She probably came to visit someone, or maybe she works here.

"It's not patient visiting time at the hospital. If she is a doctor or a nurse, she wouldn't be coming to work at this time."

"Be patient, honey! It's easy to find out. Just a moment."

Elma quickly got out of the car and approached the woman ahead. "Hi, ma'am. Are you going to the hospital to visit someone sick?"

"No, ma'am. I work here. It's not visiting time yet."

"I didn't know that."

"What's the name of the patient you are visiting? I will tell them for sure that you visited. What's your name, ma'am?" Luisa turned to Elma and stared at her.

"Have we met before? Your face, it's very familiar."

"Maybe, ma'am. But I have never seen you before. My name is Clara. My friend is being treated at the pregnancy ward. I have come to visit her."

"I'm sorry. Unfortunately, I don't work at that department. You just need to go straight and turn right. That's where the birth department is."

"Thank you, ma'am."

Elma walked the same she described for a little while and returned back. "We need to go to the casino right away. Arnoldo is usually at the casino these hours. I need to see and tell him about this."

The information Arnoldo received was really important. He rated highly what Elma did, but he didn't act too excited about it. "It's the beginning. If you wanna make up for your mistakes, finish what you have started. It needs to be done precisely and clean. I need you to find out everything about that woman and her friend. I'm gonna find Alberto's killer very soon. I won't rest until I kill him with my own hands. I still feel remorse about the fact that Alberto's other killer is still free, living his life. I'm gonna find that bastard and kill him myself. Looks like George is under police protection. Otherwise, he would have stayed in his own home."

For some reason, Michael did not show up lately. He called his secret number from the hotel phone, but it could not be reached. To check on him, he sent someone over to Lucas Marchelo's house. The owner said that he hadn't seen Michael for a week now. Roger was worried about Michael; he disappeared all of a sudden. What if something bad had happened to him? There could be two reasons for his friend's disappearance. He either was killed or was in hideout, making plans against the enemy.

Roger Thomas returned to the hotel and called in the housekeeper. He turned on the secret phone she brought and started reading the messages. His father's message was that his mother is sick and they both miss him. His mother was being treated at the hospital. Roger Thomas started to worry for his mother. He had to finish what he started. In his message to his father, he wrote that he will be back soon to take care of the business from where he left off, turned off the phone, and handed it back to the housekeeper who brought newspapers. "Very important news. I just got these papers today. You should take a look."

Roger read the news about the criminal incident that happened in the state a few days ago. As he turned to the next page, he noticed the news of three people being murdered at the same city that he is in. There was an essay about the three drug dealers who have been killed by the same man. The killer was unknown. He handled the drug dealers skillfully and left no trace behind. The gun used in crime was not found either. The bullet shells from the crime scene were taken to the lab to find out the type of the gun and the owner of the gun. The owner of the gun was killed a year ago. The reason for his death remains unknown. Perhaps the people murdered were directly involved in this crime, and for some reason, they have taken the gun after killing the owner. The description of the killer made by the witnesses made Roger Thomas think about it. Roger had a feeling that it was Michael Grady. It looked like he was still alive. He was happy to know that. His friend Michael was risking his life fighting against the enemy all by himself. The news about his friend put ease in his mind. He drank some whisky and lay on the sofa. He was really tired. He fell asleep on the sofa thinking about everything that was happening.

A knock at the door woke him up. He looked at the time. "Come in!"

The housekeeper entered the room. "Roger, important news. A taxi driver came into the hotel asking about his relative who stays here. He described his relative. It all matches your characteristics. Looks like someone is after you."

Roger quickly stood up. "I have no relatives. How did that man look?"

"To be honest, I didn't see him either. According to the guys, he's a normal-height person."

"Has a moustache, black, sparse hair and a little ponytail behind, sharp nose, right?"

"No, some of those do not match the description. The guys said that his hair was short and brown. Nose was slightly big, not sharp edged. He is a bit taller than the average and no moustache. He had a hat."

"It's very serious information. Those descriptions don't really describe the killer, but it could be someone sent by the killer. Perhaps he was waiting in the car to avoid being seen, maybe even made changes to his appearance. You should have told me earlier, I could have followed him."

"I did it, man. The taxi they arrived in stopped in front of the casino, one of the most popular ones. While I was there, they were still waiting in the car."

"Why did you act without asking me? He's very alert. You should have told me earlier. Even if he made changes to his appearance, I still would have recognized him! I need to go now. Find me a car quickly! Hurry up, time is running out. Write down the model and the plate number of the taxi here. I need to change the way I look."

"Roger, maybe I should come with you."

"We don't have much time. Just do what I asked you to do. They might have seen you already. Don't take the enemy for stupid!"

"Roger, maybe we should call the police? I am worried for you. I don't think you should go alone. Let me come with you. I can be on the watch for you."

"Wait for my call. I need to make sure that it's the same person. Hurry!"

He made plenty of changes to his appearance as quickly as he could and headed to the casino. He parked the car on the roadside to watch the casino entrance. Since it was nighttime, there were plenty of customers coming to the casino. He got out of his car and walked toward the casino entrance. The car his friend was talking about was in the parking lot, but no one was inside it. He probably went inside. He got into the casino, took a seat near the window, and ordered a drink. He put his leg over his other leg, lit up a cigar, and started watching the people inside and outside the casino. He didn't see anyone familiar. He was nervous and angry, but he must stay calm and patient; he must not draw any unwanted attention from people around. Casino staff might recognize him.

Finally, he saw a car stopping in front of the casino. He recognized the car right away. The man who got out of the car and entered the casino drew his attention. He had made changes to his appearance, but Roger recognized him. The man looked like the photos of Carlos. Roger was certain that it was the same jeweler. It looked like he knew that he was being followed and made changes to the way he looks. There was something that was worrying Roger Thomas. Why was this man, who is being searched by the police and the feds, following him? He probably wanted to get revenge and get rid of Roger Thomas, who is a witness.

It was strange that a customer was so friendly with the casino staff, walked up to the second floor without asking for permission, ordered drinks, and did not pay the bill; it could only mean that he was an important person known in the casino and he often came to the place.

He stood up and left the casino unnoticed. He got back in his car, made a phone call to his friend, and got away from the area. He pulled over the car somewhere quiet and dark. He opened the trunk, where he put fresh clothes. He changed his clothes to new ones and put on a hat. He was in a hurry. The car he was waiting for arrived, and his friend got out of the car.

"Give me the keys quickly!"

"What's up? You look nervous."

"Don't have time. I'm in a hurry."

"Roger, don't go after these jerks alone. It's not safe. He could be a dangerous gang member. That ring is a piece of a stolen jewelry set. I think he is dangerous, a gang member. Let me come with you. I have my gun with me."

"No, we will draw attention. I need to follow him first to find out his address. I will call the police when I know for sure. We need to catch him alive. What I witnessed today is going to lead to bigger things. And I think you are right, he is a gang member."

"I will have my phone near me at all times. Gonna be waiting for your call."

"Deal!" He got in the car and drove away as fast as possible.

After driving for some time, he arrived near the casino. He switched off his phone. He parked his car in a dark spot and started watching the casino entrance. From where he was standing, he could see clearly the people coming in and out of the casino. The driver of the car that just arrived was pacing around, smoking a cigarette. He was waiting for someone. He did look like the guy who came into the hotel, but it wasn't him. Perhaps the driver changed his looks too. Roger was getting more and more suspicious. Time was flying; he had to be patient and wait. He can't let this chance go to nothing this time. After some time, Carlos came out of the casino. He looked around while he kept smoking his cigar and got in the car with the driver that was waiting for him. They left the area together. The traffic was not very tense, since it was nighttime. Not to draw attention while following, he kept changing lanes and keeping a safe distance in between.

At last, the car he was following turned into the exit from the highway into the town. The town was a region of homes located separately. Although it was a forest area, the leaves were falling off, so it was clearly visible everywhere. For safety reasons, he parked his car a little further from the place. He could see the movement of the car up ahead easily as the car turned to the right and stopped in front of a small house. Roger Thomas quickly got out of that car and hid behind one of the larger trees.

The same returned after some time. The driver was alone in the car. "So this is where Carlos lives." After the taxi left, Roger kept watching the area for some time. When it was all quiet, he started getting closer to the house. He hid behind a large tree again to have a better view of the house. For some reason, only the kitchen lights were on, and the rest of the rooms were dark. It was strange. What if the man that got out of the car didn't go inside the house? He hesitated. He checked the area; it was quiet. He was mad at himself for not taking the gun. He decided to return to the car and get the gun. As he opened the glove box to reach for the gun, a gun was pointed at his head. Roger knew that he had made a mistake, a big one. Any sudden move could be fatal. He knew his mistake, but it was too late now.

"Step away from the car, you son of a bitch! Hands up!"

Roger Thomas slowly backed away from the car and looked at the man who got out from the backseat of the car. It was the same taxi driver that left a while ago. He probably parked the car somewhere close and walked here.

"Who are you? What do you want?"

"Don't try to fool me, bastard. You thought we won't recognize you?" The driver started coming closer to Roger.

"Man, I think you are mistaking me for someone else." Roger was waiting for the driver to get even closer.

"There's no mistake. Finally, we meet."

Roger turned back when he heard the footsteps of the man approaching from behind. Carlos was pointing the gun at him and giving orders to his friend. "Be careful, man, this guy is an ex-Special Force. Don't even think about doing anything. I'll put a bullet in your head."

Roger was aware of the danger. He knew that any sudden move could result in him getting shot. Roger was waiting for the man to approach him. Both men were slowly coming closer to Roger. When Roger hit and tried to take the gun away from the man in front of him with a special maneuver, he felt a sharp pain on the back of his head and lost consciousness.

"I told you to be careful. Does it hurt?"

"I think he broke my arm," as he started kicking Roger, who was lying on the ground unconscious.

"Be quiet. Get a hold of yourself! We don't have much time. He's gonna wake up soon. We need to tie him up and put him in the car."

"What are you planning? I think we should just kill him here with his own gun."

"Not here. A lot of people live in these areas. Police can come at any moment. Let's get him in the car and drive into hills in the forest. I need him for now. I need him to answer some questions for me. After I'm done with him, we can kill him and feed to the birds."

"What about the car?"

"Hurry, go get the car. We need to clean our fingerprints from his car. Where's his phone?" Carlos went through Roger's pockets. There was no phone. He looked for the phone around the car. Carlos got excited when he saw the phone on the ground. He quickly picked it up and tried to turn it on. It was switched off. Carlos threw the phone on the ground and smashed it with his foot in anger. After tying Roger's hands and legs, they put him in the backseat of the car and drove off.

He was feeling a terrible headache, couldn't open his eyes, but he could hear people talking.

"Son of a bitch. I keep saying to this bastard that there is a suspicious man in the area. I describe him, and he just keeps screaming at me. He changed his looks thinking that I'm not gonna recognize him."

"Did Anderson tell you why you were looking for him?"

"He did. I lied to him. I told him that there's a money dispute between us. He told me that he hadn't seen anyone like that at the casino. I think he recognized the man but didn't want to give it away because he is a VIP customer at the casino. He spends his father's wealth there. Anderson would not want to lose such a customer. What he doesn't understand is that he will come after me. He wants to hand me to the federals."

"It's good that we took care of him before the boss found out anything about it. It could unveil many important details about the ring, and he could just say that the ring was the reason for his visit here. The result is obvious. We are gonna send him to hell. Not a single trace of him will be left behind."

"It's nighttime anyway. Let's take him to the place you were talking about, kill him, and dump his body there."

"It's best we do it. The area seems quiet."

"I can hear police sirens from far."

"Maybe they are looking for us. He might not be alone. Someone must have tipped the cops because his phone is turned off. Hurry."

"I think these two bastards have something to do with everything that's happening and the murder of our guys. This one came to the casino to follow the guys and kill them. He's taking revenge for his friend. Perhaps someone at the casino is feeding him information. That's why we need a quiet and safe place to do this. If you hadn't told me, I wouldn't have known that this guy is the son of the owner. Boss said that Beth had started seeing her ex-boyfriend Michael. This bastard's father knew well how much worth the jewel was. Perhaps it was this guy who took the jewelry that night. We will find out."

He opened his eyes to see the two men sitting in the front seat of the car. His hands and legs were tied; he was in the backseat of the car. He tried to move, but he couldn't. They tied him really tight when he was passed out. It was dark inside the car, so the two men could not see any movement done by Roger. Roger had learned the secrets of escaping in rigorous army training. Before the two men realized anything, Roger escaped the ropes quietly and smashed their heads into each other. They both passed out from the blow. The car spun off the road and stopped after hitting a tree on the roadside.

Roger's chest was hit by the blow; he could barely breathe. He was feeling severe pain in his head and his back. With great difficulty, he gathered his strength and took the driver's gun. Roger checked his pulse; he was already dead. Roger managed to open the ropes tying his legs and got out from the back door of the car. He held on to the car and opened the front passenger door. Carlos's unconscious body was leaning against the door. As soon as Roger opened the door, Carlos fell on the ground. He was heavily injured and unconscious. The blood from his head wound was covering his face in red. Roger understood that his condition is not good either. He reached for Carlos's phone and made a phone call to the police. He explained the area and the situation they are in. All of a sudden, he felt a sharp pain in his chest. When he turned back, Carlos shot him in the chest. Roger gathered all of his strength and hit Carlos's arm to drop the gun he was holding. Roger's second strike was to Carlos's head. After the second strike of Roger, Carlos passed out again. The gunshot to the chest was a serious injury. Roger started feeling dizzy; his head was spinning. He tried to control his balance by holding on to the door handle, but he failed to do so. Roger lost his consciousness and fell to the ground.

The two heavily wounded were brought into the hospital ICU unit in stretchers. All the necessary caution steps were taken beforehand. Resuscitation began. The ambulance doctor presented the report of all the steps taken until the hospital to the resuscitation department doctor. All the staff from the surgical and resuscitation department were fighting really hard to save the lives of these two men.

Darren Edmond was in the hallway too. He looked nervous and angry. He was waiting for the operation results. It was important that both of them make it alive. Roger and Carlos's lives could be vital in solving this crime. Roger Thomas's written statement was taken when Alvaro died. His statement of the incident was a little confusing. He stated that he suspected something about the diamond stone and that's why he agreed to pay a large amount for it to check with the photos of the stolen jewelry and make sure it was one of them. Only after that he called the police to inform them about the situation. The mistakes he made caused the police to lose a warm lead. If he informed the police as soon as he could, the suspect would have been detained by now. Unfortunately, because of the late given information, a police officer was killed and two more injured in the process of chasing the criminal, and the killer had escaped. Roger Thomas was probably feeling remorse about the mistake he had made, and his father's sarcastic words toward him must have touched him. Because of his negligence, an innocent man killed himself and the robbery investigation that has been going on remained open. Roger's mistake was a really serious one. He understood it, and to make things right, he offered his help and best of his abilities in the ongoing robbery investigation. It was declined by the police. He might make another uncalculated move and ruin everything. The criminals were being extremely careful; for the moment, they seemed uncatchable.

It was important to interrogate Carl. They traced his phones, but nothing except for broken phones and SIM cards were found. Finally, they had Carlos, but his condition was critical. It was very important for the case that he lives. Darren Edmond was trying to make a sense out of all of this. Perhaps after the police turned down Roger's hand in help, he decided to act on his own and went after Carlos to the neighboring state, and when the man Carlos sent after him gave him the news that Roger had left home for some time, Carlos got suspicious. It looked like besides the police and the feds, there was someone else after him. Carlos tried to get rid of the enemy when he found out. Somehow, the driver got killed in this clash between them, and both of them were injured heavily. Roger and Carlos were brought in with a bullet wound and serious traumas. That's why it was very important that they both lived.

Darren Edmond was the first to receive the news of the incident. It looked like while Roger was making the phone call to police, he was shot in the chest by Carlos, but Roger managed to neutralize the enemy. The gun on the side and heavy blows to the head, which led Carlos to coma, proved this. Roger had also fallen into a coma because of heavy blood loss. The next killing was big news. Consecutive murders happening in the state were raising some concerned voices around the federal bureau. For this reason, the federal agent was invited to the bureau to report on the unsolved cases.

"Mr. Darren Edmond, you have been given a certain task in a fight against organized crime and transferred to the state. It is important that you report to us about what you have been doing and what you are going to do about it. Unfortunately, none of the cases have been solved yet. And the murders keep happening in the area. Unsolved murders and killings are very concerning to the bureau. The last incident, for example."

"Several people have been killed in these incidents. None of the bodies had any ID on them. We have been unable to identify them. According to the witnesses, all of these men were known by their nicknames and they were street drug dealers. The corpses were taken to forensics, where they found high dosage of heroin in their bloods."

"Do you have any solid evidence to prove their crimes?"

"Yes. During search at their house, plenty of narcotic drugs were found and taken to the department as evidence. They were dealing heroin and cocaine. From the area of the city where they operated, there have been several calls to the ambulance regarding heroin overdose."

"They must have had suppliers. We need to get to the end of it."

"Unfortunately, after the incident, we haven't been able to get anything on them or on the people around them. We couldn't even find their phones. We found the bullet shells at the crime scene and identified the owner of the gun. The owner was a city local who was killed under unknown circumstances a year ago. That case remains open. It's my understanding that these guys were involved in that murder and they held on to the victim's gun."

"Maybe this incident that resulted with the death of three people was some sort of conflict between them and their customers?"

"We have no evidence to support that idea. The eyewitnesses state that it was the first time someone was ever seeing him around there. He took care of three people easily. He was very skilled. The other two that were with him were just regular bums from the area. Unfortunately, they have also disappeared after the incident."

"What can you say about the last incident?"

"One of the men died in the car. The other two were taken to hospital. They are in a coma. Both were taken to the ICU unit with a diagnosis of severe traumatic and hemorrhagic shock. We have identified them all. Roger Thomas, an ex-Special Force soldier, was shot in the chest. The other in critical condition is a wanted criminal, Carlos Darrick. Forensics report of the dead driver indicates that he suffered a severe skull and head trauma right before the accident. He lost the control of the car and crashed. You know the rest. They were brought into the hospital, both in a coma.

"So it looks like the third person was in the car. It was Roger Thomas. For some reason, it all happened."

"We can't know it until he wakes up from a coma."

"What could be the reason for a conflict between the officer and them? Maybe the officer was also using drugs and that was their connection to this."

"Roger Thomas is an exemplary peacekeeper fighting in Afghanistan. He fought actively against the Taliban insurgents and was discharged after being seriously wounded. He's the only son of an exemplary family. He's an honest and a brave man. He's a friend of Officer Michael Grady. His employee was involved in the ring case, who killed himself after being falsely accused of everything. Seems like Roger Thomas risked his own life by going after the enemy alone to get revenge for his friend and his employee. He did offer his help to us. I told him that this is the enforcement's job and declined his offer. Although the perpetrator that caused the death of an innocent man and an officer was wanted by us, we couldn't get any reliable information on him. The fact that Carlos had the stone of a stolen ring could mean that he was involved with the gang. Getting him to talk could unveil many important things.

"Lately, Carlos has made a lot of cosmetic changes to his appearance. He kept changing his phone numbers and address. That's how he was able to avoid our arrest operations. He is in a coma at the moment. Carlos Darrick matches the physical descriptions of the ex-owner and the criminal we have been searching for. Document of identification found in his pocket proves it. He is the former owner of the store that was robbed. He was at the casino that night. The casino owner's statement indicated that Carlos was a usual customer at the casino, and he was indeed at the casino on the night of the robbery. The search made regarding the drugs in the car and his appearance at the casino on the night of the robbery did not yield any results. A gun was shot. Officer Roger Thomas was seriously wounded in the chest. Gun was taken as physical evidence. Forensics reports indicate that the gun that was used did belong to the shooter, but the gun the driver had on him was not registered in the country. He could be an illegal immigrant who was involved in crime. Narcotic substances were found in the blood samples from the dead driver and Carlos Darrick."

"We are all citizens of this great country, and in the fight against organized crime and terrorism, we must accept the help from honest citizens. It is obvious that this gun entered the country by arms traffickers or by some criminal immigrant gangs that entered the country illegally."

"What can you say about the investigation regarding the sheriff's murder at his own house?"

"Sheriff was shot by his own duty gun. Ex-boyfriend of the earlier victim, Beth. Drugs were found in his house during search. At first, we assumed that the drugs were planted by the killer, but the forensics reports stated otherwise. Considering the amount of the heroin found in his blood, it would be safe to assume that he was a heavy user. The reason for his death remains unknown. Unfortunately, the people behind this are very skilled and cautious. They leave no trace behind. High-degree psychedelic drugs were found from the houses of the victims, which means they were probably involved in criminal activities. Sheriff was one of our prime suspects. By getting enough evidence, we could have proved his hand in all of this, but they took care of him. It is possible that he was involved with the gang and was feeding them information about the police's and the feds' operation plans. That is how we were always one step behind."

"Any updates on the Beth Francesco murder investigation?"

"Investigation continues. The reason for her death is still unknown. The expensive jewelry she had on herself before being murdered seems to be the motive. We suspect that the jewelry Beth had was one of the stolen goods. But the woman who saw it couldn't give an exact description. The safe door from the basement was open when we entered Beth's house. I think it's safe to assume something valuable was taken from there. But we have nothing certain for now."

"As the FBI, we firmly believe that you, an experienced detective, will do everything in your power to solve these cases and bring the criminals to justice sooner than later."

Darren Edmond presented every report and evidence related to the ongoing investigations to the secret bureau and left the place. He was really nervous. He rushed to the hospital right away. He asked about the operation done from the reception. As soon as he heard that the operation was over, he went to the chief doctor's room. The chief doctor informed the agent about how the operation went and the patients' condition. Their conditions remained critical. Darren Edmond gave strict orders to the doctor. "I want them both alive, and nobody must know that they were brought to this hospital. It's fully confidential. To protect them, temporarily, the hospital will have a regular work schedule of police officers."

Latest news was shocking. He found out what happened and about the search in the casino conducted by the police, through Arlen. Things were getting very serious. He had to make a final decision as soon as possible. It was important to know whether Carlos survived or not. If he did, it could be the end of the whole gang. It was really dangerous, but he had to know if Carlos was alive or not. The police were probably going to interrogate anyone who wants to visit Carlos. Maybe Carlos's ex-wife could be useful to them? Arnoldo knew that Carlos had been living away from his family for quite some time now, but the police might still be interested in what she has to say about the incident and about the people around Carlos. If Gulia gave some information about people surrounding Carlos, surely the police will go after those people too. She could also say that one of the reasons for their divorce was that Carlos lost all of his earnings at Arnoldo's casino. It was certain that whatever she had to say about Carlos's friends was not going to be something good. Arnoldo made up his mind. He told Anderson to get the casino documents in order and sell the place for a cheap price. Anderson was a legal citizen, so all the establishment was registered to his name.

Anderson was in a desperate situation. He knew that the documents inside the safe were not really in order. It was not going to be easy to sell the place. There were going to be problems with selling and big ones. There was a lot of negligence in the documents related to the state tax, and there were many facts of misappropriation. Anderson had another idea. He tried to convince Arnoldo that if Carlos wakes up, it's going to be really bad for both of them and that he should get out of the country as soon as he can with the money he made from the heist. It was a smart idea. But Arnoldo found this sudden proposition to be suspicious. Arnoldo was getting tired of Anderson's late negligent and disrespectful behavior. It seemed like what his brother was saying about Anderson had some share of truth in it.

Arnoldo came to the casino looking angry. He took a seat on one of the vacant tables. Casino could be on the police watch. The waiters were aware of the situation, so they treated Arnoldo as if he was just another customer. He asked the waiter to bring a drink and the whereabouts of Anderson. The waiter explained that considering the situation, it is impossible for Anderson to meet with the boss for the moment. After hearing what the waiter had to say, Arnoldo thought for a moment and went straight to Anderson's room. Anderson saw how angry the boss was so acted quickly and tried to explain the severity of the situation to the boss. He had to be extra cautious. Arnoldo gave a mean look to Anderson and called all the gang members to the room, including Elma.

"It's serious now. I assume that everyone knows about what happened."

Most of them were staring at him with a strict face. "Of course, you don't know. How could you know? All you do all day is take drugs, gamble, and have sex with the prostitutes. You don't even know what's happening behind your ears. Then listen to me. During the night, a television report said that Frank had died and that Carlos and Alec Castello had been taken to a hospital with severe gunshot wounds and injuries sustained in a car accident. Both of them are in a coma. Do you even know what this all means?" He looked at Anderson with menacing eyes and turned to Elma.

"Which one of them did you see in the casino last night?"

"Boss, they left the casino separately. Carlos left an hour after Alec Castello left. Carlos smoked a cigarette in front of the casino, looked around, and got into the car with Frank. They drove off somewhere. I don't know the rest. You can look at the security cameras."

"Anderson, did you know about all of this?"

"It's been a long time since Carlos came to the casino. It was strange. He came to my room directly. He asked about you. I told him that you are not there. He described someone and asked if I had seen that man at the casino. Honestly, I think he was talking about Alec Castello. I told him I might have seen someone resembling the characteristics he described. He asked me to show him the man I saw in the security camera recordings. I didn't like that. I said, if he doesn't tell me the reason why he wants to see the records, I am not going to help him in any way. He got mad and left the room and got back to his table. He left shortly after."

"You think all I do all day is getting high? I am watching all of you through the camera. Alec Castello came to the casino in an unrecognizable form. He changed everything about his appearance. Did you even notice? He was a totally different man."

"I recognized him, but I hesitated to approach," Elma replied.

"You didn't recognize him either?" He looked at his bodyguard.

Arlen Brook had his head down. "I informed him and gave him advice, but he refused me aggressively."

Arlen lifted his head and gave a mean look to Elma. "Son of a bitch, mother . . . Just look at the way he is looking. Is that why I am paying you money?" The boss slapped Arnoldo as hard as he could.

After the mighty slap, Arlen stumbled; he could barely stand straight. "You don't seem to understand the severity of the situation. Frank was killed or it was a car accident, I don't know. But for some reason, three people who left the casino at separate times ended up in the same car. For some reason, there was a conflict between them. Bullet wounds could be a proof to that. Probably that's how the driver lost control of the car and they crashed. Driver died, and the rest were taken to the hospital in a critical condition. If one of those makes it alive, you can consider yourselves in jail. Carlos had really important news when he came to the casino that day. He knew something about Alec Castello. Perhaps Alec was an undercover agent sent by the feds. If you had told me about him right away, I would have gotten rid of him the same night. I would have vanished him."

"But he didn't say why he was after that man. Alec Castello was your close friend. Perhaps Carlos knows why he was sent here. Now I'm curious why he was so personally interested in this, and he did not tell you on time?"

"That's why, if you had told me earlier, I would have sent men after them and found out where they were going. Figure out why Carlos was after that man. It's not the time to wait now. Clean up the casino right away. Leave nothing related to any kind of drug. We need to check the city hospitals. Find out at which one they are being treated and find out about their conditions. If Carlos wakes from a coma, we are screwed. The feds will find a way to get the information from him. If both of them make it alive, they will confront them and find out the truth. To be honest, I don't think Alec knows much about us."

"He knows that we do drugs. We should have suspected something when we offered him some and he refused. Now I think he was sent as an undercover by the police or the feds."

"Find me the hospital they are staying in and find out about their condition. If they are alive, we need to leave the country as soon as possible. Try not to act suspicious. If you can't get into the hospital, try to get some information from the doctors and nurses leaving their shifts. Hurry up, the night shifters will be going home early in the morning."

"Even if we know which hospital they are at, their wards will be heavily protected by the police. It's really dangerous."

"If we find the hospital, I will find a way to get inside."

"It's not possible. There will be cops guarding them. Maybe we can get some information from the staff leaving work."

"Good thinking. We need to get to work. Be very careful. Find various excuses to get into the hospitals. If there's no police protection, try to kill them both, just in case."

"Boss, considering that the police might be watching this place, I was planning to meet with you at night."

"That's even more dangerous. They will catch us both if they suspect something, but this way is more convenient. I can just say that there were problems with the payment of the money I won and that's why I came up to the office to complain to the casino management, that's it. Now, answer my questions."

"What was the reason for the search?"

"Blood samples taken from Carlos show drugs in his blood, and heroin was found in his car. Police got an order to search the casino, because the last place Carlos was that night was in this casino. But I was prepared for it. I'm never careless when it comes to drugs."

"I'm satisfied with your service. Why did they get your statements?"

"They asked me to say everything I know about Carlos. I told them that I had Carlos at the casino that day, but I don't know that customer from before. I informed the staff that he sometimes comes to the casino. I even presented them the video records of him being in the casino."

"Carlos came to your room? What did you say about that?"

"He asked the staff about the owner of the place and came to my room to introduce himself, that's what I told them, that's it."

"And the police believed you, right?"

"Looking at the camera records, it was strange that Alec had made changes to his appearance."

The boss angrily turned the security guard. "You didn't see either?"

"No, sir."

"Then tell me, how is it possible that you saw and the others didn't?"

"Boss, he was a totally different person that day. He had a hat and glasses on. He sat near the window, had some drinks, and smoked cigar. He was looking out the window, and then Carlos arrived. I was busy working. After a few minutes, when I looked at his table, Alec was gone."

"He's lying, boss."

"I'm not. You can ask the waiter if you want."

"Call in the waiter! Was someone like that here that day?"

"Sir, I approached that man and he ordered a drink. At first, I didn't recognize him, but later on I did. It was Mr. Castello. The way he was dressed was strange."

"Bastard, do you see? How are you keeping watch of the people coming in and out?"

"Boss, he has been around for some time now. We didn't notice anything strange about his behavior. We have nothing to prove that he was involved in Carlos's murder."

"He came here with a different purpose, you dumbasses. His name is Roger Thomas. Open your eyes, look around you, fools. He's an ex-Special Force. They were talking about him on the news yesterday. Maybe that jerk came here for a different reason, not just for Carlos. It seems Carlos was right. Maybe it was this guy that killed our boys. Maybe they are friends with Michael Grady and he had come to the city to get revenge for his friend? If you had told me what Carlos said right away, he wouldn't have been able to get away. Now they are both in a critical condition. Do you even think about what is expecting us if any one of them makes it alive? We need to find a way out. Go, all of you. Arlen, take Elma to Alberto's place. Elma, don't get out of the house for some. You must not be seen. I will get in touch with you. Arlen, return back quickly. Anderson, I need you for some business."

"I'm listening, boss."

"I didn't want to talk about this near them. We have lost our best men. It doesn't look good for us. Looks like they are in our tail. I thought about your proposition. It's going to take a long time selling the casino. We need to get out of here quickly once and for all. You know that my documents are fake. We have plenty of guys who are illegal in the country, plus we are wanted. I handled their fake documents too. My biggest wish is to get revenge for Alberto before going away. I haven't visited his grave to this day. Yeah, I got rid of the man who helped George, but he went there to kill George, but he is alive and in hiding. We need to try to take care of these matters quickly and get out of the country with the jewelry. We need two days at least."

"If he's in a very critical condition or dies, we don't need to hurry."

"I need solid information about their condition."

"Boss, don't worry about my end of the deal. I will try to get everything done soon. Maybe we should send some of the guys to hospital areas? Maybe we can get some information from the nurses leaving work."

"No information was given about which hospital they are being treated at. It's being kept confidential. We shouldn't get everyone involved in this. Elma knows what she's doing. We must hurry, time is short."

Arlen Booker was very mad at Elma. In his mind, it was because of Elma that the boss slapped and embarrassed him in front of everyone. He was going to get his payback time; he was biding for the right moment. He even refused when Anderson asked him to go to the hospital site with Elma. Anderson asked Elma and Freddie to keep watch on some of the biggest hospitals in the city.

Elma made plenty of changes to her exterior. They knew that she was good at what she was doing and she would be successful at this. Despite all of this, Freddie was given a special task. If Elma gets caught by the police, he is to leave the area as soon as he can to inform the boss and even kill Elma if possible. With Anderson's proposal, the boss put an extra man to watch over them.

Around most of the hospitals they visited seemed very quiet. Finally, they arrived at the hospital located in the city center. Elma knew this hospital well, since she had been here several times before. She asked Freddie to park the car a little far from the hospital. She started walking to the hospital. It looked like she found the place. Lots of police cars were in the hospital parking lot. But maybe they were here for a different reason. She made a plan to get inside and find out some information. Elma returned to the car and asked Freddie to wait. She returned to the hospital. She approached the hospital reception completely freely so as not to arouse suspicion. She felt the way the police were staring at her while talking to each; she pretended not to see.

"Hello, ma'am. I need to go to the traumatology department."

"Is it your first time here, or do you have a doctor?"

"No, ma'am. It's my first time."

"Then we will open a new medical record for you and you can approach the admission department. After an initial examination at the admission department, you will be able to see a doctor on the basis of your complaint."

"Thank you, ma'am."

There was a queue at the admission department. She took a seat to wait and watch the people in the hallway. She felt very nervous, but she struggled to control herself. She started talking to the women around her so as not to attract the attention of the police walking in the corridor. Civilian-dressed people walking around in the hallway were carefully looking around. Suddenly, Elma and one of the civilians met. She quickly turned away from him. She suspected something from his looks; he could be a federal. She got nervous; she sensed that he was still staring at her. She hesitated to lift her head up; her hands were shaking. She wanted to get up and leave, but that would raise suspicion. As soon as the second civilian dressed entered the hallway, things changed. Both of them approached the admission office and asked for the doctor. The nurse made a phone call and after told them to go to the second floor. When Elma lifted her head up, they were walking to the stairs, but that man was still staring at her. To make a distraction, she asked a question to the woman sitting next to her. "Why do you think the policemen are here? Did something serious happen?"

One of the women near Elma quietly answered. "What? Yes, it is so. I heard it on the news last night. One died and two brought here wounded. I think they are dangerous criminals. The police are everywhere. They are being heavily protected."

"They are probably very dangerous, that's why the police are guarding them just in case anyone wants to attack the hospital."

She noticed two women coming downstairs from the second floor. Their faces were somehow familiar to Elma, but she couldn't figure out exactly. Elma kept staring at them as they were passing by her. Suddenly, one of the women turned to her. Elma quickly turned her head away. She recognized them; they were the women at the birthday party. One of them saw everything as Elma was taking the jewelry from Beth's handbag. The other one was the woman Elma and Frank saw at the gas station. *It looks like they work here. They have finished their night shift and now are going home.* Elma was excited as if she had found something very valuable. For a brief moment, she didn't know how to react. She needed to follow them and find out their residence address. They could find out if the man who stole the jewelry had any connection to them and the conditions of the wounded. They could even use them to implement their plans for the wounded.

She stood up quickly and went outside. Both women were walking to the parking lot. There was no time. They had to find where those women live. Elma got back to the car and got in the backseat. Seeing Elma in such a rush excited Freddie. He quickly got in the car and asked Elma about what happened.

"Freddie, two women are walking to the parking lot. Don't let them see you looking at them. As soon as they drive off, follow them, but don't let them see you. We can't lose them. We need to find their home addresses and tell the boss about it. Me and Frank saw one of them some time ago. I came to the hospital to follow her the next day, but for some reason, she didn't show up. I waited a long time, but I didn't see her. I was not expecting to see them today. We can't let this chance get away."

"Maybe you should tell me what's going on?"

"Dumbass, just do whatever I tell you to do! I don't have to stop and explain everything to you. I said it's important. The boss will value our work here very highly. I will explain everything to you later."

"All right, as you wish."

When he opened his eyes, he realized that he was in a hospital. His head was hurting. He tried to stand up. "You are not allowed to move. I will call the doctor right away." The nurse left the room.

An old doctor with white hair entered the room. "Hi. How are you feeling today?"

"My head hurts. Where am I, may I know?"

"You were brought here in a critical condition. You suffered a severe head-skull trauma. There were cracks in the anterior wall of the thorax at the level of the ninth and tenth vertebrae. I would say, you are a lucky man. The bullet passed over a large vein. If it hit the vein, we probably would have lost you because of an internal bleeding. If the ambulance did not reach on time, you would have been dead. Your treatment continues. I should note that you are under police supervision, and because of your condition, you are not allowed to move for some time. Mr. Roger

Thomas, Special Agent Darren Edmond wants to ask you a few questions about the incident. Are you ready?"

"Yes."

Darren Edmond entered the room shortly after. "Hello, Mr. Roger. How are you feeling today?"

"Like you see."

"I'm gonna ask you a few questions. I need to answer the questions with correct, accurate, and short answers."

"Of course."

"Did you know Carlos Darrick before this?"

"Not from before. I tried to get to know more about him only after the fake diamond ring incident. You already know about that."

"You were aware that he is wanted by the police and the bureau because of that incident, right? What made you decide to go after the criminal without telling the police, despite knowing who he is?"

"After figuring out his address, I was going to call the police and inform them."

"Where did you see him?"

"I saw him at the casino. He didn't look the same. He had changed his looks. I wanted to follow him to his address and let the police know about it, but it didn't end well. They were more careful than me."

"Why did you take this action?"

"The suicide of a seriously ill worker as a result of a known incident and the tragic death of the sheriff while following the criminal tormented me morally. I blamed myself for all of it. What this criminal did touched me deeply. That's why I had to find him no matter what."

"So an act done by some criminal touches you, an ex-Special Force soldier, very deeply. I think you didn't want to give him in to the federals. I think you wanted to get revenge by yourself. But you can't underestimate the enemy, you should know that.

"Do you understand that because of what you did, this case will remain open? If Carlos Darrick dies, we won't be able to catch the criminals."

"I was after him for about a month. Until I inform the police, he could have escaped again or with our cooperation be killed. I offered you my help in this matter, but you refused rudely. I took everything you said personally. I tried to prove my worth this way."

"For how long have you been watching Carlos?"

"Like I said before. For about a month, with an alias name, I went to the popular casino every day and presented myself as a rich customer as I waited for my prey to fall into my trap."

"How did you know that he would come to that exact casino?"

"That casino is popular in the city for its customers. Carlos made good money from the diamond ring. He was going to spend it somewhere."

"According to the information we have, your father knew that he was a skilled jeweler and that's why he gave him to finish the expensive order from a rich customer. That set was very expensive, and some part of the payment was already done. That set was stolen in the robbery, and now your father faces a difficult situation in front of his customer. You got to know and follow Carlos Darrick after that incident. I think your goal was to catch him and get something done about the robbery. Am I right?"

"It's a completely baseless idea. Is he alive?"

"He is, but he is in a coma. Maybe there's a connection between Carlos and the casino owner."

"I only saw him that day at the casino. I have no idea about the relation between them."

"We can't know that. We can just assume. Mr. Roger, you are hiding something from us. I believe you understand your mistake. Because of your overconfidence in yourself, you went after a dangerous criminal, risking your life. If that wasn't enough, the criminal is in a coma now. If he dies, we won't be able to get anything from him regarding the case. You were careless. Such a skilled soldier should not make such a big mistake. It's all because of your overconfidence in yourself. Remember, you may be a master soldier, but this field is not like you think it is. Therefore, the mistake you made led to the resumption of a possible criminal case. I don't want to trouble you too much. I wish you a speedy recovery. The criminal's life is important to us now. I think we will meet again during the investigation and court."

Luisa was exhausted. She, just like everybody else in the hospital, was working an intense shift because of what happened. She was starting to feel some pain in her lower belly. She asked Bella to give her a shot of painkiller.

Considering the situation, she couldn't call George and tell him. The operation of the critical conditioned patients was done, and they were moved to the resuscitation ward. Everything seemed to be calming down. Bella advised her colleague to take a rest for some time because of her belly pain and said that she will do her part of the job as well. Shortly after, Luisa switched on her phone. George had called at two separate times. He was probably worried for her, or it could be something else. She called George right away; she didn't get an answer. She was getting nervous. Even if he is sleeping, George usually answers phone calls.

"Hello. Honey, is that you? I was worried. Why didn't you answer at first?"

"Miss, are you George Bradley's wife?"

"Who are you? Tell me, what happened to my husband? Give him the phone!"

"Miss, there's nothing to worry about. I am a doctor at the military hospital's admission. Your husband was not feeling well, that's why he was brought here to the hospital. Although health concerns related to high blood pressure have been alleviated, stationary treatment is needed. I'm gonna give the phone to your husband now. He shouldn't get excited or worried. As a fellow medical worker, I hope you understand me."

"Of course, Doctor."

"Hello, Luisa. Don't worry, honey, everything's fine."

"I'm sorry, George. We are having very intense shifts. I had to turn off my phone. They are not gonna let me come near you. Tomorrow when we meet, I will tell you everything."

"Don't worry, honey. See you."

The phone line was quiet. She wiped her tears. She stood to refresh her makeup and leave the room. At this moment, Bella entered the room.

"Luisa, when the doctor was checking on the patients, he got mad because he didn't see you there. I told him about the situation, but he didn't seem to care. He said that he will note the chief doctor about this. You have to see the chief doctor before you go home tomorrow morning."

The shift was over, but Luisa was still waiting in front of the chief doctor's office. For some reason, all the things that are happening affected her in a bad way. Exhaustion on one hand, stress on the other; she was in a lot of pain. Bella was with her. Both of them were really exhausted and sleepless. Even though she was tired, Luisa wanted to visit George at the hospital before going home.

"Good morning."

"Luisa Bradley, please sit. How are you feeling? I know your shift is over. I'm not gonna take much of your time. You are a nurse who is very responsible at work. Your skills and responsible approach to work are always in the center of attention. I don't think I need to remind you how important and vital our job is. It's enough to remember what happened last night. Critical conditions of the patients can change to worse at any moment. Your condition related to the pregnancy does not allow you to work in such a rigorous work regime. All of this is temporary. For the safety of your unborn child, you must refrain from such an intense workload. To help you, I'm gonna have to temporarily expel you from work. You must complete your pregnancy under the supervision of an obstetrician and nurse in an outpatient or, if necessary, inpatient setting. I hope you understand me."

"I'm sorry for last night. I thank you for your sincere attention."

"I will inform the management of the maternity ward about you. A healthy born child is important to us. I wish you good health and look forward to seeing you among us. I must say good-bye for now. Please write your application and confirm it with your signature."

She was sad about leaving work. Belle was there to comfort her. "Don't worry, darling. It's all for your well-being. I will talk to the doctor who's going to treat you and say I can take care of you from home. Let's go to the maternity ward together tomorrow and find out your condition. We will head to the hospital where George is, to visit him, and after that, we can go home."

"Bella, I don't know how to thank you for everything. I really appreciate it."

"Maybe we should go to my place. Brook is working tonight. I'm all alone. If you want, you can stay over."

"We'll talk about it."

They went to the hospital where George was being treated. They asked the doctor about George's condition. The doctor said that the headaches caused by high blood pressure continued. The weakening of the senses on the sides of the skull indicated the seriousness of the situation. The doctor said that while keeping his blood pressure under control, he instructed George not to move for a while. He also advised to take a break from patient visits and telephone conversations. Only Luisa was allowed to come on the condition of a short meeting.

"Hi, honey. How are you?" She kissed George on the cheek.

"Thank you. How are you doing? Your phone was turned off last night. I was worried."

"Everything is all right. Starting today, I will be at home until our child is born. Baby's health is the most important thing."

"At last, you agree with my idea. But you being alone at home is going to keep me up all night."

"Don't worry. Bella is going to be with me at all times."

"I'm asking you, please stay with Bella until I get out of the hospital."

"Take care, darling." As she kissed George on the cheek and went out to the hallway, she came face-to-face with the doctor.

"Doctor, I can't thank you enough."

"Ma'am, this is our oath. I can understand how you feel. Your husband needs some quiet time right now. Please do not come to visit the patient for some time. We will keep you informed about his health. Make short phone calls to him. Give us your phone number."

"Thank you, Doctor. I understand. Thank you for everything."

"This is our job."

After visiting George, she came back home with Bella. Bella called her husband about Luisa's condition and told her that she would be a little late. Luisa was tired and felt a slight increase in pain in her lower abdomen. She asked Bella to bring her painkiller medicine.

"Be patient, honey. You didn't even eat anything."

"I can't forget what happened last night during our shift. I wonder how the wounded are? There were a lot of policemen at the hospital. Federals were there too. It's probably something very serious."

"These things happen at the hospital. You didn't worry this much back then. Looks like you really do need to rest. Be patient. When I go to work tomorrow, I will find out about their condition and tell you when I come back."

"I'm gonna be alone tonight. I have this scary feeling inside me."

"Don't worry, Luisa. We'll think of something. Perhaps we should go to my place. You can stay with me until George comes out of the hospital. You won't be alone when I'm not home. I have a very nice and friendly neighbor. Very easygoing. Most of the time she's here, won't let you get bored."

"All right, Bella. Let's do it."

Bella sat on the edge of his bed and stroked her hair. "I see that these kinds of things touch you deeply. I worry that you are troubling yourself too much. Consider the chief doctor's words sincerely. You are pregnant. This much work is not good for you. Why do you make yourself suffer so much? You've got everything you need. Think about your unborn child. Trust me, if your doctor knows that you worry too much, he won't let you work either. You need to be careful about other things too. You see what's happening in the state? Until the criminals are caught and put to jail, the situation is going to remain like this. The chief doctor made a good decision for your benefit. Brook told me everything about you two. He asked me to be extra careful too. I think he suspects something too."

"Bella, to be honest, I was tired of George's demands for my resignation. I understand the difficulty of the situation. Maybe the wounded from last night were members of the same gang. I'm terrified enough going out to the street after what happened. It is not pleasant for me to be driven from my home and stay at someone else's home. All this affects me badly. I used to live alone in my home, and nobody bothered me. I was just minding my own business. I was happy when Michael and my husband returned from Afghanistan. Then these things happened. Without even realizing, Michael and George came face-to-face with the criminal gang. He loved Beth very much.

Her death was out of nowhere. Her lavish lifestyle, expensive car, and jewelry showed that she was not on the right track. Everything that happened to Michael and George, as well as to me, happened because of the dishonest actions of this dishonorable woman. I'm fed up."

"Luisa, I don't want to make you mad or anything, but what you are saying is that it all happened because of Michael? I'm sorry, but you are wrong. To say the truth, I don't know him personally, but Brook has told me a lot about him. He's a very brave and an honest man. It's according to what Brook told me. He fell victim to Beth's nasty little games."

"I have a lot of respect for Michael. He loves me like a sister. After all of this, I'm worried for him too. We haven't been able to get in touch with him lately. We don't even know if he is alive or not. He has nobody in his life. We were the closest people to Michael. He risked his life to protect George. If it wasn't for Michael that night, they would have killed him. Sometimes I get mad at him, but later I regret doing so. One of the main reasons George worries so much is Michael disappeared. After his house burned to the ground, Michael was nowhere to be found. This was seriously affecting George's health."

"Be positive, be patient. Trust me, everything will be fine again. Maybe he's alive, you never know."

"All right, Bella. I must contact the doctor and be checked tomorrow. My child's health is more valuable and more important than anything else. I will go to the doctor's appointment with you."

"OK, honey. Take some rest, forget about the pain. We will go to my place later and discuss all of these things."

"Why not go now? We can both rest then. I know you are tired too. I need just a couple of things. The pain has gotten less after taking the medicine."

"All right, as you wish."

Bella thought it was important not to leave her alone for a moment. She could get anxiety attacks again. She was always nervous.

George was worried for Luisa. He tried to hide his main health concerns so that she would not have to worry. He even told the doctor that she was pregnant and asked to tell his wife that he was only suffering from high blood pressure. Actually, it didn't look good for him. His headaches were increasing lately. The doctor gave him an immobile treatment regime. Complications from the traumatic brain injury of the war were recurring. Failure to follow the doctor's instructions could result in complete loss of senses. This would put him in a wheelchair for life. Therefore, he had to follow the doctor's advice.

Luisa went with Bella to her place. She had a doctor's appointment in the morning. Bella's home was near the clinic. Bella would be home alone because Brook Cletus was at work tonight.

She parked the car in front of the house with a small yard. A man in a police uniform greeted them, and they went inside home. Freddie parked the car a short distance away, and they watched as Bella went in. Elma recognized the sheriff greeting her. It looked like it was Brook Cletus's house.

"We need to be extra careful. He's a good sheriff. He knows what he's doing. He might suspect something. We need to get out of this area and tell the boss about it immediately."

"Looks like they are friends. They work at the same hospital. Beth worked at a different hospital. She told me about Luisa—that they were friends with her until she broke up with Michael. After that, they have lost touch. Fortunately, I remember the looks of the women who were with Beth on her birthday. A few months ago, the boss told me to go to the hospital and ask about Luisa. I presented myself as her relative. The receptionist said Luisa had resigned temporarily because of her health condition. For some reason, she was staring at me strangely. I knew she suspected something and got out of there quickly. Later on, the boss cautiously kept me away from these things. It won't be good for us if Carlos wakes up from the coma. That's why we need to get information about what's going on at the hospital. But it's not safe. I think the boss is going to do something before he wakes up from a coma. At first, the boss asked me not to leave Alberto's house. Then, for some reason, he wanted me to get some information about Carlos's condition, and I saw this nurse again. I think the boss is going to be satisfied with our work here."

"Carl Caster used to be partners with this sheriff. Now he is partnered up with another sheriff. Because of them, our sales have decreased significantly. After the Carlos incident, Anderson instructed us to stop working altogether."

"Freddie, I think the situation is really, really bad. At night, I came home with Arlen. Early in the morning, Arnoldo came to the house and gave strict orders for you and me to do this serious task. I think there are some questionable points here. They are probably making a new plan and waiting for news from us. I need to let Arnoldo know about this as soon as possible. Looks like we are going to solve some problems today."

"You better go. I will keep watch here. What are you going to say if he asks about Carlos?"

"I'm gonna have to say that we haven't been able to find anything on Carlos. This is more important than that. If this woman is really George's wife, the boss is going to appreciate it."

"Then hurry and inform the boss about this. Let's find out what they are going to decide about this."

Arnoldo thought a lot. This was very important information. After the death of his brother, they searched George's house but could not find him. So he left home and lived with his wife at another address. Although Carl Caster promised to find George's address soon and provide information, he was later assassinated under unknown circumstances. After some thought, Arnoldo announced his decision to Anderson.

"We are unaware of the situation at the hospital. The patients are probably not doing so well. A statement from any of them will be sufficient enough to conduct a thorough search at the casino and arrest the employees. It's quiet for now. Carlos is more dangerous to us if he survives. We can get detailed information about the situation through nurses. We can even speed up Carlos's death with their help. We will set a condition for them. We will threaten to kill their husbands if they don't fulfil our request. We have to go to that area immediately. It is important how many people are in the house now. We must be extremely careful and speed up the work. Talking on the phone is strictly forbidden. We must solve the problem on the spot and lose track."

"It seems to me that these women have secrets about lost jewelry, and the main organizer of this work was Carl Caster himself. I told you in time that I doubted this bastard, but you did not hear me out. Maybe he was an undercover agent sent by the police. He had a well-thought-out plan. By telling the password to Beth, he had to deliver the jewels in the safe to these women from the birthday party. His main goal was to sell us out after Beth was eliminated as a witness. As a result, they would both become rich and gain the respect of the police as a capable sheriff. We rushed into killing Beth. We should have done it after we found out the truth from her."

"Apparently, Elma thwarted their plan. But why didn't they kill Elma when they took the jewelry from her? They would have killed Elma too to get rid of any trail left behind. The house that woman went into was Sheriff Brook Cletus's house. He used to work together with Carl Caster. The woman whom Elma recognized and gave a statement to the police is Sheriff Brook Cletus's wife. But Sheriff Carl Caster didn't tell me about it at the time. What was his plan? So that's it. Looks like both sheriffs were in on it together. Apparently, the sheriff would give the jewelry to Bella through Beth so that the boss would not suspect him. Elma's arrival at the birthday party disrupted their plan. Bella informs her husband that the plan did not work out and that Beth went with a blonde woman. Following them, Brook Cletus enters through the open kitchen door and, in the darkness, quickly takes the bracelet from Elma's hand and leaves."

"But the night of Beth's murder, Sheriff Cletus was on duty with Caster."

"Did you see them together that evening?"

"No!"

"It's all a part of Caster's plan. What I said will be true. We will make those bitches talk now, and they'll say everything as it is. Trust me. I think my arrival at the scene ruined their plans. Because he couldn't use his duty gun to commit the crime. Beth's gun was in her handbag upstairs. Because of lack of time, he had to leave with the jewelry." Anderson spoke out his mind.

"These assumptions don't make any sense." Arnoldo called in Elma from the next room.

"Are you totally certain that those are the same women?"

"Of course. I think one of them is pregnant. I overheard them talking to each other. That's when I heard their names."

"You are hesitating, boss. The idea that was just told seems logical to me. Perhaps Brook and Carl had some kind of argument and Brook ended up killing Carl."

"So Brook didn't come to the sheriff's house by chance the day we were there. Apparently, he felt that we were in Carl's house and changed his mind."

"How could he have known that we were in the house?"

"From the cigar on the ashtray. We should have taken away the cigar from the ashtray when we went downstairs."

"We turned it off, though."

"Even if it is so, Carl doesn't smoke cigars. That's enough of a reason to assume that there are other people in the house."

In fact, Elma was glad they thought so. Doubts about jewelry would be put to an end. It was too late to see Carlos and talk about it and try to learn regarding the jewelry. There was a reason Carlos stayed away from her, even from all the gang members. His hospitalization in critical condition and Frank's death were a mystery. Apparently, there was a mysterious connection between Carlos and Aldo, and the survival of both would shed light on many mysteries and remaining issues. That's why Elma was hoping that Carlos wouldn't make it out of the hospital alive. If he survived, the situation would not be good. Elma wanted this more than the gang members.

Arnoldo asked Elma to wait in another room.

"According to what you say, I came to the conclusion that these women and both sheriffs were involved in the stolen diamond. Carl gave Beth the password. He did this not to arouse suspicion."

"There are many dubious points. We need to hurry, Tonight we are gonna get answers for many things. I will go there with Arlen and Anderson. Elma is going to be with us too. Hurry."

The door opened. The sheriff kissed one of the women and left. It was probably his wife.

"We need to know exactly how many people are in the house. Elma's attention was drawn to a woman walking toward the sheriff's house."

"Boss, let me handle."

"Be careful."

Elma quickly got out of the car and tried to approach the woman in front.

"Good evening, ma'am. Do you live here?"

"Talk louder! I can't hear you."

"I'm sorry to disturb you. I come from the neighboring state. There is a courtyard house where my relative lives on this street. I know the exact house is located in this street. But I forgot the address. It's been a long time since I last came. Does Sheriff Eddick Osvaldo live around here?"

"There's some other sheriff living in my neighborhood, Brook Cletus. He and his wife Bella have been living there for a long time now. They are very dear to me."

"His wife's name is Gulia. They have three kids."

"No, ma'am. Unfortunately, they do not have kids. You must have mistaken your address."

"I'm sorry, ma'am. Perhaps it's another address. Thank you."

Elma happily approached the car.

"Boss, I think we can handle the rest of the business. I don't want Elma to participate in this. She's being wanted anyway. Allow her to go."

"Tell Freddie to take her home. We definitely need to take her with us. She has been very helpful. Call Freddie over. I have an assignment for him. You, get out of the car, go talk to Elma outside."

A few minutes later, Freddie was in the car with the boss. "Listen to me carefully. First, take Elma to the casino and then to Alberto's place. Take one of the guys you trust with you and head to the forest. You know the rest. I don't want to lose time there. As soon as we are done, we will come straight to the forest. They are gonna wait for us around five o'clock in the morning near the border. We might miss it. Every hour we spend here is dangerous. Hurry up. Call Elma."

Elma quickly approached the car. "Listen, go to the casino with Freddie urgently. Take these keys and open the safe there. Take all the documents and money. Wait at Alberto's place. I will send men after you."

"Boss, maybe we can get away from here quietly now?"

"No, I'm not going anywhere without taking revenge on my brother's killers. I'm not, even if I die. One more thing— we should have killed Carlos when we had the chance. Now it's impossible to kill him. If he wakes up, they will find out everything from him."

"But we are leaving the country."

"That's why I'm leaving this country, but if we can't cross the border, we are going to have to hide in this country's area. With the information Carlos is going to give, it won't be possible. I'm sure he would want us to end up in jail."

The doorbell rang. "Bella, are you expecting someone?"

"Don't worry, girl, it's probably Brook. He forgot something."

Bella got up from the couch and went to the door. She looked through the peephole. There was a pizza delivery man waiting at the door with a pizza in hand.

It was strange. Bella opened the door. "I'm listening, what do you want?"

"You didn't order pizza, ma'am?"

"No, you have the wrong address."

"I'm sorry, ma'am."

"And that's a large pizza. There's only two of us." She laughed.

"It's all right. Maybe we can be helpful and help you find the address."

"There's no need, because it's the right address." He pointed his gun at Bella from under the pizza box and demanded that she step back from the door. At that moment, with great pressure, the door opened inward, and two masked men outside entered the house with guns in their hands.

"I'm telling you the truth, believe me." Bella began to tremble in fear when she saw two masked gunmen in front of her.

"Who are you?"

"Get inside. You'll know soon enough," said one of the masked men, poking Bella with the gun in his hand and asking her to sit on the couch.

"What, ma'am? You don't know us? But we know both of you very well. Don't act like you don't know. First, you must do as you are told. Tell us about Roger Thomas and Carlos Darrick, who are being treated at the hospital."

"Sir, our shift finished in the morning. We can only know about them tomorrow."

"Pick up the phone and call the department! Ask your colleagues about the patients!"

"Sir, but that's not right. The police are watching everything about them. They might get suspicious over our phone call."

Arnoldo pointed the gun at Luisa's head. "Sir, calm down right away," she said and dialed the phone number.

"Put it on loudspeaker. If you try anything stupid, consider yourself dead."

"Hello, is this the admissions office? I'm nurse Bella Cletus. I would like to contact Yuan Lee, a nurse on duty at the intensive care unit today."

"Ma'am, I'm gonna connect you with the room. Wait a moment, please."

"I'm listening."

"I'm Bella Cletus."

"Bella, do you have something important to say? You know the rules."

"Yuan, Luisa and I are very worried about the patients' condition. How are they?"

"Roger Thomas woke up from a coma this evening. Carlos Darrick opened his eyes an hour ago. But the doctors don't allow them to talk yet. You have seen plenty of things like this. Why are you worried?"

The sound cut off. Anderson was staring at Alvaro. "Unfortunately, I couldn't catch that bastard. It's all right, I have his favorite woman with me. But a man should come face-to-face with a man. I'm gonna revenge my brother. There's only one way for you two to stay alive. Just do as I say quietly, that's it. You will not get hurt in any way. Understood?"

"Sir, you can have all you want from the house."

"What do you have at home, tell me."

"Some money and some jewelry."

"You see, my friend? Looks like our visit has a purpose. Bring them."

Bella went to the next room with one of the masked gunmen and opened the small safe. She took all the money and jewelry and placed the money and some jewelry on the table. "This is all I have."

Luisa was shaking in fear.

"This is it? Where's the necklace?"

"What necklace, sir? You must have mistaken us with someone else."

"Don't act stupid, bitch. I'm talking about the necklace and the earring you saw at the birthday party in the woman's purse!" said Arnoldo and slapped Bella. Bella collapsed on the couch, dizzy from the blow.

"Believe me, I have nothing else." Luisa started crying.

"You don't know anything too?" When Arnoldo wanted to slap Luisa, Bella got up with difficulty and stepped forward.

"Guys, she is my guest. Please don't touch her. She is pregnant. She's having troubles anyway. I have seen the jewelry you are talking about, but those women left the party together. I simply helped the drunk woman to the car. Her name was Beth. She used to be a nurse at the clinic. Luisa was her neighbor."

"Which woman was falling?"

"I was in the kitchen. I saw the woman who arrived late to the party hit Beth in the bedroom. She fell unconscious. Then that woman opened Beth's handbag, and when she took out the jewelry, I saw it."

"So this woman is pregnant. I'm so happy to hear that. That bastard George is going to have a child. What a nice coincidence. My brother is rotting in the cemetery of the unknown."

"Sir, we don't know you. What's her fault? Hurting a pregnant woman is the biggest sin!"

"She's pregnant. You see what she's saying!" he yelled, grabbing Bella by the hair again.

"Stupid cunt. My mother was pregnant. She gave birth to her children in the old hut without a doctor, and she died of heavy blood loss. She entrusted her son to me in her last breath. Her husband took my brother from me. Now his child is going to be birthed in the most beautiful hospital. And I'm just gonna grieve for my brother till the end of my life, is that right?"

"Sir, believe me, I feel your pain. Her husband can't kill anyone. He was heavily injured in the war. He is sick. His only wish is to hear his child's voice. I swear to God, take everything you want, just don't touch her."

"Don't try to fool me. Where did you hide the jewelry from Beth's bag at the party? The pregnant woman you are protecting was there too. I don't have much time. I'll kill both of you. Return the goods!"

"Please believe me. I know nothing about these things. At the police station, I reported seeing only jewelry and the women's appearance."

"You don't know either?" He pushed Bella aside and stepped toward Luisa. Frightened, Luisa retreated and fell on her back.

"You bastards, I told you she is pregnant and her husband's sick. He suffered a severe trauma in the war." She cried, trying to lift Luisa off the ground. Arnoldo grabbed Bella's neck with one arm, pulled her back, and began choking her with all his might.

"Stupid woman! What was your crippled husband doing at Beth's house in the middle of the night!"

Bella reached out and removed the mask from Anderson's face, but she began to gasp and gasp. Gathering all her strength, Luisa got up and tried to take Bella from Anderson's hand. "Let her go. She's going to suffocate! Please, I'm begging you, don't kill her! We don't know anything."

"Don't tell me what to do, bitch!" Anderson let go of Bella and slapped Luisa with all his might. Luisa fainted and fell to the ground.

"Boss, they gave everything they have. Looks like they have nothing left. I don't believe that in a situation like this, they would lie about it and hide it."

Arnoldo was trembling with rage. He leaned over and grabbed Luisa by the hair and slapped her in the face. "Don't you dare to try to fool me, stupid woman! Where's he? Tell me where that war veteran is!"

"I am not going to kill you. He's not at the hut that you two were hiding in, is he?"

Bella gathered herself with all her might and tried to pull Luisa away from Arnoldo. "Quick! Tell me, where's her husband hiding? And tell me where the jewelry is, or I'll kill you."

"Her husband is at the hospital, getting treatment. He's not doing so well."

Unable to bear what was happening, Arlen entered the room from outside. "Let go of her, don't you see her condition, how bad it is? She needs an ambulance!"

"What are you saying, jerk? Did I bring you over to just watch?"

"Boss, calm down. She's pregnant. She's doing good anyway. As you see, they have nothing!"

Arnoldo slapped Arlen as hard as he could. "Son of a bitch, I told you to wait outside and stay watch. Get the hell out. If I ever see you coming in again, I'm gonna kill you!" He grabbed him by the collar and pushed him to the wall.

Arlen went outside. He was fed up with everything happening. He thought about getting back inside and killing them both. At the sound of police cars heard in the distance, he realized that the situation was not good. He went back inside again. "Boss, we need to get out of here quickly. It's not good. I heard police sirens approaching. I think they are coming this way."

"Looks like bastards are tracing the phone calls to the hospital."

Arnoldo pulled out the gun and handed it to Arlen. "It's up to you. If you don't do it, you will die with them. Anderson, watch him. My brother was a child too. That orphan kid was all I had. Your bastard husband with his friend took him away from me. A mother gave birth to him. Hurry up! Quickly! His husband will leave the hospital soon. I'm gonna find that bastard no matter what happens!" Arnoldo yelled and went outside.

"Anderson! What do we do? We are running out of time," he said, pointing to the blood flowing from where Luisa lay.

"He got his revenge. This will be a suffering for him all his life."

Bella didn't know what to do. Luisa was losing a lot of blood; it did not look good. "Anderson, we are not killers! Let's not kill her. She has suffered enough. She's losing her baby anyway. At least let me call an ambulance so that the mother can live." He started begging.

Anderson took the gun from Arlen's shaking hands and fired twice. They quickly went outside and got in the car. "I'm gonna ask you a favor. When you are going after Elma, kill her and destroy all the casino documents. The police are going to be here any minute now. Hurry up."

Arlen was pleased with the assignment he was given. "Did you kill them?"

"Yes, boss. The cars are getting closer. We must hurry. What do we do?"

Arnoldo looked at Arlen. "I'm going to the forest with Anderson. Go to Alberto's place right now and pick up Elma and come to the area. Hurry! Time is running."

She barely managed to get up. She had a terrible headache; her head was spinning. The cell phones were broken, and the home phone's lines were cut off. Luisa was losing blood. Calling for help would take too much time. She tried to get up with difficulty but fainted and fell on the sofa. Talking sounds came to her ears. "Hurry! Looks like they are in critical condition."

"Bastards! How could they do this to a woman?"

She didn't hear the rest of it. After receiving first aid, both patients were taken to hospital by ambulance. Darren Edmond left the scene and headed straight for the department, driving very fast.

The police department and the federal government had already mobilized all their forces in search of the criminals.

Brook Cletus was not well. He arrived in the area as soon as he received information about the incident. However, he was not allowed near Luisa and Bella. They were taken to the hospital emergency. Seeing that his colleague was not well, the sheriff took him to the hospital. Brook Cletus was having a nervous breakdown. He needed psychological help for some time.

Michael was happy. Finally, after a long search, he found out about the house where Elma was hiding, and it took a long time to find the place. So the place she was staying in was Alberto's place. He got the information from one of the gang members before killing him. So Elma changed her image, hid in Alberto's house, and came to the casino at night to work. However, he could not find the house based on his searches because he did not have an exact address. He had to find Elma and track her down exactly when she went home. Roger informed Michael about the appearance of the woman he suspected, and he identified the information, albeit partially, with Elma. Some signs certainly proved that she was Elma. He had to meet with Elma alone and clarify certain issues. This woman was very mysterious. Through her, he would be able to obtain accurate information about the gang and the cause of Beth's death. Probably the man near her was her bodyguard.

With this purpose, several times, Michael kept watch around the casino to see how everything works around there. But he did not see anyone with similarities. Apparently, he did not get to see her because she came to the casino from time to time or this woman often changed her image very often. On the other hand, Michael was cautious about being seen around the casino. His appearance around the casino for a long time could have attracted attention. Michael decided to continue his observations for three days in a row. During this time, he would follow the woman with the similar signs to the house where she lived. If she was Elma, she would tell him the truth, and he would record everything on the phone. But there was a problem—he needed a cell phone. He urgently looked for a way to get a new number and phone. It was not very easy, because his passport and other documents burned in the house fire. Only way left was to ask his neighbor for help. This time, he was going to ask about Sarah's condition. After leaving Sarah, he learned that she had been taken to the hospital in critical condition by ambulance through a woman who sometimes spent the night at his house. The woman spoke to Michael about a girl she saw on TV who was taken to hospital in critical condition. Following the news, Sarah's parents came to the hospital and confirmed that the girl was their daughter. That girl was Sarah Marchelo, who went missing a few months ago.

He looked around. When he made sure that there was nobody around, he approached the house. He rang the doorbell. They were happy to see him.

"I was shocked when I heard. How's Sarah?"

"She was taken to the hospital in critical condition. She was in a coma for three days. Thanks to the doctors, she's feeling much better now. After receiving treatment in the hospital for a while, she will be sent to a drug treatment center."

Sarah's mother could not hold back her tears. "The bastard who threw my child into the desert in critical condition called an ambulance. Who committed this remains unknown. But what is strange to me is why they called an ambulance if they wanted to kill her. Perhaps an honest man was among them who did this out of pity for Sarah."

"What does the owner of the car say about this?"

"There's information about the owner of the car, but the driver isn't found yet."

"What does Sarah say?"

"She doesn't know the place she was being held or the driver. She will probably need a long-term treatment. She loves you very much. She's waiting for your arrival. Maybe you should visit her."

"Of course, ma'am. I will go to visit her soon, but now I have some other things to do. I need some time to conclude some things."

"Michael, you are probably hungry. You should eat something."

"Thank you, I'm not hungry. I need to go. It's really important. Me staying here at a time like this would be dangerous for you too. I need a favor from you. I need a cell phone. It doesn't have to be new."

"I'll give you one of our phones."

"I need it for a short time. Temporary. I'm sorry for bothering you. Soon, Sarah will get better and get out of the hospital. Then we will celebrate together."

"Michael, I need to talk to you in private. It won't take long," said Lucas, and they went to the next room.

"I wanted to give you information about Roger Thomas. I know you are really worried for him." Lucas spoke about the incident. "I heard that he got up from a coma today. They are keeping the information about his condition confidential. I just want to say that he is alive."

"I was saddened to hear what happened. If I'm still alive after concluding my business, I will meet with him. For certain reasons, I operate in secret. My enemies don't know that I'm alive. Please try to get more detailed information about Roger Thomas's condition. I need one more favor from you, Mr. Lucas.

Take this letter. Everything is written in detail about what happened. Get the letter to Agent Darren Edmond. It's life, you never know. If I die, I don't want people to have the wrong idea about me."

The entrance of the casino was clearly visible from where it was. It's been a long time. The clocks are already showing the night. During this time, many strangers came and went to the casino. But there was no one like Elma among the women. Elma was a relatively small and medium-sized woman. His friend told him that her hair previously was blonde; later she dyed her hair black. She was using another name at work. It seems she changed her name too. Finally, Michael noticed a woman who got out of a car and rushed into the casino. She looked like Elma. The driver, with his hand on the steering wheel, often leaned over and looked at the casino door. Apparently, he was in a hurry, waiting for someone. Michael began to get excited. He needed a vehicle. He looked around. Among the cars lined up in the parking lot a short distance away, an old brand Ford Bronco drew his attention.

Shortly afterward, the woman reappeared at the casino gate. She looked nervous. The folder and bag in her hand drew Michael's attention. She hurriedly put the bag in the backseat of the car and sat in the front with the folder in her hand. Michael was getting suspicious. It looked like the gang was on the move and they were using this woman with that purpose.

Finally, the car started moving. Michael took the license plate and quickly walked to the parking lot. He knew that there was a long highway ahead and that the car would go straight for a while without turning. But another thought came to his mind. Maybe this woman was not Elma? Or the car could go to another address. He opened and started the car with a small trick he learned, quickly drove to the highway, and kept following the car ahead from a safe distance.

Time was passing. The car in front was speeding along the highway. Michael kept a fair distance to the car as he followed. At last, the car turned into the town on the opposite side of the road. Michael knew that town. So it seems Alberto's house is located in this town. To avoid suspicion, he stopped the pursuit and parked the car on the side of the highway and watched the traffic ahead. In the moonlight, everything was clearly visible. The car in front stopped in front of the two-story house after a while. The woman got out of the car and went inside. Michael sat on a bench and waited for the car to return from town. It was about a kilometer away. He planned to walk that road. Gradually, he was approaching the area. He hid his gun under his coat, ready to shoot as a precaution. This weapon belonged to the villain he killed, and he would use it if necessary. The lights were on, and it looked like she's home. He stood, looked around, and listened intently. He was nervous; he got fairly close to the house. He wanted to make sure that Elma was alone in there. He went to the side of the house to watch the kitchen where the light was on through the window. She was alone. She was busy with something in front of the gas stove. Sometimes she put the cigarette she was smoking in the ashtray and got back to work.

He approached the door and picked open the lock. He went inside. Loud music was playing. He went into the kitchen. While singing, Elma opened the refrigerator door and took something. She turned back and saw a man standing in front of her. With shock, she dropped the whisky bottle on the floor. She wanted to scream, but Michael pointed the gun at her and told her to be silent with his finger.

"Am I dreaming? But they killed you? What do you want from me? How dare you come into my house!"

"If I'm here, that means I'm alive."

"What do you want from me? They are coming here. They will kill you. Get out!"

"Maybe. But before we die, we will clarify a few issues with you."

"I don't know anything!"

"You know very well. Maybe you just forgot. All right, I guess I'm gonna have to make you remember. Get in the room and sit. I don't have much time."

"I don't know anything about this. It's better you just leave quietly. They think you are dead anyway. I won't tell them anything."

"Don't try to scare me with death and bums around you. I have questions to ask. Try to answer correctly. Because the moment I feel that you are lying, it will cost you dearly."

"I'm begging you, please. I have nothing to do with this."

"Listen, I didn't come here to hear you beg. Time is short. I'm just an ordinary citizen like you. I'm here only to clarify some issues. You will answer my questions correctly, and I will leave you alone. That's it. Understood?"

"OK, Michael, I'm gonna tell you everything. You're not gonna kill me, right?"

"Answer the questions."

"All right."

"Who killed Beth?"

"Anderson."

"Who's he?"

"He's the boss's right hand."

"Who's the boss?"

"Originally he is from the neighboring country. They say he changed his name. I don't know his real name either. His current name is Arnoldo. He's the leader in the gang. Everybody calls him boss."

"Why did you kill Beth?"

"They found out that she met with you and got suspicious of her."

"Why would they suspect Beth?"

"Stolen jewelry was being kept at her house. Sheriff Carl Caster is the boss's one of the loyal and close assistants. The boss and the sheriff found Beth's house to be suitable for storing the goods. The sheriff spent most of his free time with Beth, so it was a better place to store jewelry at her house."

"Who did the jewelry belong to, and when was it stolen?"

"We didn't know about the robbery. We didn't even know that the jewelry was being stored at her house. Looks like they were cautious with women. Beth revealed all the secrets to me about this, and we later learned from the jeweler Carlos that the jewel had been stolen by a gang."

"You killed Beth. Instead of getting the hell out of here, why did you ruin innocent people's lives? What was the reason?"

"The disappearance of precious jewels, the value of which was measured in millions, among the stolen goods, angered the boss. Beth took the most expensive set from the safe, and a man took it away from my hands in a dark room. Carl claimed that Beth's neighbor George was in there and he took the jewelry. He even said that he personally saw the earrings of the jewelry set before an official search was done. They linked all of this to George and his friend, meaning you. Caster told the boss that you are George's friend. The search conducted in George's house was a result of Caster giving the wrong information in the department. Sheriff was playing two sides. On one hand, he tried to get back at his enemies by feeding the boss false information. On the other hand, he tried to give the impression to the police that George was behind the robbery by planting the earrings in his house and turning him into a prime suspect."

"Although the earrings were not found at George's house, it was enough to get him detained as a suspect. George could not do this alone because he was ill, and I must have been the one who helped him. Son of a bitch! Who killed him?"

Carl Caster was a vital member of the squad. The chief periodically informed the boss about the processes taking place at the station, during his shift, boss's boys deal drugs in the street easily. They deal the worst drug, heroin. They made a lot of money. Sheriff got his cut too. His death is unknown. He was killed with his own gun."

"Who did the robbery and how?"

"It was done by the boss's gang. Two of the guys were working at the restaurant for about a month that time. The sleeping pill added to the drink ordered by the security guard and the sheriff's colleague at the restaurant prevented them from interfering with the work, and the crime was committed without hindrance. Former owner of the place, Carlos, explained to them all the secrets of the place. He was the one who told me about it too. Me and Beth found out about the robbery and the stored goods from Carlos."

"Why was Carlos giving you this information? After all, the robbery was being kept a secret from the women in the gang."

Elma didn't respond. "You must tell accurate information."

"He was my lover."

"So the two of you wanted to seize the jewelry and that's why you killed Beth, is that so?"

"The man who took the jewelry from me did not look like Carlos at all."

"If it wasn't Carlos and wasn't the man Carlos sent, then it was someone else. Why didn't he kill you then?"

"I don't know."

"Who told them about me and Beth's meeting?"

"We were being watched at all times. Probably they saw you with her and informed the boss about it."

"The information was correct—that we were lovers before, that I served in the army. An accurate information about all of these could have only been given by someone who knew Beth and me closely. That could only be you and Caster. Sheriff's side, I understand—we had beef. What problem did you have with Beth? She was your friend. Why did you get rid of her?"

"I have nothing to do with this."

"Tell me the truth. I'm talking to you."

"It was all because of that damn jewelry. It's true, Carlos and I planned to kill Beth, seize the jewelry, and sneak out of the country. But for some reason, Carlos did not arrive."

"Why did Anderson kill Beth?"

"After they found out that you were meeting with Beth, everything would be at risk. She was hard to recognize lately. They always had fights with the sheriff. After Beth found out that the letters you sent to Beth were torn apart by Carl before it reached her, she got really mad at him."

"How could that be?"

"Yeah, Beth told me about it. Each time, Carl Caster picked up the mail himself and used every means at his disposal to make Beth fall in love with him. Beth was under the impression that since she doesn't receive any letter from you, it means that you don't love her anymore. She started leaning toward Carl. He fell into Beth's trap at the end. Arnoldo needed a police outpost to carry out his ugly intentions across the country. That man was Sheriff Caster. Using Caster, he skillfully carried out all his plans for robbery and drugs. At the end, he was killed under unknown circumstances."

"That bastard! So that's how me and Beth fell apart. Where was Sarah being held?"

"That girl worked at the restaurant. They were supposed to kill her on the night of the robbery. But Alberto liked the girl, so he didn't let them kill her. Alberto was the boss's little brother. Boss repeatedly criticized his brother and demanded that he kill the girl. After Alberto was killed, the girl was kept for some time in a house he rented near the forest. I don't know what their plan was. They were probably waiting for the boss's orders. Boss was busy with women and drugs at the time. I don't know what happened to the girl later."

"How many are in the gang?"

"How could I know that?"

"Tell me about the ones you know."

"The ones I know? Ten of them were killed by unknown men. Boss's brother Alberto, his friend Carlos, his driver friend, the sheriff, and finally three drug dealers were killed at home by some homeless man. Two of them were men sent by Arnoldo to Alberto's rented house that time to finish off Sarah. They were supposed to go to the rented house by a stolen car, kill Sarah and somewhere in the forest bury her body, and burn the car to lose any trail. However, the unidentified man who killed both of them managed to kidnap the girl in the car. To prevent the corpses from being found, the boss ordered them to bury the bodies in the forest. The girl was saved. Police arrived at the scene and saw nothing but an empty house. The sheriff told the boss that it was you who killed his brother. He also thought that he burned you to death in his house. You are alive. He repeatedly sent people to kill George, but they could not find him at home. I heard that he was hiding with his wife."

"So that's how. Bastards."

A car stopped in the street. "Was someone supposed to come here?"

"Only a guard named Arlen. Boss assigned him to watch over me. But someone else brought me home today. Have you seen him? I don't know who it is this time."

Michael took his gun and prepared to leave out the kitchen door. "Aren't you going to untie me? But you promised!"

"Whoever is coming will help you. One more thing, you were supposed to tell me everything. This conversation is not over. Till next time," he said and turned off the microphone of the phone he had taken out of his pocket.

"Bastard, son of a bitch! You were recording my voice? God damn you to hell! They are going to kill you like a dog!"

Michael hurriedly put the phone in his pocket and walked out the kitchen door.

It was strange to Arlen to see that the door was unlocked. He took out his gun. After searching all the rooms, he entered the kitchen. Arlen, who came in, shouted angrily when he saw Elma with her hands tied.

"What is this? Who did this? Who was here?"

"Michael. He's not dead. He's alive. Michael."

"Have you lost your mind, stupid woman? It's not possible."

"What? I'm telling you the truth. He left after he tied my hands and searched the house."

The last sentence she said on purpose. She knew that Arlen usually checks the closed room upstairs. Elma knew that Alberto's belongings were being stored there. To see Arlen check that room every once in a while made her suspicious.

"What was he looking for? What did you tell him, bitch? If you hadn't opened the door, how could he have entered the house?" He kicked Elma's stomach with all his might. Elma sobbed in pain and cried.

"I told him nothing! I don't know how he opened the door either. I was making some coffee in the kitchen. When I turned around, I saw him standing in front of me!"

"Where did he go? That bastard!" Arlen quickly went out of the kitchen door with a gun in his hand and returned again after a while.

"Wish I was here! Why didn't he do you any harm? Perhaps there is something going on between you two. Answer me!" He slapped Elma.

"Tell me, bitch, what did you tell him? I've got my hands dirty today anyway. Don't make me send you after those bitches."

"I swear to God, I don't know. He tied me and searched around the house. He was just here. Perhaps he was planning to do something with me, but your arrival ruined his plan. I'm begging you, don't do anything to me."

"We will decide later whether I'm gonna do something or not." He quickly got upstairs and returned quickly. Elma was shocked to see the jewelry in his hand.

"What is that? Why do you have that?"

"Yes, it was me who stole it from you that night."

"That was you!"

"Yes, you wanna know the real story? I'm gonna tell you all of it. You should know it before you die and know that I'm not killing for no reason. I was working for Alberto. He wasn't happy with the boss's relation with Anderson. He gave me money for the information I gave him. After the news you gave me, I told Alberto about Anderson and the boss's plan for Beth. Alberto had his own jewelry plans, and this decision was prompted by his brother and Anderson hiding the jewelry from him. Anderson's decision on Beth hastened Alberto's plans. He asked me to come to the house, find the password and the keys, kill you and Beth, and take all the jewelry before Anderson got there. For some reason, he came earlier than he was supposed to. I found that out later. You called and informed him about the jewelry in Beth's bag and that you were going home together. I hurried to the house, and when I saw the lights of a car coming from afar, I knew Anderson was approaching, and I took the necklace in your hand and ran away. With Alberto's orders, I hid the set in his house. I later found out that there were earrings in the set and that they had disappeared when the sheriff informed the boss. It seems the earring set fell down when I took it from you. That Caster was using that earring to implement his nasty plans."

"Then why didn't you kill all of us?"

"I didn't have the keys or the password. I was going to get it from you and be done with both of you. I was fed up with your insults anyway. I would not forgive you for the insulting words you used against my mother, who died bleeding giving birth to me. That night was going to be your last night. Anderson's arrival was a problem. If there was a shootout between us, the result would be worse. If any of us got caught by the police, the whole gang would be captured. Then I would not have had this necklace. Now it's the best time to fulfil my plan. Otherwise, I wouldn't go after these bastards. I might have forgiven you, but you were the one who caused what happened tonight. Several people died along with Beth because of you and that wicked Anderson. You slandered innocent people. At least you shouldn't have sent Arnoldo after defenseless human beings, especially after knowing that she is pregnant. She lost her unborn child, and her life is in danger too. Fortunately, her wife was at the hospital. Arnoldo would have killed him too. Don't get me started on the woman she was with. After all, why did you and that vile Anderson want to carry out your ugly intentions by slandering innocent people? That bastard sheriff Caster. I killed that bastard. Because you told him you suspected me and told him to come here at night and search around the house. He saw me when he came here at night. Everything could have been uncovered if I hadn't killed that bastard."

"I swear. I won't tell anyone. Don't kill me, please! There was no secret between me and Carlos about the jewelry."

"Stupid woman! You deserve what you get! Arnoldo told me to take you with me to the forest. Anderson, to whom you kept feeding wrong information, told me to kill you. What you did to the pregnant woman hastened your end. Where are the documents?"

"I will tell you. Untie my hands, I'm begging you."

"They are going to be inside the house. I need to destroy them."

"If Arnoldo finds out about it, he will kill you."

"Boss has got his own problems right now. He and his gang went after the gold they stored in the hunter's hut. He will take his property and cross the border if he manages to. Anderson ordered me to destroy the paperwork." Arlen pointed his gun at Elma.

"Ah, you bastard! Damn you to hell!"

The bullet hit Elma in the shoulder. Arlen himself fell to the ground before the second bullet was fired. Michael's accurate shot touched his heart.

Elma bleeding on the floor was trying to say something to Michael. Michael Grady quickly dialed the numbers and called the police department.

"It's Michael Grady calling. Sheriff Brook Cletus's house was attacked by criminals. Lives of two women inside the house are in danger. Send a medical team to the scene urgently. They are going to try to escape the country with the stolen goods tonight. Do what's necessary right away. In addition, send the police and ambulance to the address I mentioned. There are two members of the criminal gang. One of them is dead, and the other is seriously injured. I'm going to switch off the phone. Don't forget to take the phone and valuables under the refrigerator in the kitchen. If I die, you will have the truth."

Michael untied Elma and laid her on the floor. He quickly reached for the first aid box and took out a bandage, trying to attend to Elma's wound. He got a pillow from the bedroom and put it under Elma's head.

"I understand what you said. You became a victim of your own ill doing and greed. You ruined the life of an innocent, pure-hearted woman who loved the man who was in a hell of fire day in, day out by pulling her into your own dirty world. You dragged her into the mud you were drowning in and ruined her future. What did you gain? Nothing. People who were using you left you behind. Soon enough, they will get their punishment too. Justice always prevails. Innocent people die and suffer in between. God will take you to hell with such torments. You will receive the punishment you deserve. If you survive, the hell in this world is waiting for you. If you die and there really is heaven and hell, you will go straight there. I am a little comforted by what I heard today. If I survive, I will go to Beth's grave again. I have so many things to say to her."

Michael took out the earrings from his pocket. "Do you see this? Look, the sheriff took revenge for his enmity with me and took my love away from me. That wasn't enough for him. He wanted to arrest a handicapped person who is close to me as my own brother in life by planting these in his house. Fortunately, George reacted on time and was able to dodge the threat. In life, you can't have what's not yours. This will get back to its owner. But you and people around you will burn in the fire of hell."

Michael dropped the earrings on the necklace and quickly grabbed the phone to make a phone call.

"Hello, Lucas! It's me. Thank you for the phone. I assume our conversation is being recorded. If you hadn't given me this phone, I wouldn't have been able to clarify many things. Now my heart is at ease. I saved Sarah. I do not regret killing those addicts and criminals. It's thanks to that I was able to locate Sarah. My goal was not to kill but to surrender to justice so that they could be held accountable before the law. But they asked for it. Something comforted me. I rescued a friend of mine captured by the Taliban in Afghanistan and managed to return home crippled but alive. But I could not allow him to become a victim of some villains and criminals. I killed two men sent by the gang to kill him. I had to act in secret because of Sheriff Carl Caster. I had a feeling that he is somehow involved with the gang. However, I could have been prosecuted if the information provided to the department with unproven evidence was considered unfounded facts and evil against the police officer. I knew the plans of my enemies to eliminate me, and I had to go underground. If it wasn't for you, I would have been the victim of my own mistake. Now I am going after the rest of the gang to fulfill both my military and my civic duty. We shall meet again, if I make it. Give a kiss to Sarah for me. I informed the police about the place where I put my phone and jewelry. I can already hear the police sirens approaching. I need to get out of here. There are still some things I need to do. Good-bye, my friend!"

The phone switched off. Lucas Marchelo took a seat on the couch and started crying. So he was the one that saved Sarah. Now he was up against the enemy, alone.

He had a phone with a lot of necessary information in his hand. With this important information, it was not smart to go against the enemy. If something happened, the records could be destroyed or lost. He hid the phone with the jewelry under the refrigerator and left the house. The police cars were already nearby.

Upon receiving the news, the chief doctor immediately gave serious instructions to the doctors of the intensive care and surgery department. "Quickly prepare the operation rooms. Create a rapid task force. The whole team should be ready to receive patients in critical condition at a high level."

The two were brought by ambulance in a critical condition. One of them was taken to the emergency room with a diagnosis of severe hemorrhagic shock. The blood reserve bank for all groups was ready. All preparations for emergency blood transfusions were made in the laboratory. The second patient was transferred to another operating room because of cerebral hemorrhage and trauma. The diagnosis was confirmed after an MRI.

The doctor on duty gave information about the patients. "Patient Luisa Bradley, thirty-two years old. Initial diagnosis, twenty-four to twenty-five weeks of pregnancy. After the separation of the placenta and heavy uterine bleeding, she was admitted to the department with a diagnosis of severe heart and lung failure. She already is taken to an operation. In addition to blood transfusions, other important resuscitation measures were performed. The fetus was surgically released to stop the bleeding. Her situation remains severely critical.

"Second patient, Bella Cletus, thirty-three years old, entered the department with a diagnosis of blunt trauma of internal organs and cerebral hemorrhage. After the diagnosis was confirmed by MRI, she underwent emergency surgery. The patient's condition is considered to be a variable critical."

Doctors fought a life-and-death struggle for the survival of Luisa and her son. Emergency surgery was performed under general anesthesia to stop the bleeding. Three minutes later, the twenty-four-week-old baby, who was born in critical condition, was connected to an artificial respiration machine in the emergency department, and appropriate resuscitation measures were started. Although it was possible to save the life of the mother and child after a hard struggle, the situation remains critical. Immediately after the operation, the final opinion of the patients on the condition of the patients was heard, and discussions were held in the room of the chief doctor.

The chief physician informed the representative of the department about the condition of both critically ill and the baby.

"I would like to note that the condition of the mother and the baby remains critical. Ms. Luisa Bradley was admitted to the department with third-degree hemorrhagic shock and difficult reversible processes in vital organs. The main cause is uterine bleeding, which occurs with the separation of two-thirds of the placenta after trauma, and therefore the nutrition of the fetus, and acute intrauterine hypoxia because of disorders of the respiratory system. The condition is critical because of incomplete formation of internal organs in the fetus and pulmonary insufficiency. Although we were able to save Ms.

Bella's life, her condition remains critical. We are trying to resolve the treatment of both patients in high condition with the latest achievements of medical science."

"Doctor, you and the medical staff of the clinic have a hard and responsible job. We believe that your team will be able to cope with this difficult task, and we wish you success.

"Boss, there's no news from him. Maybe something happened?"

"We are late, but I need to know what's going on there. Arlen is very talented. He uses all kinds of weapons skillfully. I can't leave without him. If Elma is captured, the police will get all the information from her. She even knows our plans to leave the country. There's a reason Arlen is being late. I need to know what's going on in Alberto's house. Send someone over quickly. The rest, come with me. We're losing time."

The sound of approaching police cars frightened him. He took a hidden and dark waiting position and took control of Alberto's house with binoculars. For some reason, the cars stopped around Alberto's house, and the police hurried inside. After a while, ambulances arrived at the scene. The scene was horrible. Arlen's and Elma's dead bodies were removed from the house and placed in the ambulance. One of the policemen in the area was talking to another officer in front of the house, holding phones and a bright object. He was surprised to see three phones in his hand. Who did the third phone belong to? What was the shiny, bright object in his hand? He immediately informed the boss about the situation.

"I'm gonna lose my mind. What's going on! Who could have killed them both? There's some mystery here."

"Boss, calm down. We need to get out of here quickly. It seems that the whole police department and the federal agents have been activated regarding this incident. Men are waiting for us in the area. These latest incidents are a mystery to us."

"Maybe that jewelry is the lost necklace? If the person who killed them did it out of greed, then why didn't he take the necklace? How could that necklace have ended up in Arlen's and Elma's hands?"

"I think there's nothing strange about it. The lost necklace was a doing of Elma and Arlen."

"I'm tired of these bullshits!"

"Boss, we must hurry. We need to get to the forest. We need to be at the border before 5:00 a.m. Our boys are waiting for us there. If we make it, we will have a lot to think about these issues."

The chief of the police department announced an emergency meeting. After a while, the police were waiting for Jonas Nilford's order to carry out the next operation plan.

"Gentlemen, we have received very important information about the Mexican criminal Fidel Jonathan and his criminal gang. According to the information received, he, nicknamed Arnoldo Columbus, has long been convicted of drug trafficking, robbery, and murder of innocent people in the country. They intend to leave the country as soon as possible after committing another serious crime. We were informed about this by a former Special Force Michael Grady. For many of you, this may sound strange. You are right. Unfortunately, until now, the public considered him killed by these criminals. Although he was alive, he disappeared for a long time, and he gave us this important information. We found his phone in the house where the bodies of the two murderers were located, and an expensive set of jewelry stolen during the robbery was also seized as evidence from the scene. We will be investigating this later. However, it seems that our brave officer still risked his life and attacked the enemy alone. Gentlemen, we need to make haste. The place we are going to is an old hunter's hut in the woods. The police will be working on intensified mode. According to the secret information we received, the criminal group intends to cross the border and leave the country tonight. Probably someone is helping them in this. We don't have much time. The bureau is already involved in this operation. Help is definitely needed. The operation must be carried out in strict secrecy."

A car coming from afar was rapidly approaching the area. The police coming after them ordered them to stop the car. Their arrival was unexpected.

"Bad news, boss! They are gonna ruin everything."

"Act calm and confident. I'll handle this. Don't do anything without my approval."

The police car stopped behind them.

The sheriff, pointing a gun, ordered the driver, "Stay in the car! Don't move! You're not allowed to leave the car."

The sheriff approached and asked the driver for license and registration documents.

"Here you go, Sheriff. May I know why you pulled us over?"

"You were going over the speed limit."

"It was dark, so I could not see the road signs."

"If you break the law one more time, your car will be confiscated and taken into a penalty area."

"Thank you, Sheriff! I'll try not to do it again."

"Have a safe trip."

The car drove off. The sheriff quickly informed the center on the radio. "Mr. Jonas Nilford, Anderson's car with license plate detained. The car, which included the suspects, was speeding on the seventieth kilometer of the highway and headed toward the area. Continue the pursuit. Set up traps in the area. The object is closing into the area."

Apparently, the information is solid. The head of the department gave another task to the police officers in the area.

The car entered the woods area and stopped on the side of the road. "Boss, it could be dangerous for us all to go there at once. Two people will go ahead and inform me about the situation. The police and the federals might have traps set up for us to ambush us. That's why I think you should wait at the area I showed you with two men. You must be extra careful. We must hurry."

Anderson was moving cautiously. After a while, everyone was in the area. Near the hunter's hut, the gang members noticed a small flashlight flashing three times in the dark. "It's me, Anderson. Everything is in order?"

"We also brought weapons. We took all precautionary measures. The goods are ready. Where is the boss?"

"Boss is going to wait for us at the preplanned destination. We must try to easily deliver all the goods and money to the intended area. Everybody will get their cuts after we cross the border. Time is short. We have to pick up the jewelry and leave immediately."

It was quiet all around. The moonlight illuminated the plains, but the forest was dark. Except for the sound of owls, there was silence everywhere. For some reason, Anderson did not like this silence. He motioned for the support to stop for a short time, and after listening for a while, they resumed their traveling.

"The boss's not coming with us?"

"He will be waiting for us at the bottom of the hill."

Shortly afterward, Anderson gave out orders. They were to be divided into two groups and move in different directions and meet in the area near the border. Someone waiting for them at the border would help them leave the country by boat through a relatively safe part of the border.

"Why are you separating the group? Why can't we go together? We can withstand it better together. Maybe you have other plans? I don't see the boss anywhere around. Where's Arlen?"

"Freddie, it's too dangerous to go everyone together. If they see us separately, they might think we are hunters. That's why I think it's better we divide into two groups. You know the area. Arlen is with the boss, like always."

"All right, Anderson. We believe you."

Anderson was happy. He made a plan with the boss. Although the area was difficult to navigate with the map, the road they had to take was short. They would reach the area faster than the other group. When the second group arrives at the area, they would find nothing. Arnoldo didn't want to create more problems by gathering more people near himself. On the other hand, the police and the feds might be on to them. That way, the second group, when they arrive, will see police waiting for them. It could win them some time to cross the border unnoticed. Leaving the group, Anderson met Arnoldo, who was waiting for them at the bottom of the ravine, and entered a forest surrounded by hills. Time was short. They were in a hurry. They had a long way to go. They could come face-to-face with the border police at any moment; even coast guards could be following them. But they were unaware of another danger that awaited them.

"Stop! Hands up! You are arrested for violating U.S. law. Any sudden movement, and you are dead. Give up the guns. Each of you has been sentenced to life imprisonment for the crimes you have committed in the country. If you do not obey the law, you will be shot on the spot. Your resistance is meaningless. Surrender your weapons. Otherwise, you will be shot at."

Everyone was stunned; they didn't know what to do. Nothing around was visible. Any sudden movement could be death. Special police and federal agents, along with border guards, surrounded them from all sides and clearly monitored their movements with night vision devices. The gang members were shocked; they had nowhere to go.

"How did they find out?"

"I think it has something to do with Anderson and Arnoldo."

"So you are saying that they trapped themselves too? Because after they get us, they will go after them."

"You're wrong. Anderson made this plan because he thought we would meet them. He would win some time to reach the area and lose track. The federals and the police will assume that we are the whole gang, and with all that distraction, they would cross the border easily."

"Guys, let's not resist. We are either going to die and Anderson and boss will escape, or we get arrested and stay alive. We can give information to the police about them to help arrest. Maybe they can reduce the length of our imprisonment."

"I don't know about you, but I don't plan on surrendering to these assholes." Freddie ordered his men to stand quietly and shoot only when he said. Fully armed Special Forces were approaching and could be seen.

"Fire!" They went behind the tree in front of them and began to fire back at those who approached. The silence of the forest was disturbed by the sound of bullets fired from a machine gun.

"You see, boss? Just like I said. We must hurry."

"Apparently, they are following us," Arnoldo replied.

"Anderson, you are very smart. Hurry. If any of them gets caught alive, they will give us away. It's safe after we cross the river."

"Not much distance left. We will be there very soon. But it's hard to move in the dark forest. We must use the plain area. We must reach there before the military helicopters arrive."

After a while, gunfire sounds stopped. It looked like the other group was incapacitated.

They paused and listened for a moment. Silence didn't last long. Sound of dogs barking was approaching. They needed to make haste; they would be at the destination very soon.

Sensing that the situation was not good, Arnoldo carried the bag on his shoulder and began to move down the stream with the gang members.

"We must cross the river at all costs."

"The water is cold and frightening."

"Let's find a relatively shallow place and go through there. Hurry up."

Anderson stumbled on a rock and started rolling down. When he reached the bottom of the ravine, he hit his head on a rock and fainted. Arnoldo approached and checked his pulse. His heart was pounding. It was impossible to carry him in such a situation.

"Boss, what are you thinking?"

"We're gonna leave him behind."

"But that's not right!"

"Are you stupid or what? How can we carry him anywhere in this condition?! Never mind, hurry!"

Arnoldo had to determine the shallow part of the river to cross. They went down the river. Finally, finding a suitable place, holding each other's hands, they crossed the river with difficulty and hurried to meet the person waiting for them.

The police and the bureau agents had already tracked down the fugitives. Time was short. They needed to get to them before it's too late. There was a long distance to the border area. The dogs that easily detect traces by sniffing the ground hurried forward. However, the large river ahead prevented the animals from advancing.

"I don't believe that they could pass through this river. We need to search the area quickly."

"Wish it was morning soon enough. With helicopters, we could conduct the pursuit."

"They might have hidden in the woods."

"I can already see them. They are in the desert area. Three men are approaching the border."

"Can we get them with a sniper?"

"No, they are too far away to shoot."

"We must continue the pursuit and cross the river at all costs."

"Hurry up, guys! I see something down there. I can't stop the animals."

"Sir, there's someone in a critical condition here. Maybe he fell down, or maybe he was traumatized with a weapon. Only a medical helicopter can come here, hurry. Let the other groups hurry. We have little time. They cannot be allowed to cross the border."

Arnoldo was moving forward. The more tired he became, the more difficult it was to keep moving.

"Boss, hang on. They are still far away. We are already here."

"Hurry up! The man waiting for us should be around here. Call, search, I don't know what you're doing, find it. We don't have much time. The sound of a helicopter is coming. It may be a military helicopter."

Arnoldo was not feeling well. His heart was pounding; he was exhausted.

"Sir, the boat is in the area. We couldn't find the man."

"Be quick, sons of bitches, don't make me shoot you! Find him and bring him here. Look to see if the keys are in the boat." He began to walk around nervously.

He turned around, feeling as if someone was coming after him. It was quiet. He paused for a moment with his machine gun ready in his hands and looked around. After making sure of the silence, he wanted to continue on his way and could not believe his eyes when he saw the man in front of him. For a moment, he felt the revived spirit in front of the eyes of the man he had killed. That spirit was coming toward him. Before he managed to fire with the gun, his weapon fell to the ground because of the heavy blow he received. He lost consciousness after the second strike. Michael moved quickly, tied his hands behind his back, picked up the gun on the ground, grabbed

Arnoldo's arm, and lifted him to his feet. Arnoldo looked around but saw none of his men.

"So you're not dead, bastard! I should have cut you into pieces that night. What have you done to the boys?"

"They are looking forward to the police's arrival. The man who was waiting for you with the boat ran to his mother crying."

"I am being punished for the mistakes I made. Let it be. We will live to see. If I make it, I will find a way to make it even with you."

"If you are alive!"

"So you did all of this?"

Michael did not respond.

"Listen, there are millions here. We can get on the boat and escape together. I'll be your best friend. We'll divide this in two. What do you say? It's enough for you till the end of your life."

"You have lost your pride and honor. Now you lose all that you have gained because you have gained that wealth by shedding blood. You have given tears to many families by selling drugs to their children. In the blink of an eye, you stole everything from people who worked hard all their life. You even sent your blood brother to kill innocent people and sacrificed him to your ego, and even his death did not deter you from his ugly deeds."

"God damn you! You son of a bitch!"

Nine gang members were killed. The rest were arrested. The three wounded among police and special agents were sent to the hospital with first aid for gunshot wounds. FBI agent Darren Edmond was concerned. He looked through the binoculars. "No one is visible in the area. I wonder what is happening there? There are no reports from police or federal agents tracking the remaining members of the perpetrators. The border zone in the area falls on the water area. Probably the harbor patrol has already started working. If they don't arrest him quickly, he will cross the border."

A federal agent approached and gave him important news. "Mr. Darren Edmond, someone wants to contact you from a radio station in the area."

"Mr. Darren Edmond, we lost them after pursuing them for a long time. After a while, we saw two people coming toward us. I have a feeling that their hands are tied from behind. This may be a trap. The action to take depends on the decision you make."

"Be patient. Nobody opens fire without my order. Wait for them to get closer. The man in the back is limping. He looks familiar. Take a look."

"Yes, sir. He does limp. The one in the front has his hand tied. Whoever that is, looks like he caught the criminal and wants to hand him to us. I think I know this man. He looks so much like the former officer Michael Grady, who was murdered."

"Give me the binoculars." Darren Edmond looked through the binoculars again.

"It can't be! I can't believe my eyes. Apparently, he was fighting the enemy all along, and alone."

"So he is alive? How could that be?"

"Well done, you hero! Yes, he lived and fought like a zealous and brave son who loved his homeland and his people."

"What are you saying? Is that really him?"

"Yes, yes, it is."

The operation was over. Most members of the gang were killed, and Anderson was in critical condition. The villain Arnoldo Columbus has been charged along with the surviving gang members.

Darren Edmond headed straight to the hospital. He was going to ask about the current condition of both patients in critical condition in the intensive care unit. He recognized the man walking in the hallway. It was Brook Cletus. He looked nervous and angry. He came and greeted him and asked about the situation. The sheriff said Bella's condition was not good. Together they went to the intensive care unit. They would meet with the doctor in charge of the department and get detailed information about the current condition of the patients.

The head of the department, Andrea Eduardo, welcomed them. He gave detailed information about the current condition of both patients brought in critical condition and the course of postoperative treatment. Patients' situation remained as stably critical. Darren Edmond told Brook Cletus that he regretted what happened.

George was being treated at the neurology department for a nervous breakdown. Psychological help was being given to him.

Five days passed after the incident. During this time, Michael went to the hospital every day to visit George and inquire about the condition of other patients.

Today, for some reason, he felt weak and had a severe headache. He didn't get out of the bed all day. He hardly managed to get up in the evening. Alongside with being hungry, he was having difficulty breathing. He took a drink from the refrigerator, approached the window, and opened it. It was getting dark. The sun's rays were gradually fading on the horizon. He opened the window and breathed in the fresh air. He stared at something and thought deeply. He recounted what had happened in his mind for a moment. The phone call distracted him. He could not recognize the number.

"Hello. Am I speaking to Michael Grady?"

"Yes, I'm listening."

"I'm calling you from the hospital. This is the resuscitation doctor Suzanne Harland. Mr. Michael, Mrs. Luisa woke up from a coma. I wanted to give you the good news. In her first words, she asked about her husband and the baby. When I told her about you, for some reason, she was surprised and said she definitely wanted to see you. She asked me to call you and find out how you are doing."

"Doctor, I don't know how to thank you enough. Thank you very much, ma'am. Can I come and visit the patient?"

"It's not possible for now. Approach the admission office tomorrow."

"Thank you again."

The good news was unexpected. He was so excited; he didn't know what to do. He wanted to call George to share the good news, but he changed his mind because the doctor wouldn't let him. Tomorrow he would go to the hospital where George was being treated and give him the good news.

A call came from a number that belonged to federal agent Darren Edmond.

"Hello, Mr. Grady. How are you?"

"Hi. Thank you, Agent Edmond. I'm listening."

"In the morning, you must be at the headquarters of the Federal Bureau of Investigation."

"Thanks for the invite."

"Good night."

He arrived at the headquarters in the morning. They greeted each other. Darren Edmond ordered him to wait in front of the general's room and entered the room with permission. He returned a few minutes later and went in again with him. After giving the military salute, the former officer Grady met with the general and sat down. The general asked Darren Edmond to report on the outcome of the operations.

"Sir, General, I would like to say that the investigation is nearing completion. I would like to briefly inform you about the course and results of the investigation. The investigation revealed that Fidel Jonathan, a fugitive from the territory of a neighboring country, was wanted for a long time for a serious crime. Together with a group of criminals, he raided the house of a well-known businessman out of greed. After killing him, they wanted to enter the territory of our country illegally and secretly, crossing the border with fake documents and the wealth they received. One police officer was killed, and two others were taken to hospital in critical condition during the shootout in the border. We were able to save their lives. Two criminals were killed. The rest managed to escape into hiding.

"In fake documents, his name goes by Arnoldo Columbus. He was able to gather a large group of criminals around him in a short time. The gang members have long been involved in the illicit drug trade in the state. Unfortunately, I can say that Sheriff Carl Caster also helped them in this matter. He met Fidel through his mistress Beth Francesco's girlfriend, Elma Carmelo. Elma was Fidel's mistress. Fidel captured him with all the money and gifts given. He then trapped Carl to carry out his ugly plans. To this end, Fidel systematically organized a fake gambling game. Carl, who gambled at a casino with a friend of Fidel's brother Alberto, lost a large sum of money. As a result, Carl faced a difficult situation.

"To act like he was protecting the sheriff, Fidel claimed the debt. Thus, it made him dependent on himself. He promised to help the sheriff pay the money. In return, he asked Carl to create a suitable situation for illegal drug trafficking and dealing. On the other hand, the sheriff's drug addiction worsened the situation, and he agreed to Fidel's terms. Fidel reminded Carl Caster how dangerous the man he lost money to was, and if he failed to pay his debt, he will get him killed. Facing a difficult situation, the sheriff asked Fidel to help him with the debt. Carl promised to help Fidel deal with drug trafficking in the country if he paid his debt. As a result, the sheriff informed the gang leader in a timely manner about the entire operational plan for the arrest of criminals at the state police department. Thus, the gang took the necessary measures, being aware of the danger that awaited them in time. The sheriff worked closely with criminals to rob the state's largest jewelry store and workshop, while facilitating sales in an area controlled by the drug trade, alongside controlling the area and facilitating drug trade.

"The stolen jewelry was stored in the basement in Beth's house for some time. Because Carl Caster spent most of his day with his mistress Beth and was a sheriff, the house was considered safe for jewelry. Because of the necessary conditions in the house, it was a convenient place to hide the jewelry. Only the sheriff, the casino owner Anderson, and Fidel knew about the location of the jewelry. It was kept a secret from the rest of the gang members. This caused dissatisfaction among the gang members. Thus, groups started to form inside the gang. The boss, who made a lot of money, left Elma, and she joined former jeweler Carlos to make plans to seize the jewel. He talked about a safe in the basement of Beth's house and suspected that the jewelry was hidden there. After some time, he found out that his suspicions were correct. On Carlos's advice, Elma convinced Beth to agree on the plan to switch the jewelry with fake ones piece by piece. As a result, they would make a lot of money by reshaping expensive stones through a jeweler. The proposition excited Beth, and she agreed.

"However, a jeweler in a neighboring state carelessly sold the stone to its owner. The businessman's father found out through pictures that the stones belonged to the stolen jewelry and informed the police. Police got involved right away, but Carlos managed to escape. Both women and the sheriff were killed under unknown circumstances. The investigation revealed that Elma's murderer was Arlen Booker, Fidel's bodyguard. Fidel's brother Alberto and his right-hand man, Anderson, did not get along much. For this reason, he formed another group within the gang. Because of his brother's craziness and carelessness, Fidel kept all secrets from him. Alberto was not satisfied about that. Alberto was outraged about the fact that his brother was keeping the location of the goods a secret from him. Through his close friend and security guard at the casino, Arlen Booker, he learned all about Anderson's plans on time. Arlen conveyed to Alberto all the conversations that took place in the casino's meeting room. Alberto's main plan was to find the jewel, capture it, and cross the border with his gang and leave the country. His brother was already making plenty of money from the drug trade.

"On the other hand, he was wary of Anderson. Alberto was concerned about his brother's drug addiction and the fact that he had given over the management of the casino to Anderson. Anderson could kill his brother and get away with the jewel at any time. Anderson was the real reason why the boss kept the jewelry hidden from Alberto. Arlen informed Alberto about the location of the jewelry. In return, Alberto promised his friend a large sum of money from the future sale of jewelry.

"On the other hand, the unrest among the female members of the gang led the issue in a different direction. Although Fidel's girlfriend Elma considered Beth her friend, she later considered her as an opponent. Elma was outraged by being left alone by the boss and expensive gifts given to Beth to capture the sheriff. After seeing the boss shower Beth with expensive gifts, she started to get jealous and got into the idea that the boss and Beth had some kind of intimate relationship. In fact, all this was part of a plan to control the sheriff.

"Knowing that the stolen jewelry was kept in Beth's house, Elma made a plan. She met Carlos, the former owner of a jewelry store who was involved in the theft of jewelry. Taking advantage of Carlos's negative attitude toward Fidel, Elma started having romantic relations with him. Their warm relationship grew and Elma told Carlos about her secret plans. They agreed on a plan to eliminate Beth and seize the jewel. First, they got Beth to agree to their plan—seize the keys to the door to the basement and the safe through her, and give Carlos the expensive ring that Beth brought, and share the money made from stone replacement. However, when the police and the federal government found out about the incident, they were unable to catch Carlos before he managed to go into hiding. Police officers died. Carlos went underground. He, with his friend and Elma, planned to attack Beth's house, kill her, and seize the jewel.

"Elma lied to the boss and sheriff to create a suspicion that Beth's ex-boyfriend Michael was the killer. She gave false information to Anderson and the sheriff about Beth's secret meeting with Michael. In fact, this information was satisfying to the sheriff, because it was a good time to put an end to his enmity with Michael. Beth made her own plans. She hid the stolen necklace and earrings in her handbag and left the house. She wanted to leave the country with the expensive jewelry after calling Carlos on the phone. But Carlos, cautious over being followed, could not come to the place. Beth, afraid of being followed by the police, put the jewelry in her bag and went to the birthday party. When Elma found out that Beth called Carlos to a meeting without her, she got mad, and through Carlos, she found out that Beth had gone to the birthday party.

"Arriving at the birthday party, Elma saw the jewelry in her bag and called Anderson. The news hastened the gang's decision to kill Beth. Anderson got orders to go to Beth's house, seize the jewelry, and kill Beth. Elma came home with Beth. Beth lay in the bedroom on the second floor. When Elma went downstairs with the expensive jewelry in her hand, the person whose face she could not see in the kitchen asked her to open the safe and enter her password. For some reason, the headlights approaching the house hastened the unknown man. He hurriedly stole the precious jewel in Elma's hand and ran away. That's when the earrings fell to the ground. Hearing the noise downstairs, Beth came down to the kitchen, where Anderson killed her. Anderson and Elma swept everything from the safe, and they left the house in a hurry. Elma's plan failed because Carlos was supposed to arrive before Anderson. But the stranger in the kitchen got away with the jewelry. That's when the earrings fell.

"After Beth was killed under unknown circumstances, Sheriff Caster threw the set of earrings at George's house and wanted to arrest him on trumped-up charges. George, who was going to the hospital, returned home suspecting something because he saw the earrings in Beth's house and the sheriff's unauthorized entry to his house raised suspicions. A search of George's home yielded no results because George threw the earrings out of the window. Despite that, the police arrested George as a suspect. After several unanswered phone calls to George's phone from his friend Michael, Michael decided to come to George's house where he saw the police at the scene. Hearing Carl's false and ugly assumptions, Michael couldn't take it anymore and attacked Carl. Michael was arrested for resisting an official civil servant.

"Later, I got involved and came across some suspicious moments. Michael Grady was released. I later understood the sheriff's help in all that happened. Sheriff Carl Caster convinced Arnoldo that the jewel was stolen by George Bradley. However, a plot by the gang to assassinate George failed, and Michael killed Fidel's brother and his friend. The sheriff told the boss that Michael Grady was the killer. Then the gang members attacked Michael's house at night, beat him up real good, tied his hands and legs from the ceiling, set fire to the house, and left him to burn to death. Michael's neighbor saved him, and he went underground after that. He risked his life to fight the criminals, killing some of them and overcoming this crime. Michael Grady's services and extensive details of the incident are detailed in this investigation."

"Mr. Darren Edmond, that is plenty for now. You are exhausted and you need some rest. Yours and Michael Grady's heroic contributions in solving this case are undeniable. On behalf of the bureau and myself, I would like to thank you and Officer Michael Grady once again."

After leaving the department, he picked up flowers and went to the hospital to visit Luisa. After permission, he entered Luisa's room. Luisa could not control her tears when she saw

Michael. She thought she was dead, and Michael's survival was a miracle. Michael took her weak hands and kissed them, placing the bouquet she had brought on her windowsill. They were both crying. These were the tears of joy. Since Luisa was not allowed to talk much, Michael briefly told her about George and wished him a speedy recovery and return home with the baby. Going straight from the hospital to the hospital where George Bradley was treated, he shared with him the good news he had received. George was over the moon with news; he didn't know how to thank Michael enough. Michael, dreaming of the day he and his friend could go to the hospital to visit Luisa and the baby, left George's room.

A day later, Michael Grady attended the next meeting at the FBI headquarters. The meeting was opened by Col. Benjamin Clinton of the U.S. Federal Bureau of Investigation.

"Gentlemen! Today I would like to introduce you to former special services officer Michael Grady. Captain Lieutenant Michael Grady and his battalion fought heroically against Taliban groups in Afghanistan, carrying out their peacekeeping missions. He was discharged from the army and returned home after being seriously wounded in one of the battles. Unfortunately, Mr. Michael Grady lost one of his legs after being wounded in one of these battles. Continuing his military service with dignity to his homeland, Michael Grady has played a key role in neutralizing a criminal group operating in the country. Mr. Michael Grady, we thank you very much for your assistance to the police and the federal bureau in neutralizing the long-running criminal gang in the country. You will again be awarded a medal of honor for your services to the country."

The floor was given to Gen. Barton Coleman, chief of staff of the U.S. Army.

"Gentlemen, one of the main characteristics of every patriotic person is love for the motherland, respect and love for its people. The patriotism, self-sacrifice, heroism, and invincibility that characterize each of the U.S. Special Forces stem from love of people and country. Love for the motherland strengthens the sense of trust to win the intense struggle for truth and justice, and increases hatred against the enemy. Patriotism is the basis of heroism. Although this feeling is innate, it needs nurturing and is strengthened in this way. Michael's father died when he was a child, and he was raised by his mother. The mother raised her only child in a patriotic spirit. Michael Grady is brave and a real patriot. These expressions can be applied to thousands of sons of the fatherland. Michael Grady and Roger Thomas are just a couple of them. Today, they have shown their true patriotism not only in the peacekeeping struggle of our country but also in the neutralization of criminal groups operating in our territory for the benefit of our country. We bow before the souls of our heroes who sacrificed their lives for the prosperity and well-being of the country.

"Mr. Michael Grady, your services to the homeland have always been highly valued, and today you are again awarded the highest award of the homeland. This is an honor for us. I thank you once again for your dedication to maintaining peace in the country and wish you success."

After the meeting was over, Darren Edmond and Michael Grady left the building together and went to a restaurant to have lunch.

"What now, my friend? What are you thinking?"

"I miss my home. I'm sure my parents are waiting for me to come back. I will return back to work again. I hope to see you again as a friend. Take care, my friend. See you around."

Michael was really tired. Tomorrow he would go to the hospital where Roger Thomas was being treated again and pay him a visit. He got in the car and drove to the address he had long dreamed of.

He bought some flowers before arriving at the destination.

There was a knock at the door. He knew that she was home. Today, the American people are celebrating a holy holiday.

Few seconds passed. The door opened. The mother, who had seen the soldier in front of her before, paused. His face was familiar, but the military uniform he was wearing was strange to her. She stared at the soldier in front of her with confused eyes.

"Who are you looking for?"

"You probably did not recognize me. I stayed at your house a while ago. You took care of me."

"I can't believe it. Am I dreaming?" said the mother, hugging Michael, and could not hold back tears.

"Yes, Mother. That man is me. We will still have a lot of time to tell you what happened."

"Come on in, son, you must have served in the military."

The bouquet of flowers on the table did not escape Michael's notice. So the mother was preparing to visit someone.

"Looks like you are preparing to go to visit someone."

"The war took the light of my eyes, my only existence, Buster, from me. I am going to visit his grave. I bought these flowers for him." She took a picture of her son in a military uniform from the wall and kissed him in tears.

"I knew him."

"How so? Did you serve together?"

"Yes," he said, handing the talisman to his mother. This was the talisman I gave to Buster when he was sent to military service. During the difficult days of my life, I protected this talisman like the apple of my eye."

"You knew my son?"

"Yes, he was going to Afghanistan with me that day. We met in the plane." Michael told his mother in detail about everything that had happened.

As Michael spoke, his mother could not hold back her tears.

"Now I understand why you cried when you saw my son's picture on the wall. Today is a holy day, so I wanted to visit his grave. My son's dreams did not come true. The girl he was going to marry was next door to us. She got married a year after. That day was the worst day of my life. I couldn't stop crying all day, and I cursed the war. So many young people died in this war. Everyone is a child of a mother like me, whether Afghan, American, Muslim, Christian, regardless of their race. May the Holy God not shed any more tears of any mother. May the Blessed Virgin Mary protect all people. May the God himself curse those who enter the skin of man and enter the devil into their hearts. We are all guests in this world. We are all going to die sooner or later. The greed for power, wealth, gold, and money destroys people. Everything needs to be achieved in a civil manner. Democracy is the key to peace. If they came to power in a civilized way, they would not ask any state or NATO for help to quell the uprising in the country. No state or NATO would have interfered in their internal affairs if they had not revolted in their countries, killing thousands of people, regardless of age or gender. Even today, mothers like me would not have shed tears over the unfinished destiny of their children. Sons like you would not have lost their legs or arms and be crippled and lose the light of their young lives, and would not be dependent on someone's mercy just to get across the road. My heart aches thinking about it." The mother cried.

Michael got up to give her a hug. "May God give you patience. The loss of a child is a great sorrow, and I regret that your child died in the war. I will go with you to visit your son's grave."

"You came from the cold. Have some hot tea. We can go after that."

After some time, they were at the graveyard. The mother placed the flowers she brought to her son's gravestone. She could not hold back her tears when she tried to wipe clean her son's picture on the gravestone. "You have a guest, my child. Look who has come to visit you. Fortunately, there are still good people left in this world. Now, Michael is dear to me as much as you are. Rest in peace, my child. You were always worried for your old mother. Now there's a strong man like you near me. I will consider him as my son from now on. He returned the talisman to me. I will keep it under my pillow till the end of my days."

Michael knelt down and hugged the mother, lifting her from the grave of her son in tears. "Have patience, Mother. His death is a sorrow for each one of us."

"Let's go, son. I won't let you go anywhere. You will stay with me. I will care for you as I cared for Buster."

Michael hugged her again. "Of course, ma'am."

Three months have passed. A lot has changed during this time. Roger Thomas recovered and returned to his state. He sat at the marriage table with the girl he loved. Michael, George, and other military comrades eagerly attended the wedding. Roger opened a new store in the state where Michael lived and entrusted the management to a friend.

Michael Grady spent most of his day at Buster's house. A real mother-and-son relationship formed between them. Sometimes he and George went to the hospital to visit the baby. He liked the nurse taking care of the baby, and in the depths of his heart, he felt a renewed sense of love. Sometimes he waited impatiently in the hospital yard for the nurse to finish her shift. He could sense that the nurse had feelings for him too. Larisa was from Russia originally. After graduating from college, she worked in a hospital as a nurse. She also felt that she loved Michael; she was looking forward to the end of work. The sparks of love between them were growing.

Luisa was happy to hear from the doctor about her baby's condition. Luisa could not hold back her tears of joy when she was told that she would be released a week later.

Michael woke up early in the morning. It was one of the best days in his life. He drove directly to his friend George's house.

He was still ecstatic about the good news he heard yesterday. At the sound of the car, George and Luisa looked out the window to see Michael arriving, and they both went out to the street. He recognized the woman sitting in the front of the car. It was Buster's mother. Michael got out of the car and hugged George and Luisa. "Congratulations, my dears. Today is one of the best days of my life. We will go to the hospital soon and bring little Brandon home. There will be a real party in the yard today."

Four people were waiting impatiently in the lobby on the first floor of the maternity ward of the hospital. The elevator door opened. Nurse Larisa came to them with the baby in her arms and the doctor. George Bradley could not hold back his tears. Michael stepped forward, picked up the baby, and walked over to George and Luisa, placing the little Brandon in his friend's open arms. Luisa came closer and thanked the nurse and the doctor. Michael Grady presented the bouquets of flowers to the medical staff.

A year later. The door opened. Larisa was back from work. She went into the bedroom. Michael was still asleep. Larisa kissed her husband on the face and tried to wake him. "Honey, wake up. It's time. We are going to have guests over tonight. We need to make preparations."

Michael looked at the time. He got up quickly, dressed, and after washing up, entered the kitchen. Larisa was sitting in the kitchen.

"You look upset. What's wrong? Looks like you are really tired." He gave her a kiss.

"Michael, I'm pregnant."

Michael hugged Larisa tightly. "Congratulations, honey. I love you very much."

Today they would celebrate the holiday together. Everyone gathered at Michael's house. Everyone dear to him was there. Sarah looked very happy and sincere. She took little Brandon by the hand and helped him take his first steps in life, while Lucas Marchelo and George were arguing about different ways to cook turkey. Sheriff Brook Cletus put an end to their argument. "One day I will take you all to the good kebabrestaurant in the city. They add some kind of special herb to the meat that increases the tenderness and the taste of the meat. They take out the barbecue from the fire and pull it out of the needle with a piece of bread. It's so delicious."

"We definitely need to go to that restaurant one day. I will definitely taste your glorious kebab." Michael invited all the guests to the table.

Everyone had a smile on their faces today. Michael rejoiced, sometimes grieving deeply remembering the days gone by. Tomorrow, he and Larisa would go to the cemetery to visit their mother's grave. Finally, everyone got up to go home. Lucas Marchelo came closer to Michael and gave him a hug. "Michael, today is a dear holiday. I wish that the baby's voice will come from this hearth, which is dear to you, on the next holiday, and that these voices will increase every year." Everybody laughed out loud.

Michael's mother passed away when he was in Afghanistan. Her only wish was to see her son come back safely from war and hear the cries of his baby in his household. "I wanted to remember Mother Clara's wish on this beautiful day. We will all go there tomorrow with Michael's family to visit Mother Clara's grave. Let the mother's soul feel that her loved ones are always with her."

The next morning, the mother's grave was painted red with tulips. Michael left the group and walked a little through the graves with a bouquet of flowers in his hand. Everyone understood his intention.

Beth's grave was located further down the cemetery. It was covered with grass, and the board was bent again. It was as if she was alone in that world, a stranger. Michael bent down, cleared the weeds from the tomb, and straightened the plate. He planted the flowers in his hand on the ground above the grave. "Sleep in peace. I will not leave you alone. I will come visit often." Saying good-bye, he stood up and returned, wiping away his tears.

Years passed. Sarah got married and had a happy family. Baby voices began to be heard in Brook Cletus's house. Although George Bradley's health improved significantly after his treatment, he was still having problems regarding his high blood pressure. Luisa was very happy; a third child is going to come into their lives.

Michael Grady was sitting in the yard. The weather was really hot. Larisa would be home for a while for her next vacation.

"Darling, perhaps we should go to the park with the kids."

"All right. I need you to rest in such a situation. We will definitely go to the doctor tomorrow."

"The kids will be back from the school soon. I should get prepared." She kissed her husband on the cheek and went inside the house.

Michael sighed deeply. He was happy; all of his pains and sufferings were left behind. The next piece of news made him happy. Under a peace agreement between the Taliban and the Afghan government and Allied Forces, the U.S. government and NATO have agreed to withdraw their peacekeeper troops from the area. The country would soon hold democratic presidential elections. He rejoiced because the peace agreement would bring joy to thousands of families. He had been waiting for this good news for many years; at last, his dream had come true. He got up, picked up his mobile phone to share the good news with his friends, and dialed the numbers . . .

Lightning Source UK Ltd.
Milton Keynes UK
UKHW041930200121
377415UK00001B/52